Lint Boy

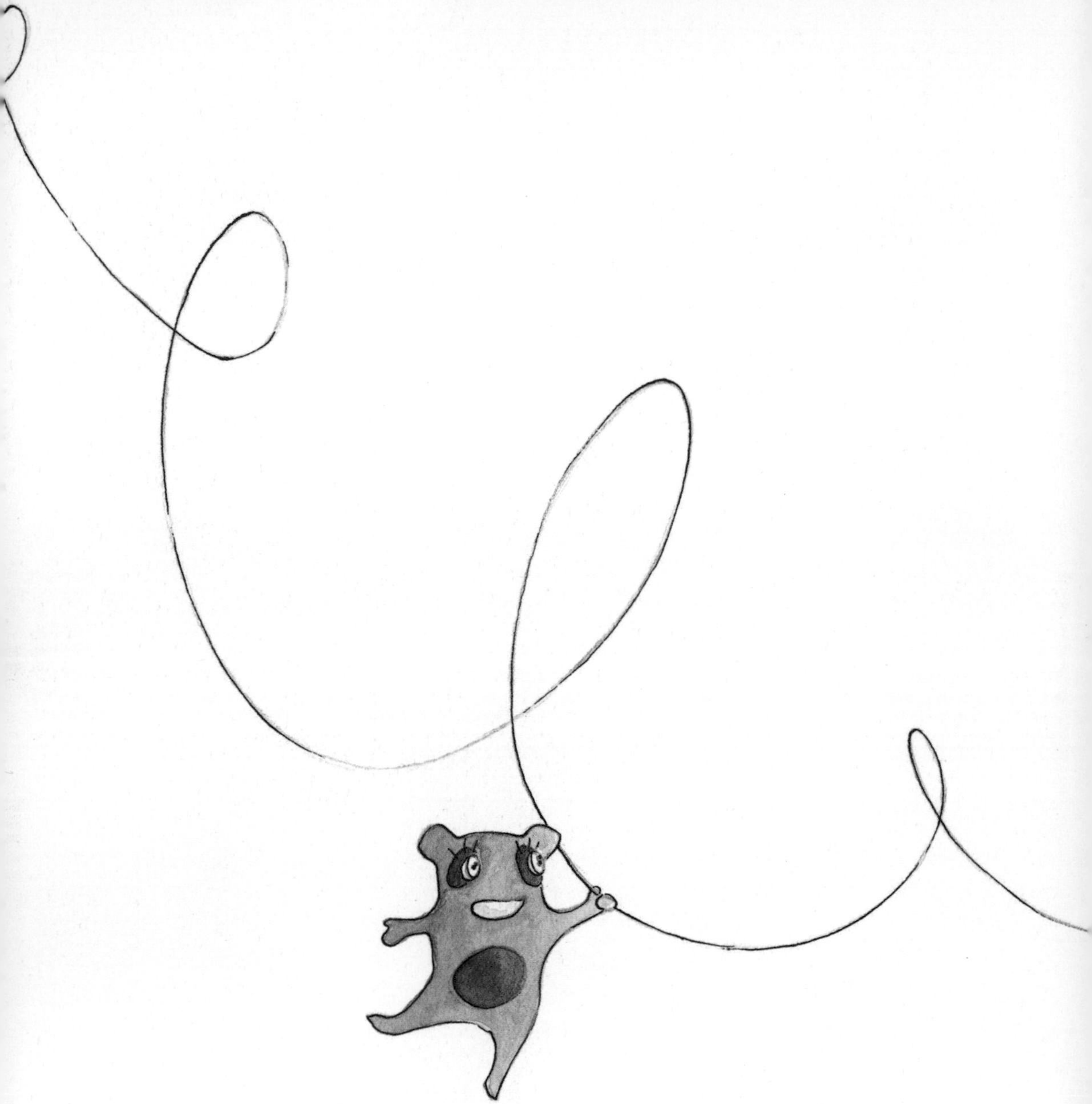

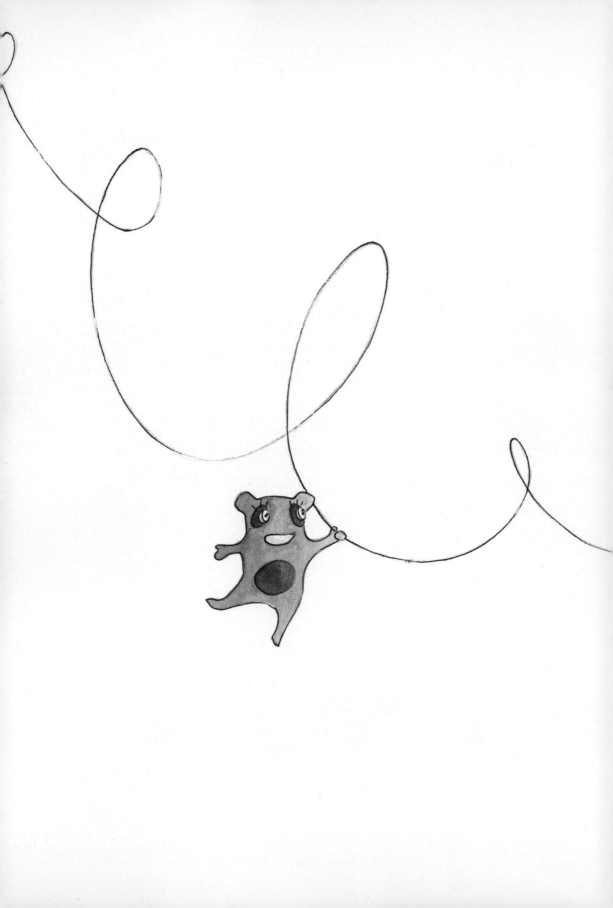

Lint Boy

by Aileen Leijten

CLARION BOOKS
Houghton Mifflin Harcourt
Boston New York

For my daughter, Alaya

Clarion Books
3 Park Avenue
New York, New York 10016

Copyright © 2017 by Aileen Leijten

Clarion Books is an imprint of Houghton Mifflin Harcourt Publishing Company.
www.hmhco.com

The text in this book was set in Tekton Pro and Filmotype Brooklyn.

Library of Congress Cataloging-in-Publication Data
Names: Leijten, Aileen, author. | Title: Lint Boy / by Aileen Leijten.
Description: Boston : Clarion Books-Houghton Mifflin Harcourt, [2017] |
Summary: A band of dolls, led by the brave and noble Lint Boy,
tries to escape the clutches of an evil woman who is the sworn enemy of doll-kind.
Identifiers: LCCN 2016003668 | ISBN 9780544528604 (paper over board)
Subjects: LCSH: Graphic novels. | CYAC: Graphic novels. | Dolls—Fiction.
Classification: LCC PZ7.7.L455 Li 2017 | DDC 741.5/973—dc23
LC record available at https://lccn.loc.gov/2016003668
Manufactured in China
SCP 10 9 8 7 6 5 4 3 2 1
4500646553

Table of Contents

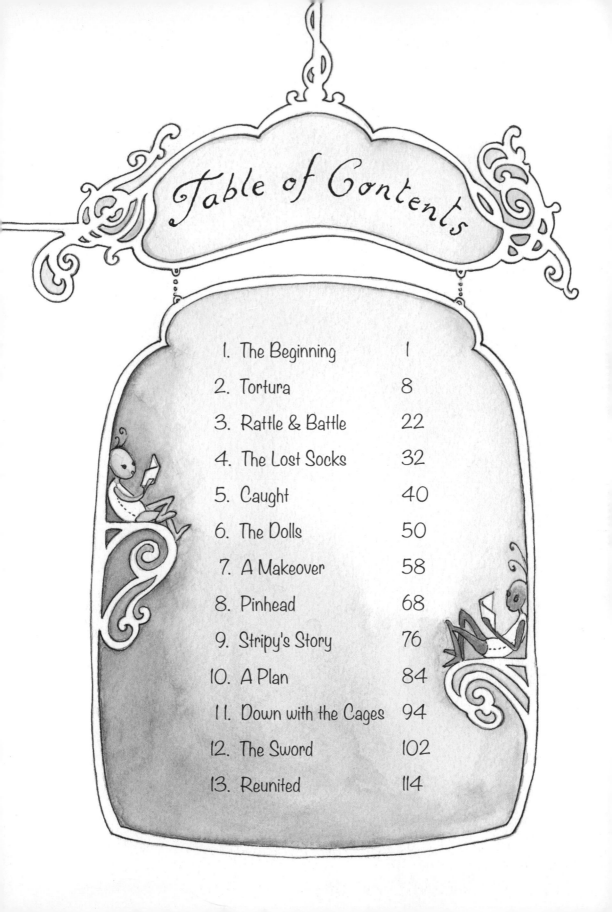

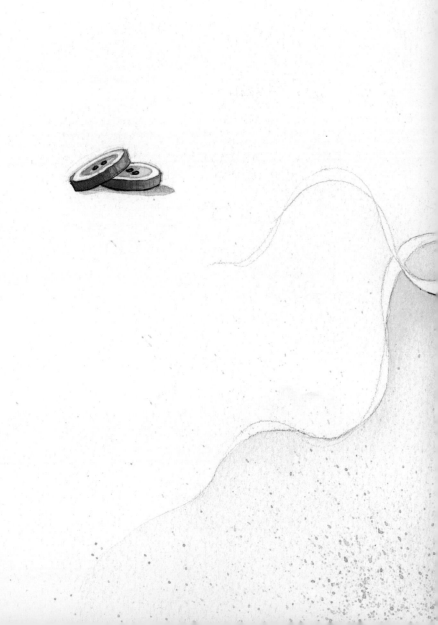

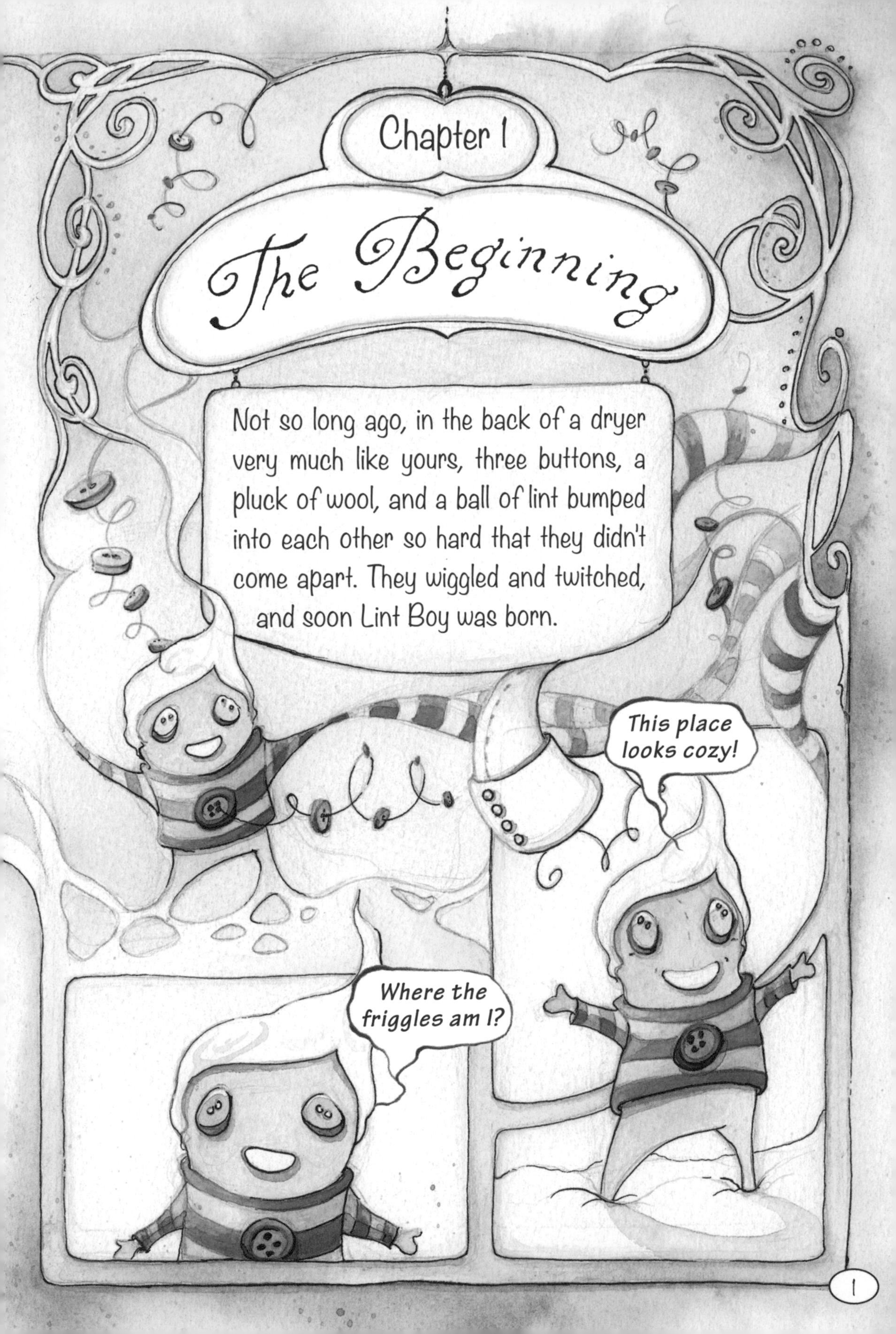
Chapter 1
The Beginning
Not so long ago, in the back of a dryer very much like yours, three buttons, a pluck of wool, and a ball of lint bumped into each other so hard that they didn't come apart. They wiggled and twitched, and soon Lint Boy was born.
Where the friggles am I?
This place looks cozy!

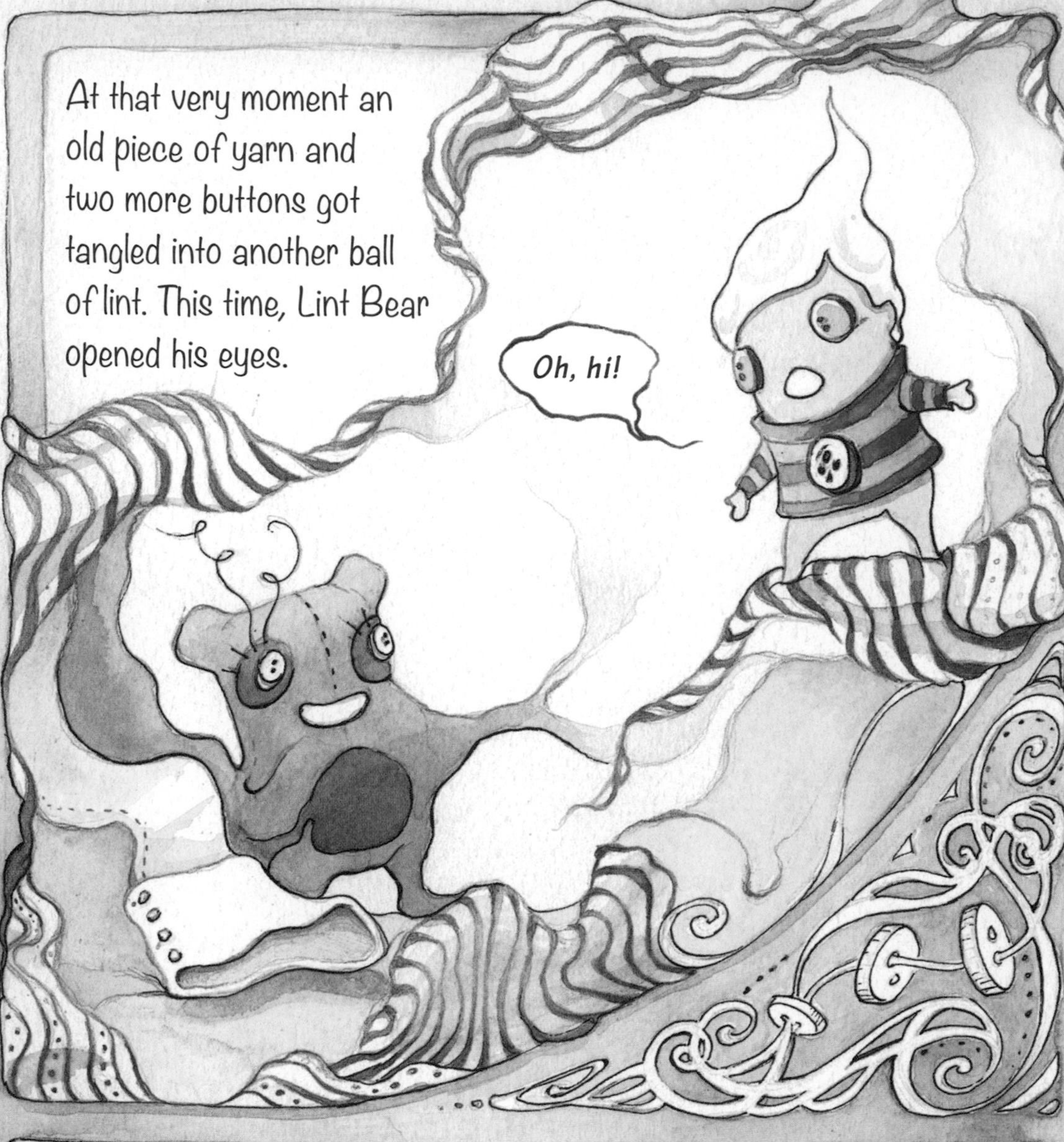
At that very moment an old piece of yarn and two more buttons got tangled into another ball of lint. This time, Lint Bear opened his eyes.
Oh, hi!

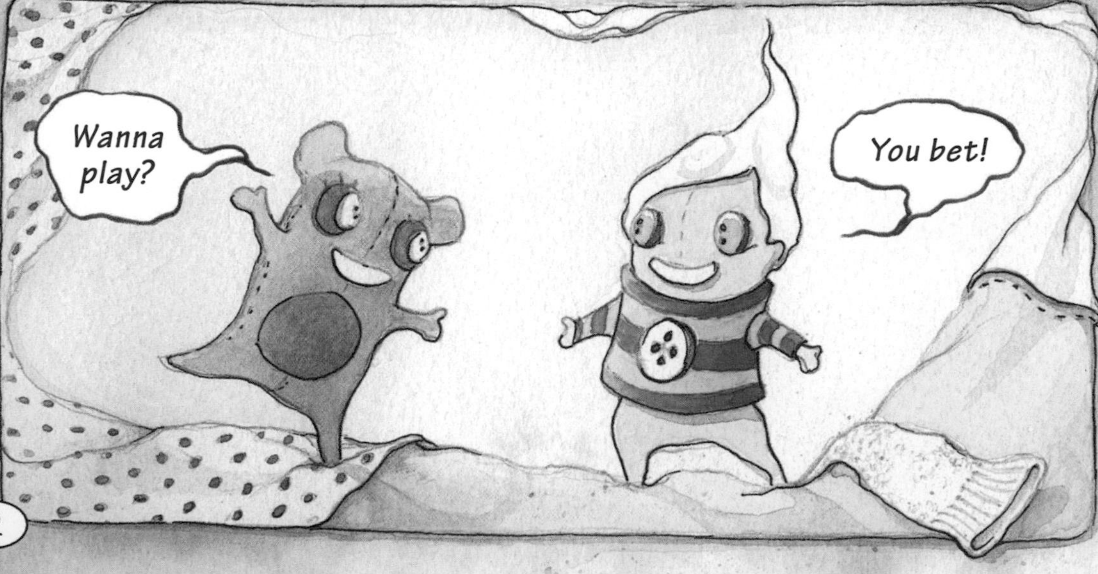
Wanna play?
You bet!

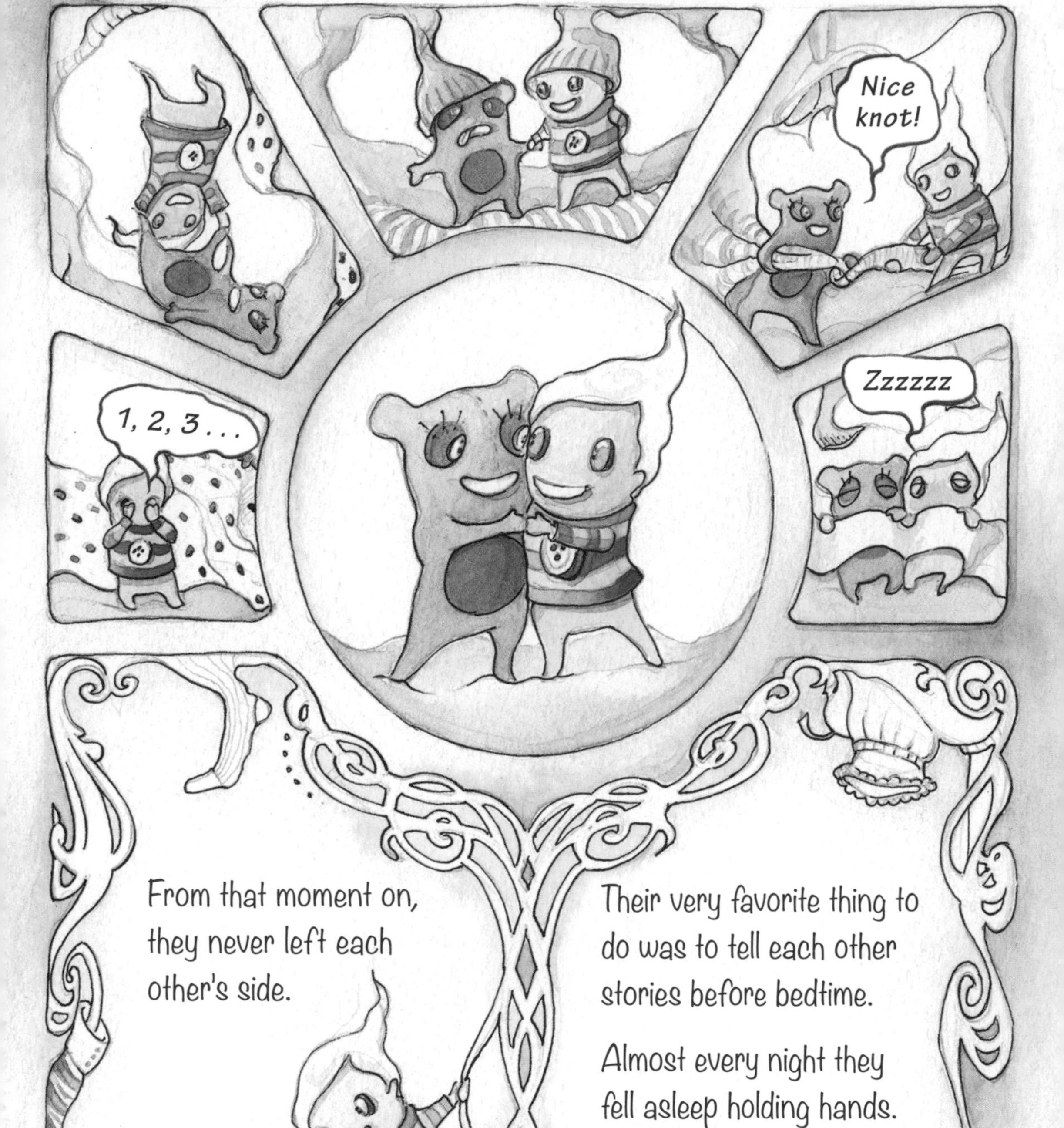
Nice knot!
1, 2, 3 . . .
Zzzzzz

From that moment on, they never left each other's side.

Their very favorite thing to do was to tell each other stories before bedtime.

Almost every night they fell asleep holding hands.

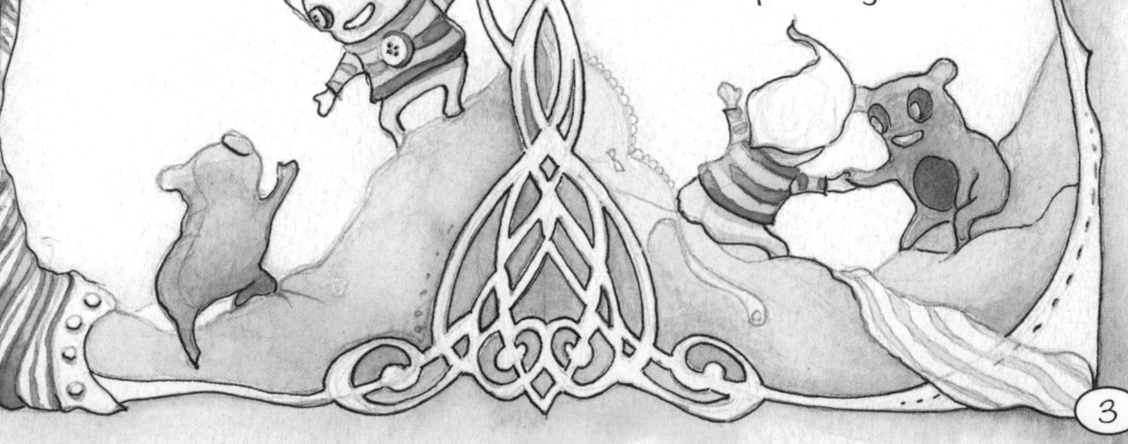

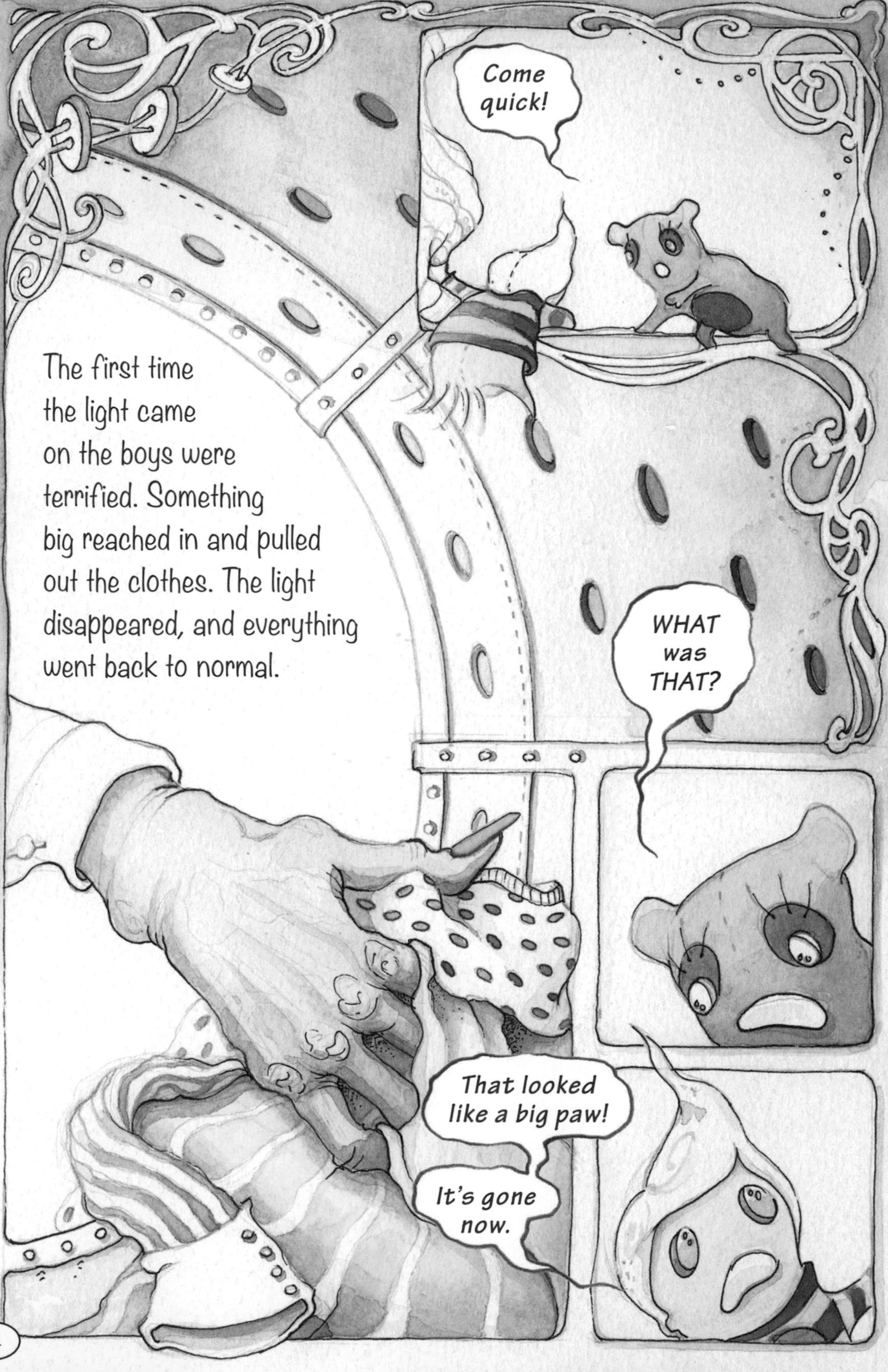
The first time the light came on the boys were terrified. Something big reached in and pulled out the clothes. The light disappeared, and everything went back to normal.
Come quick!
WHAT was THAT?
That looked like a big paw!
It's gone now.

Days and weeks went by. The boys got used to the short episodes of bright light. Lint Boy was always quick to climb up and away.

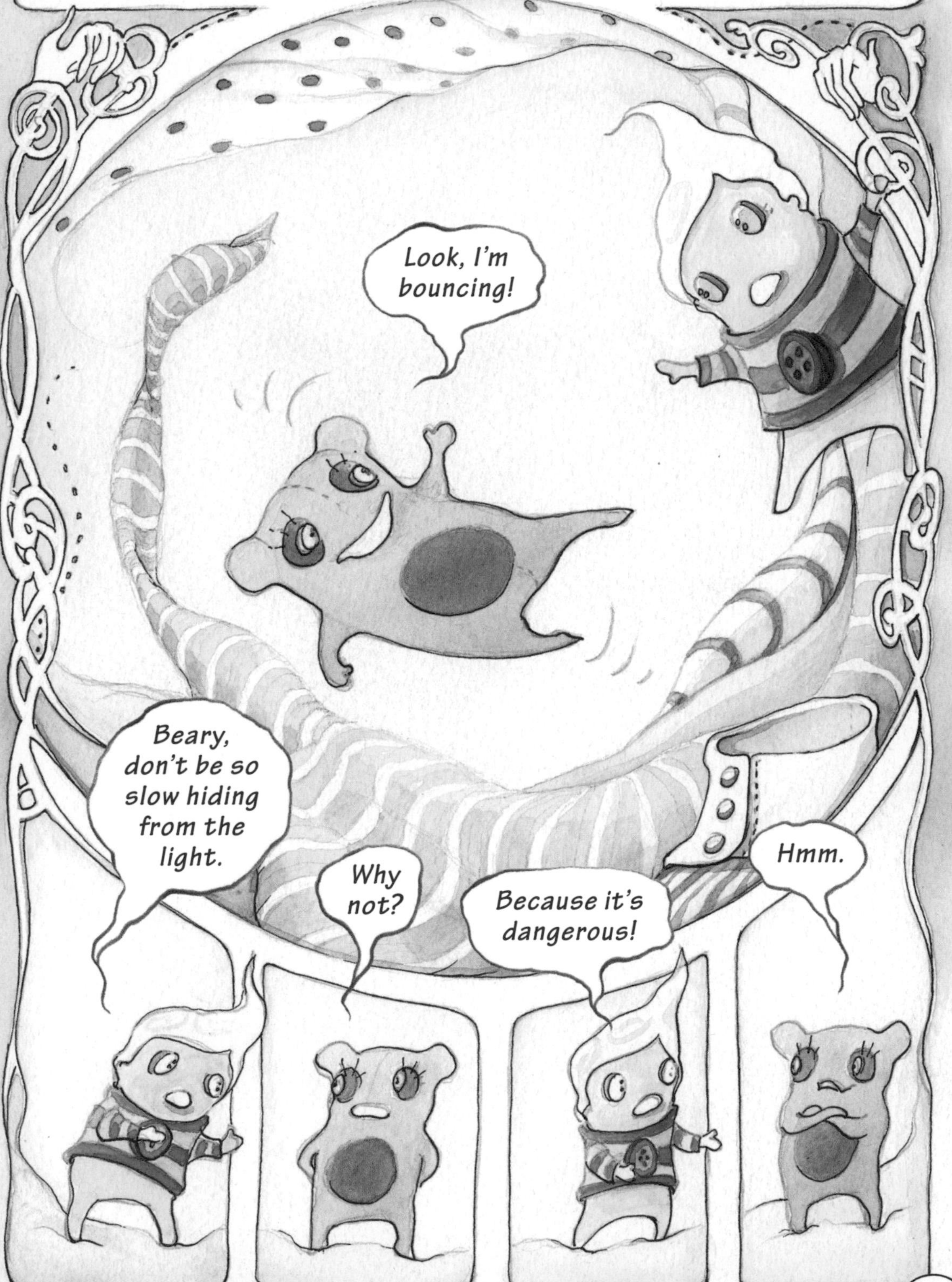
Look, I'm bouncing!
Beary, don't be so slow hiding from the light.
Why not?
Because it's dangerous!
Hmm.

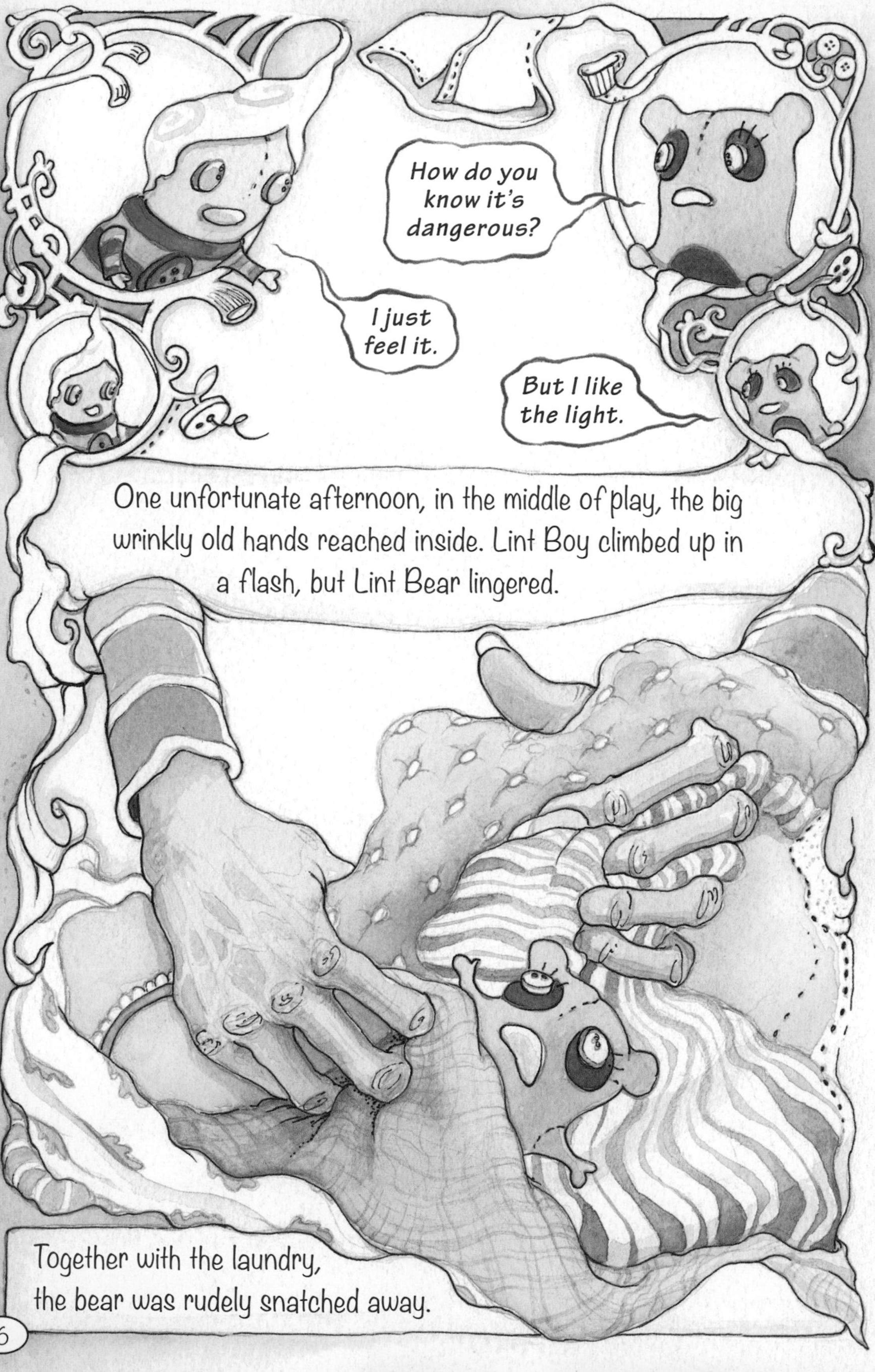
How do you know it's dangerous?
I just feel it.
But I like the light.
One unfortunate afternoon, in the middle of play, the big wrinkly old hands reached inside. Lint Boy climbed up in a flash, but Lint Bear lingered.
Together with the laundry, the bear was rudely snatched away.

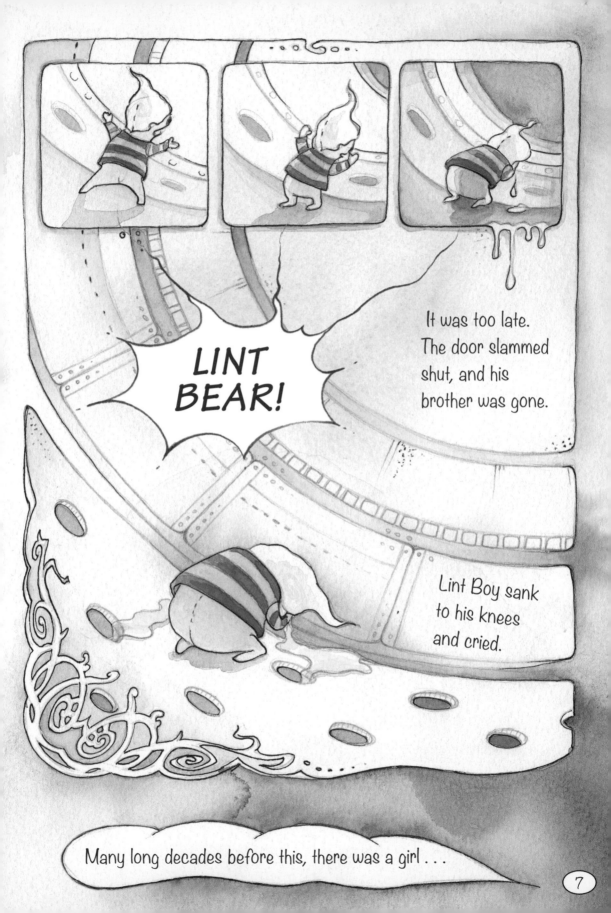

LINT
BEAR!

It was too late.
The door slammed
shut, and his
brother was gone.

Lint Boy sank
to his knees
and cried.

Many long decades before this, there was a girl . . .

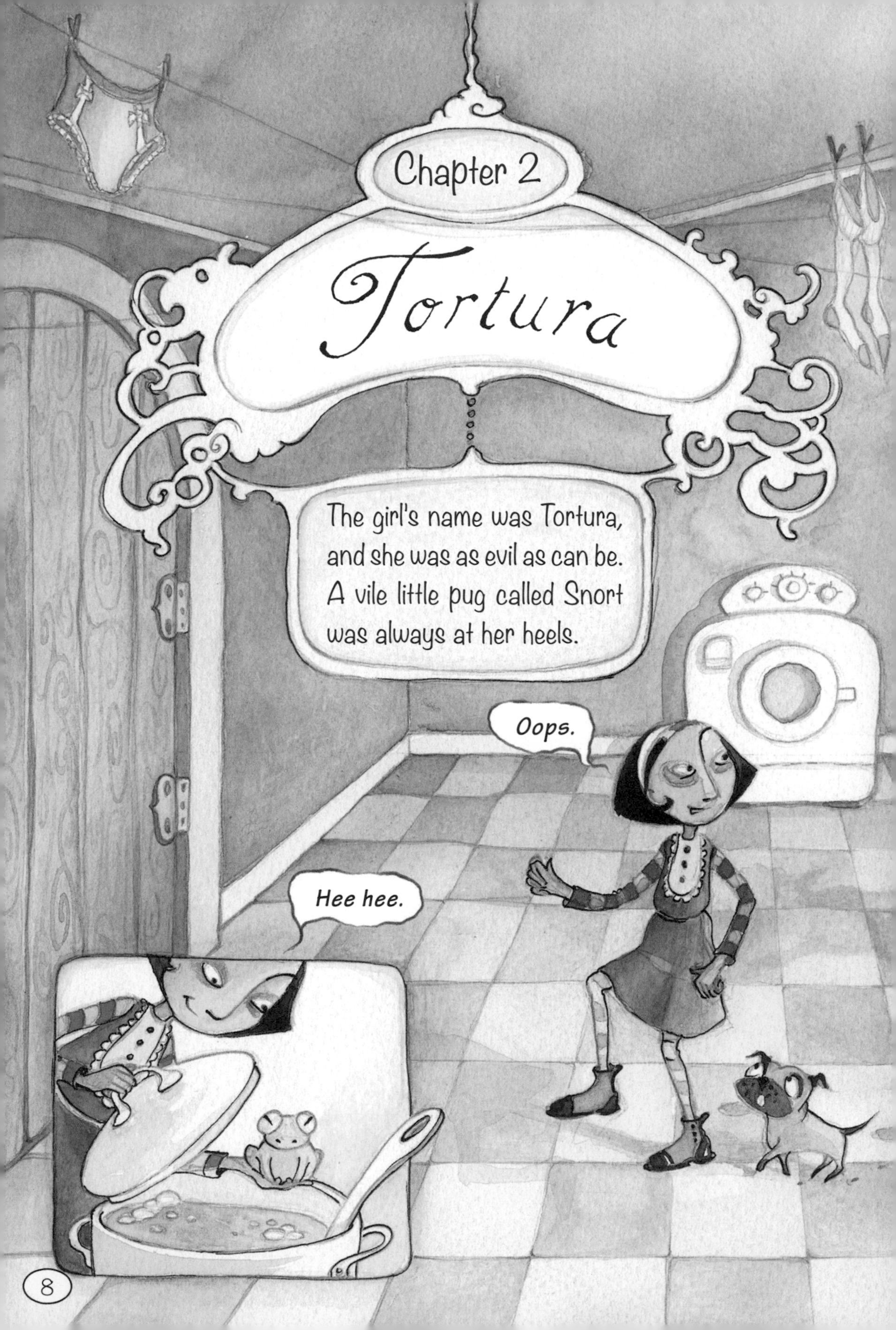
Chapter 2
Tortura
The girl's name was Tortura, and she was as evil as can be. A vile little pug called Snort was always at her heels.
Oops.
Hee hee.

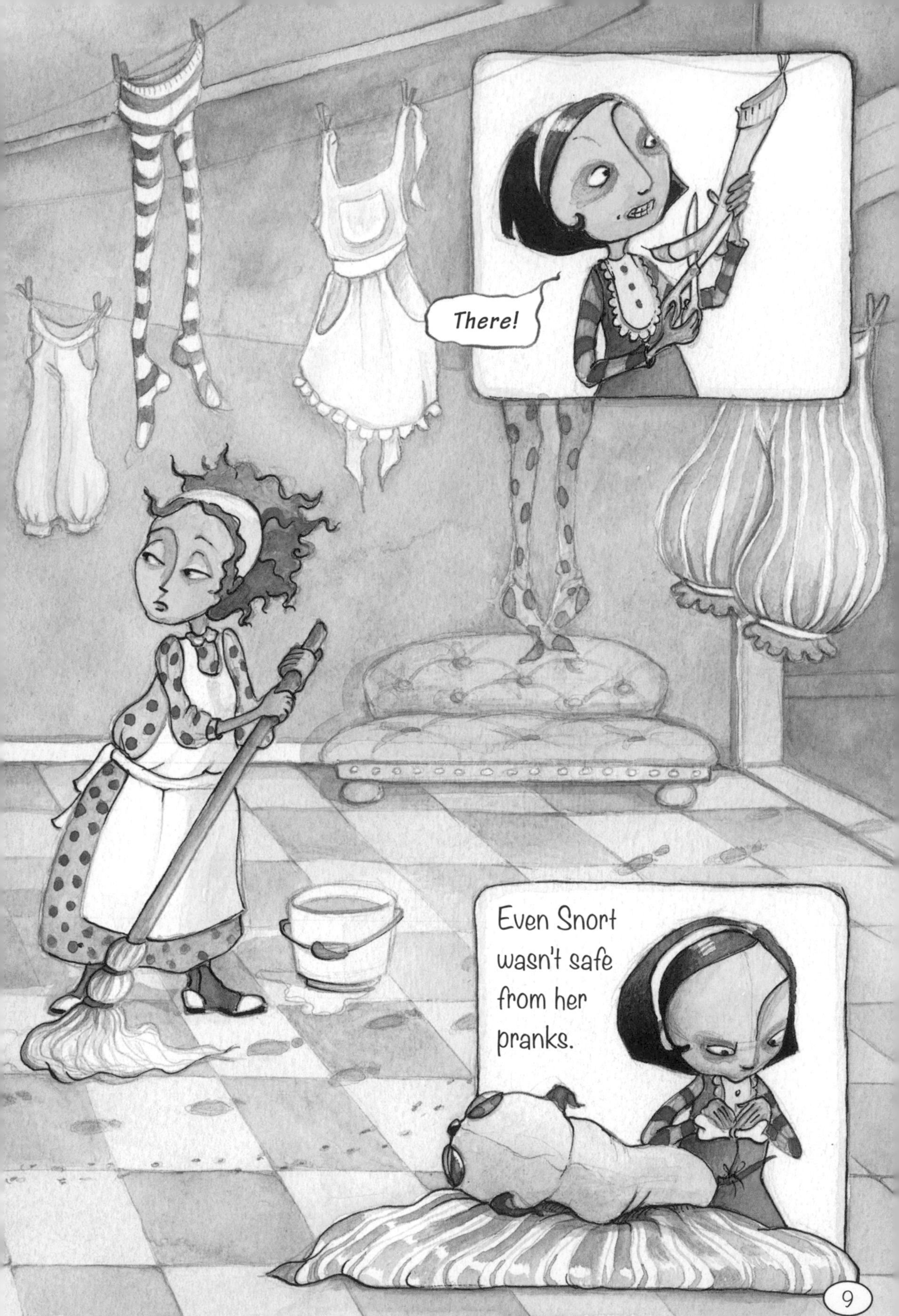
There!
Even Snort wasn't safe from her pranks.

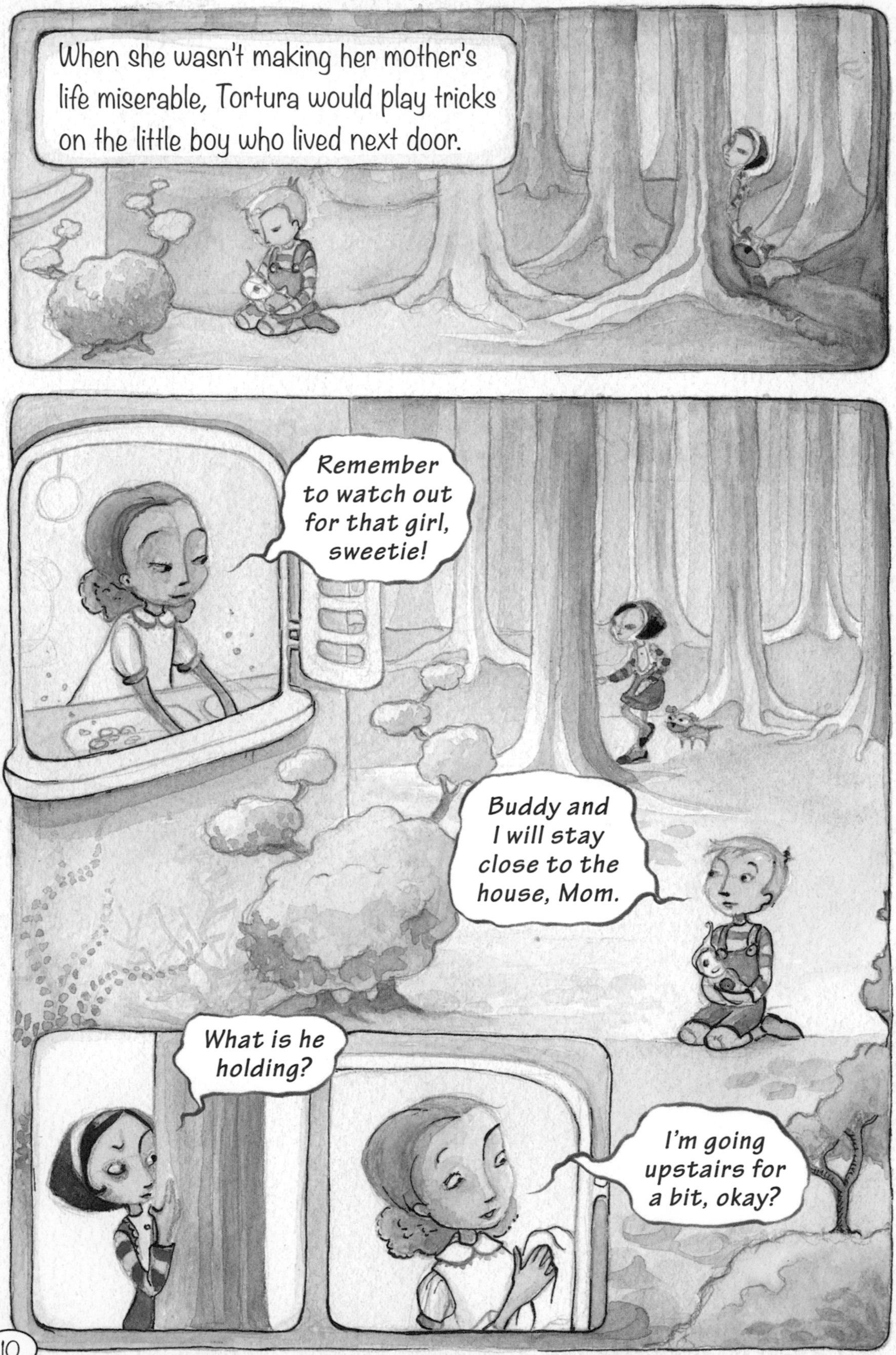
When she wasn't making her mother's life miserable, Tortura would play tricks on the little boy who lived next door.
Remember to watch out for that girl, sweetie!
Buddy and I will stay close to the house, Mom.
What is he holding?
I'm going upstairs for a bit, okay?

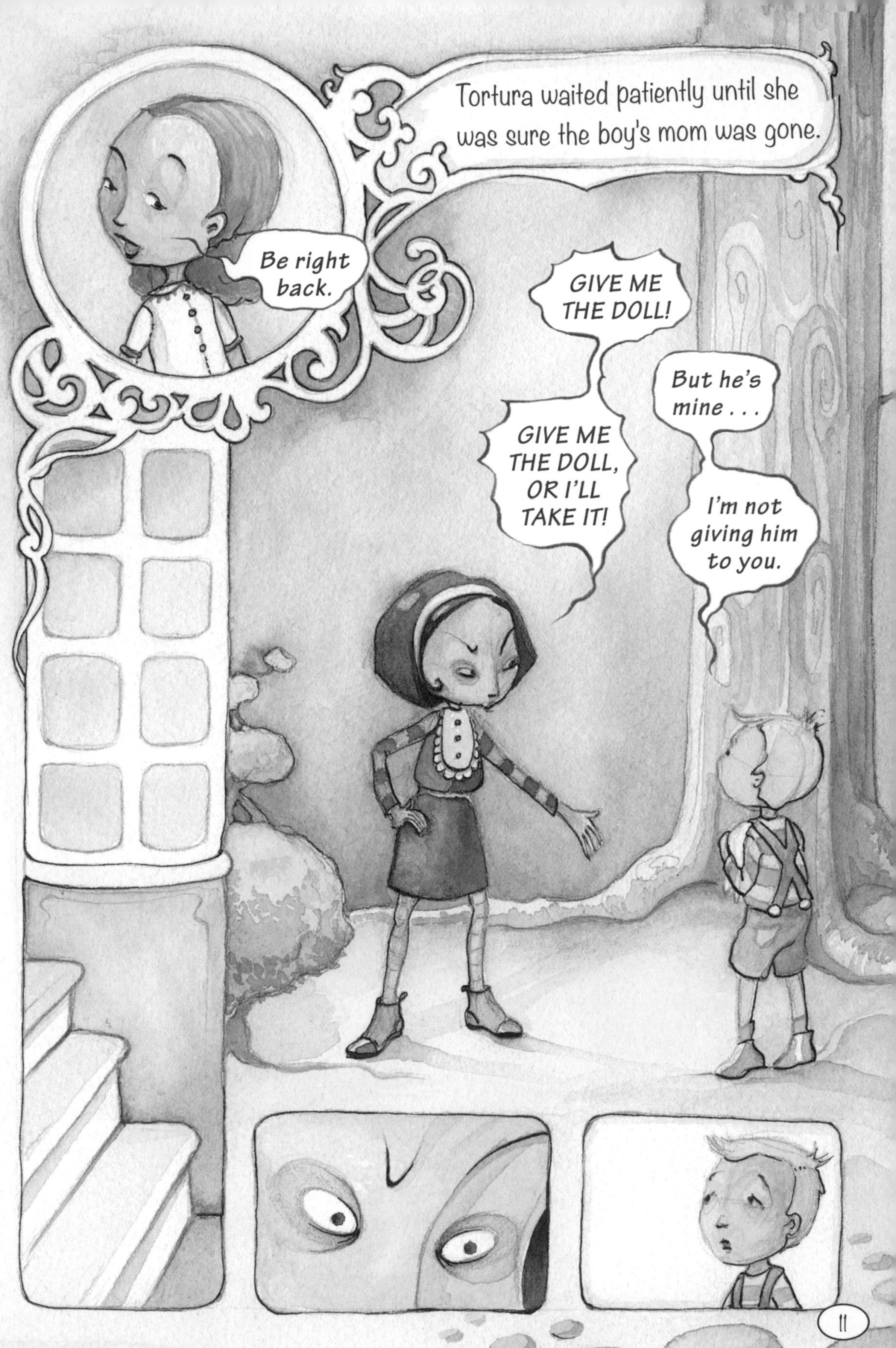

Tortura waited patiently until she was sure the boy's mom was gone.
Be right back.
GIVE ME THE DOLL!
GIVE ME THE DOLL, OR I'LL TAKE IT!
But he's mine . . .
I'm not giving him to you.

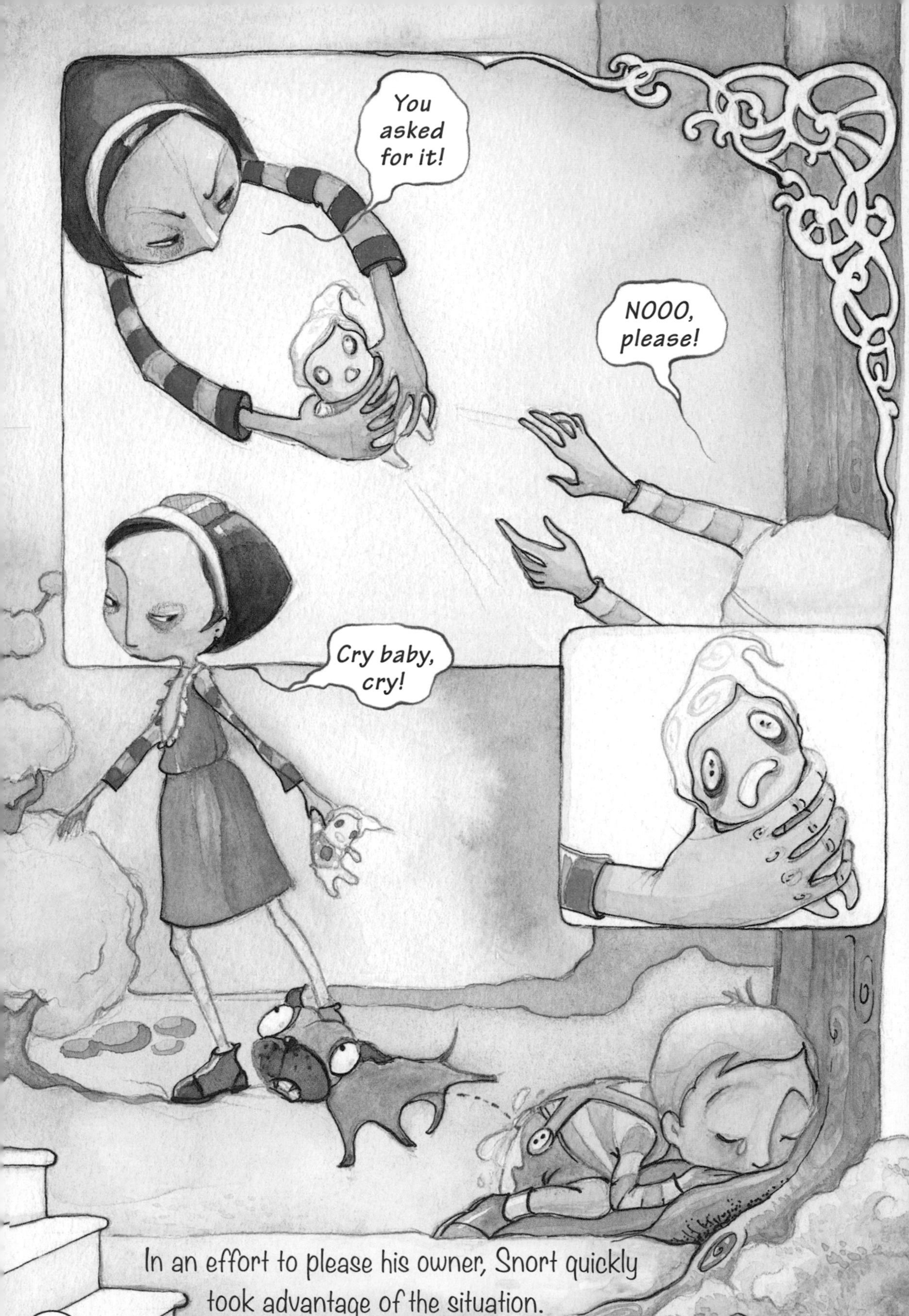
You asked for it!
NOOO, please!
Cry baby, cry!

In an effort to please his owner, Snort quickly took advantage of the situation.

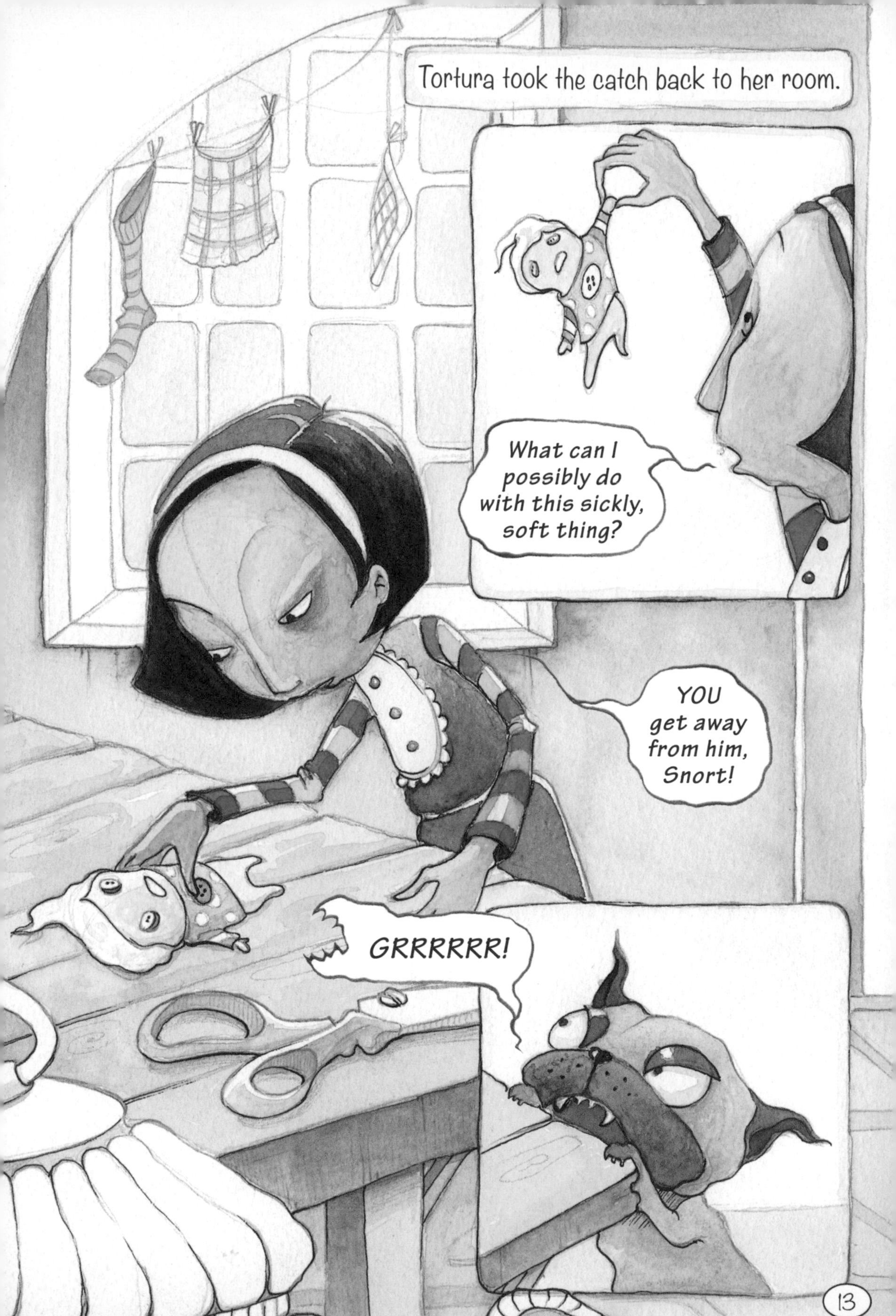
Tortura took the catch back to her room.
What can I possibly do with this sickly, soft thing?
YOU get away from him, Snort!
GRRRRRR!

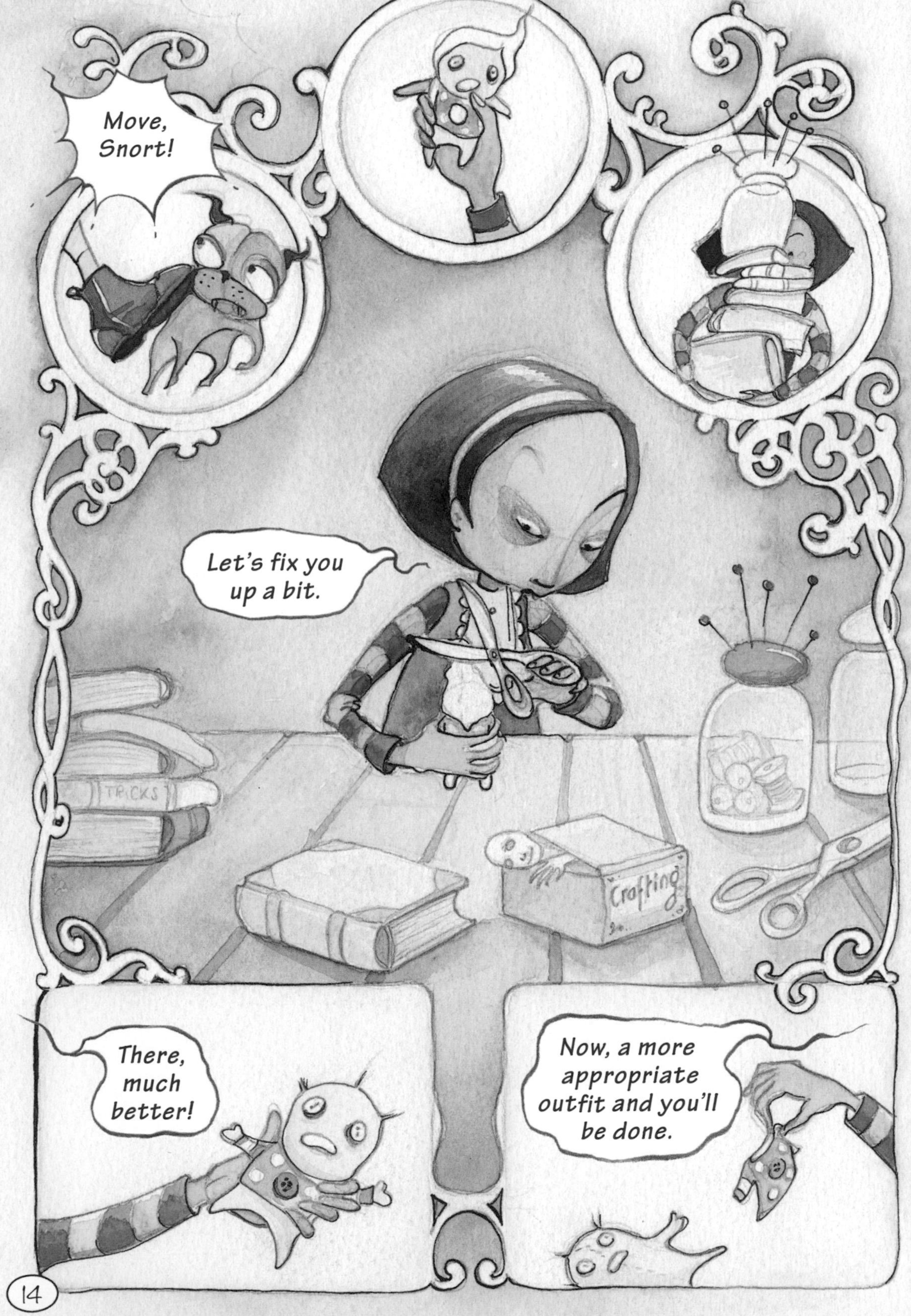
Move, Snort!
Let's fix you up a bit.
TRICKS
Crafting
There, much better!
Now, a more appropriate outfit and you'll be done.

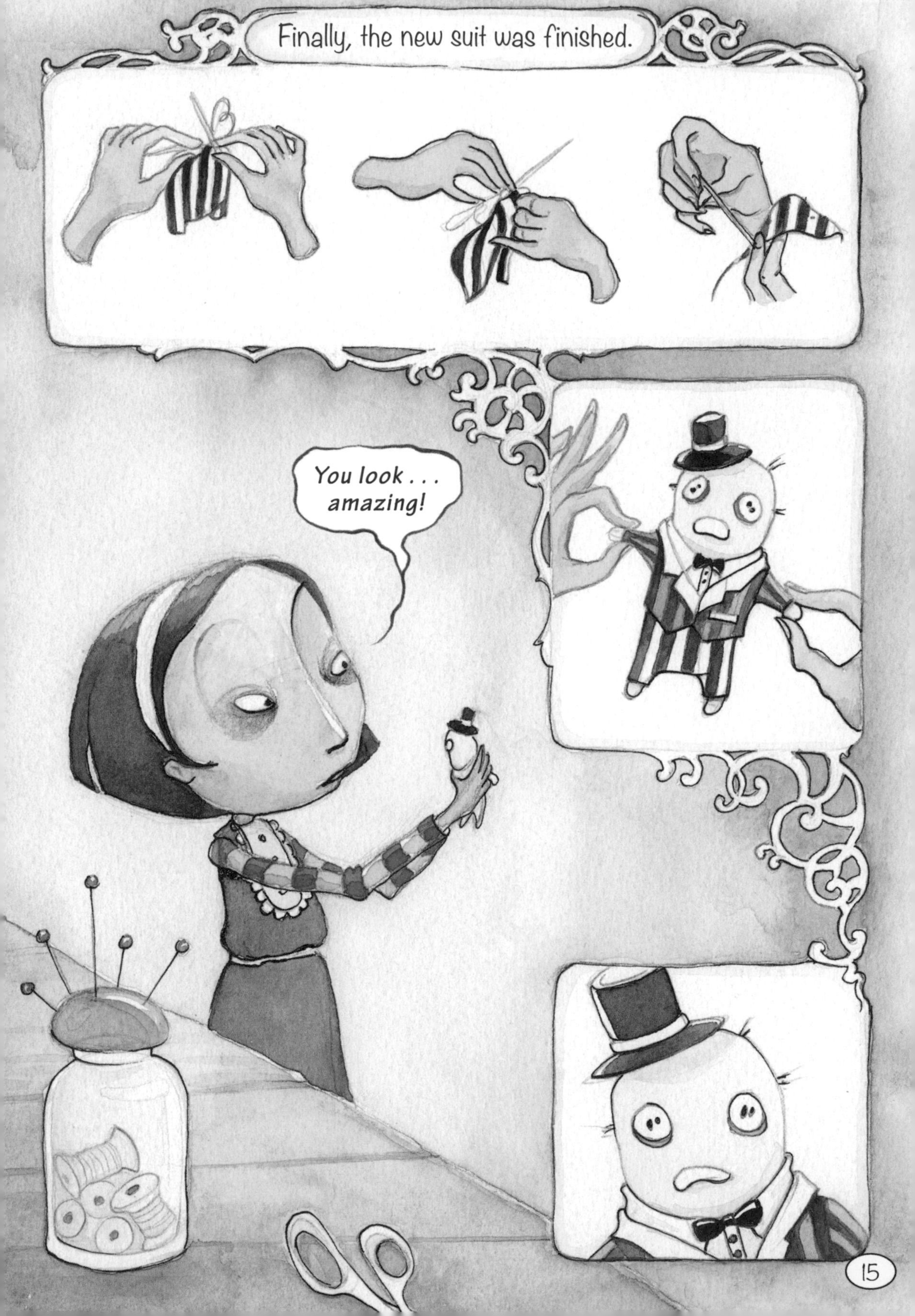
Finally, the new suit was finished.
You look . . . amazing!

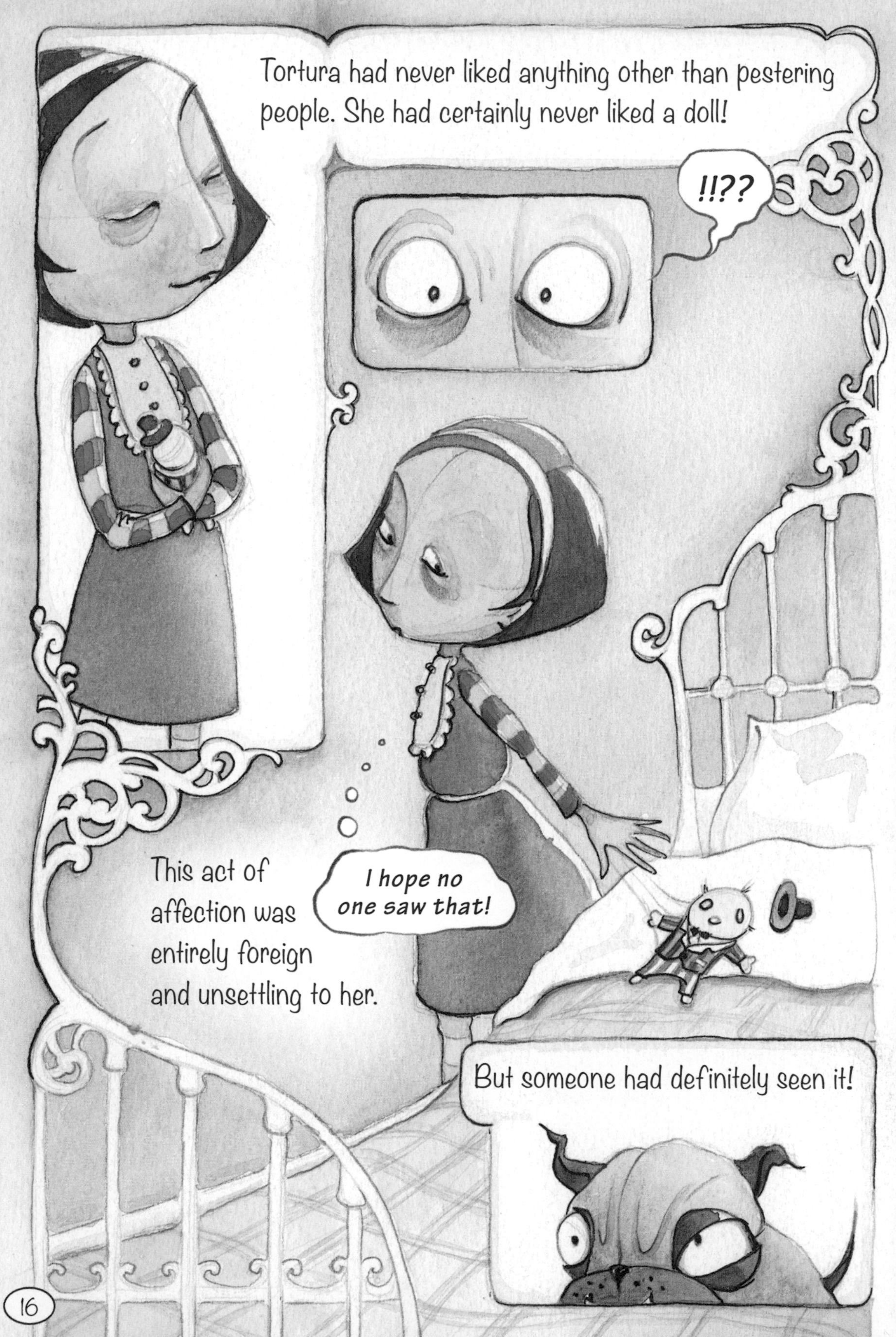
Tortura had never liked anything other than pestering people. She had certainly never liked a doll!
!!??
This act of affection was entirely foreign and unsettling to her.
I hope no one saw that!
But someone had definitely seen it!

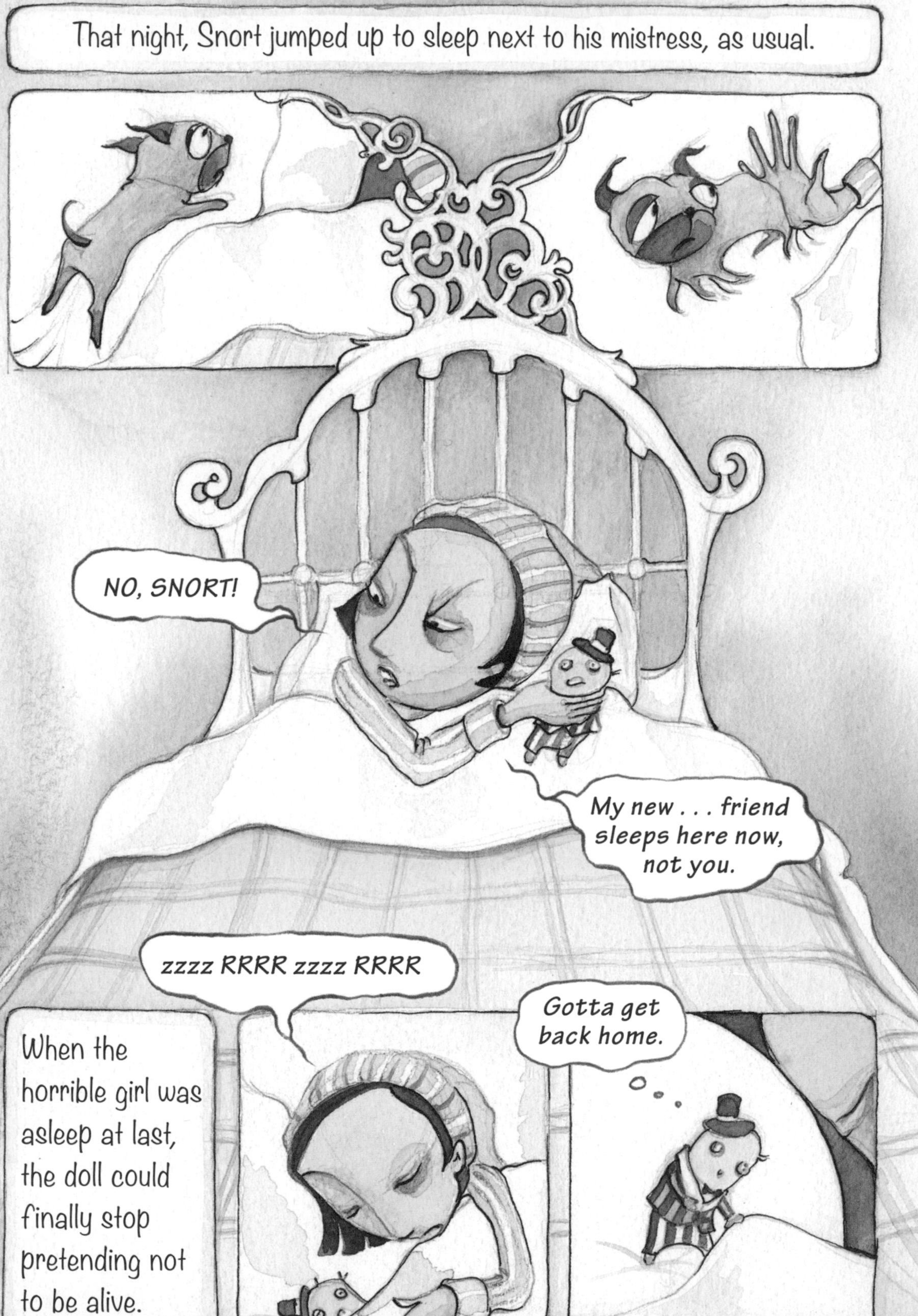
That night, Snort jumped up to sleep next to his mistress, as usual.
NO, SNORT!
My new . . . friend sleeps here now, not you.
When the horrible girl was asleep at last, the doll could finally stop pretending not to be alive.
zzzz RRRR zzzz RRRR
Gotta get back home.

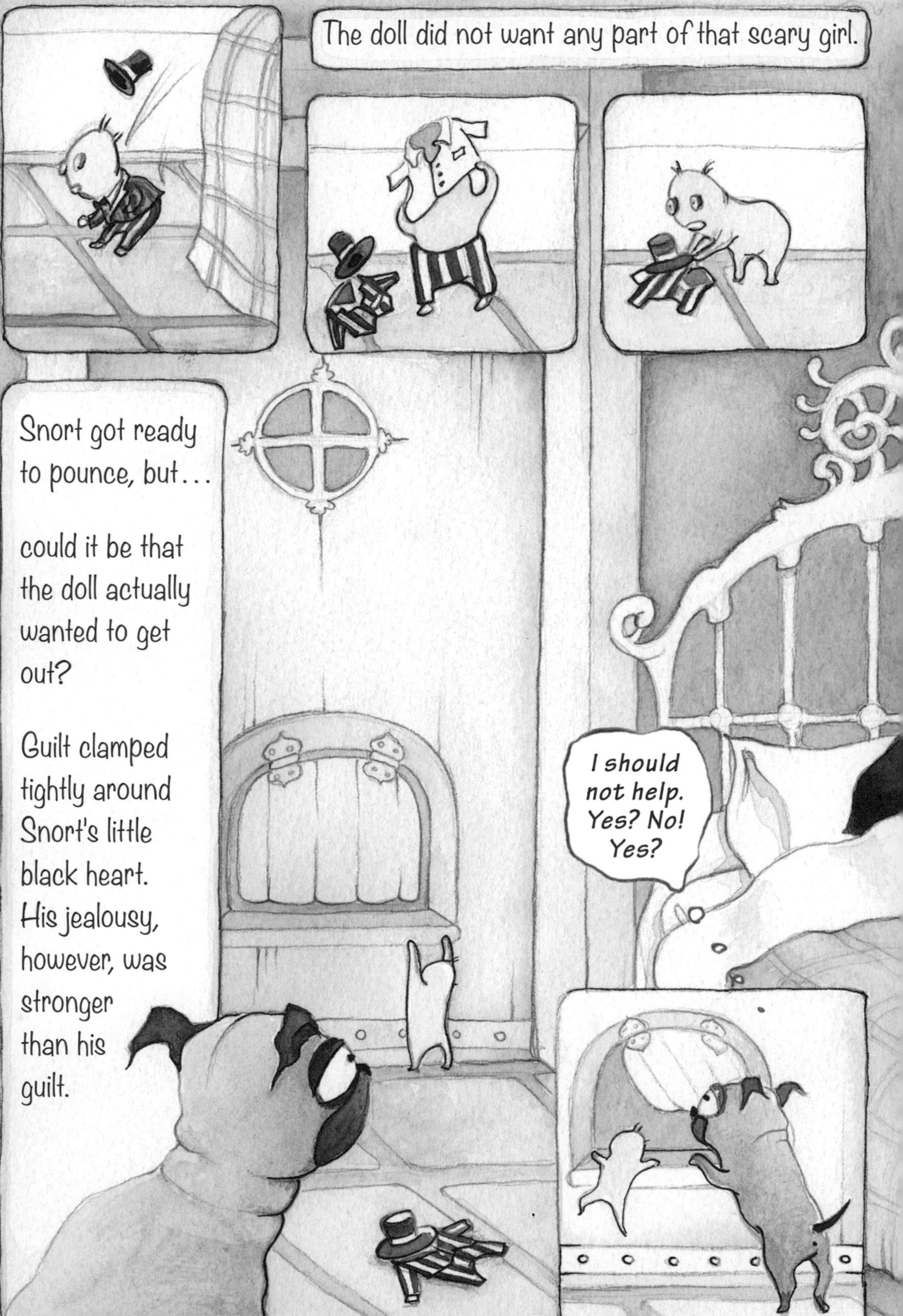

The doll did not want any part of that scary girl.
Snort got ready to pounce, but...
could it be that the doll actually wanted to get out?
Guilt clamped tightly around Snort's little black heart. His jealousy, however, was stronger than his guilt.
I should not help. Yes? No! Yes?

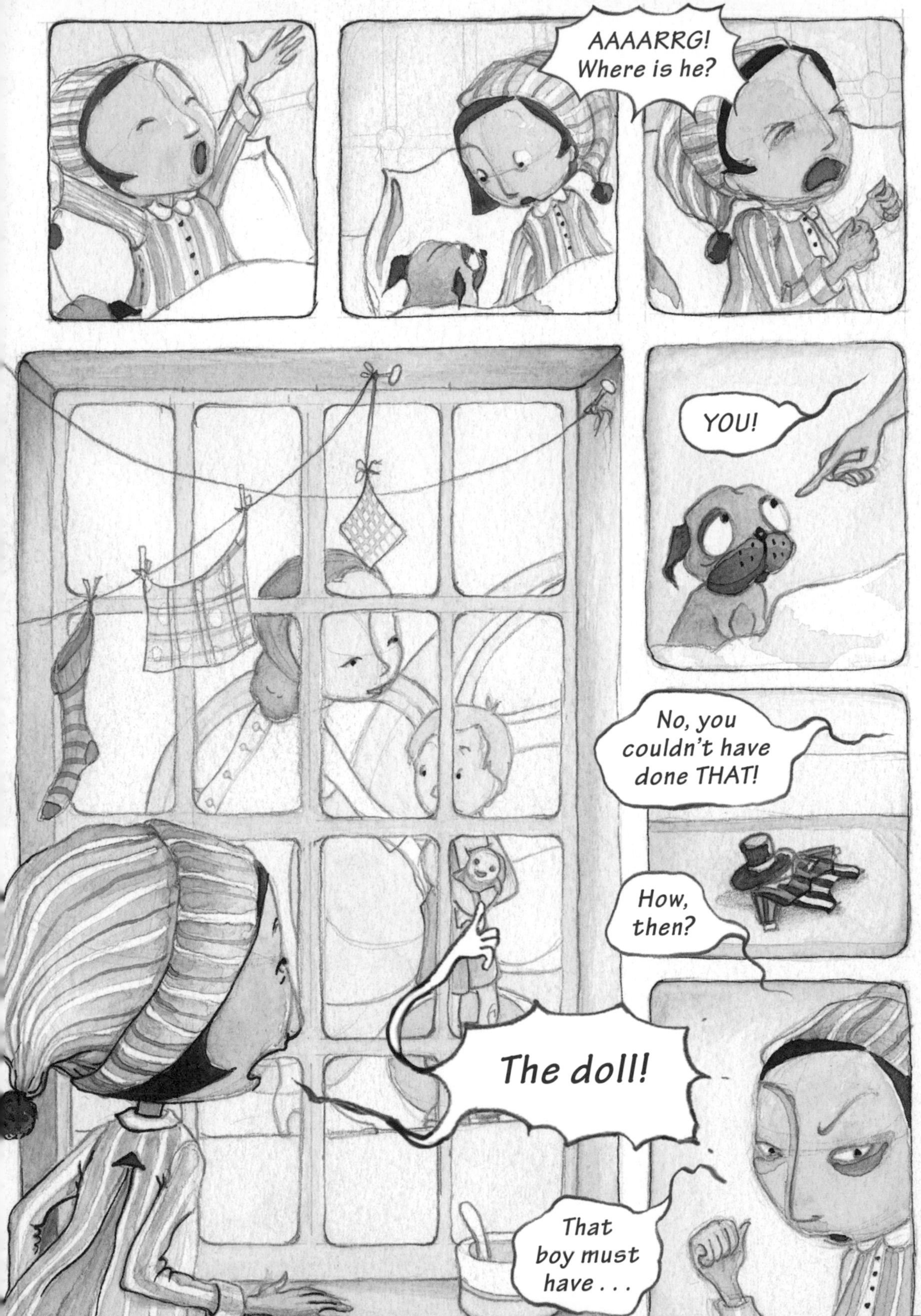
AAAARRG! Where is he?
YOU!
No, you couldn't have done THAT!
How, then?
The doll!
That boy must have . . .

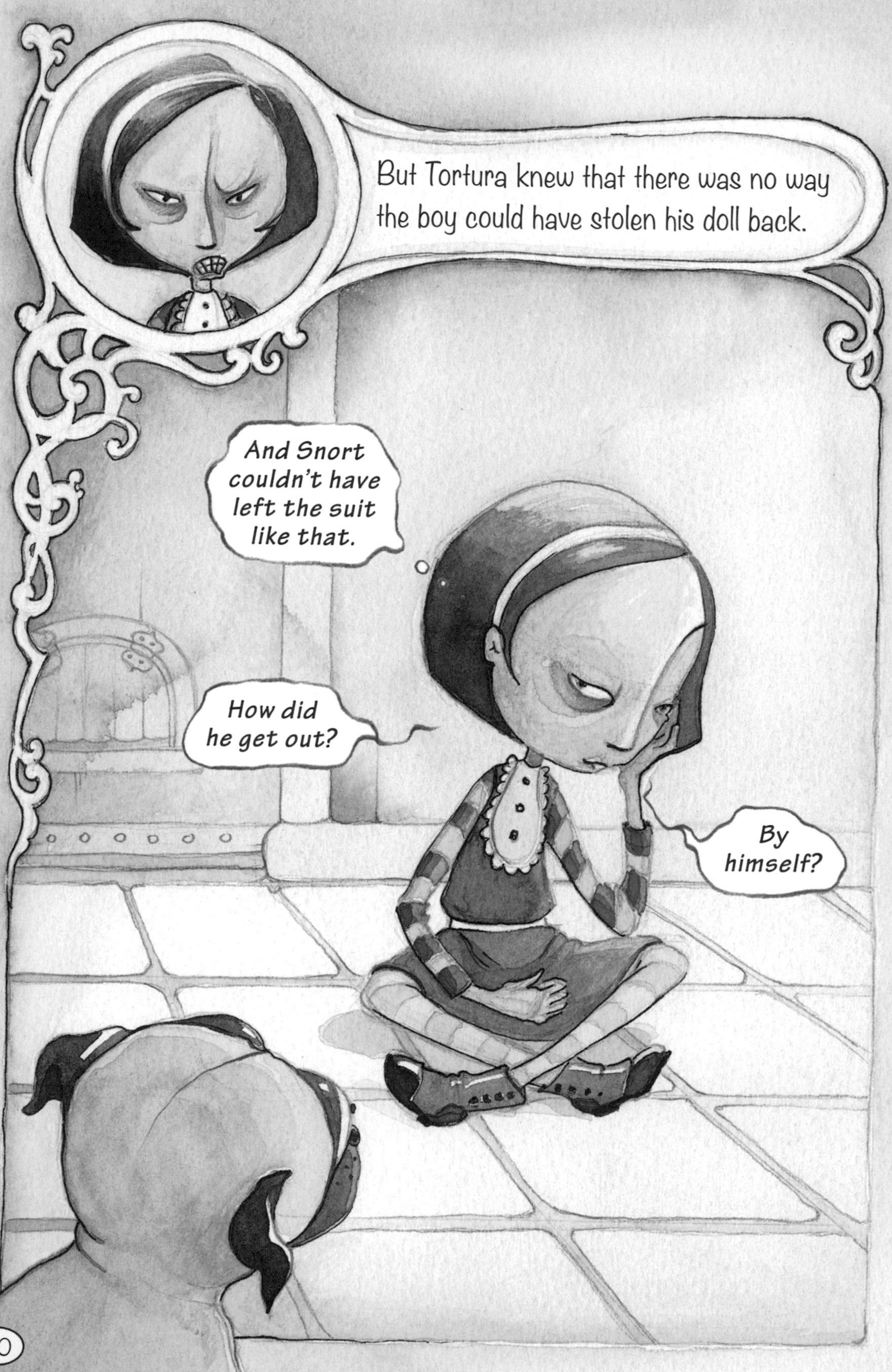

But Tortura knew that there was no way the boy could have stolen his doll back.
And Snort couldn't have left the suit like that.
How did he get out?
By himself?

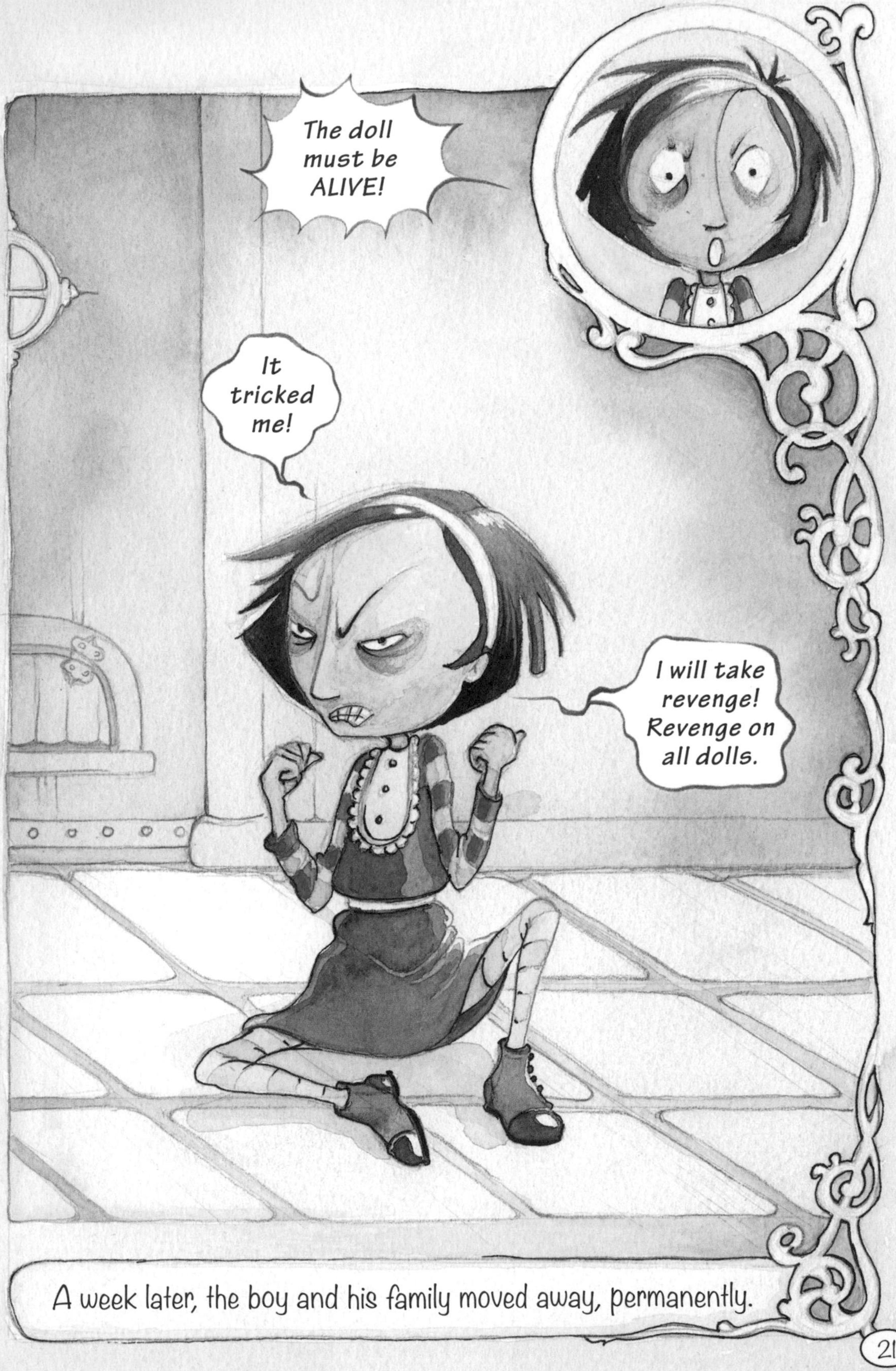
The doll must be ALIVE!
It tricked me!
I will take revenge! Revenge on all dolls.
A week later, the boy and his family moved away, permanently.

Chapter 3

Rattle & Battle

It so happened that the cruel hands that had snatched away Lint Bear belonged to Tortura.

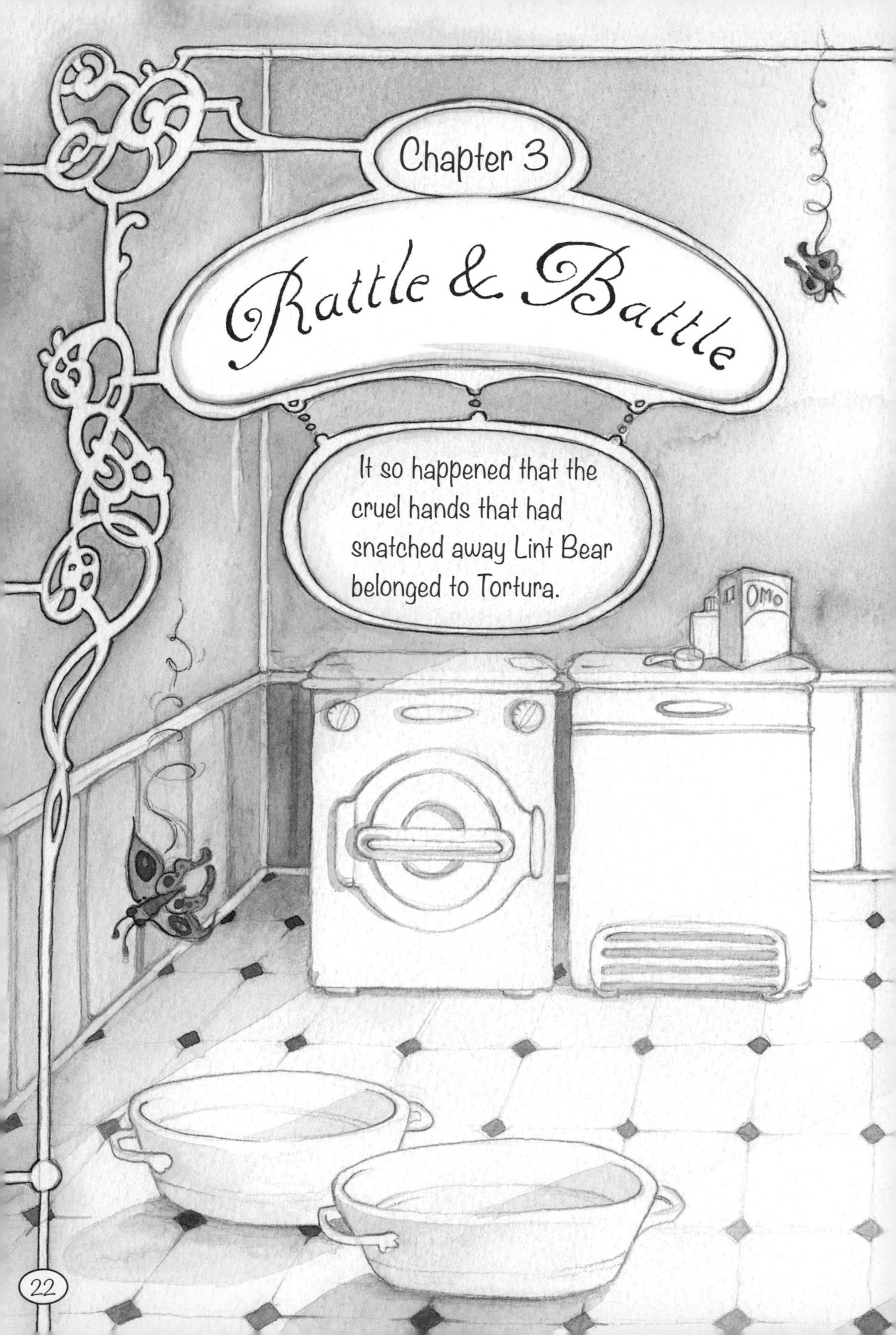
OMO

Tortura had grown up into a wicked old hag, Mrs. PinchnSqueeze. She lived with her snappy little puppy, Snort Junior the Seventh, in an abandoned toy store, and she was as mean as can be. She was so mean that even moths shriveled up when she looked at them.

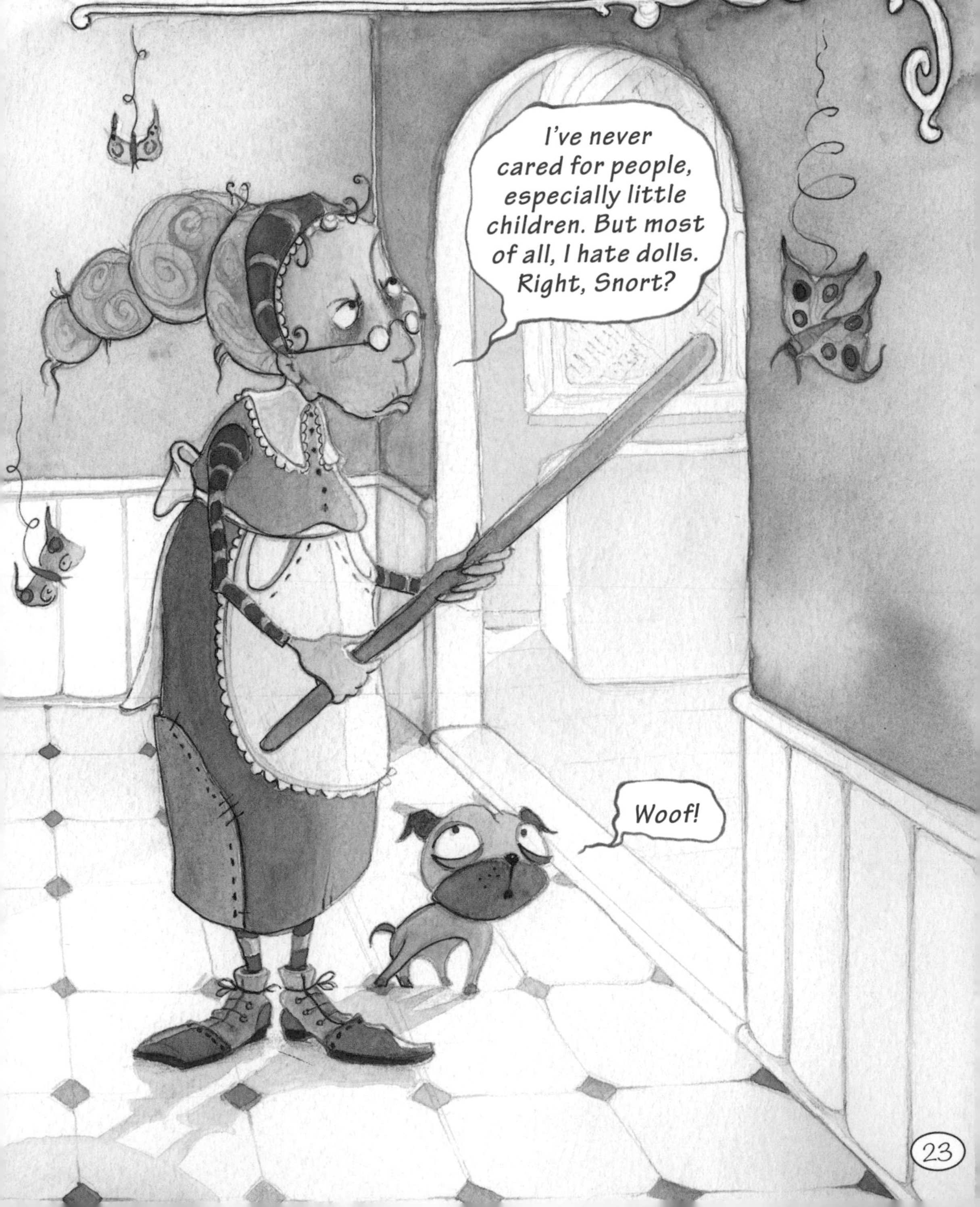
I've never cared for people, especially little children. But most of all, I hate dolls. Right, Snort?
Woof!

On this unfortunate day, Lint Bear appeared in the laundry.

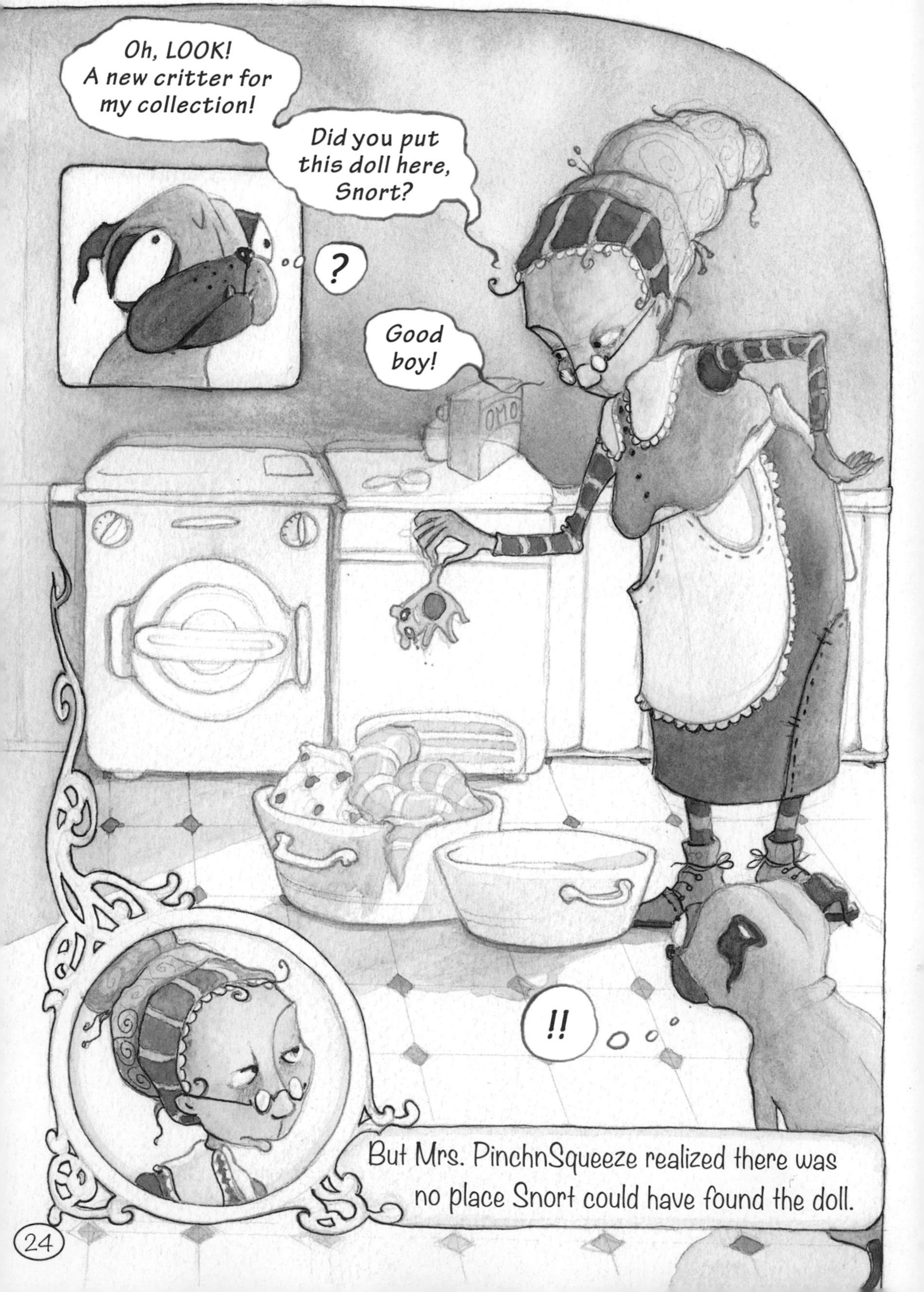
Oh, LOOK! A new critter for my collection!
Did you put this doll here, Snort?
?
Good boy!
OMO
!!

But Mrs. PinchnSqueeze realized there was no place Snort could have found the doll.

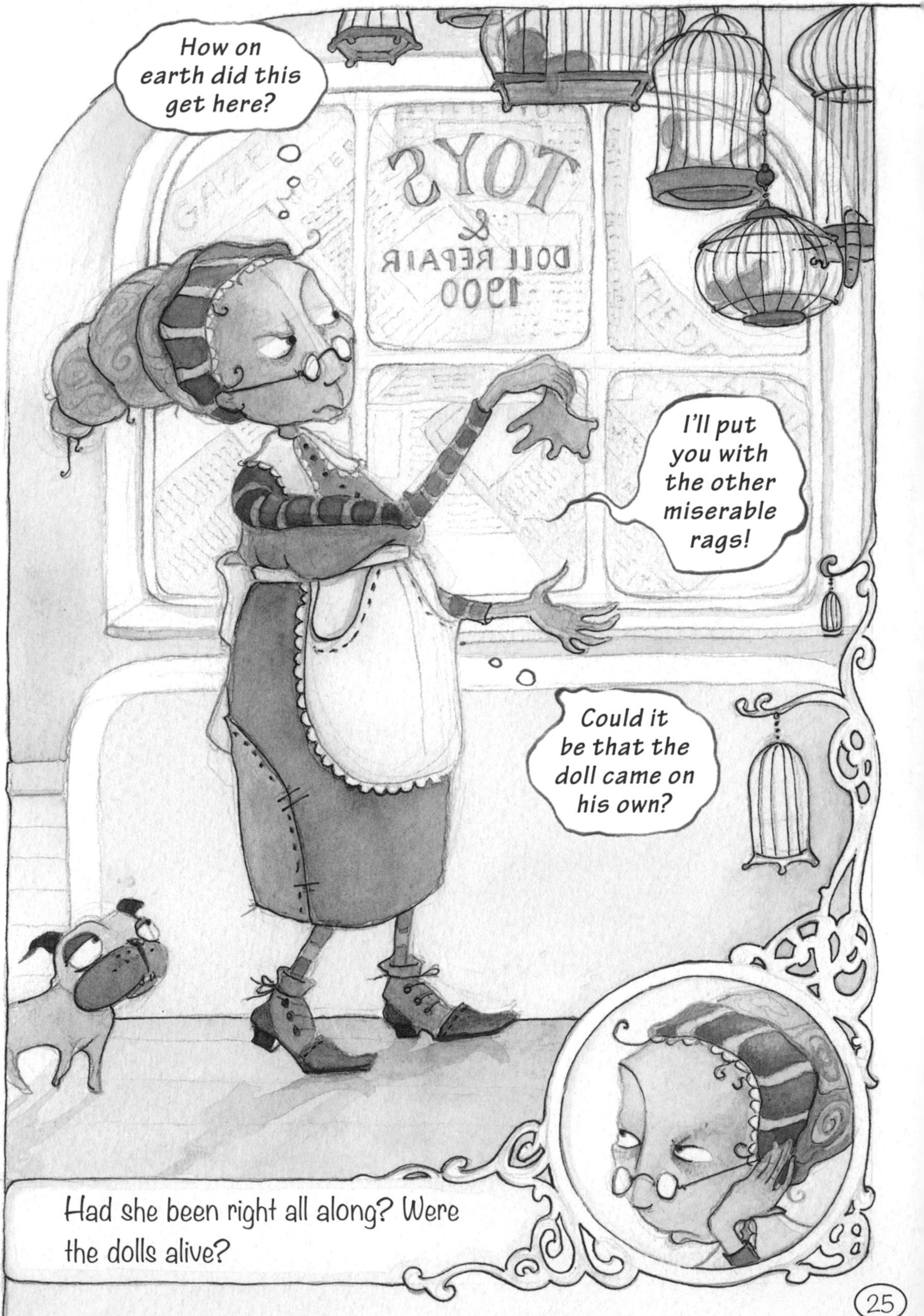
How on earth did this get here?
TOYS & DOLL REPAIR 1900
I'll put you with the other miserable rags!
Could it be that the doll came on his own?

Had she been right all along? Were the dolls alive?

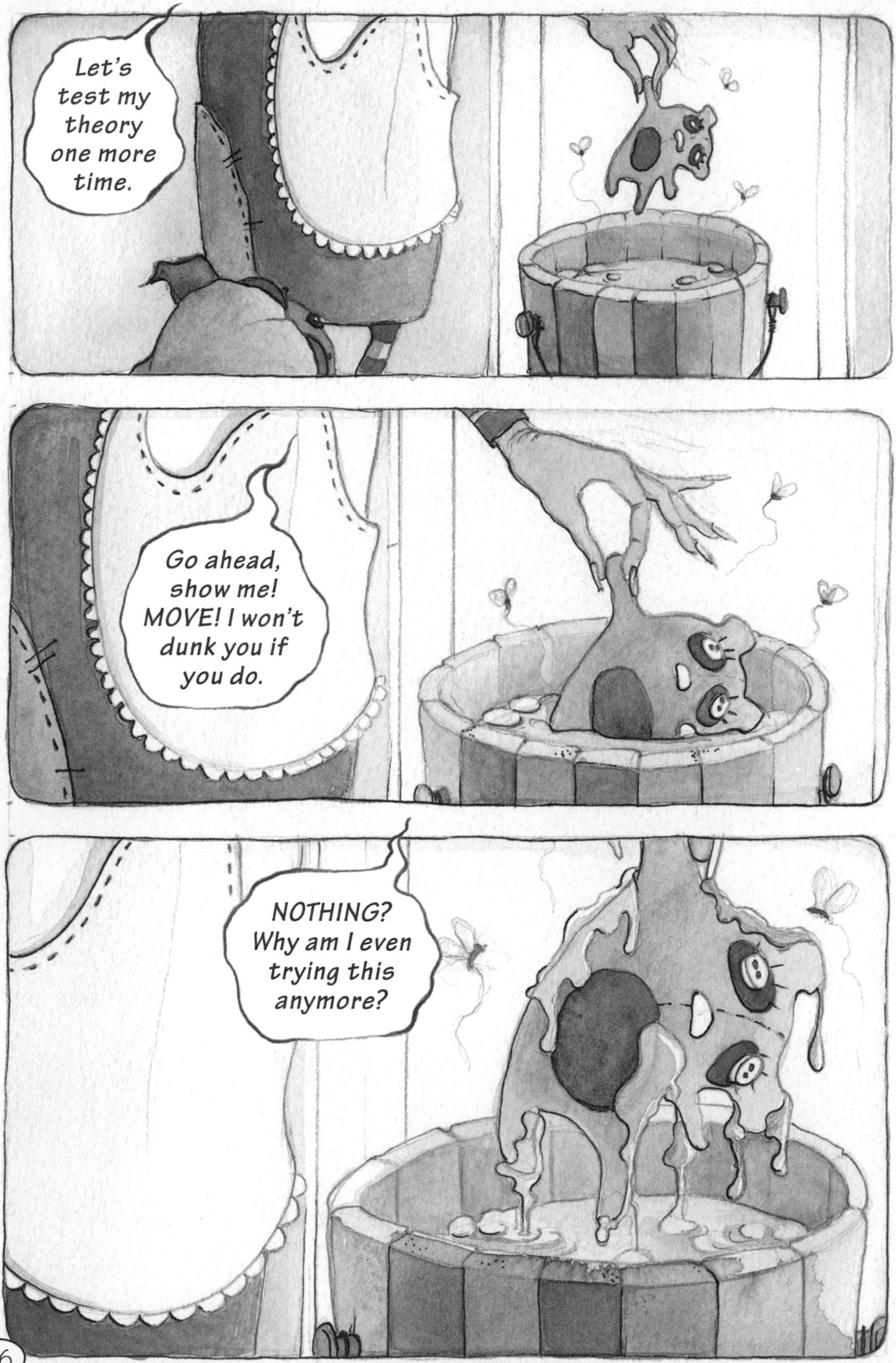

Let's test my theory one more time.
Go ahead, show me! MOVE! I won't dunk you if you do.
NOTHING? Why am I even trying this anymore?

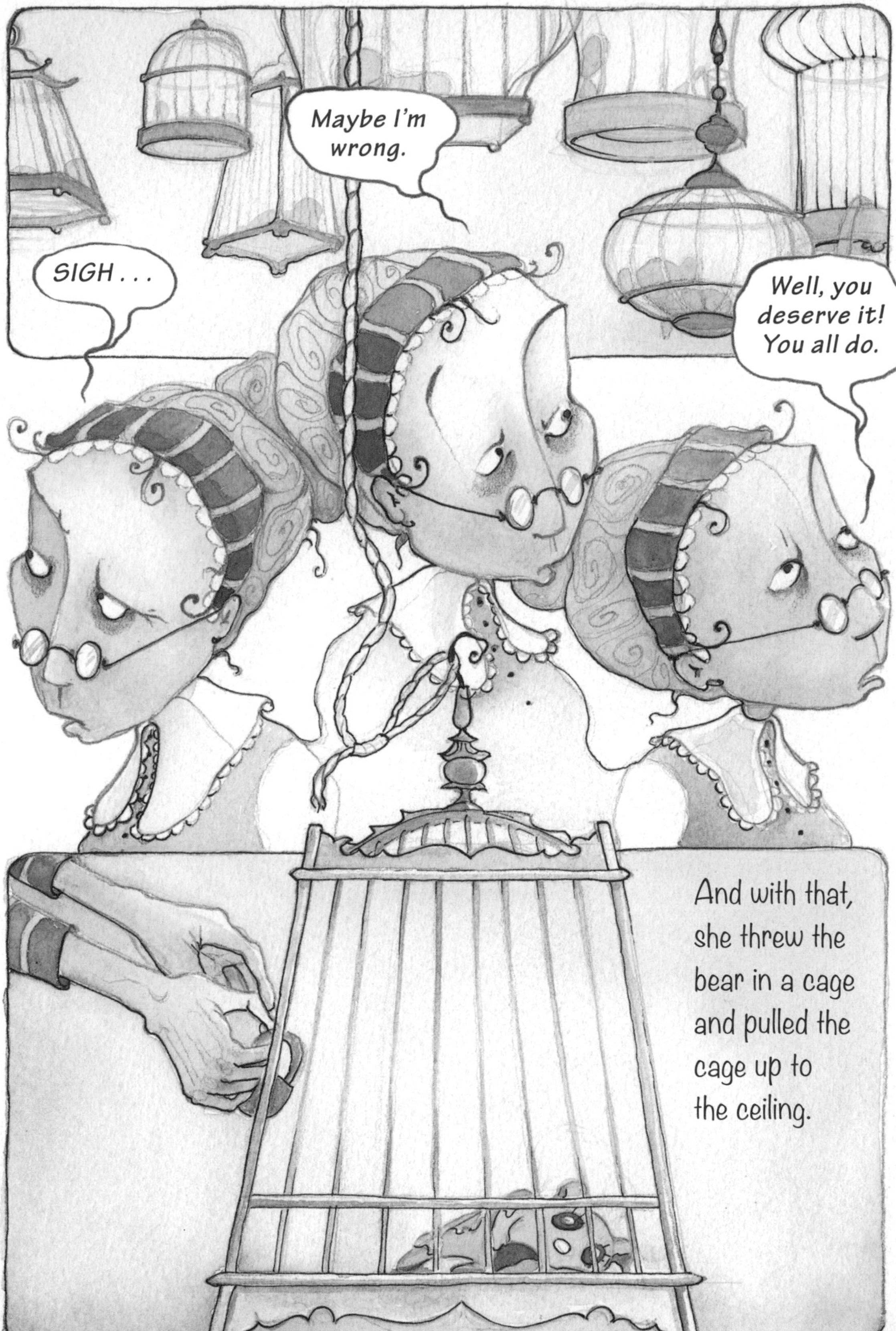
SIGH . . .
Maybe I'm wrong.
Well, you deserve it! You all do.
And with that, she threw the bear in a cage and pulled the cage up to the ceiling.

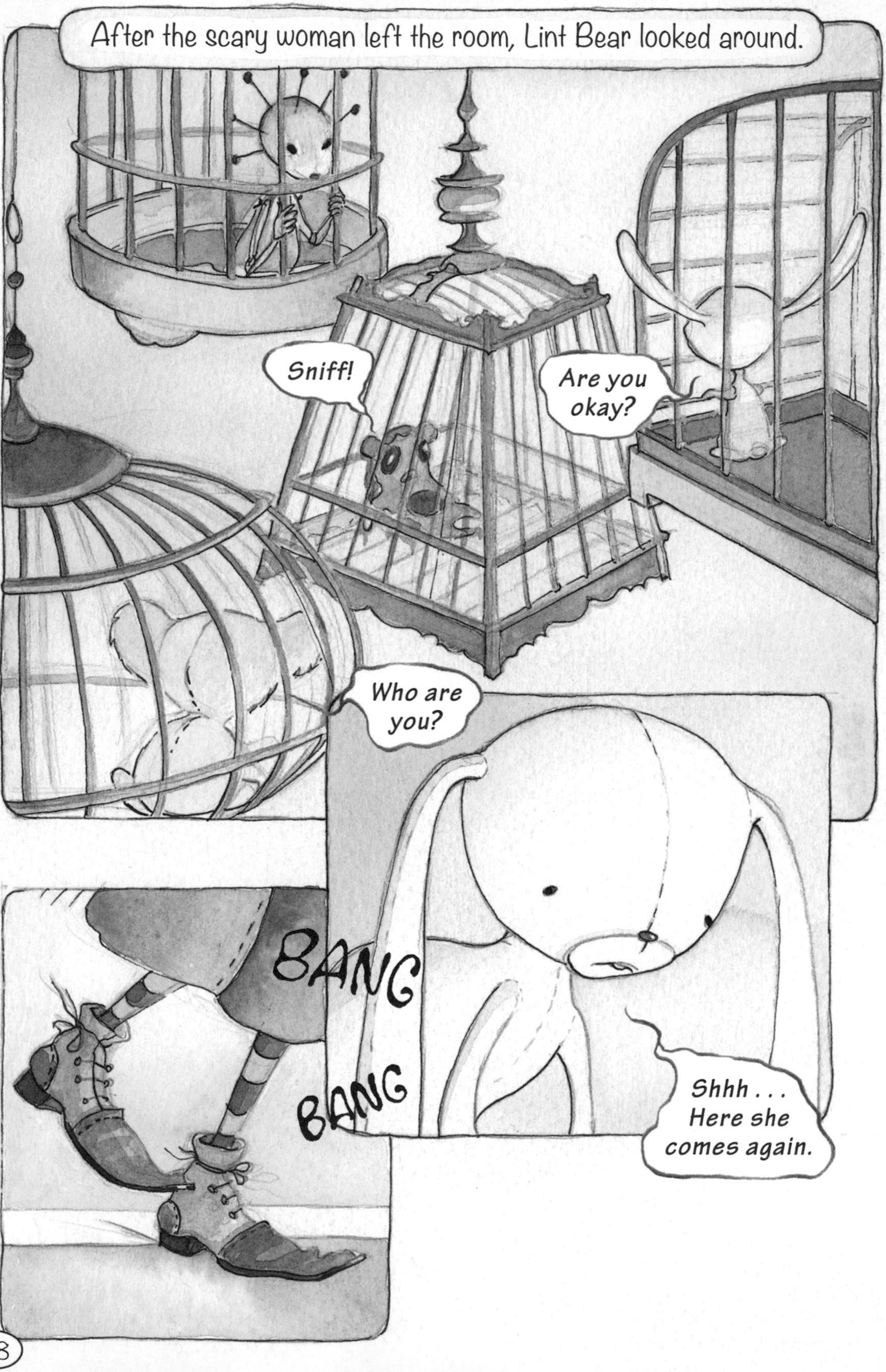
After the scary woman left the room, Lint Bear looked around.
Sniff!
Are you okay?
Who are you?
BANG
BANG
Shhh . . . Here she comes again.

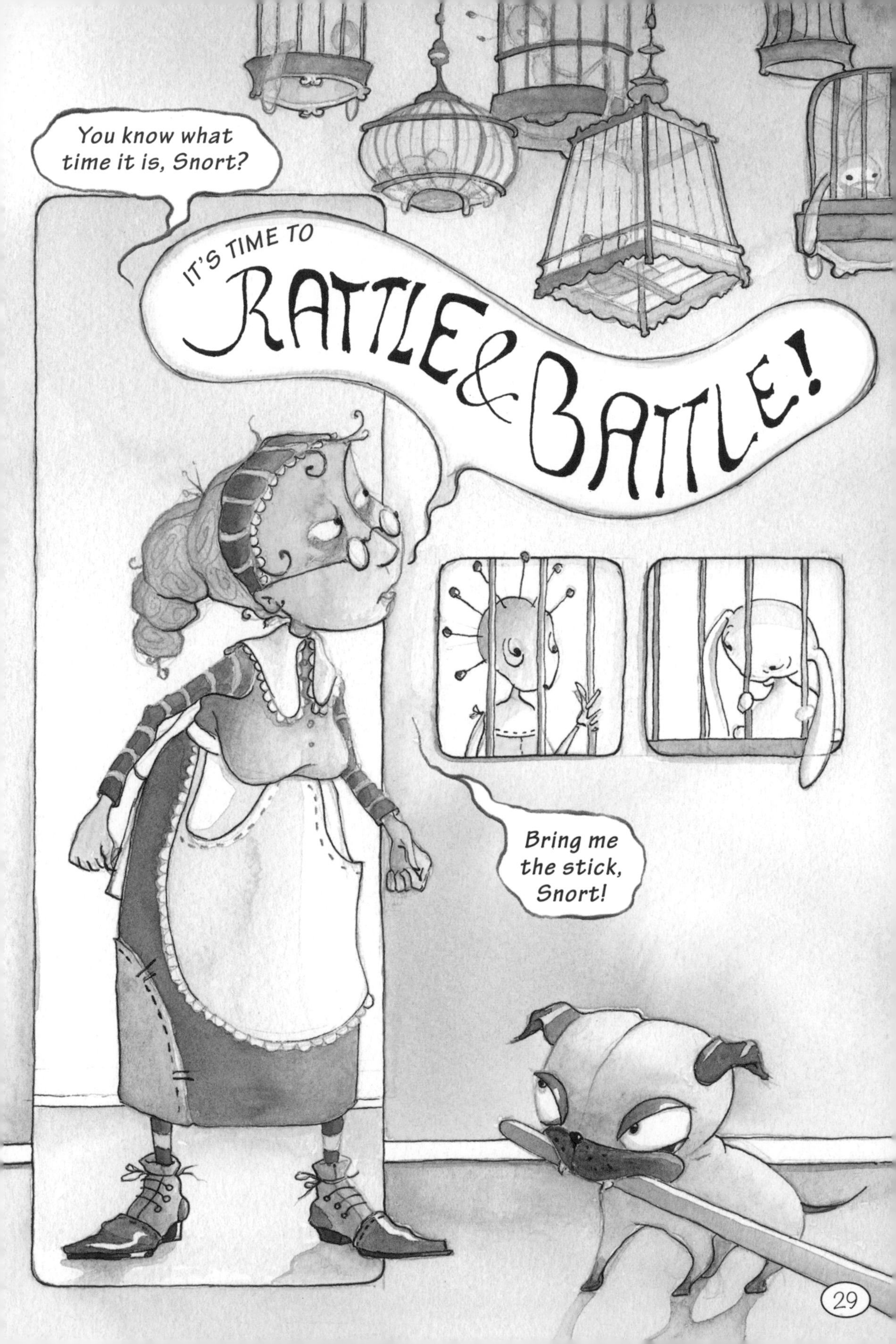
You know what time it is, Snort?
IT'S TIME TO RATTLE & BATTLE!
Bring me the stick, Snort!

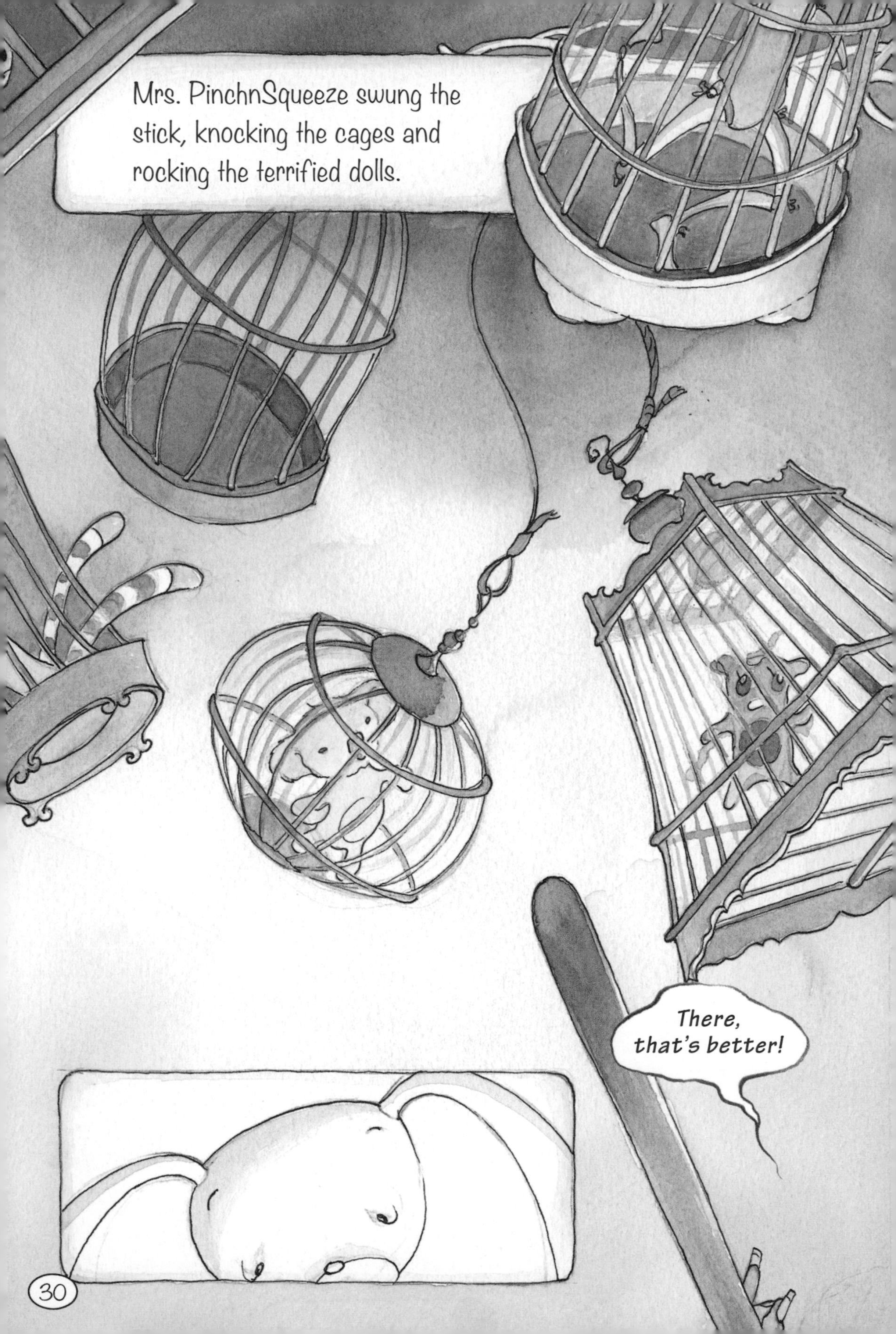
Mrs. PinchnSqueeze swung the stick, knocking the cages and rocking the terrified dolls.
There, that's better!

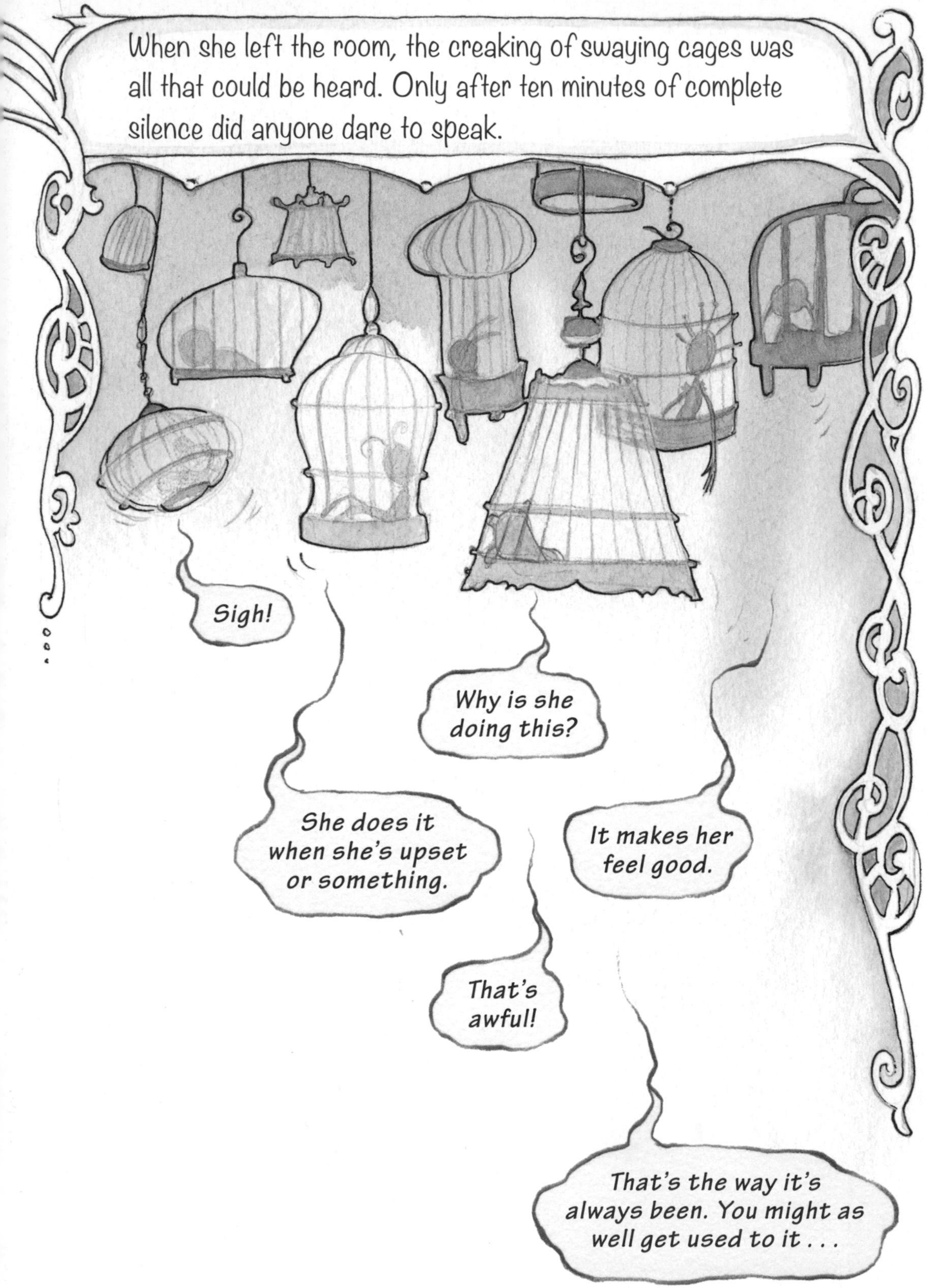
When she left the room, the creaking of swaying cages was all that could be heard. Only after ten minutes of complete silence did anyone dare to speak.
Sigh!
Why is she doing this?
She does it when she's upset or something.
It makes her feel good.
That's awful!
That's the way it's always been. You might as well get used to it . . .

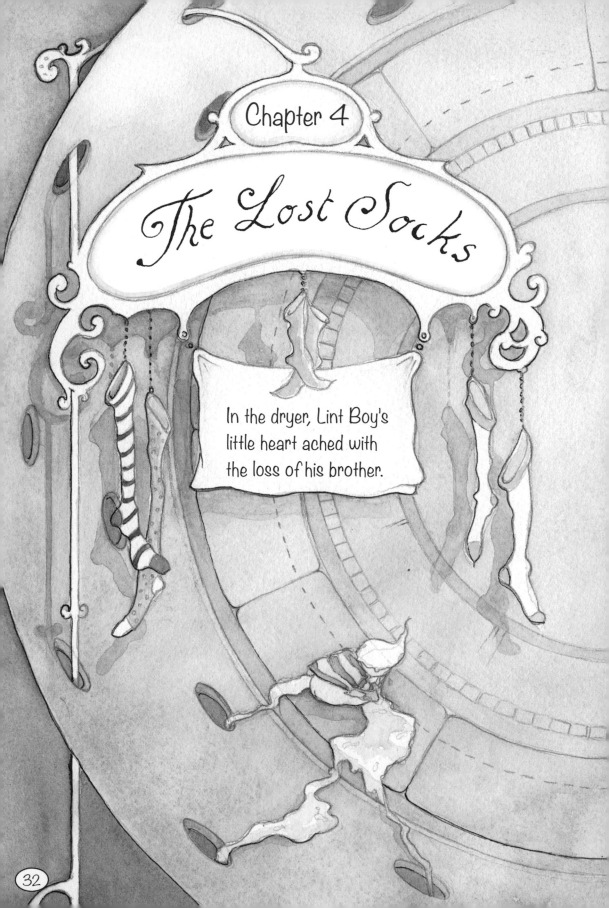

Chapter 4

The Lost Socks

In the dryer, Lint Boy's little heart ached with the loss of his brother.

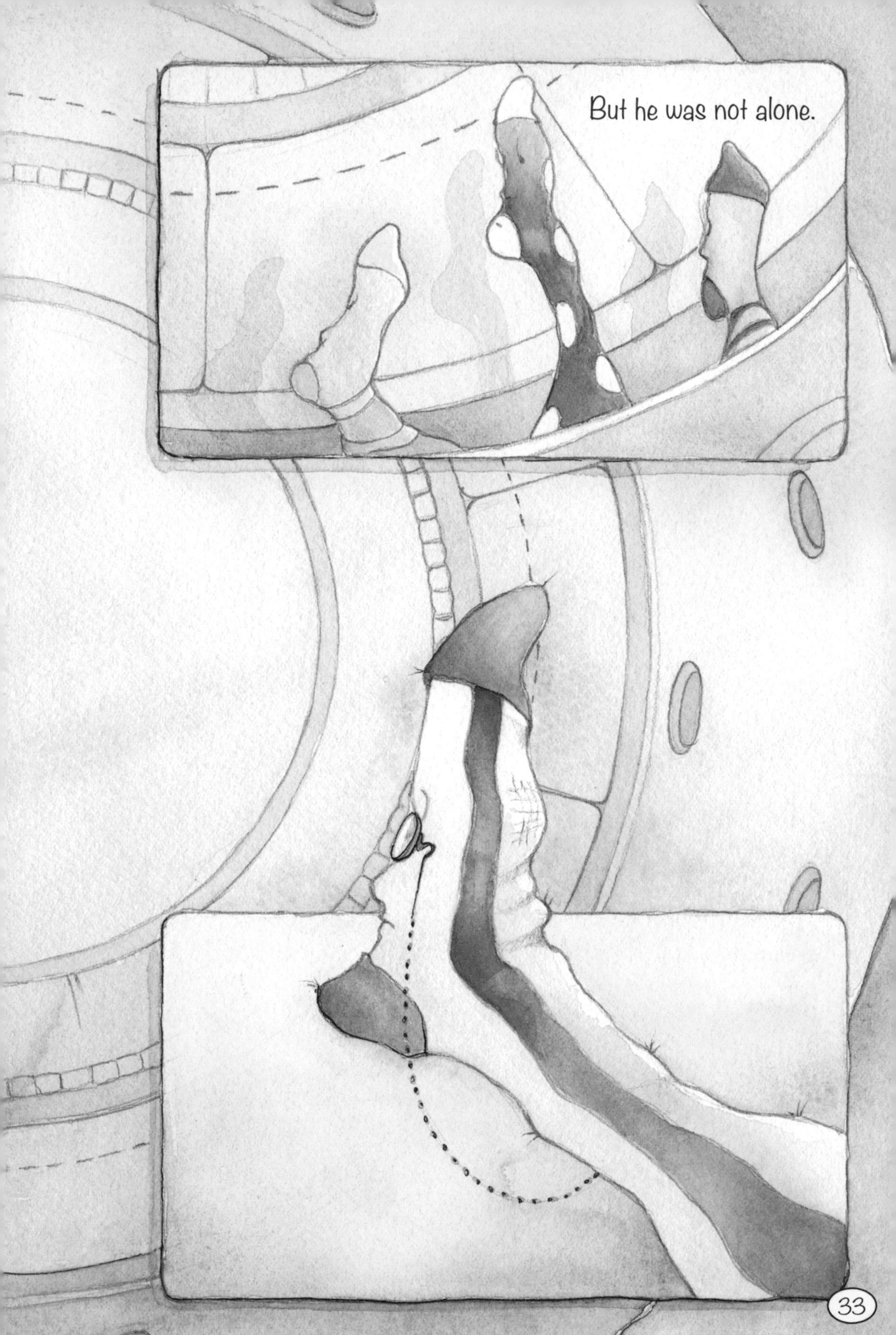
But he was not alone.

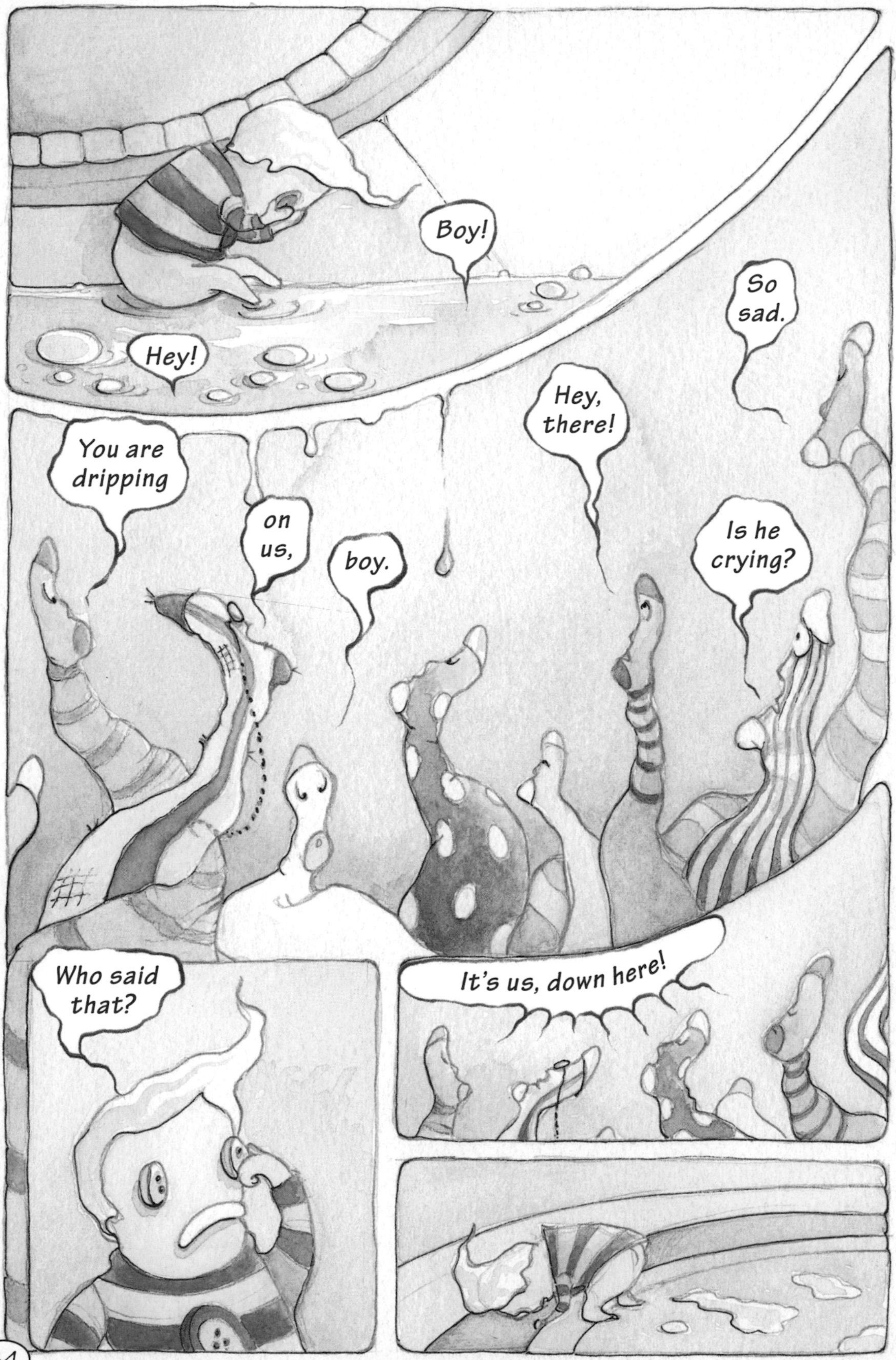
Boy!
Hey!
So sad.
Hey, there!
You are dripping
on us,
boy.
Is he crying?
Who said that?
It's us, down here!

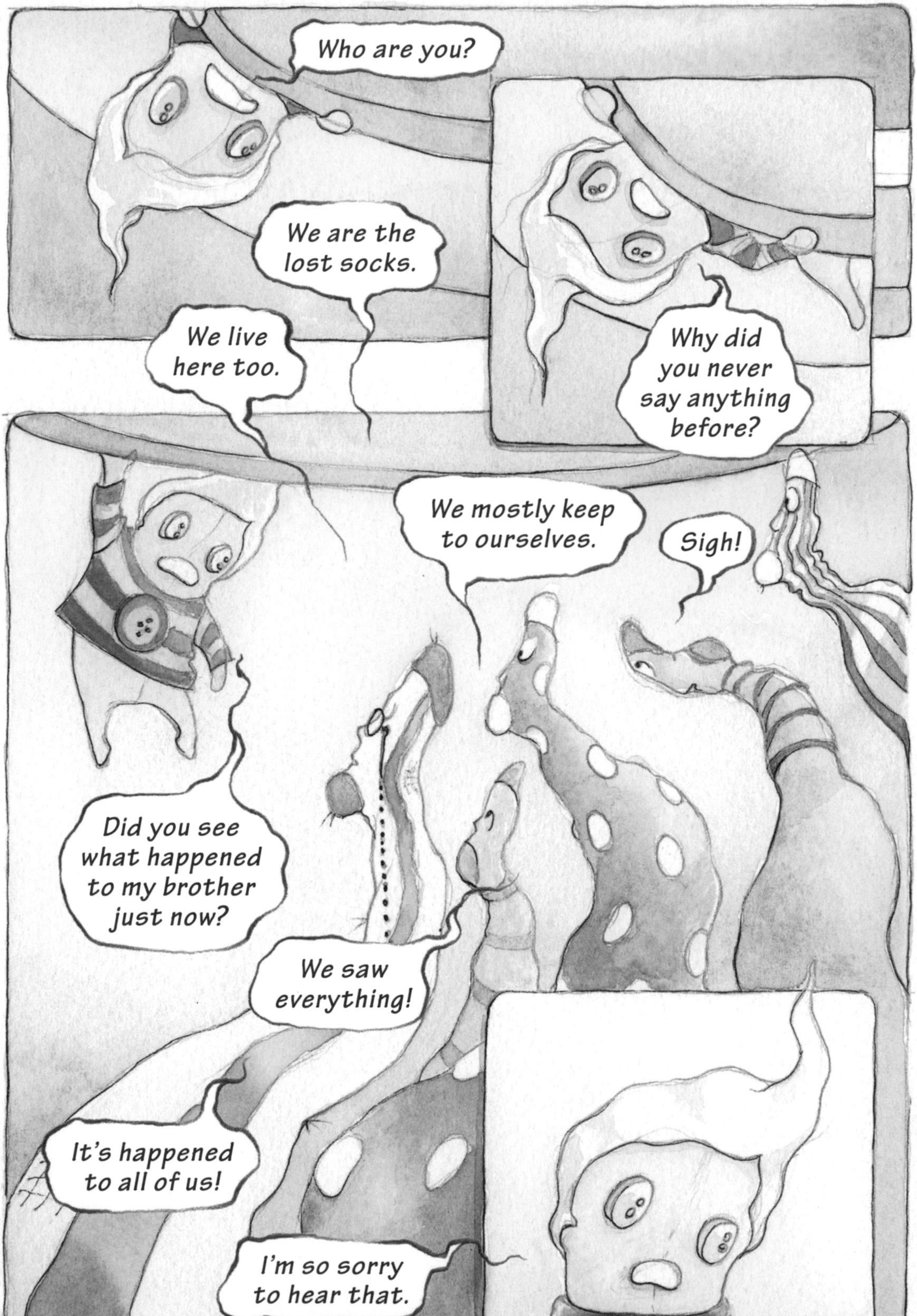
Who are you?
We are the lost socks.
We live here too.
Why did you never say anything before?
We mostly keep to ourselves.
Sigh!
Did you see what happened to my brother just now?
We saw everything!
It's happened to all of us!
I'm so sorry to hear that.

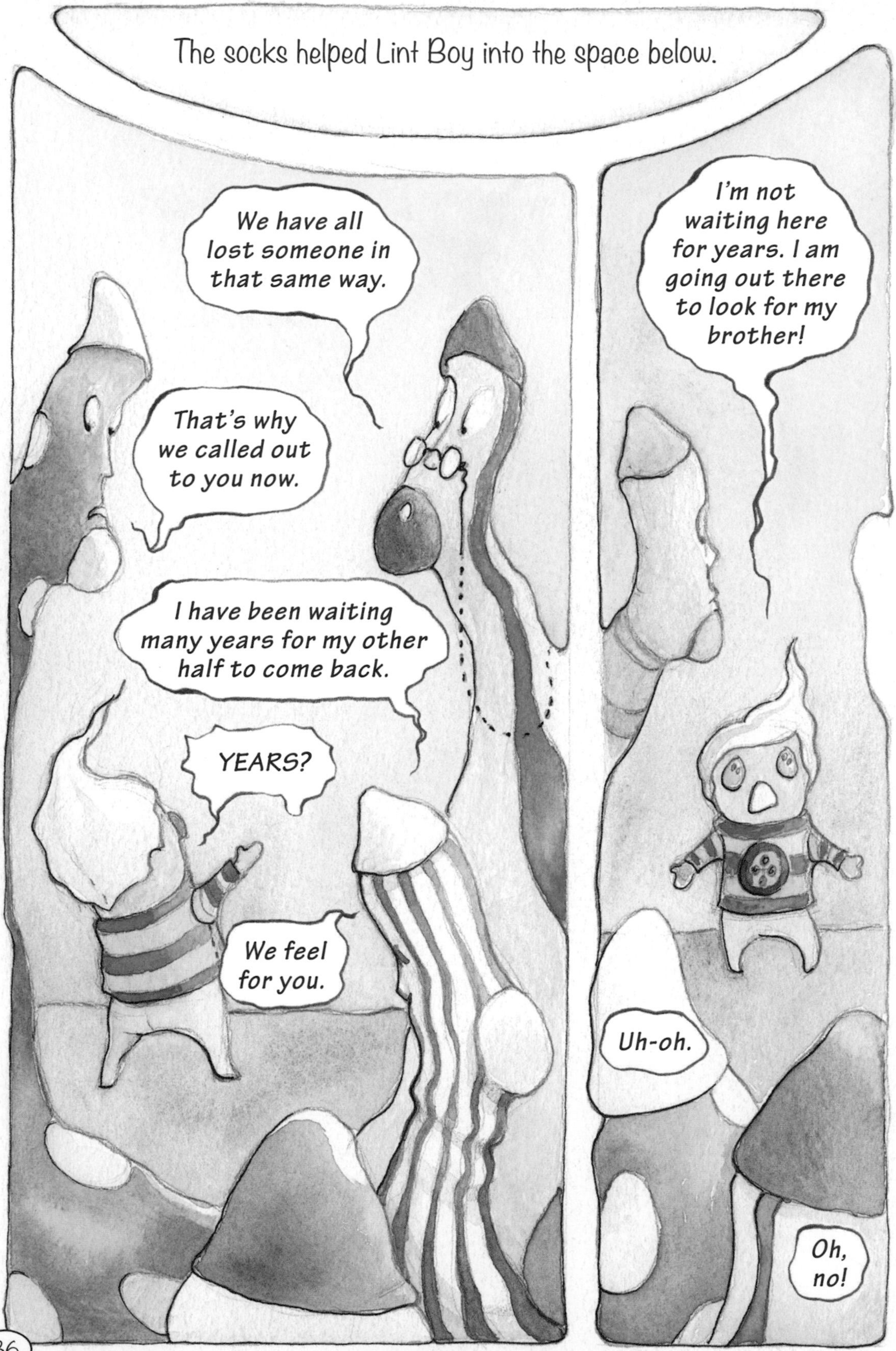
The socks helped Lint Boy into the space below.
We have all lost someone in that same way.
That's why we called out to you now.
I have been waiting many years for my other half to come back.
YEARS?
We feel for you.
I'm not waiting here for years. I am going out there to look for my brother!
Uh-oh.
Oh, no!

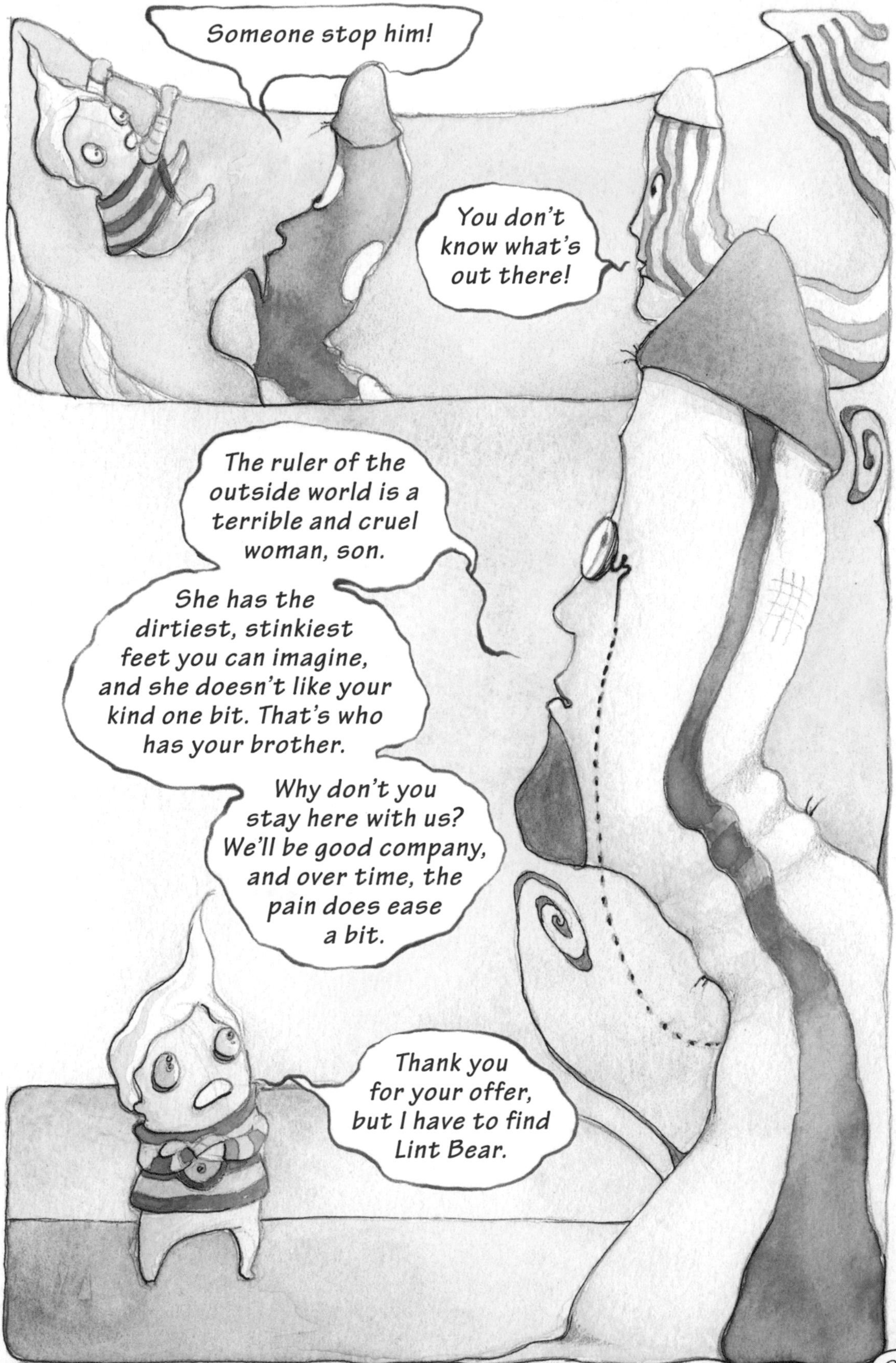
Someone stop him!
You don't know what's out there!
The ruler of the outside world is a terrible and cruel woman, son.
She has the dirtiest, stinkiest feet you can imagine, and she doesn't like your kind one bit. That's who has your brother.
Why don't you stay here with us? We'll be good company, and over time, the pain does ease a bit.
Thank you for your offer, but I have to find Lint Bear.

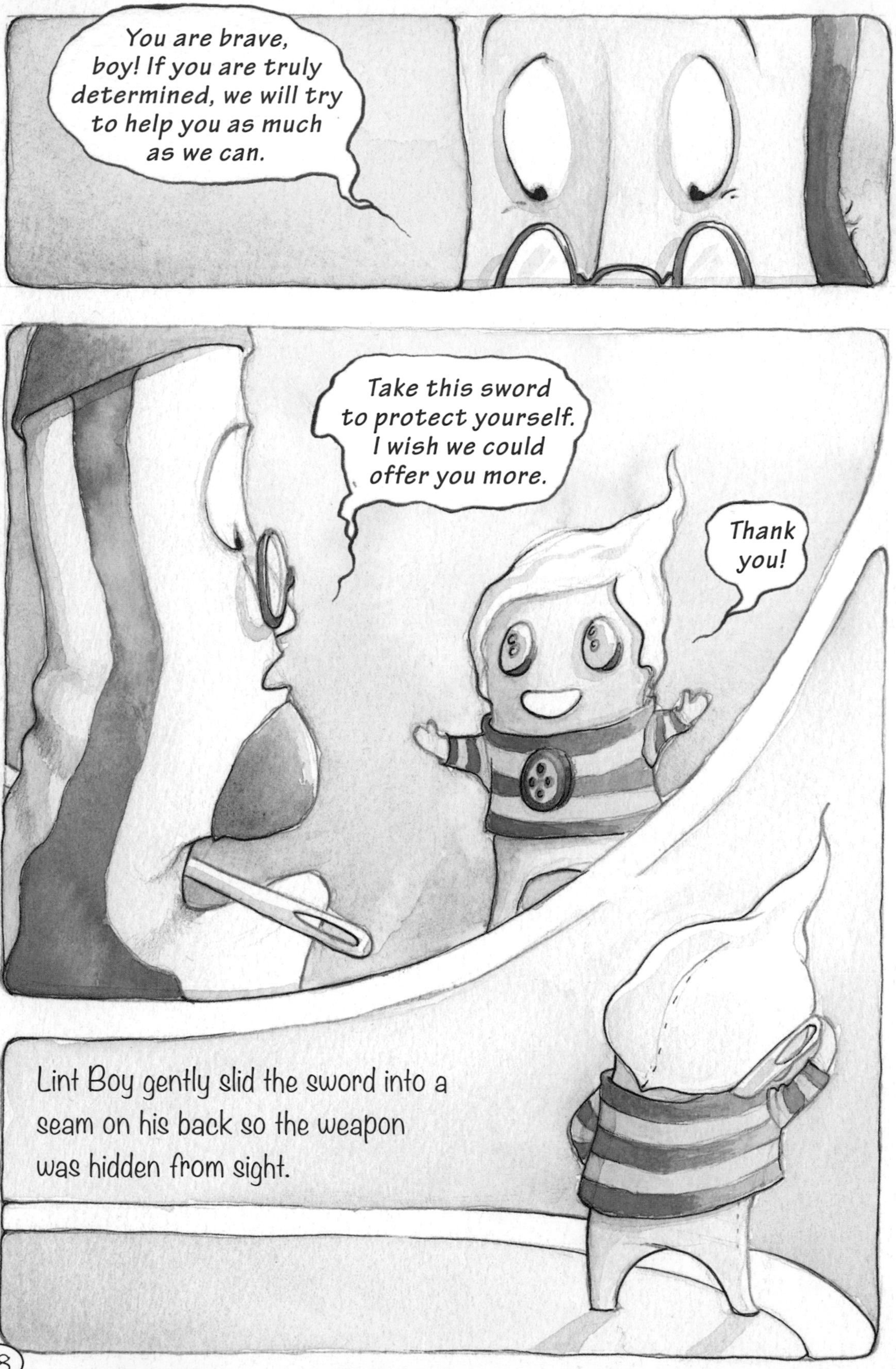
You are brave, boy! If you are truly determined, we will try to help you as much as we can.
Take this sword to protect yourself. I wish we could offer you more.
Thank you!
Lint Boy gently slid the sword into a seam on his back so the weapon was hidden from sight.

He waited cautiously until everything seemed safe. Then he pushed the dryer door open and . . .

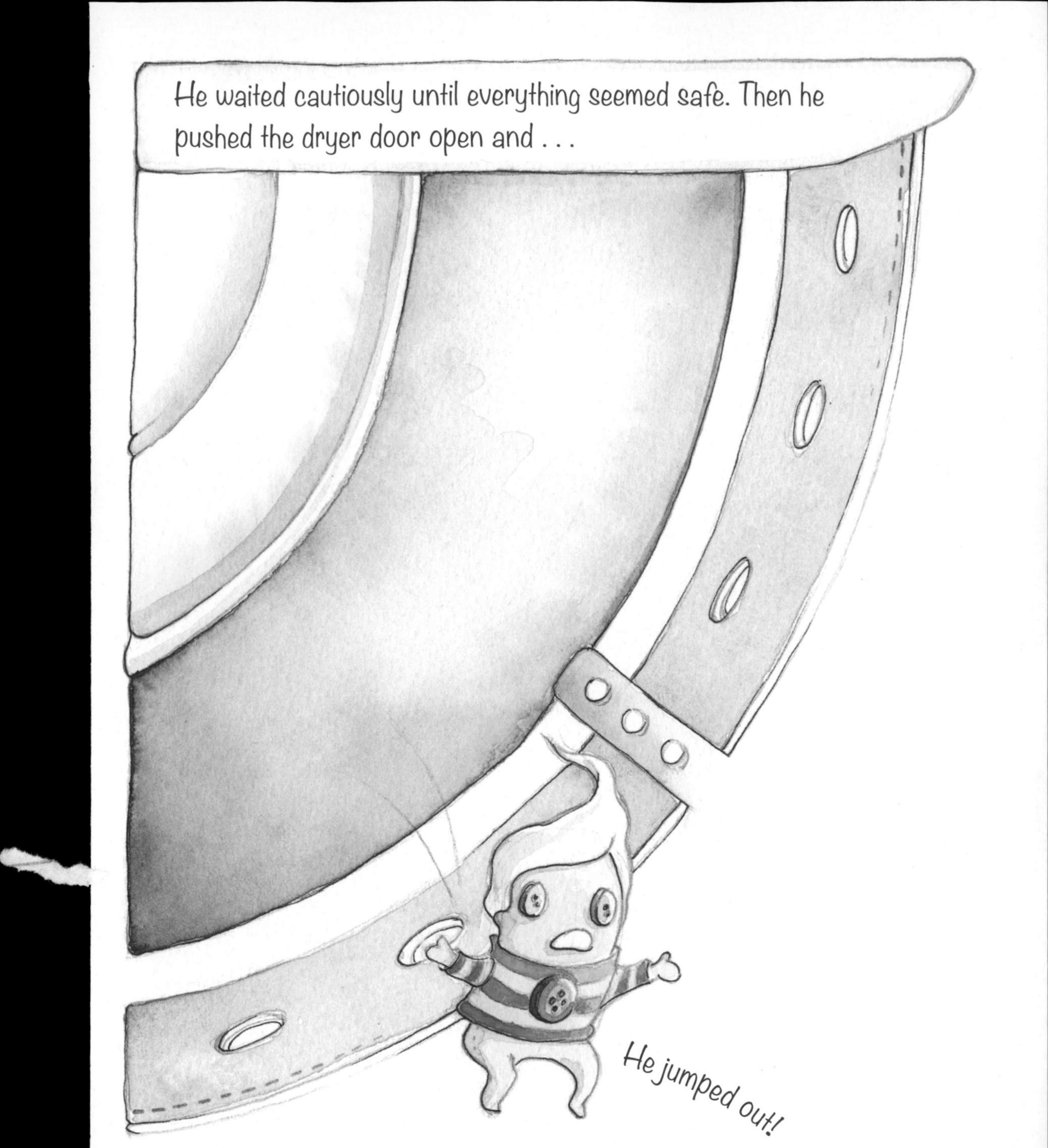
He jumped out!

Chapter 5

Caught

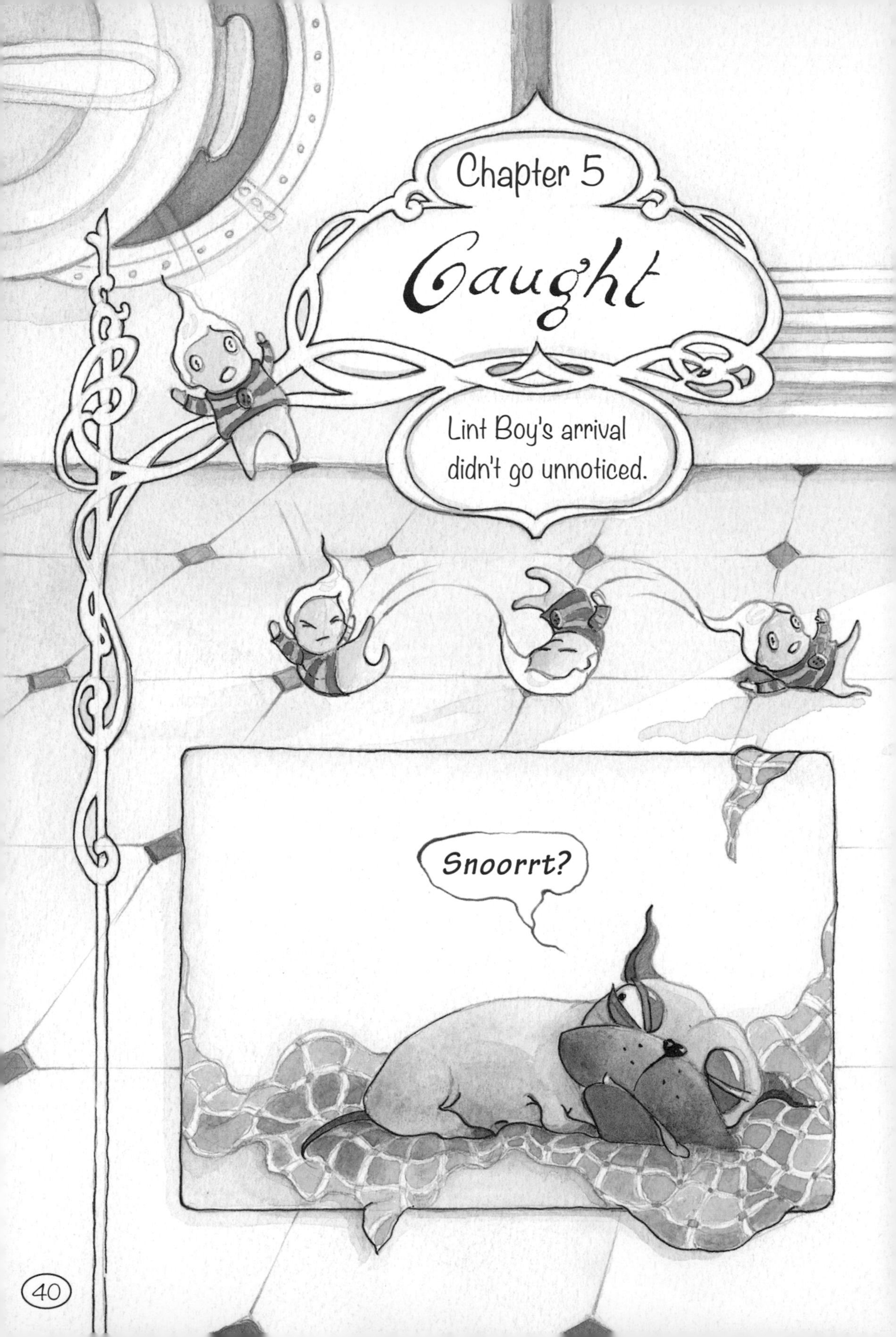
Lint Boy's arrival didn't go unnoticed.
Snoorrt?

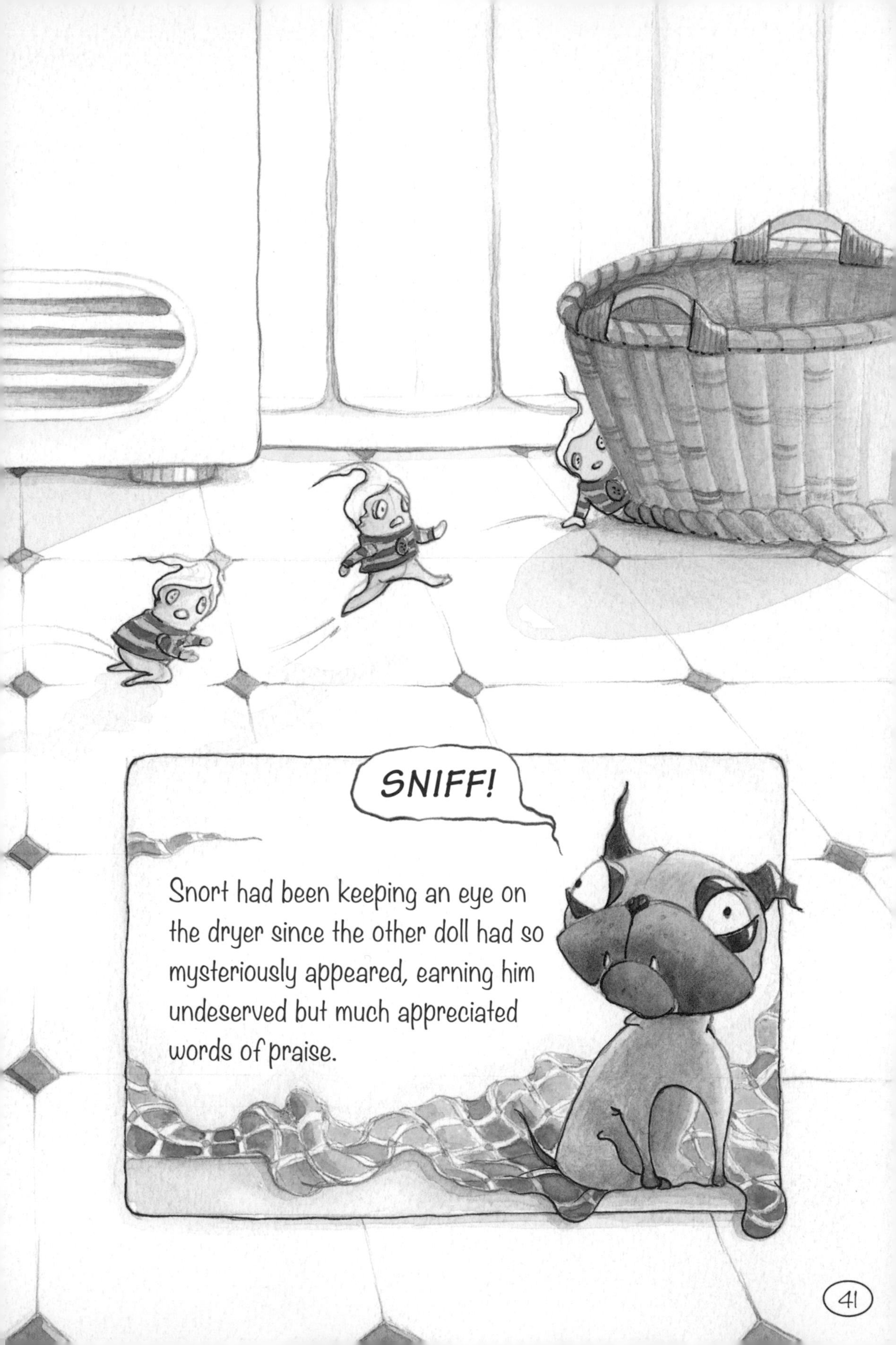
SNIFF!

Snort had been keeping an eye on the dryer since the other doll had so mysteriously appeared, earning him undeserved but much appreciated words of praise.

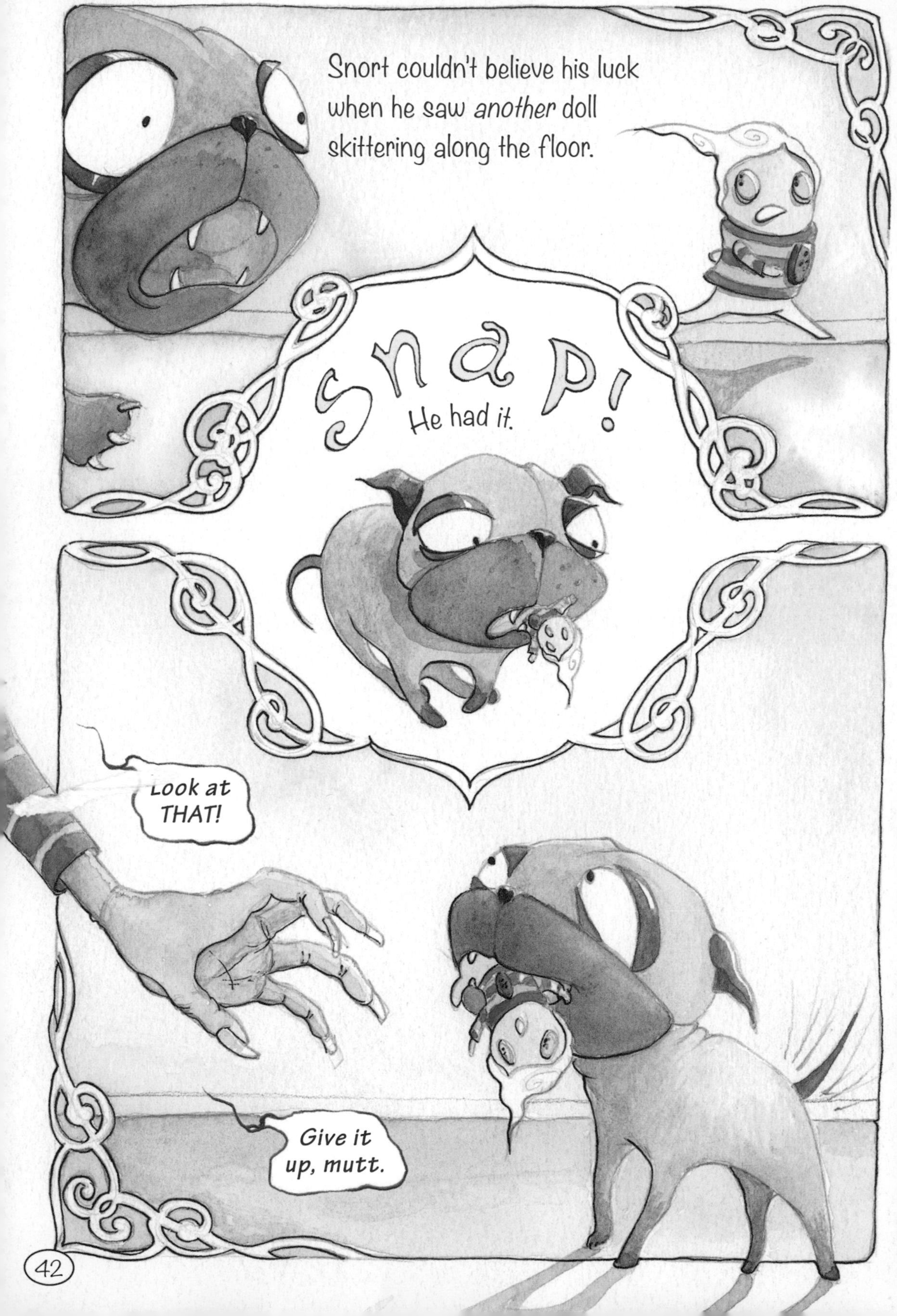
Snort couldn't believe his luck when he saw *another* doll skittering along the floor.
SNAP!
He had it.
Look at THAT!
Give it up, mutt.

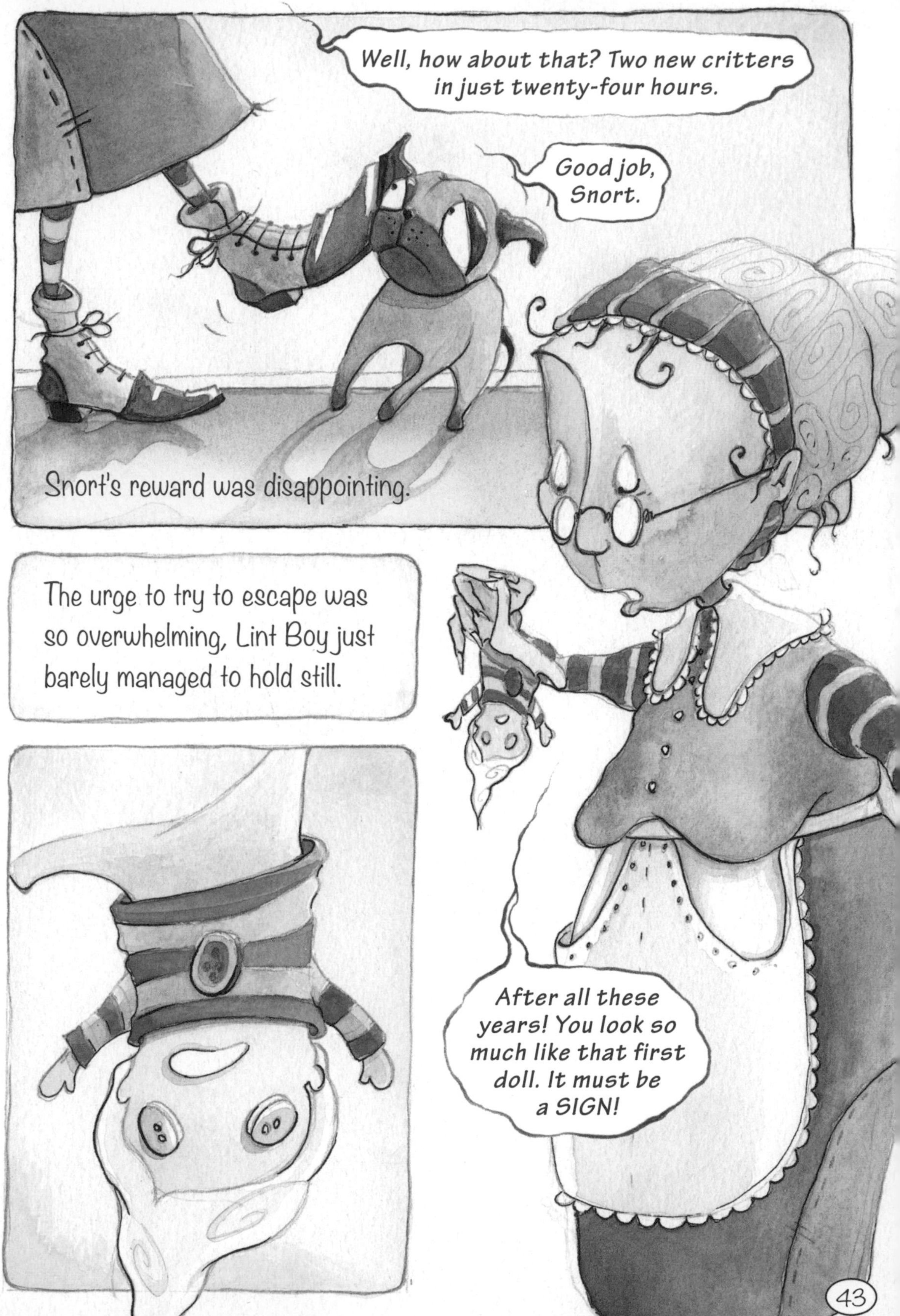

Well, how about that? Two new critters in just twenty-four hours.
Good job, Snort.
Snort's reward was disappointing.
The urge to try to escape was so overwhelming, Lint Boy just barely managed to hold still.
After all these years! You look so much like that first doll. It must be a SIGN!

Mrs. PinchnSqueeze had always believed that dolls were alive, but in decades of trying, she had not been able to prove it. Over time, doubt had set in.

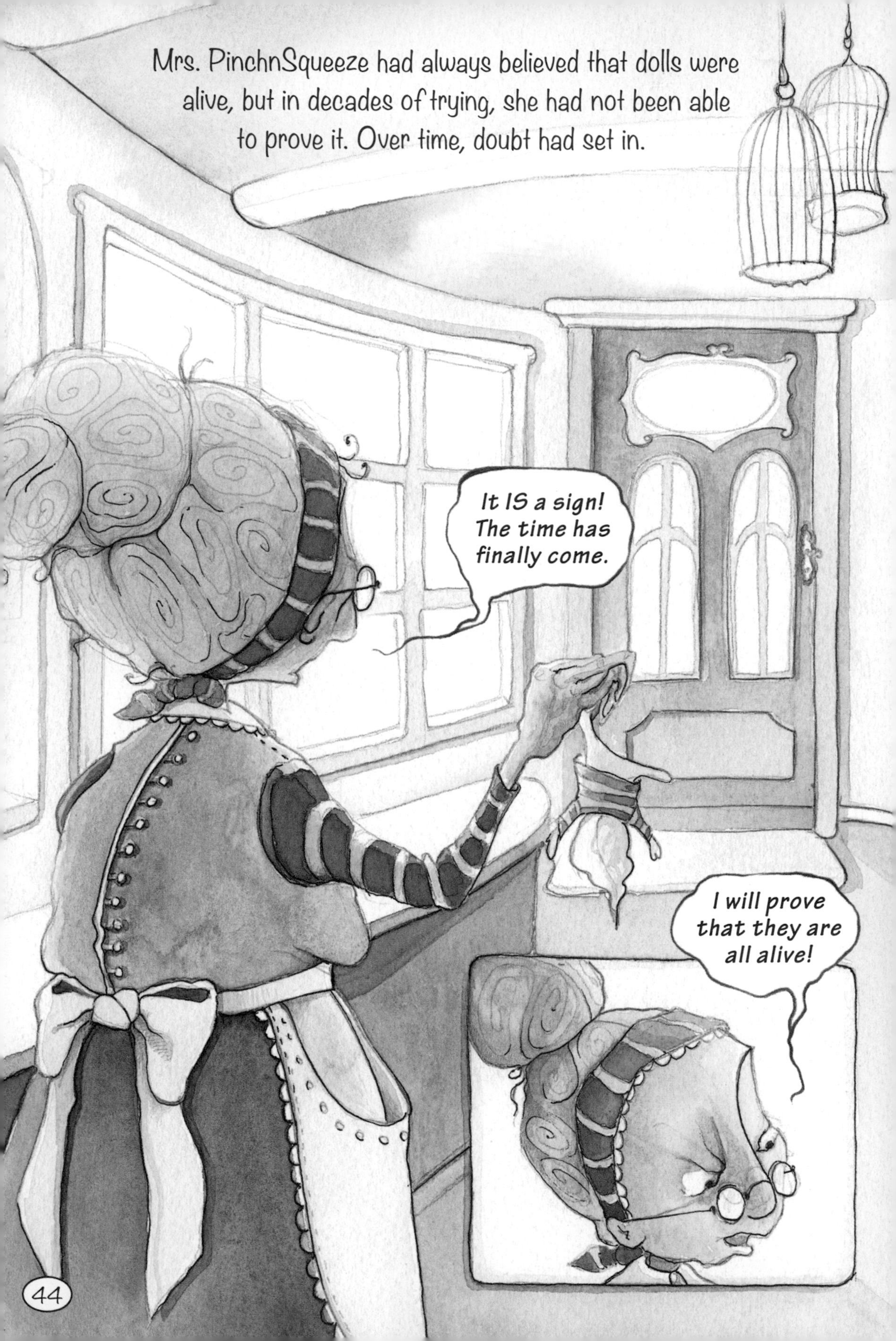
It IS a sign! The time has finally come.
I will prove that they are all alive!

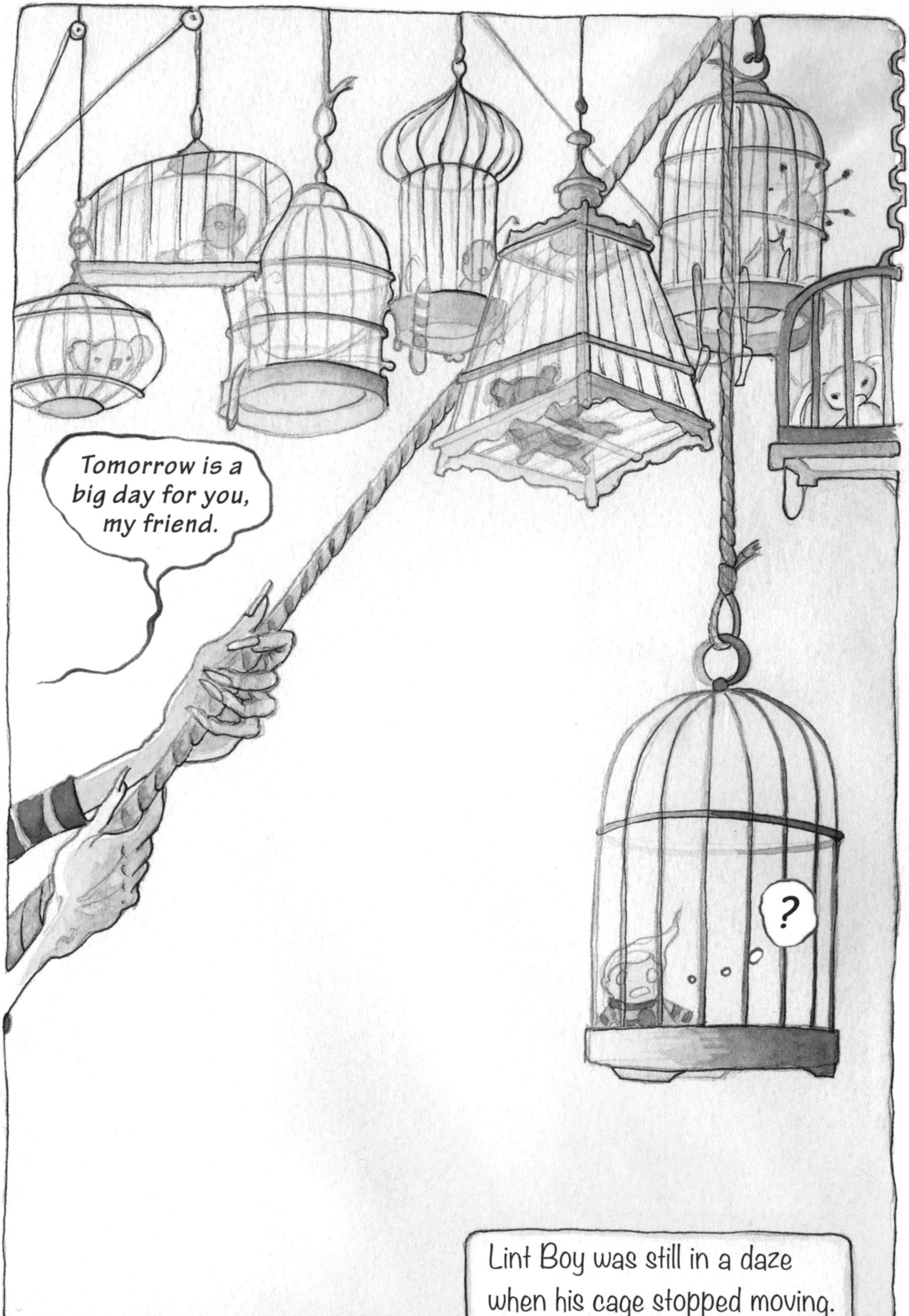
Tomorrow is a big day for you, my friend.
?
Lint Boy was still in a daze when his cage stopped moving.

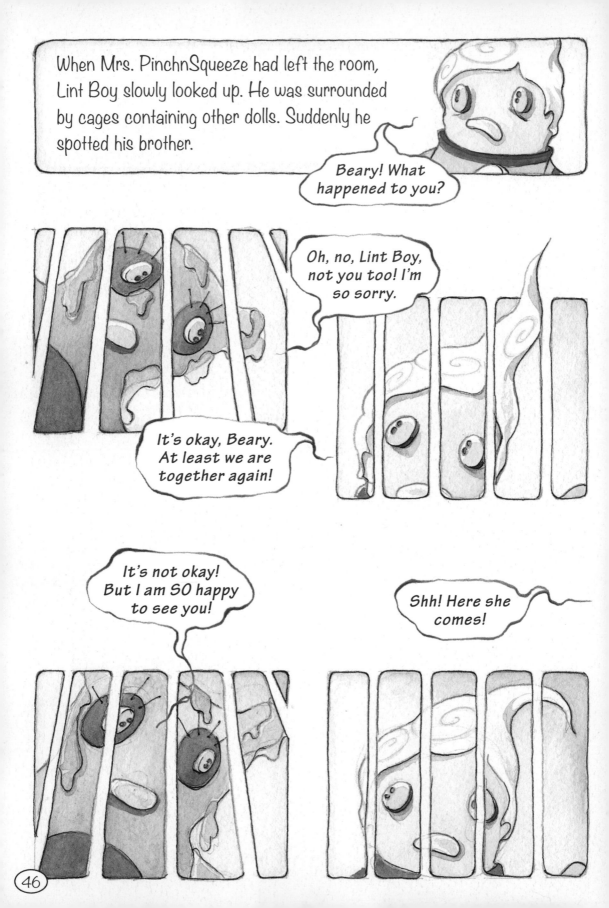

When Mrs. PinchnSqueeze had left the room, Lint Boy slowly looked up. He was surrounded by cages containing other dolls. Suddenly he spotted his brother.

Beary! What happened to you?

Oh, no, Lint Boy, not you too! I'm so sorry.

It's okay, Beary. At least we are together again!

It's not okay! But I am SO happy to see you!

Shh! Here she comes!

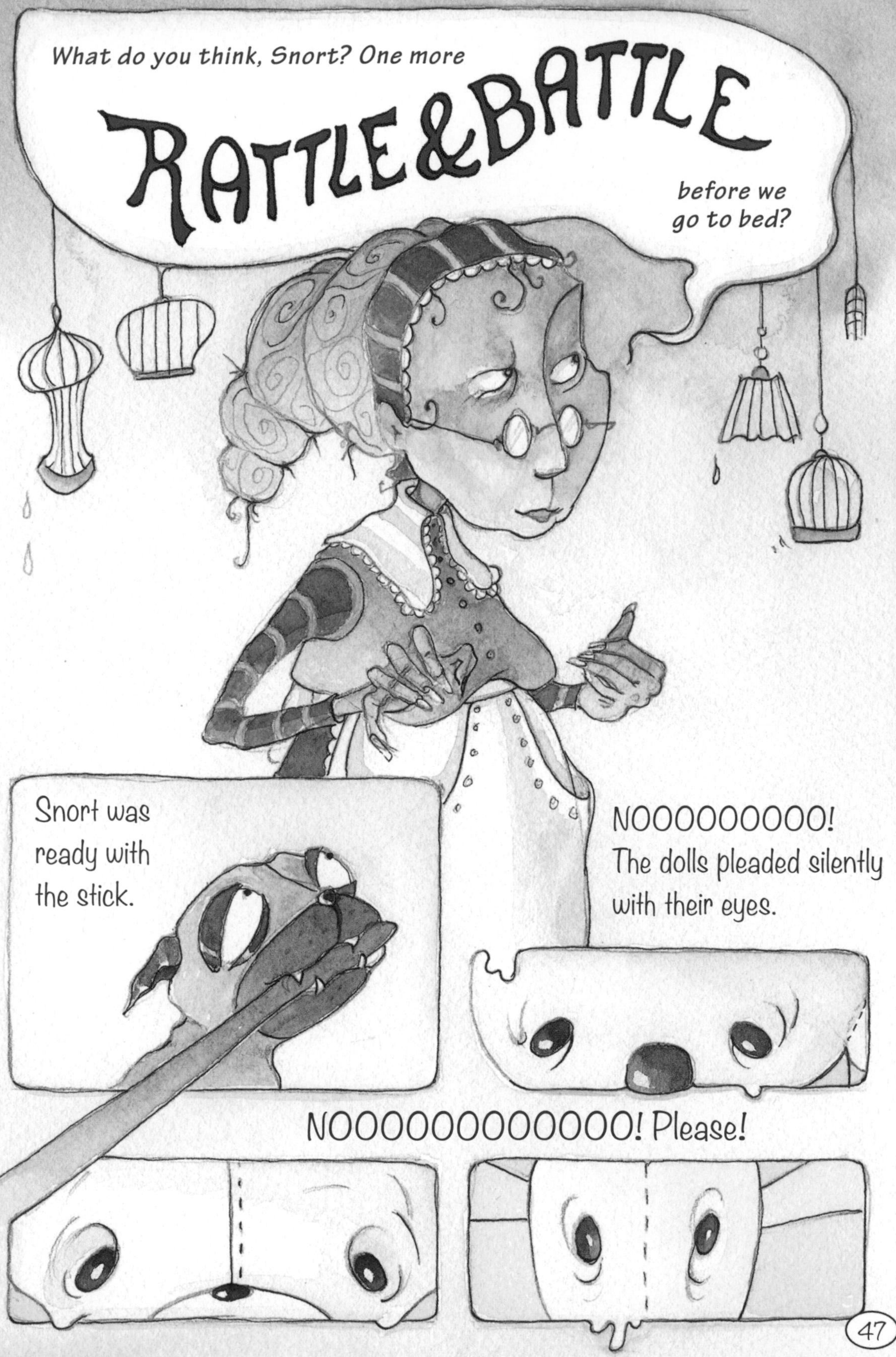
What do you think, Snort? One more
RATTLE & BATTLE
before we go to bed?
Snort was ready with the stick.
NOOOOOOOOO! The dolls pleaded silently with their eyes.
NOOOOOOOOOOOOO! Please!

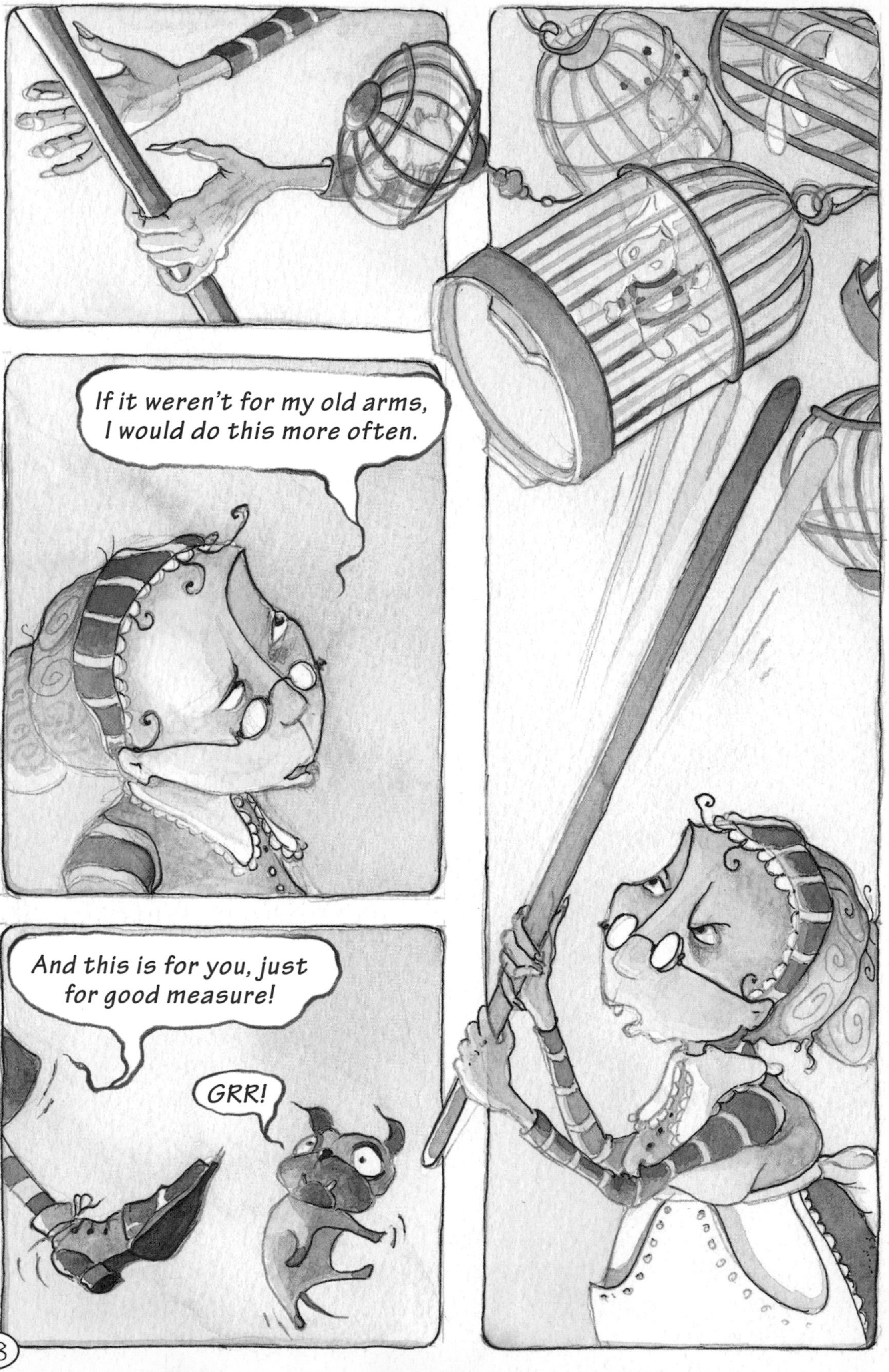
If it weren't for my old arms,
I would do this more often.
And this is for you, just
for good measure!
GRR!

It was late. Mrs. PinchnSqueeze was tired from thinking wicked thoughts. Together with a resentful Snort, she retired to her sleeping quarters.

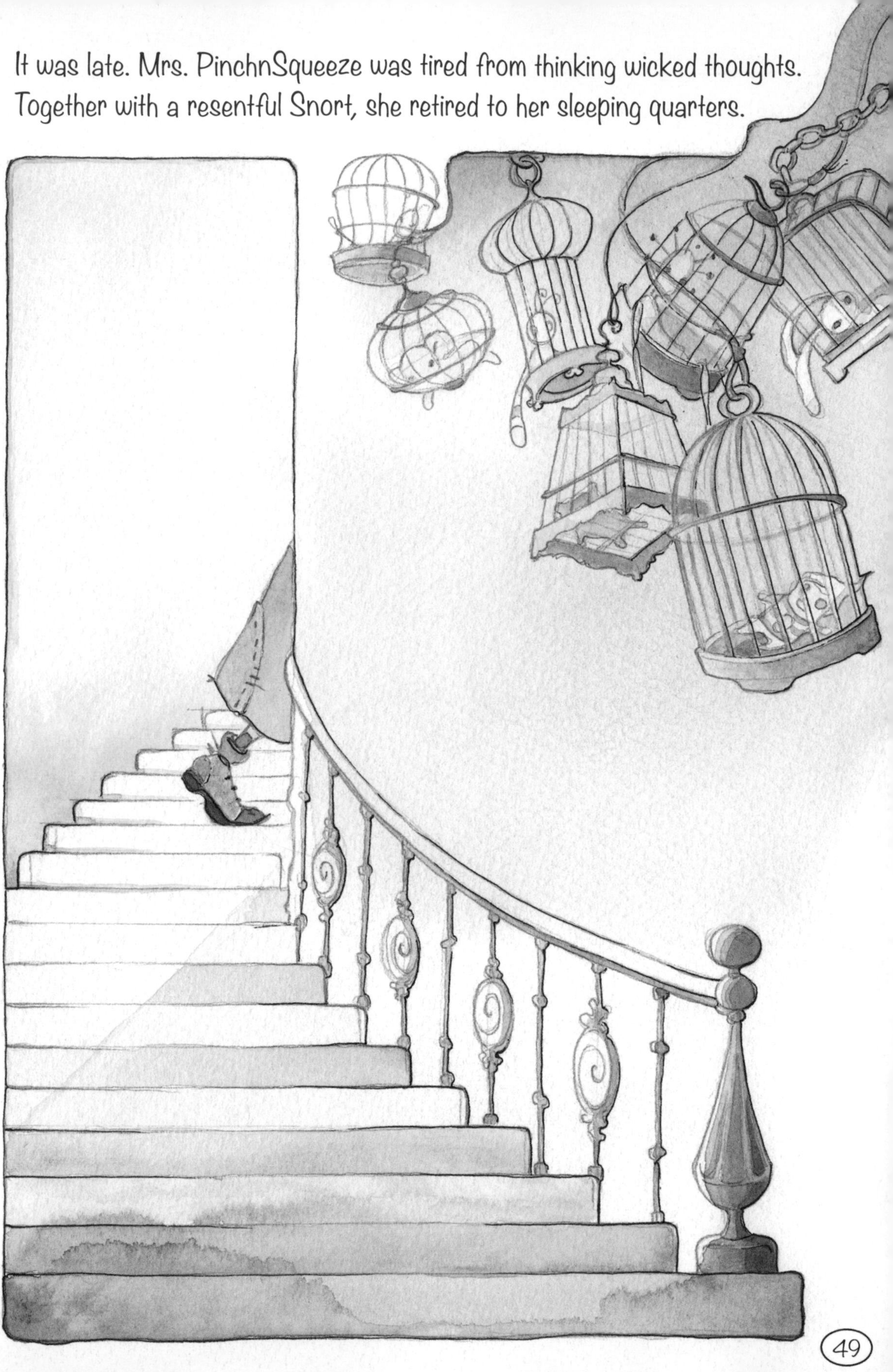

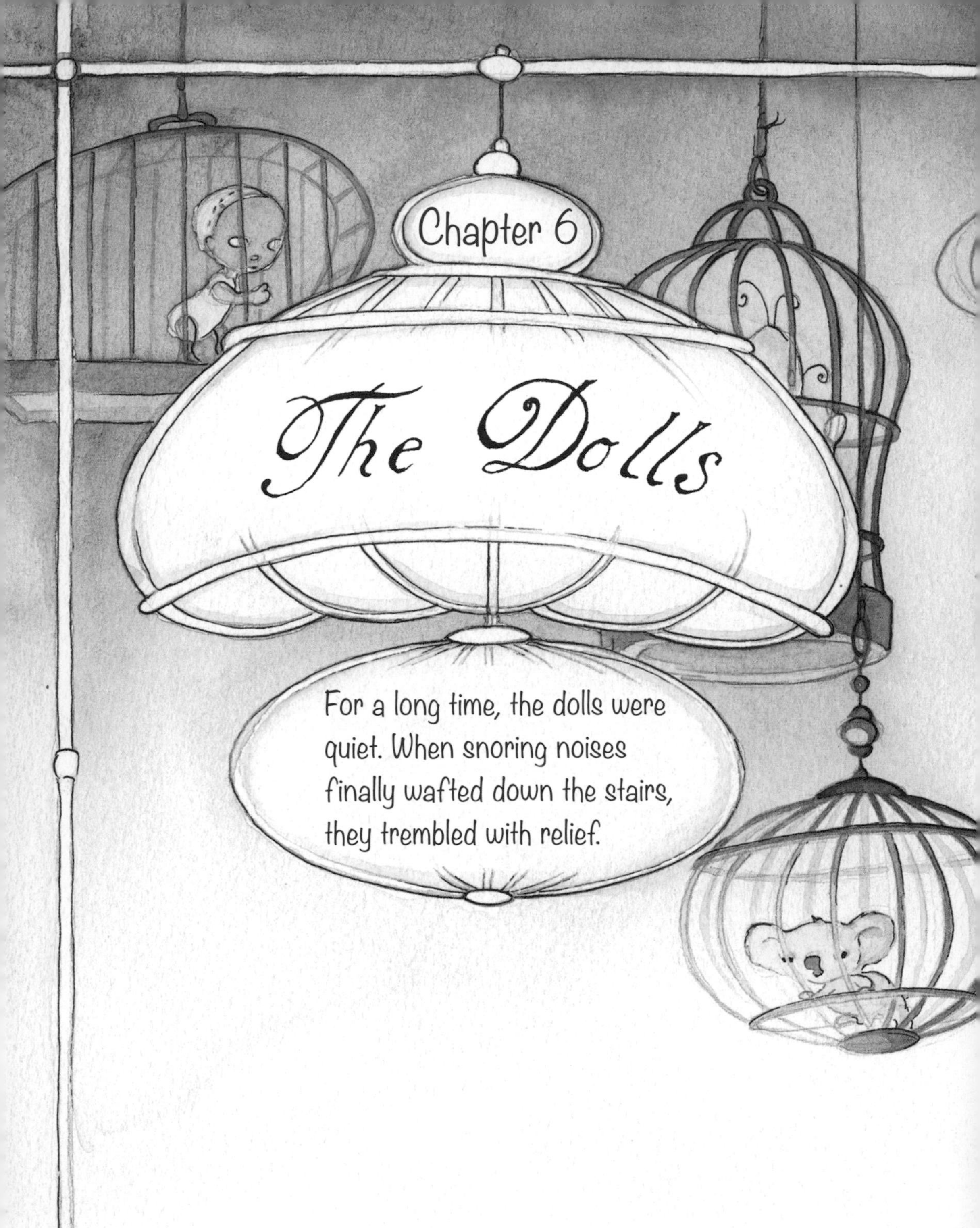

Chapter 6

The Dolls

For a long time, the dolls were quiet. When snoring noises finally wafted down the stairs, they trembled with relief.

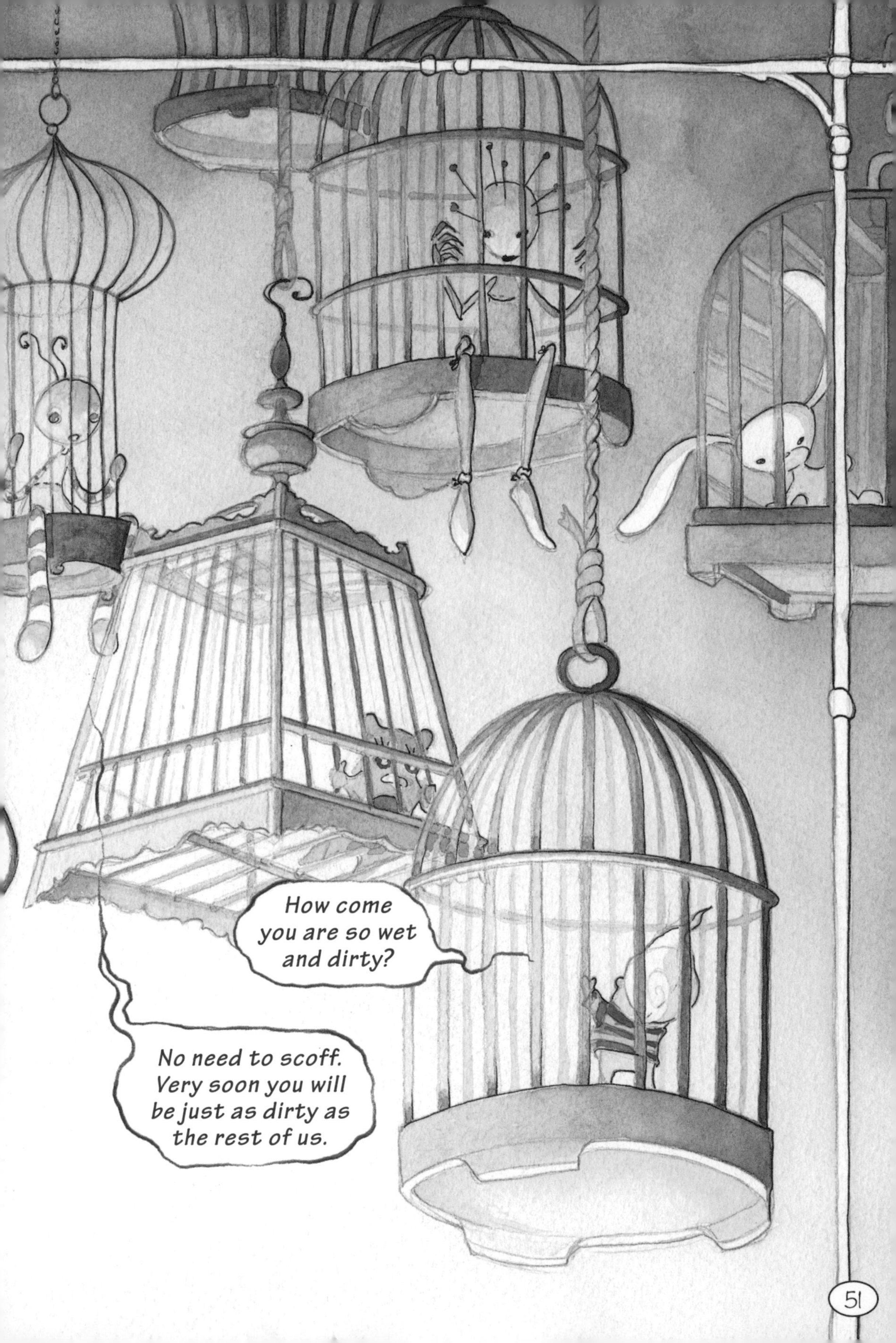
How come you are so wet and dirty?
No need to scoff. Very soon you will be just as dirty as the rest of us.

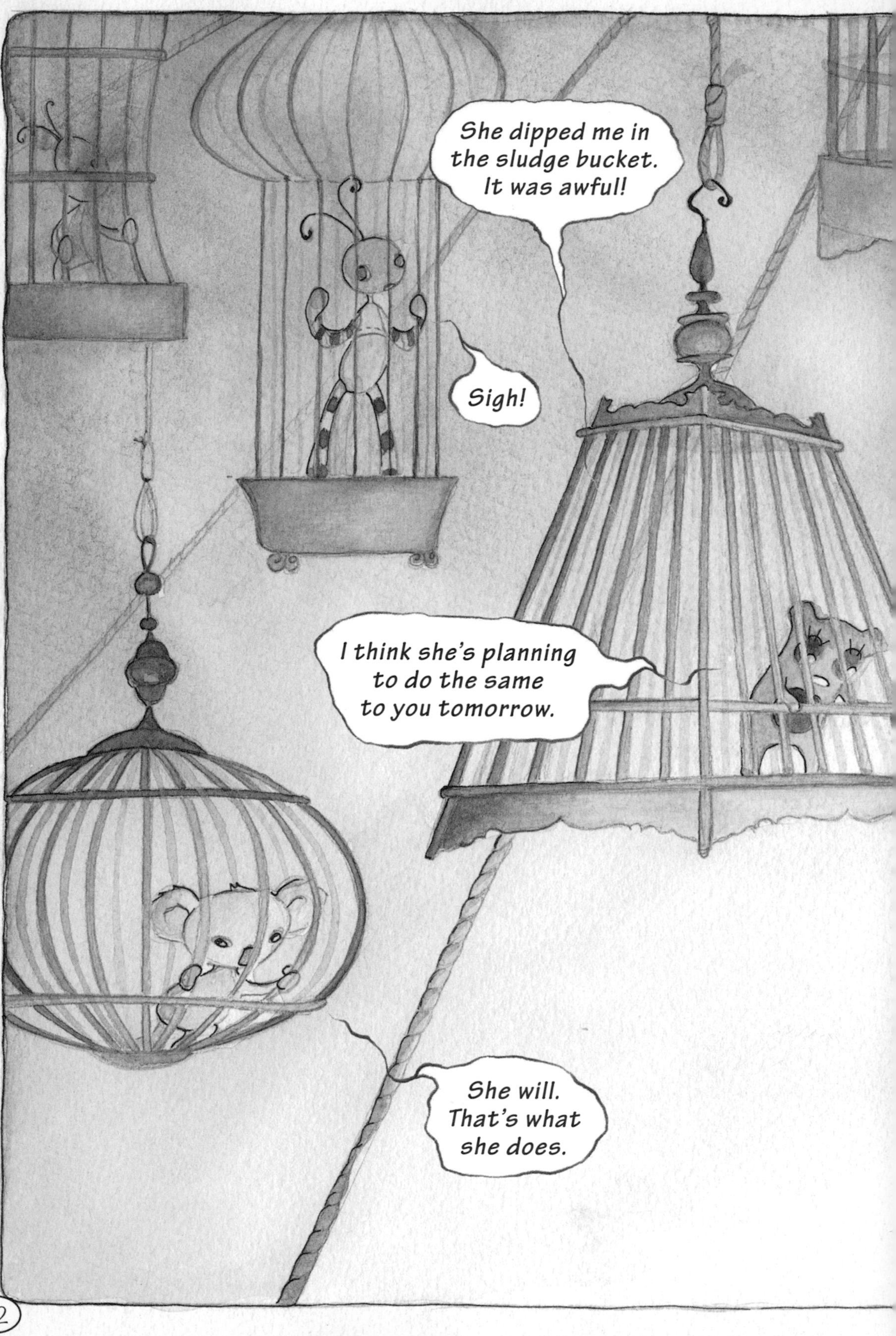
She dipped me in the sludge bucket. It was awful!
Sigh!
I think she's planning to do the same to you tomorrow.
She will. That's what she does.

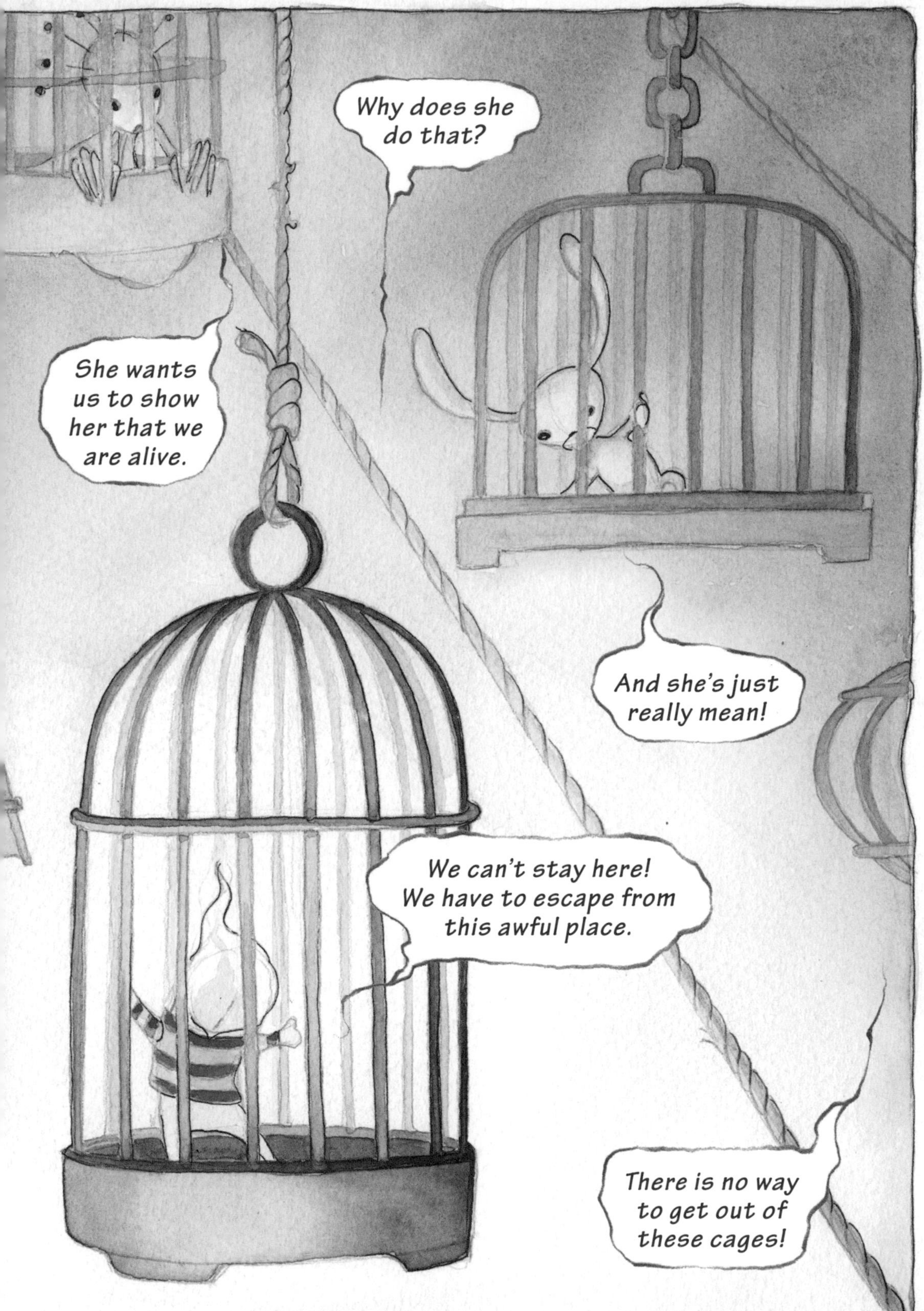
Why does she do that?
She wants us to show her that we are alive.
And she's just really mean!
We can't stay here! We have to escape from this awful place.
There is no way to get out of these cages!

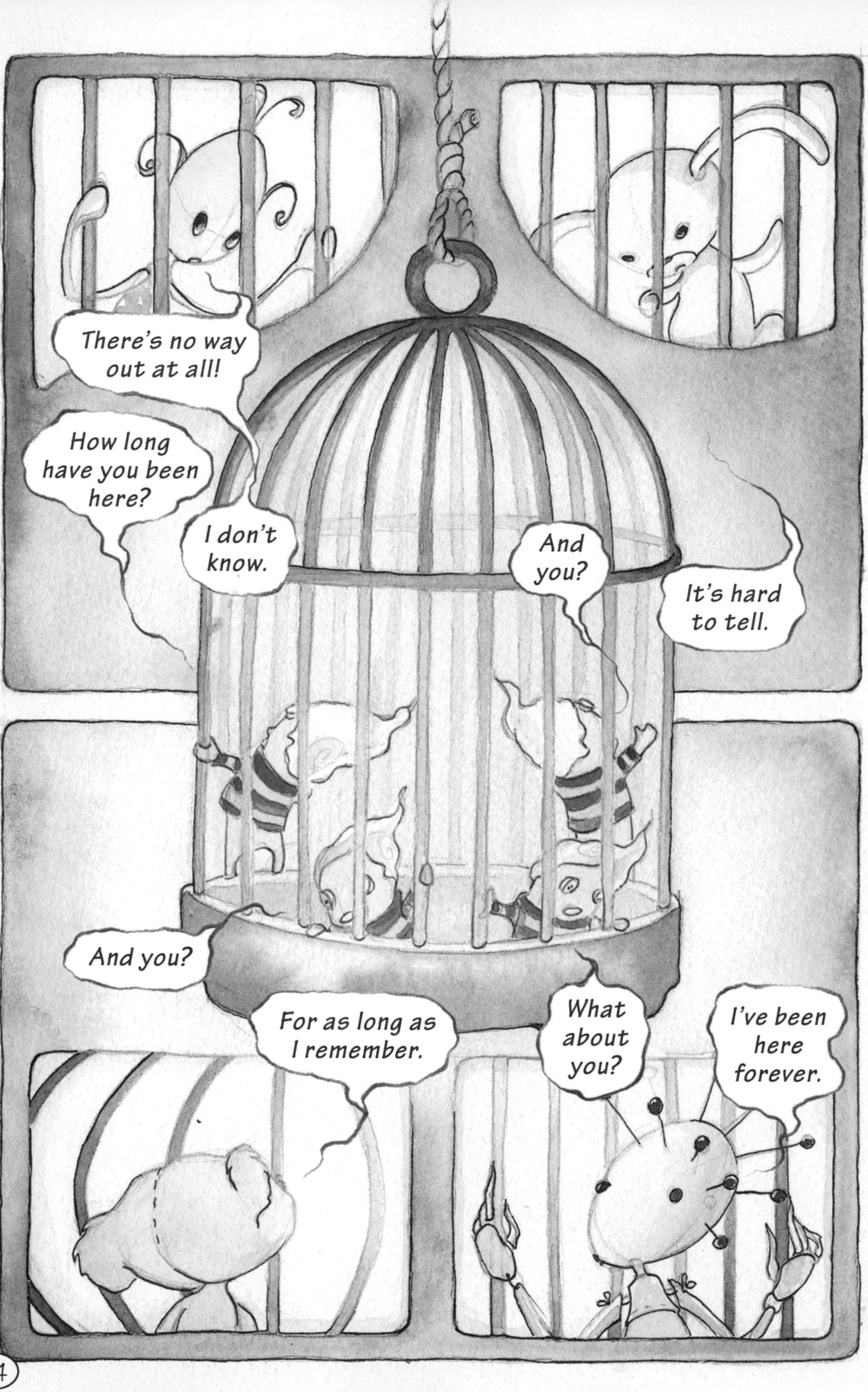
There's no way out at all!
How long have you been here?
I don't know.
And you?
It's hard to tell.
And you?
For as long as I remember.
What about you?
I've been here forever.

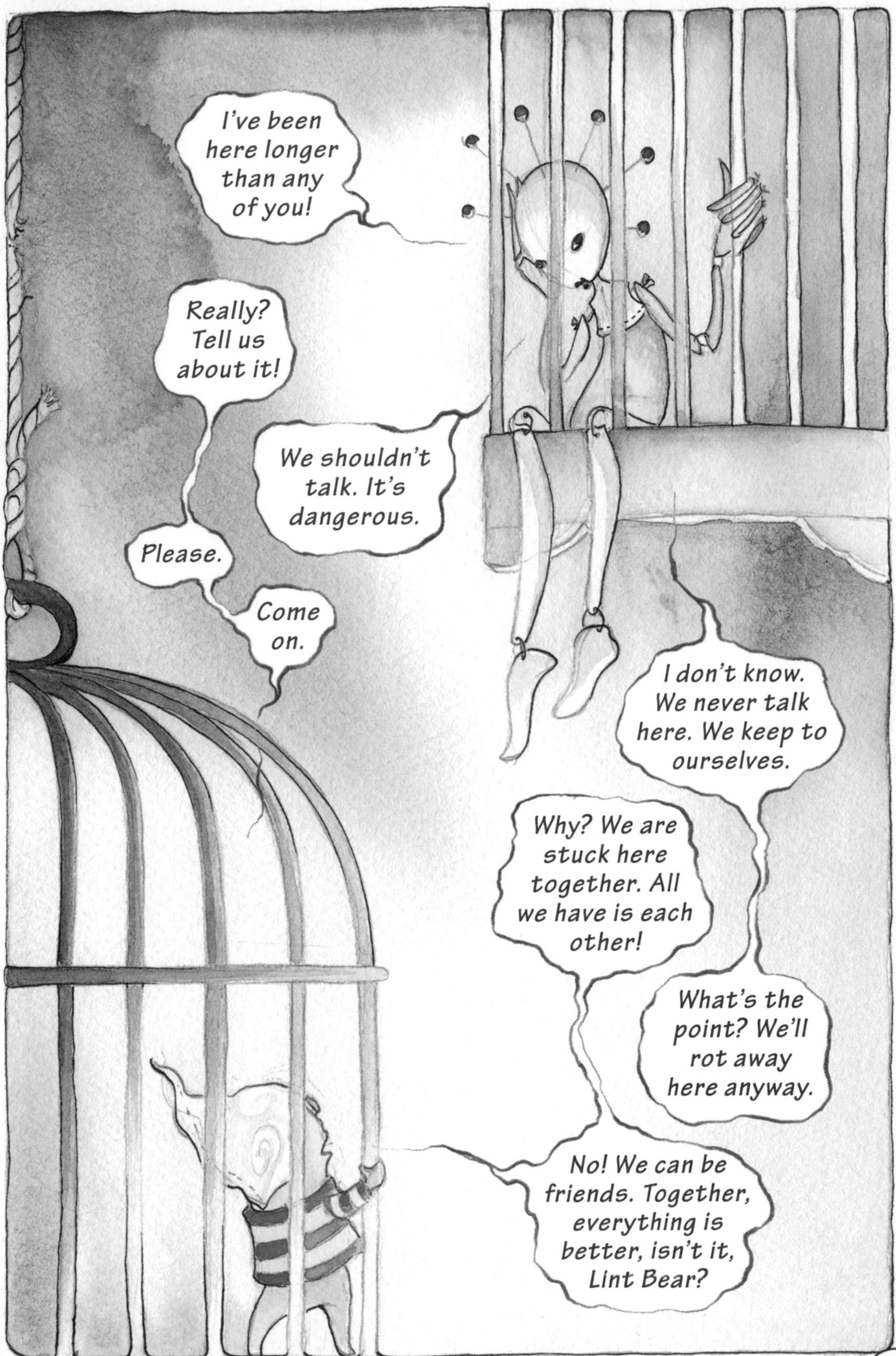
I've been here longer than any of you!
Really? Tell us about it!
We shouldn't talk. It's dangerous.
Please.
Come on.
I don't know. We never talk here. We keep to ourselves.
Why? We are stuck here together. All we have is each other!
What's the point? We'll rot away here anyway.
No! We can be friends. Together, everything is better, isn't it, Lint Bear?

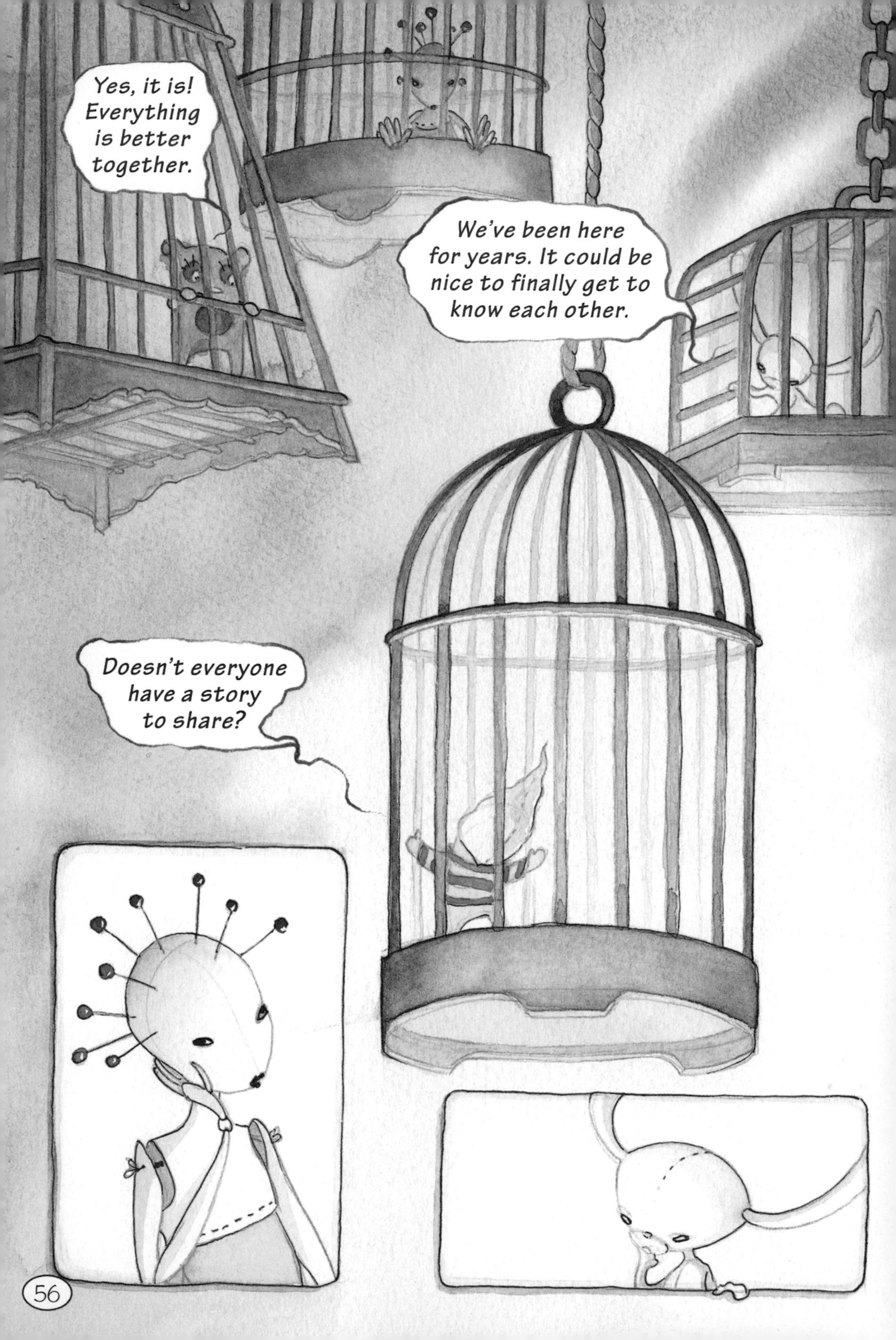
Yes, it is! Everything is better together.
We've been here for years. It could be nice to finally get to know each other.
Doesn't everyone have a story to share?

No one had asked about the dolls' stories before. Unexpectedly absorbed by their own memories, they were quiet. Finally Lint Boy, exhausted from the day's happenings, drifted off into a fitful sleep.

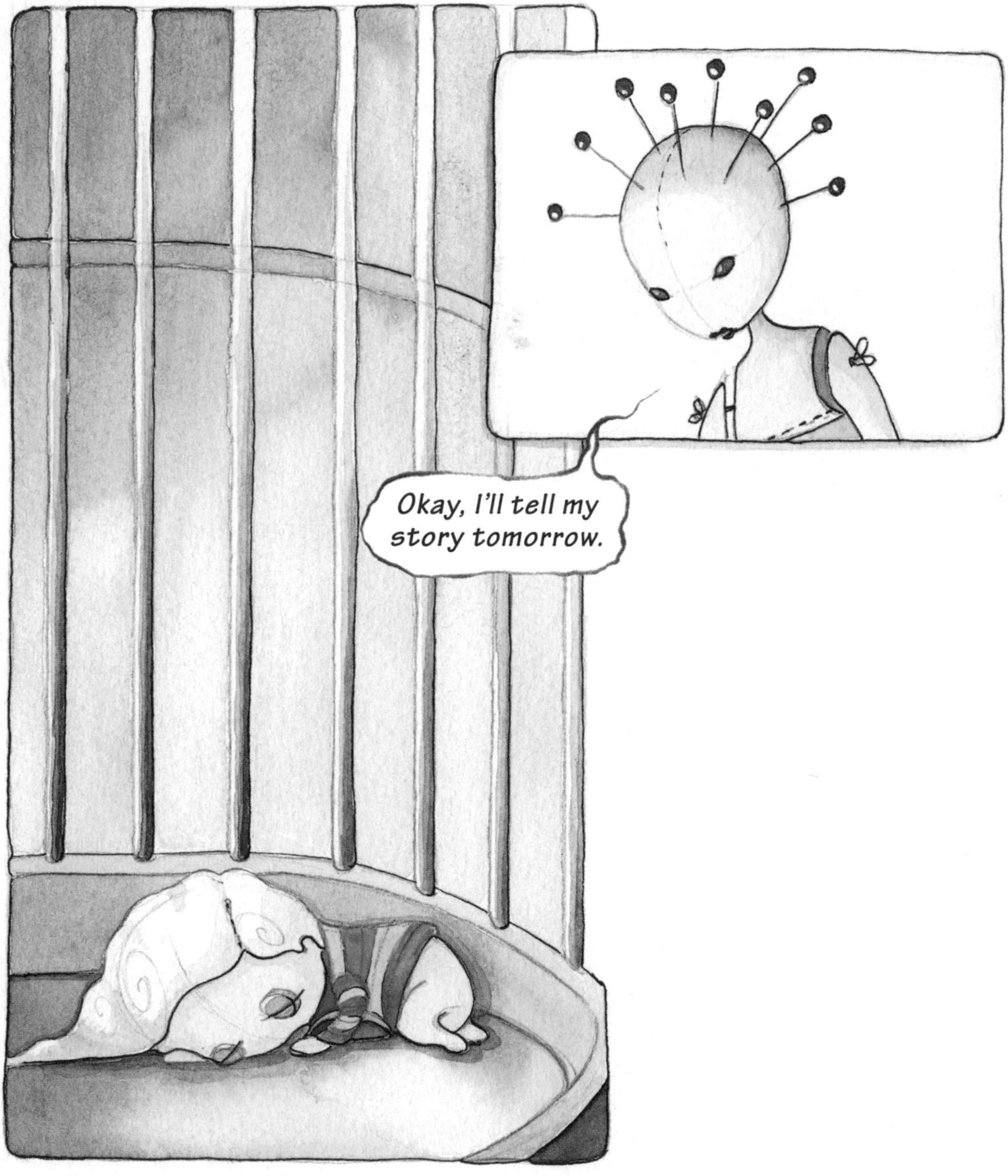
Okay, I'll tell my story tomorrow.

Chapter 7

A Makeover

Lint Boy woke up feeling cold. Where was the cozy warmth of the dryer? With a start, he remembered where he was.

Before long, a pair of disagreeable boots came banging down the stairs.

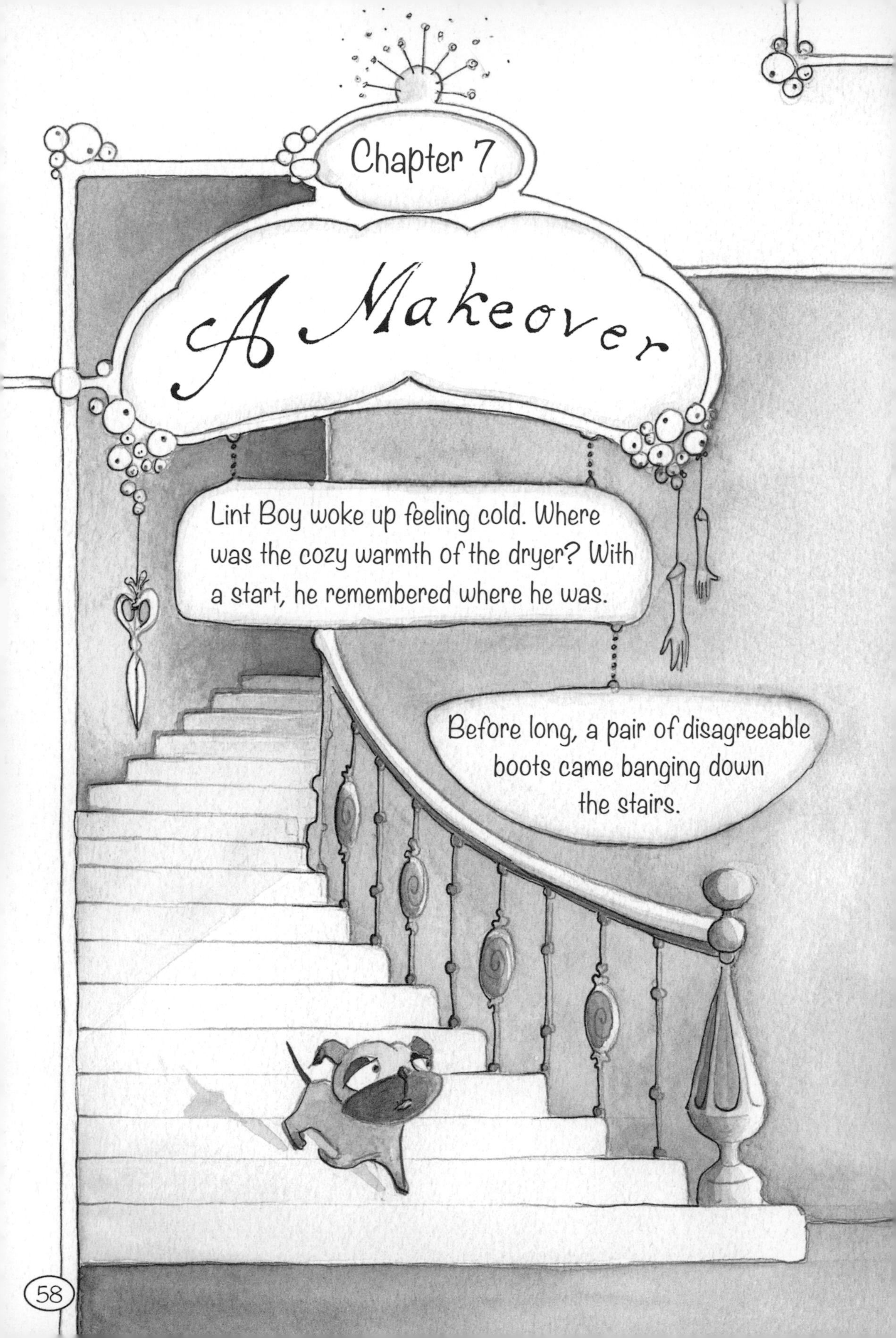

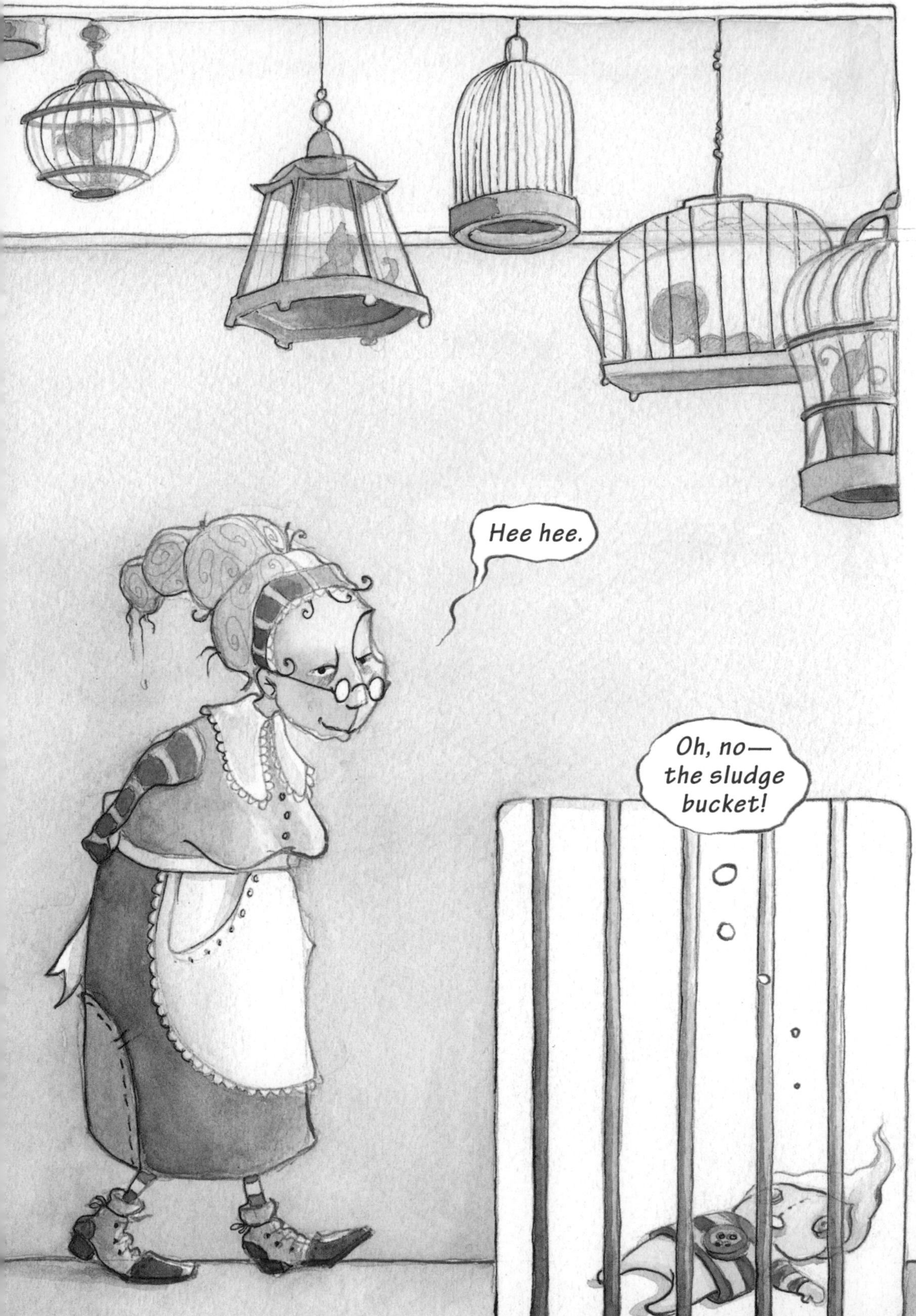
Hee hee.
Oh, no— the sludge bucket!

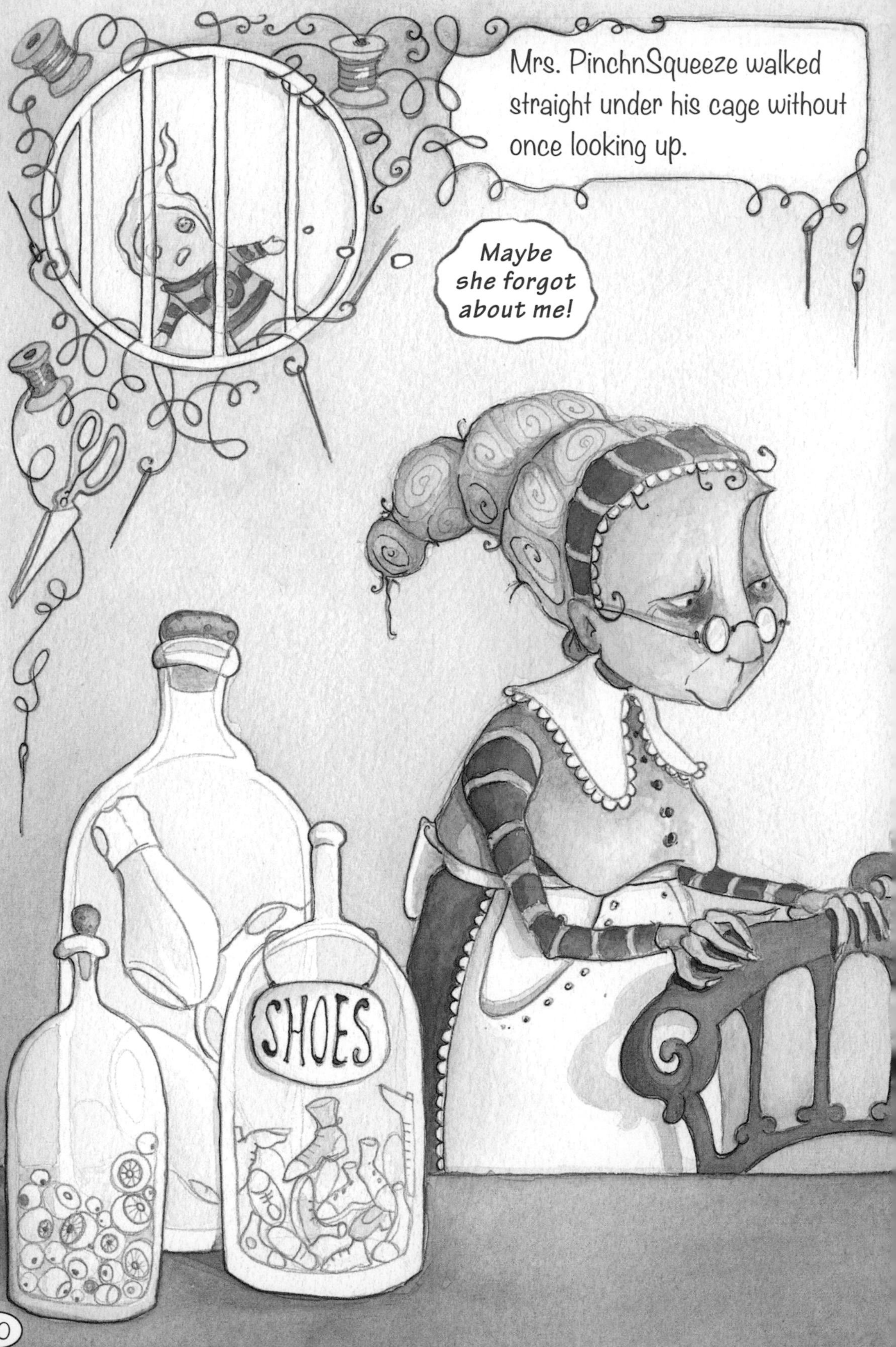
Mrs. PinchnSqueeze walked straight under his cage without once looking up.
Maybe she forgot about me!
SHOES

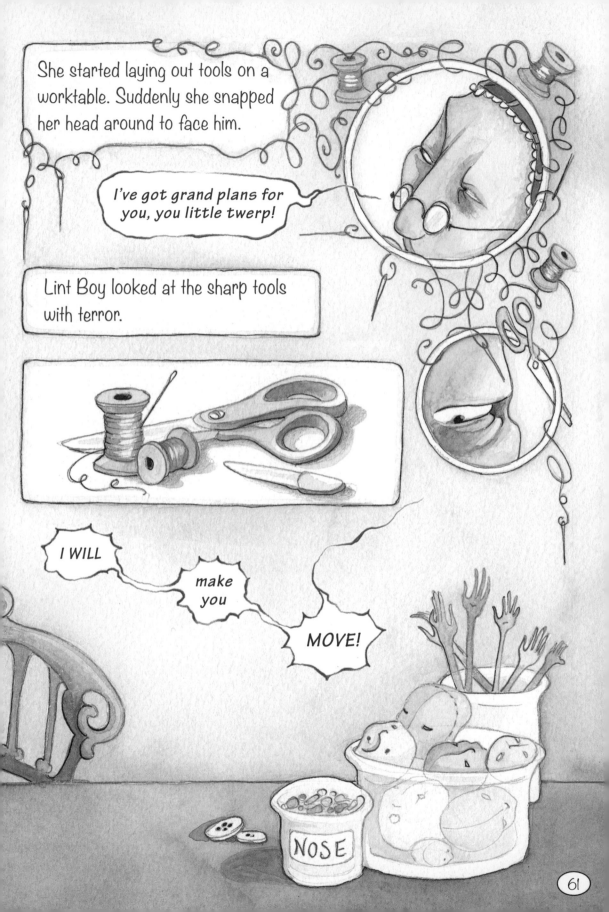

She started laying out tools on a worktable. Suddenly she snapped her head around to face him.

I've got grand plans for you, you little twerp!

Lint Boy looked at the sharp tools with terror.

I WILL

make you

MOVE!

NOSE

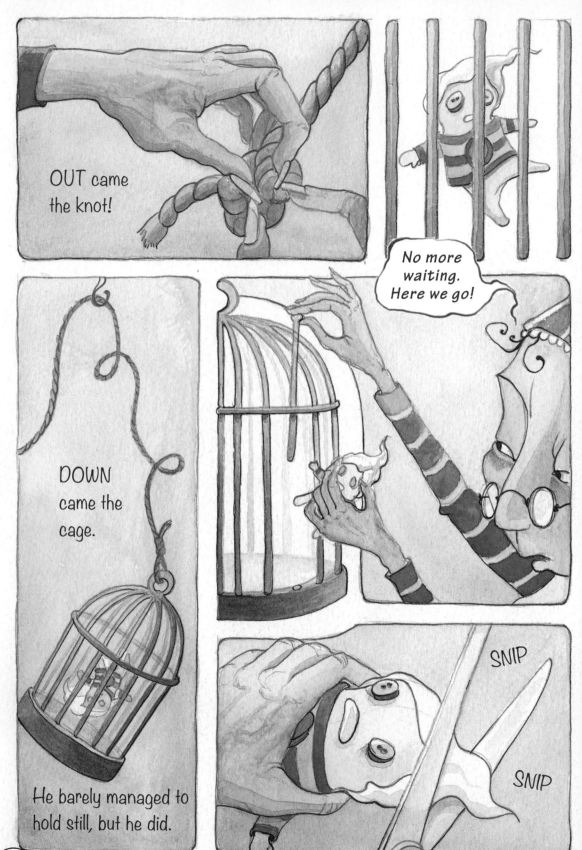

OUT came
the knot!

No more
waiting.
Here we go!

DOWN
came the
cage.

He barely managed to
hold still, but he did.

SNIP

SNIP

62

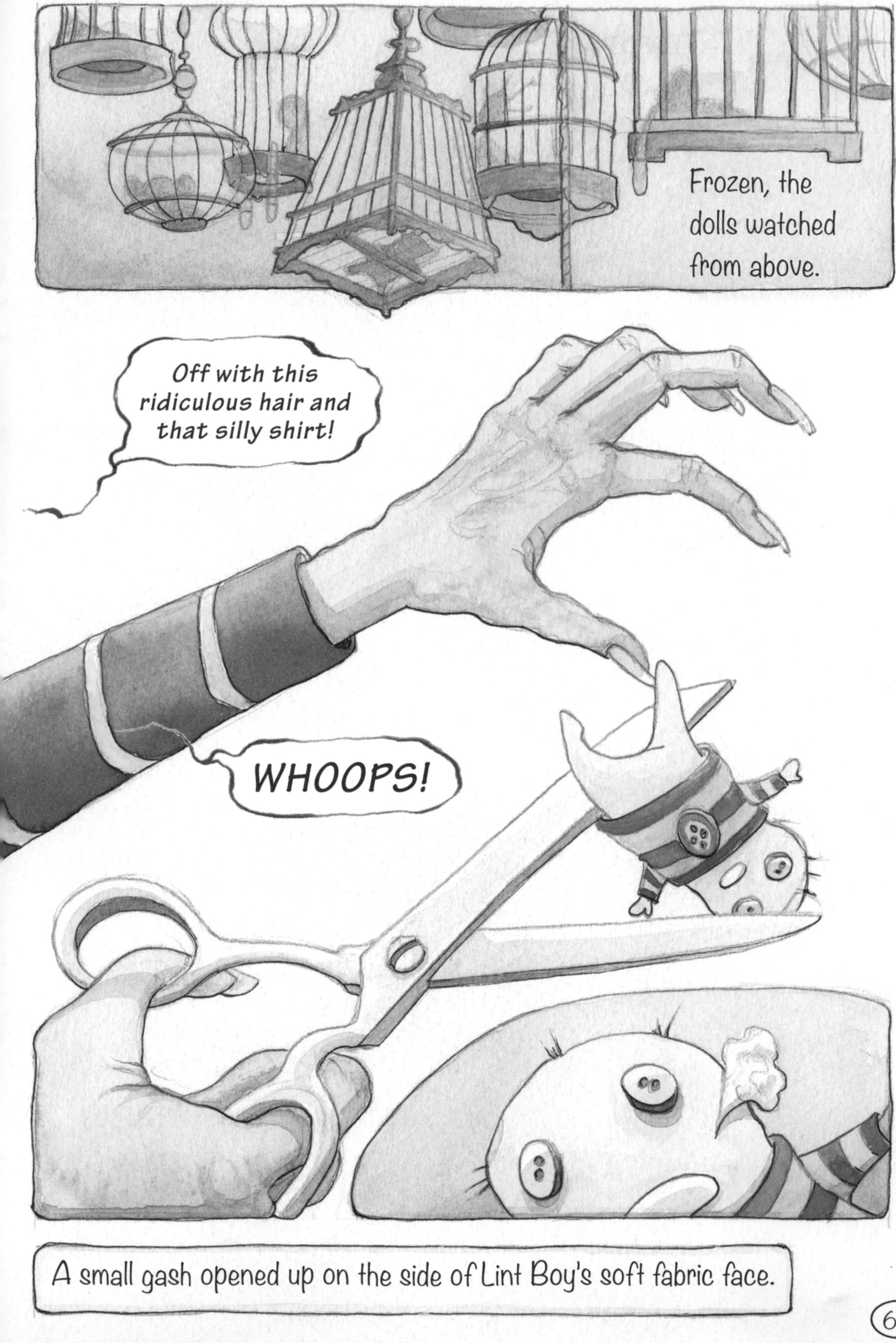
Frozen, the dolls watched from above.
Off with this ridiculous hair and that silly shirt!
WHOOPS!
A small gash opened up on the side of Lint Boy's soft fabric face.

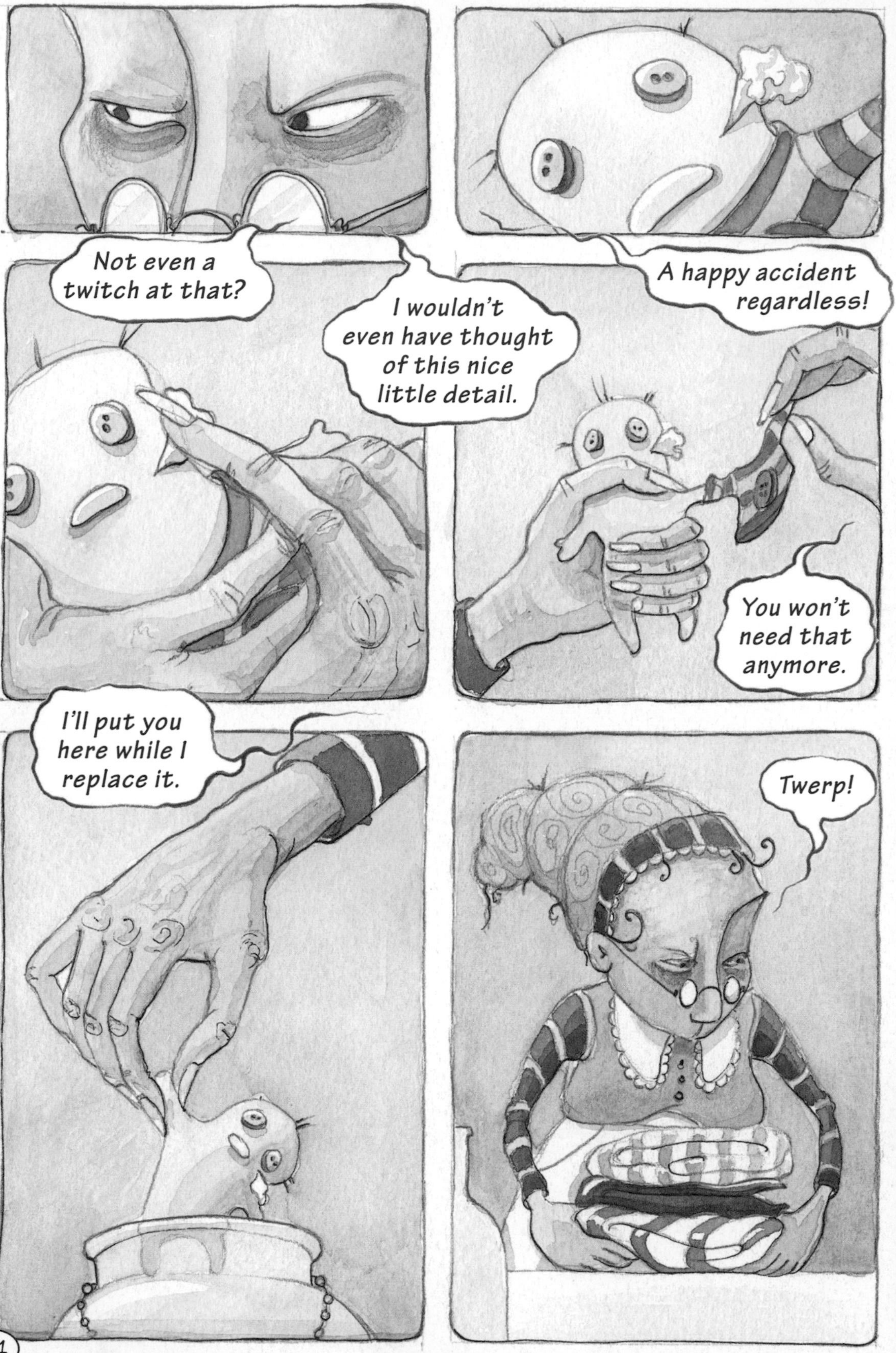
Not even a twitch at that?
I wouldn't even have thought of this nice little detail.
A happy accident regardless!
You won't need that anymore.
I'll put you here while I replace it.
Twerp!

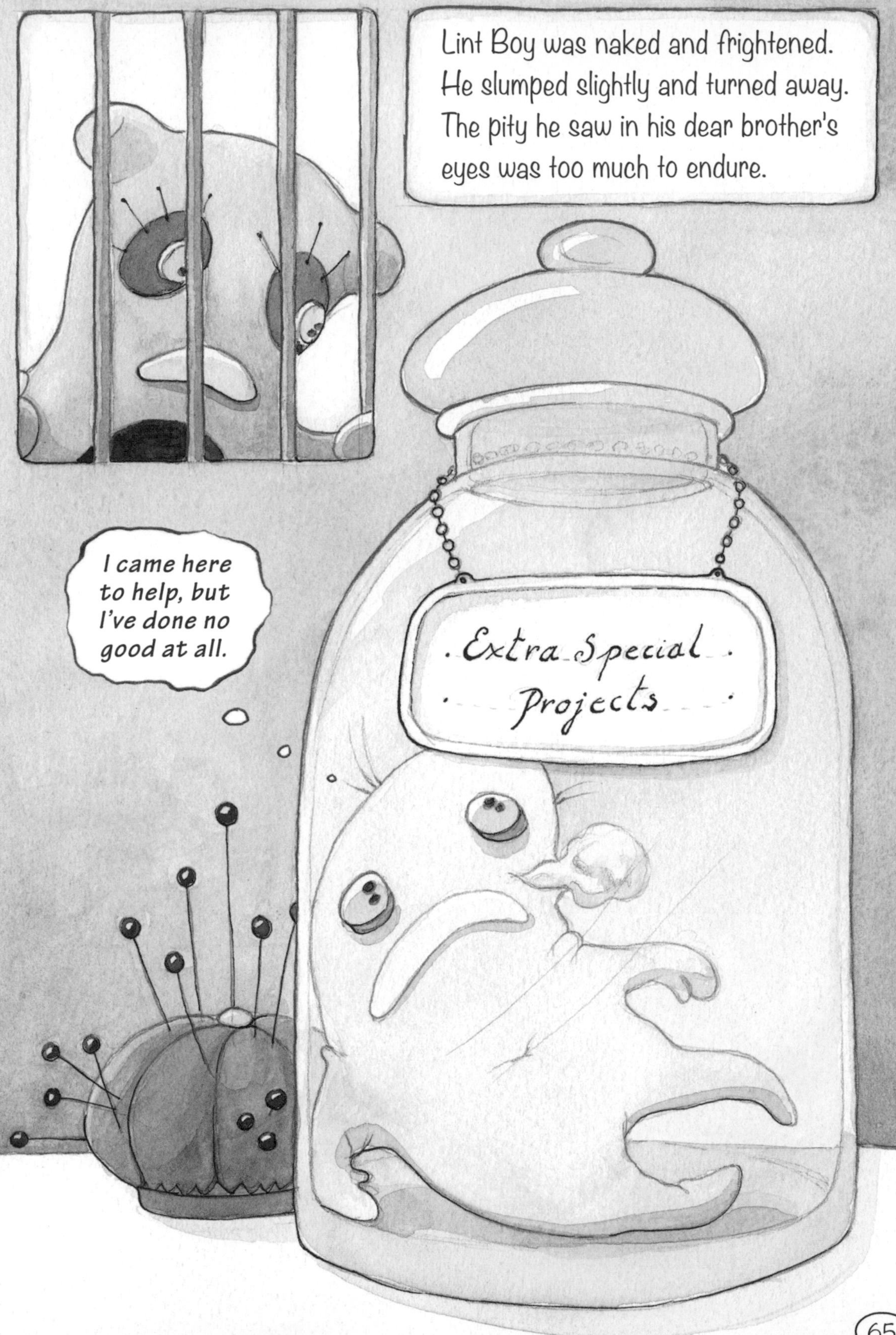
Lint Boy was naked and frightened. He slumped slightly and turned away. The pity he saw in his dear brother's eyes was too much to endure.
I came here to help, but I've done no good at all.
Extra Special Projects

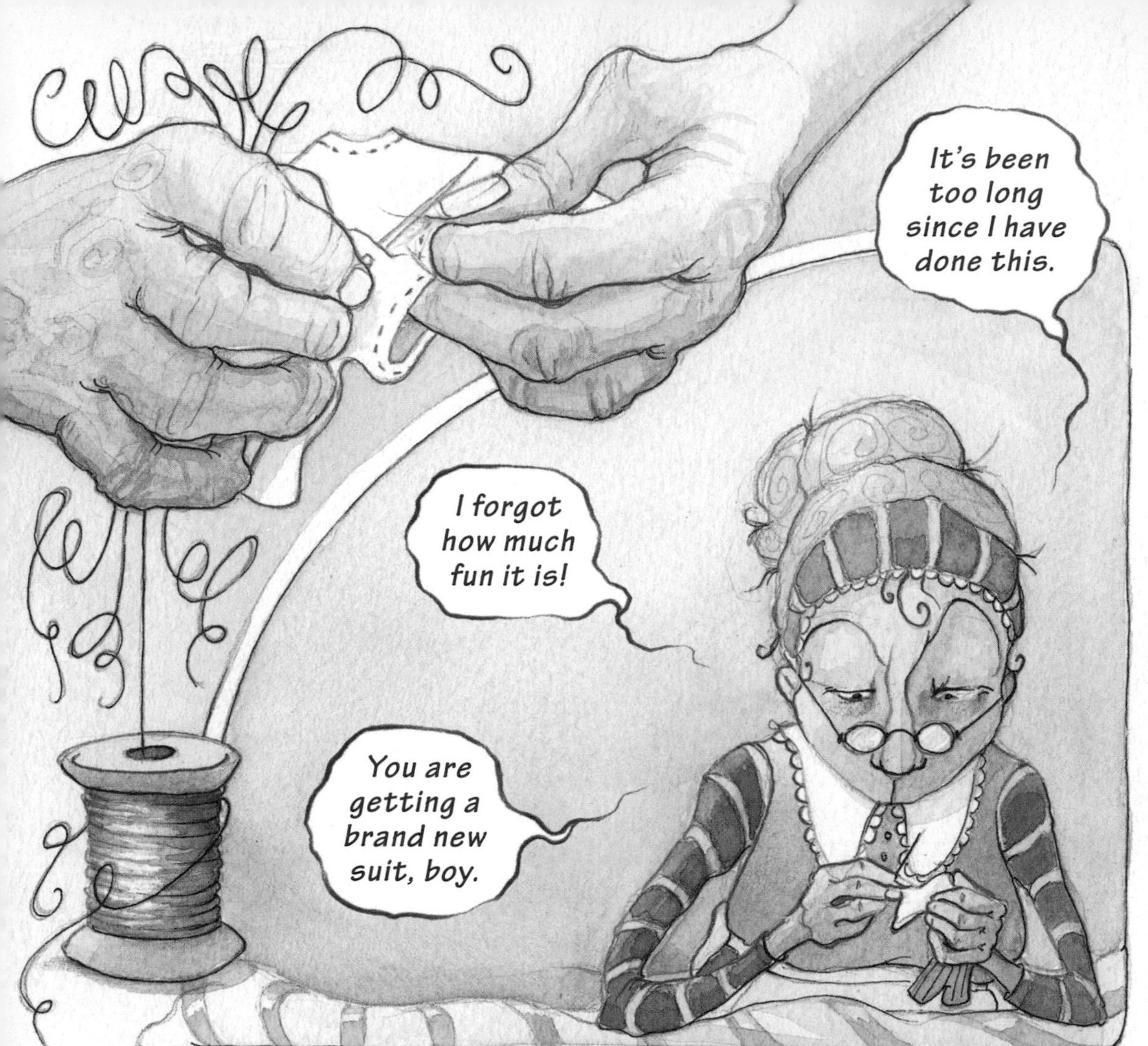
It's been too long since I have done this.
I forgot how much fun it is!
You are getting a brand new suit, boy.

Quickly, a small, dark, perfectly tailored pinstriped suit emerged.

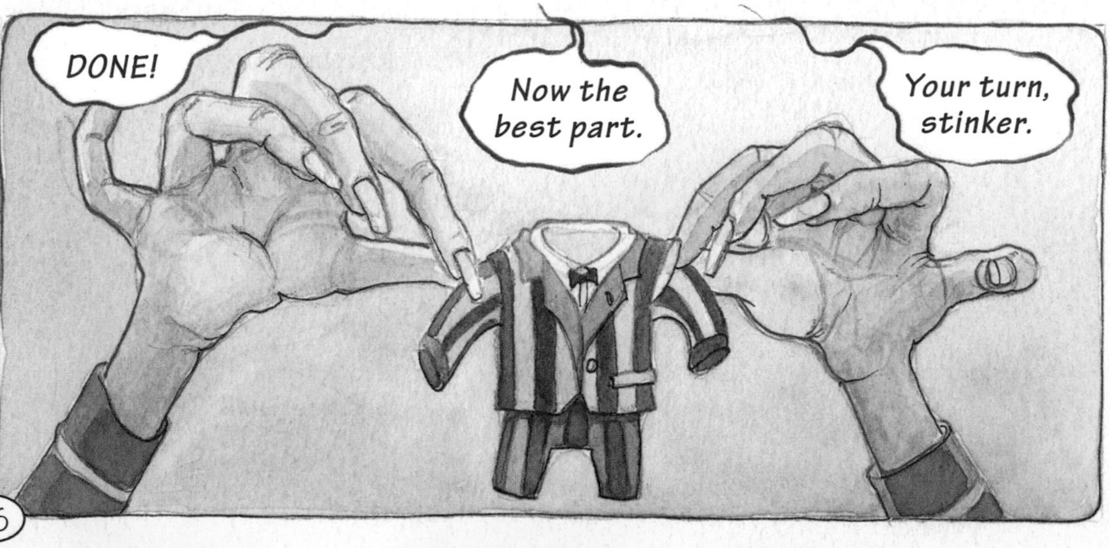
DONE!
Now the best part.
Your turn, stinker.

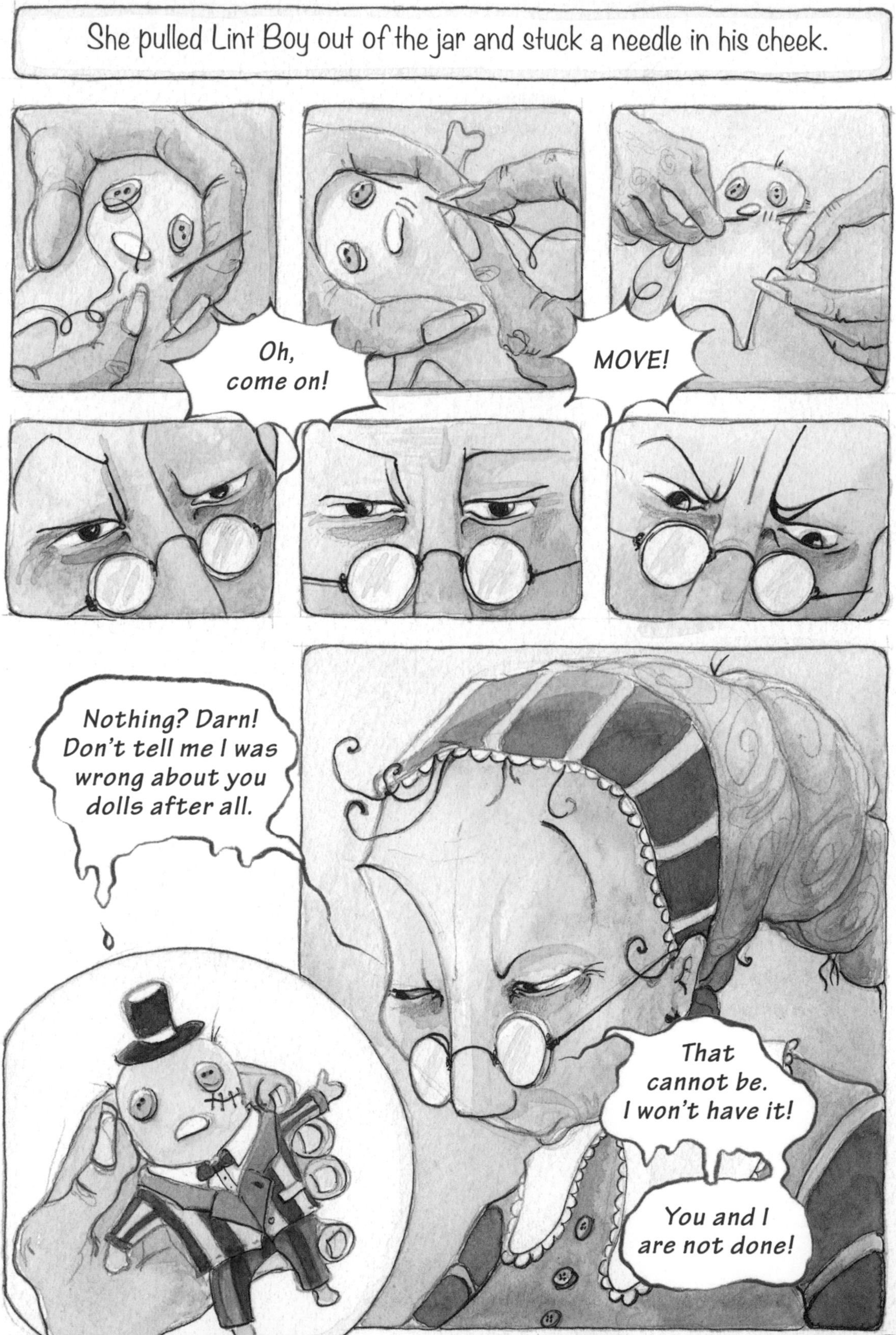
She pulled Lint Boy out of the jar and stuck a needle in his cheek.
Oh, come on!
MOVE!
Nothing? Darn! Don't tell me I was wrong about you dolls after all.
That cannot be. I won't have it!
You and I are not done!

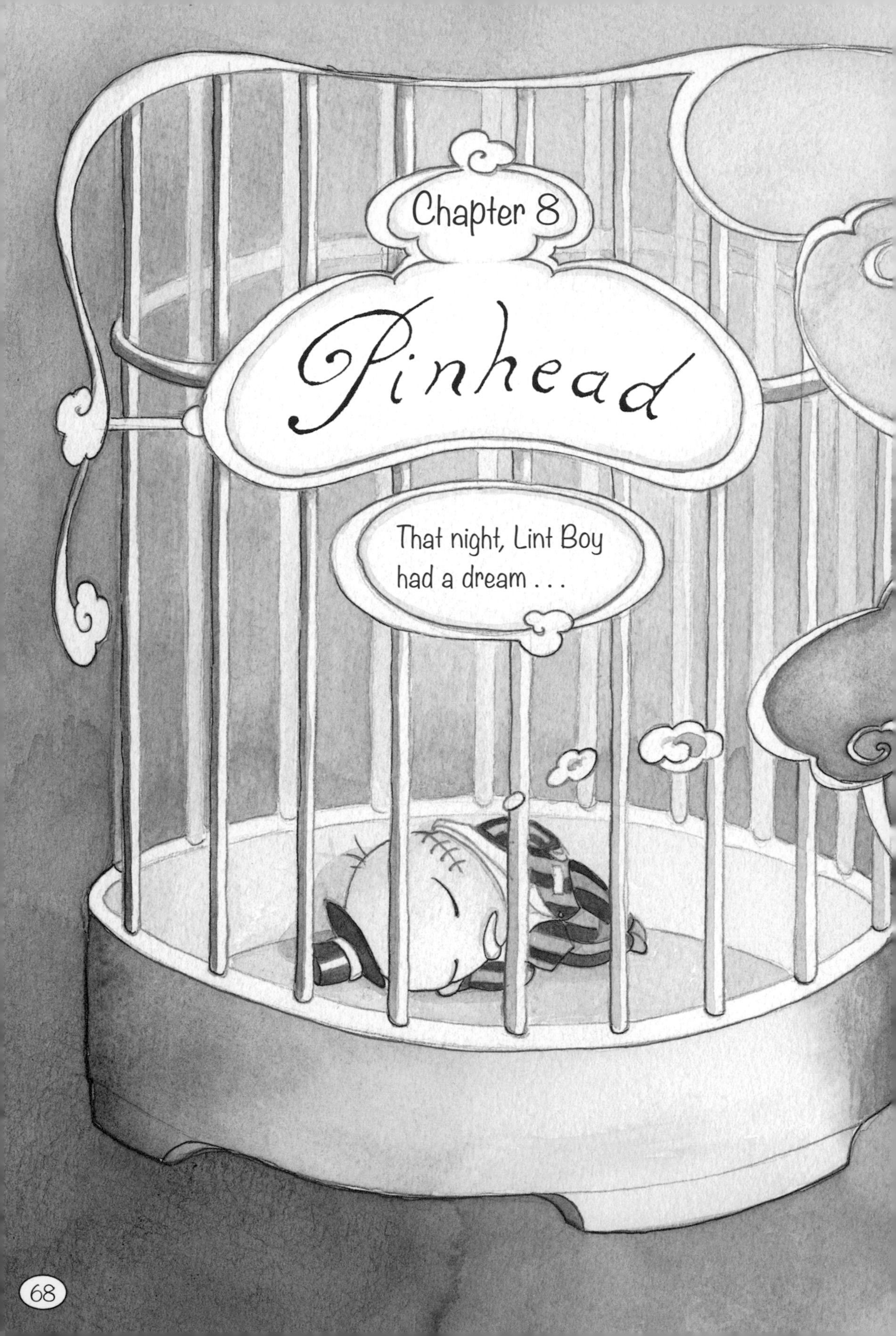
Chapter 8
Pinhead
That night, Lint Boy
had a dream . . .

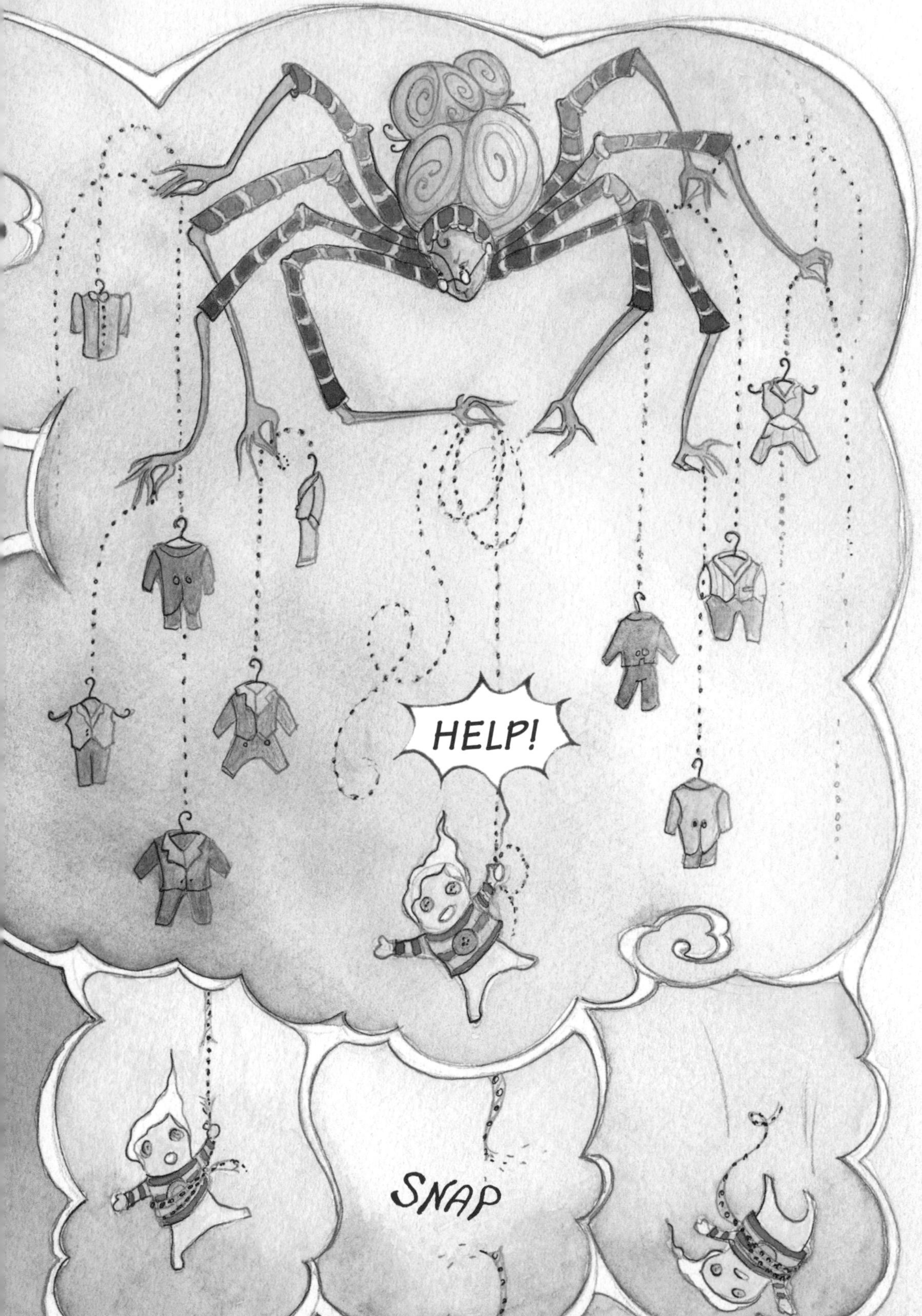
HELP!
SNAP

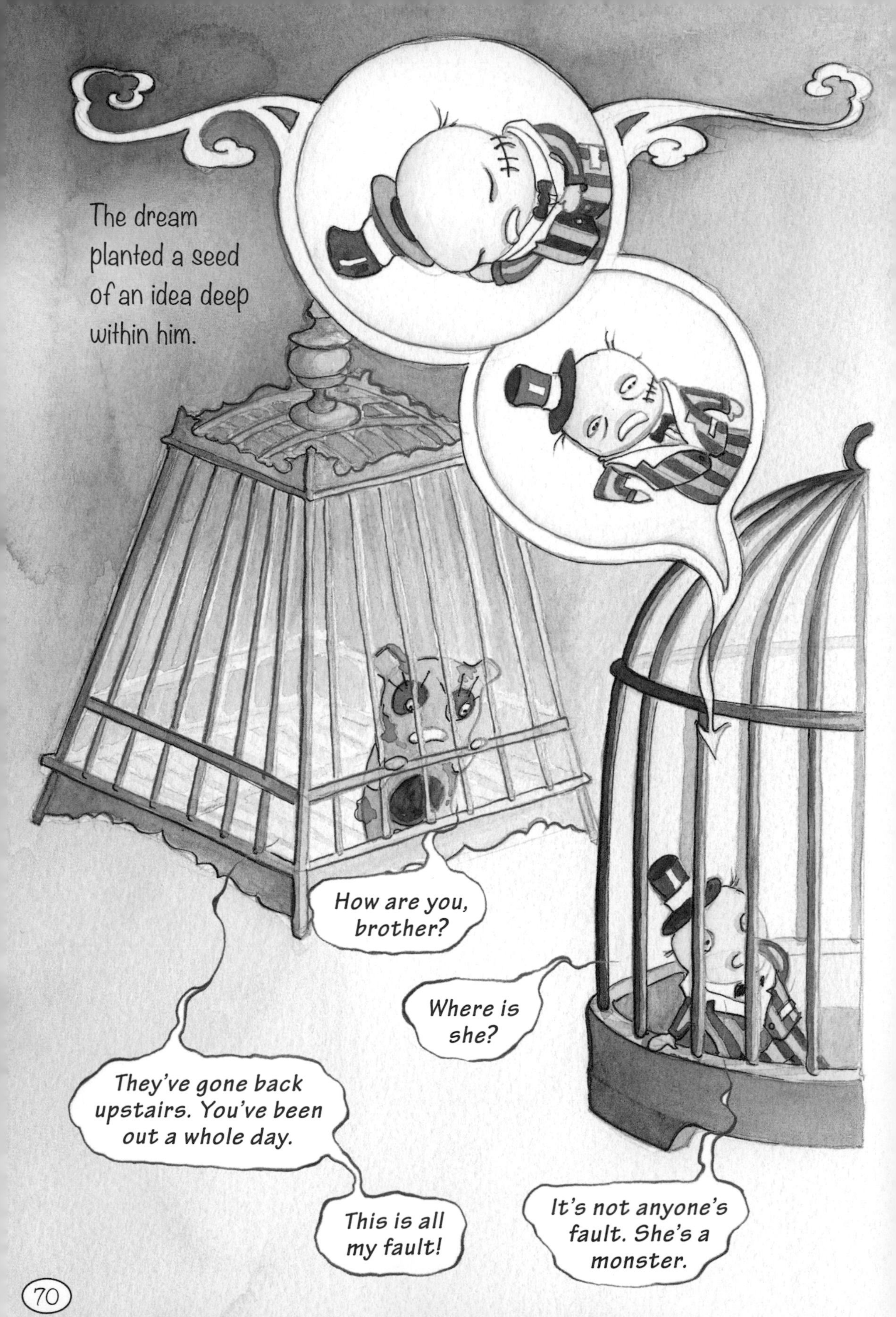
The dream planted a seed of an idea deep within him.
How are you, brother?
Where is she?
They've gone back upstairs. You've been out a whole day.
This is all my fault!
It's not anyone's fault. She's a monster.

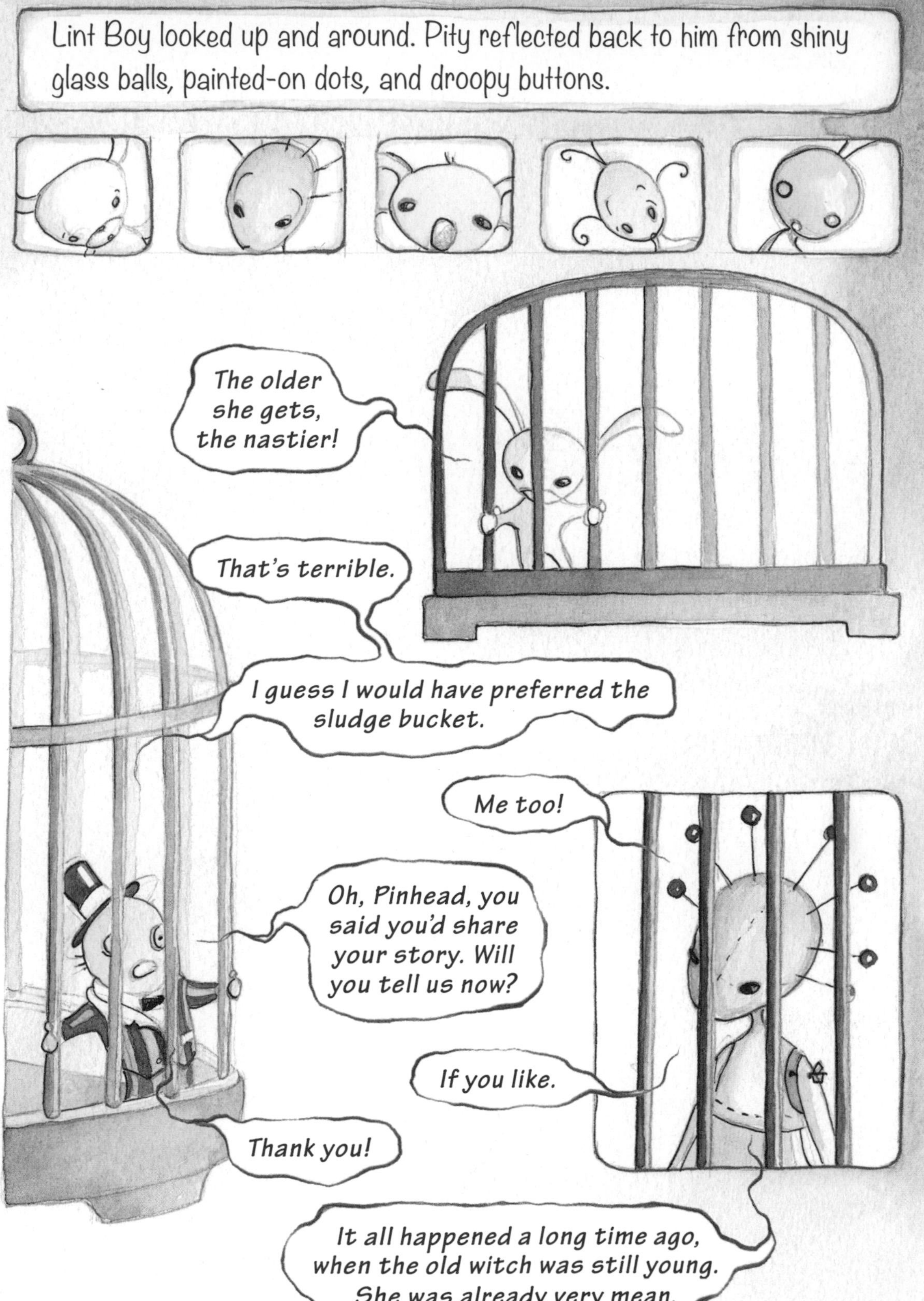
Lint Boy looked up and around. Pity reflected back to him from shiny glass balls, painted-on dots, and droopy buttons.
The older she gets, the nastier!
That's terrible.
I guess I would have preferred the sludge bucket.
Me too!
Oh, Pinhead, you said you'd share your story. Will you tell us now?
If you like.
Thank you!
It all happened a long time ago, when the old witch was still young. She was already very mean.

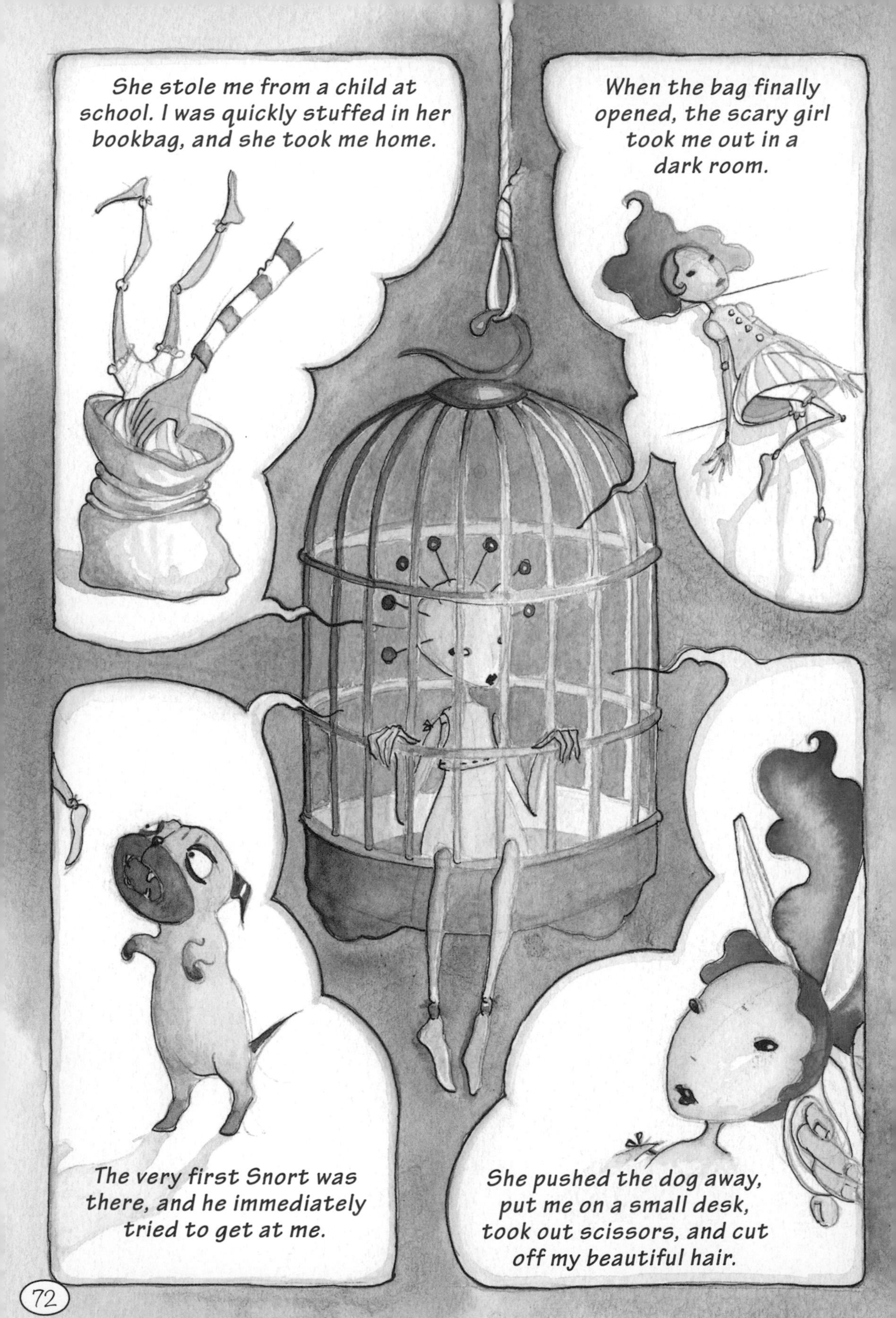
She stole me from a child at school. I was quickly stuffed in her bookbag, and she took me home.
When the bag finally opened, the scary girl took me out in a dark room.
The very first Snort was there, and he immediately tried to get at me.
She pushed the dog away, put me on a small desk, took out scissors, and cut off my beautiful hair.

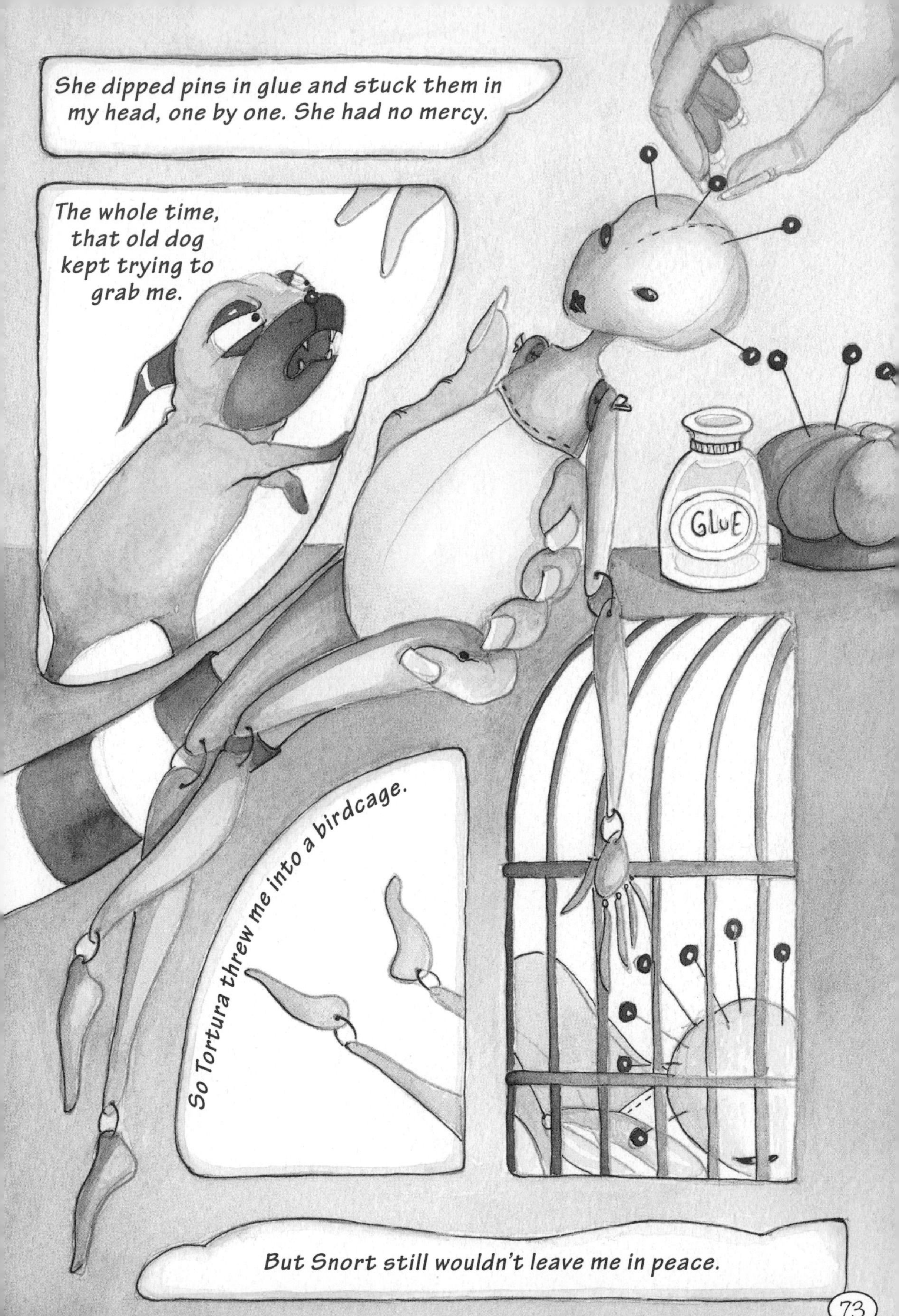
She dipped pins in glue and stuck them in my head, one by one. She had no mercy.
The whole time, that old dog kept trying to grab me.
GLUE
So Tortura threw me into a birdcage.
But Snort still wouldn't leave me in peace.

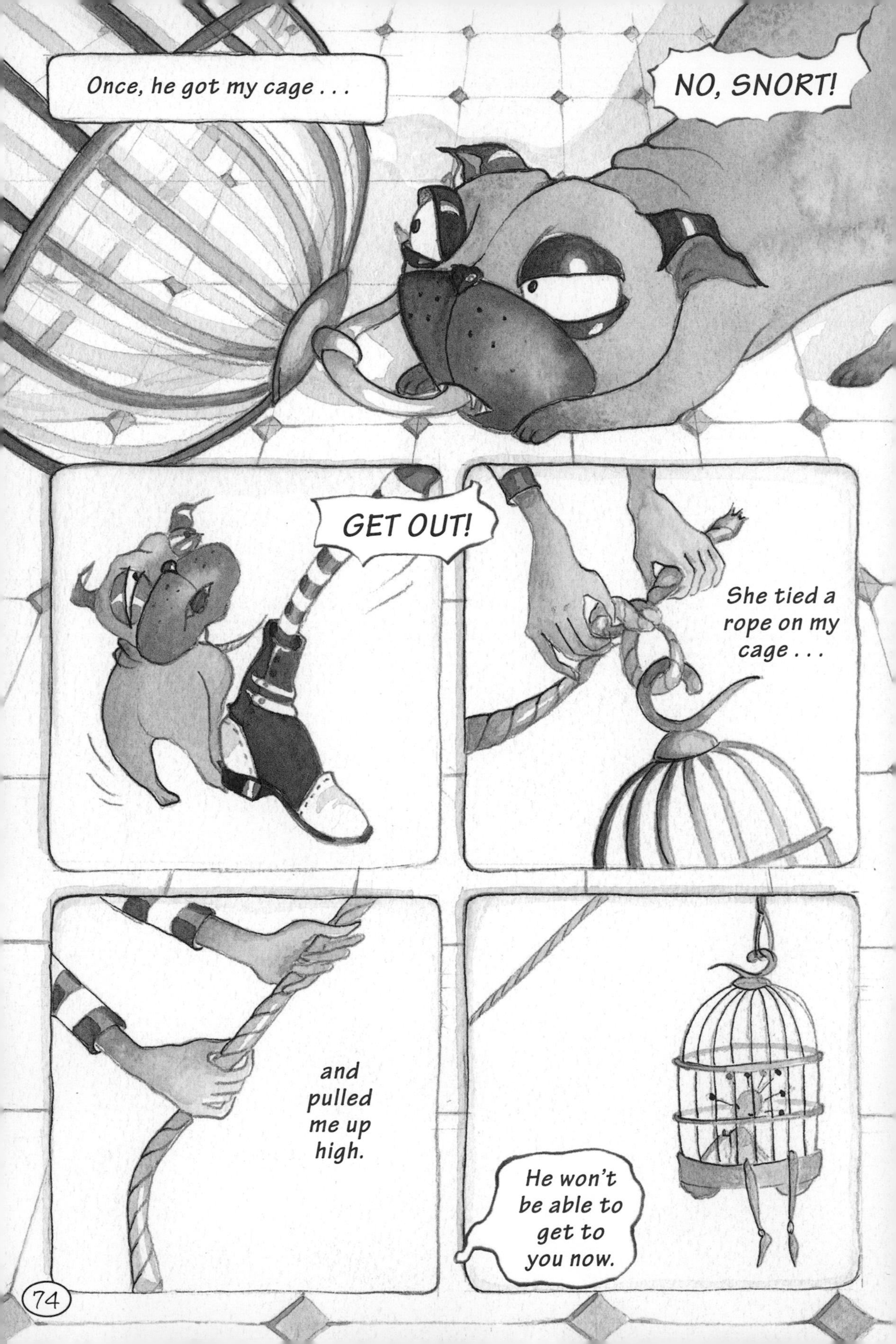
Once, he got my cage . . .
NO, SNORT!
GET OUT!
She tied a rope on my cage . . .
and pulled me up high.
He won't be able to get to you now.

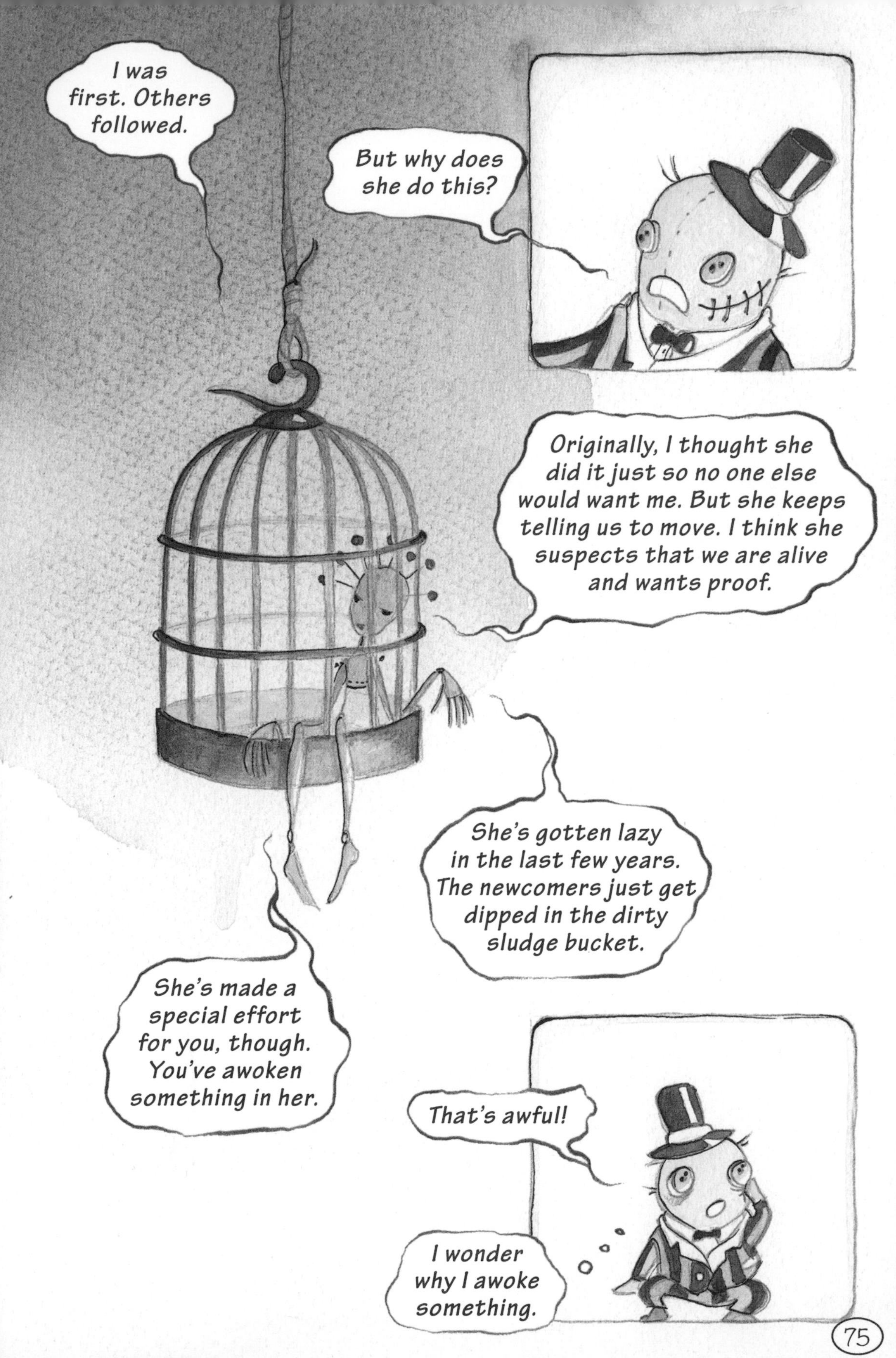
I was first. Others followed.
But why does she do this?
Originally, I thought she did it just so no one else would want me. But she keeps telling us to move. I think she suspects that we are alive and wants proof.
She's gotten lazy in the last few years. The newcomers just get dipped in the dirty sludge bucket.
She's made a special effort for you, though. You've awoken something in her.
That's awful!
I wonder why I awoke something.

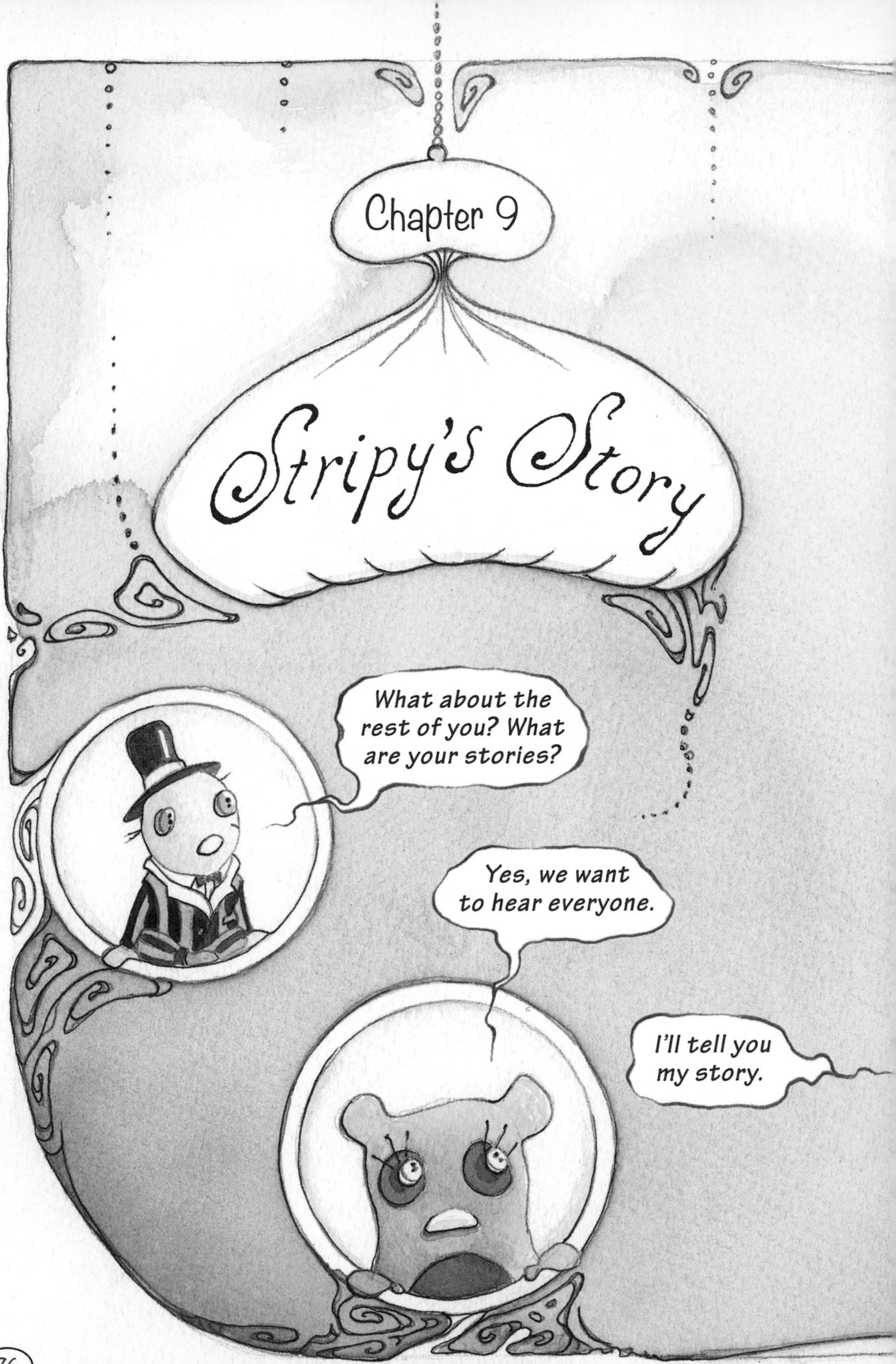
Chapter 9
Stripy's Story
What about the rest of you? What are your stories?
Yes, we want to hear everyone.
I'll tell you my story.

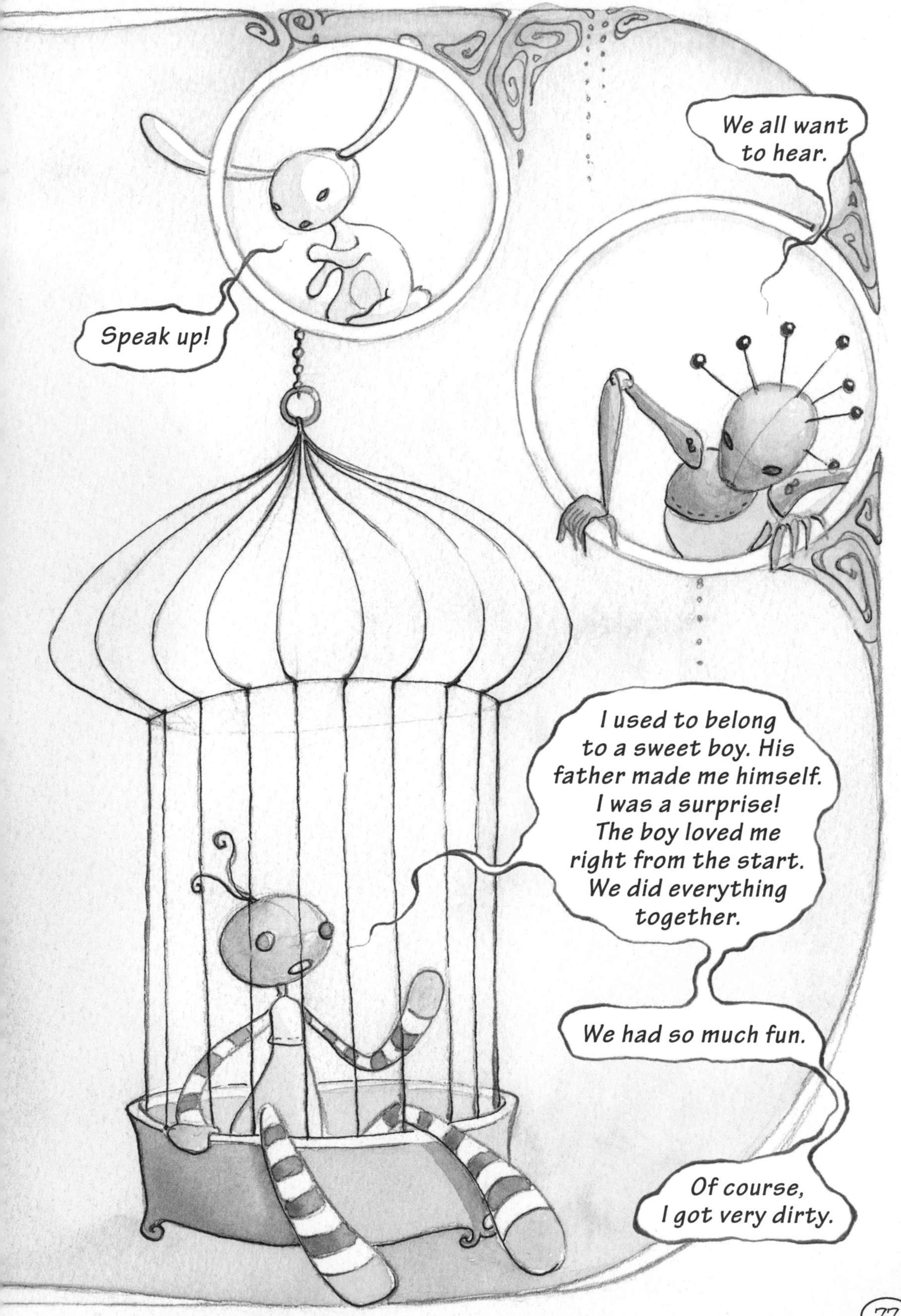
We all want to hear.
Speak up!
I used to belong to a sweet boy. His father made me himself. I was a surprise! The boy loved me right from the start. We did everything together.
We had so much fun.
Of course, I got very dirty.

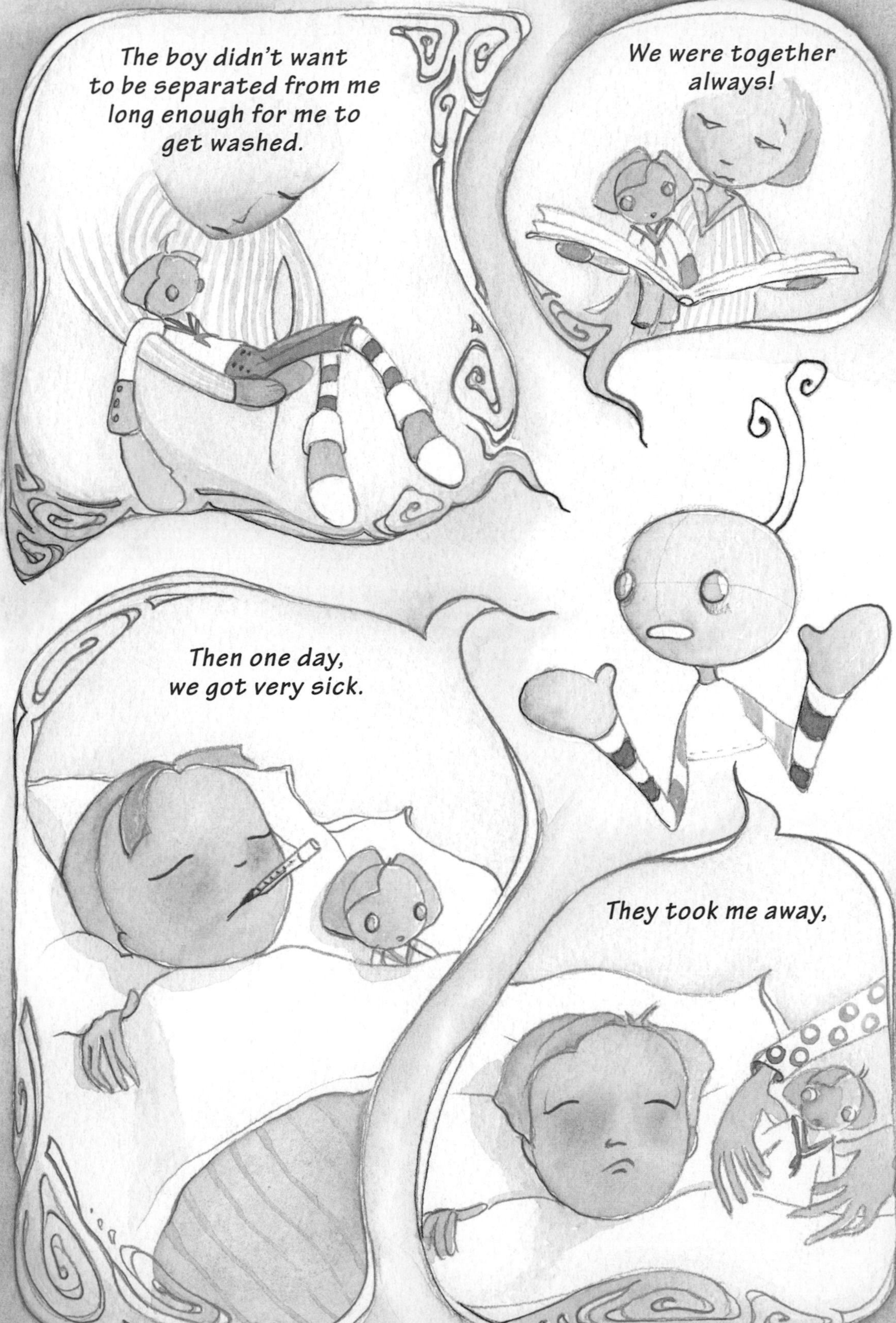
The boy didn't want to be separated from me long enough for me to get washed.
We were together always!
Then one day, we got very sick.
They took me away,

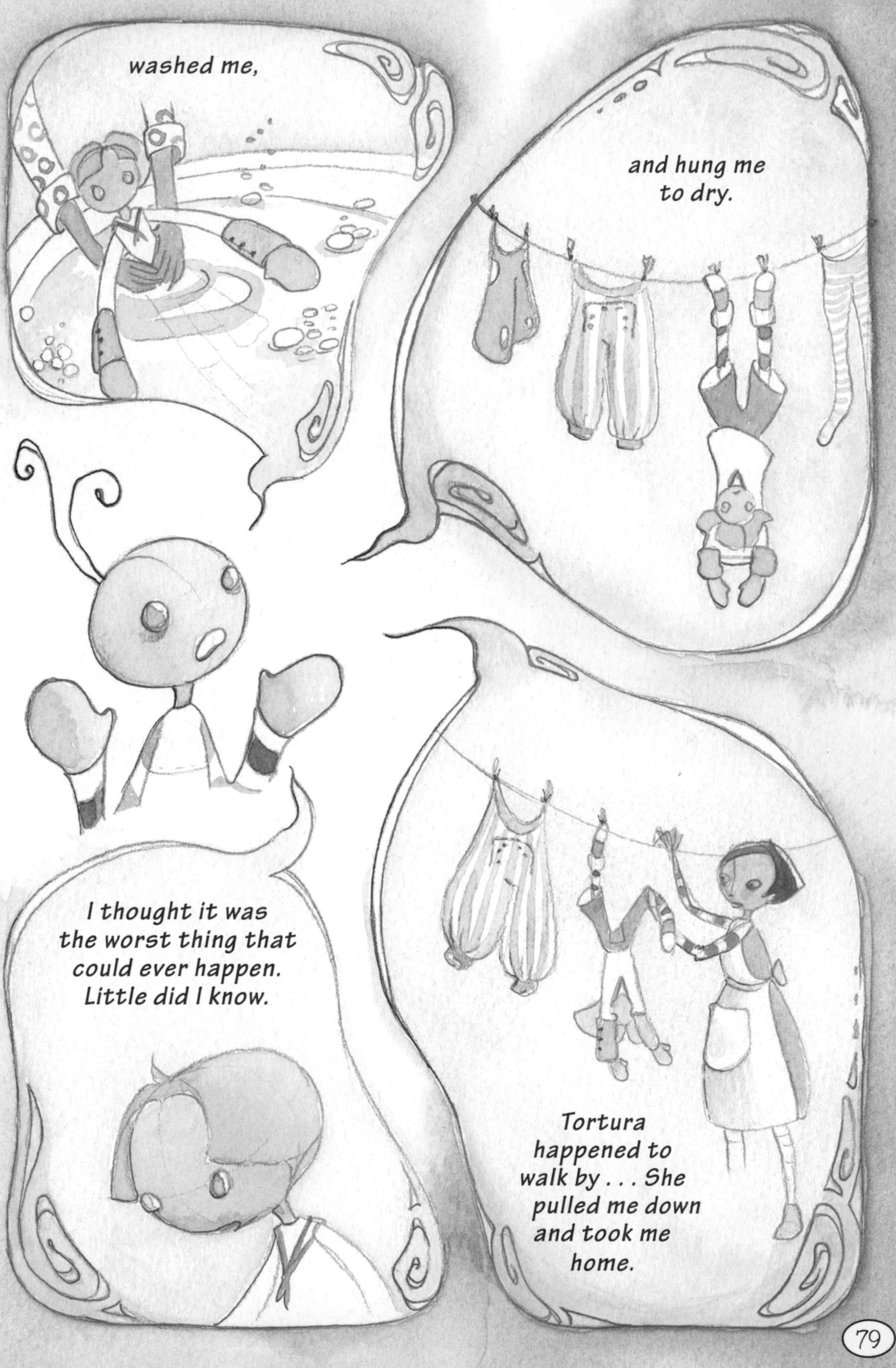
washed me,
and hung me to dry.
I thought it was the worst thing that could ever happen. Little did I know.
Tortura happened to walk by . . . She pulled me down and took me home.

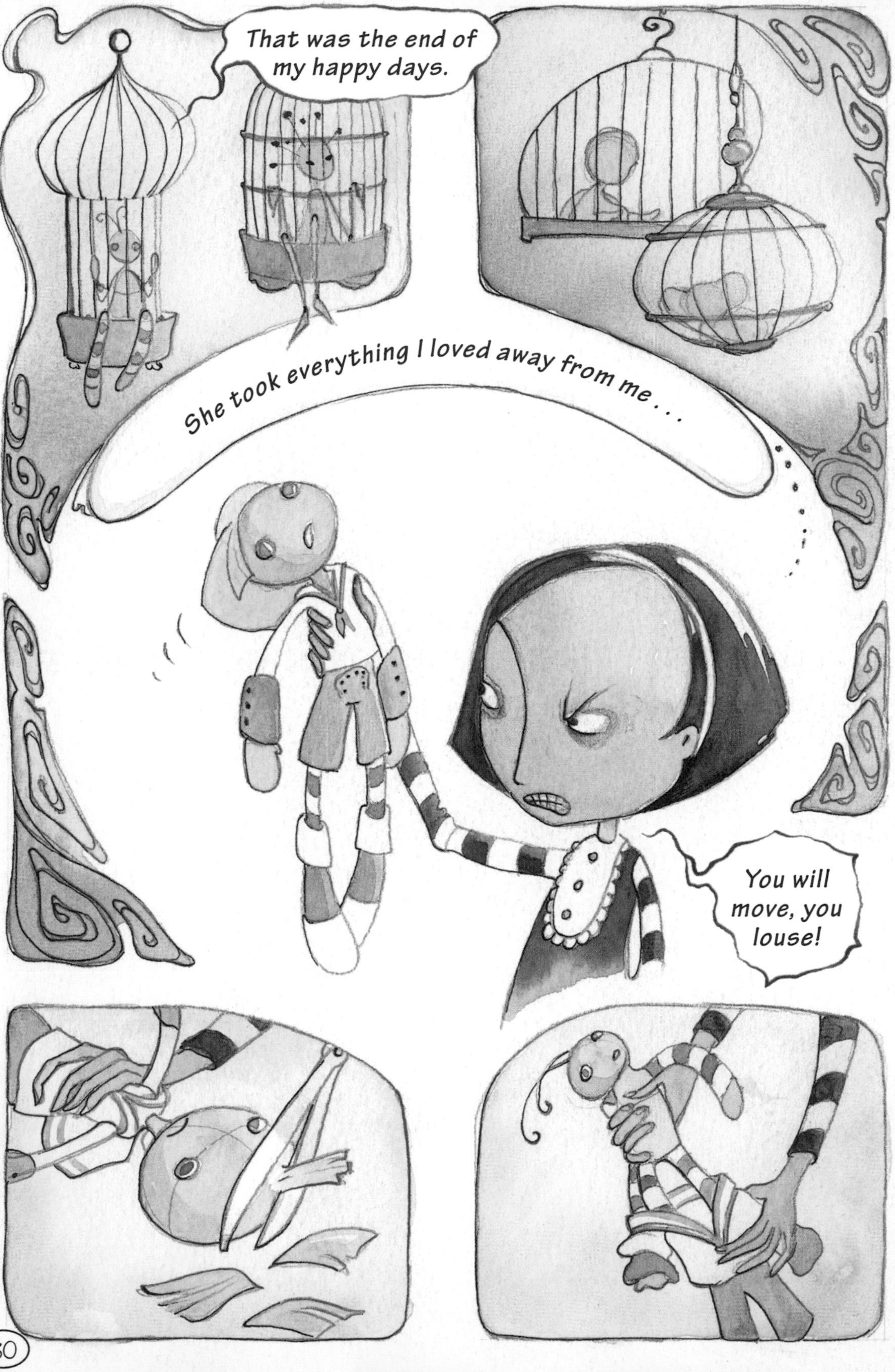
That was the end of my happy days.
She took everything I loved away from me . . .
You will move, you louse!

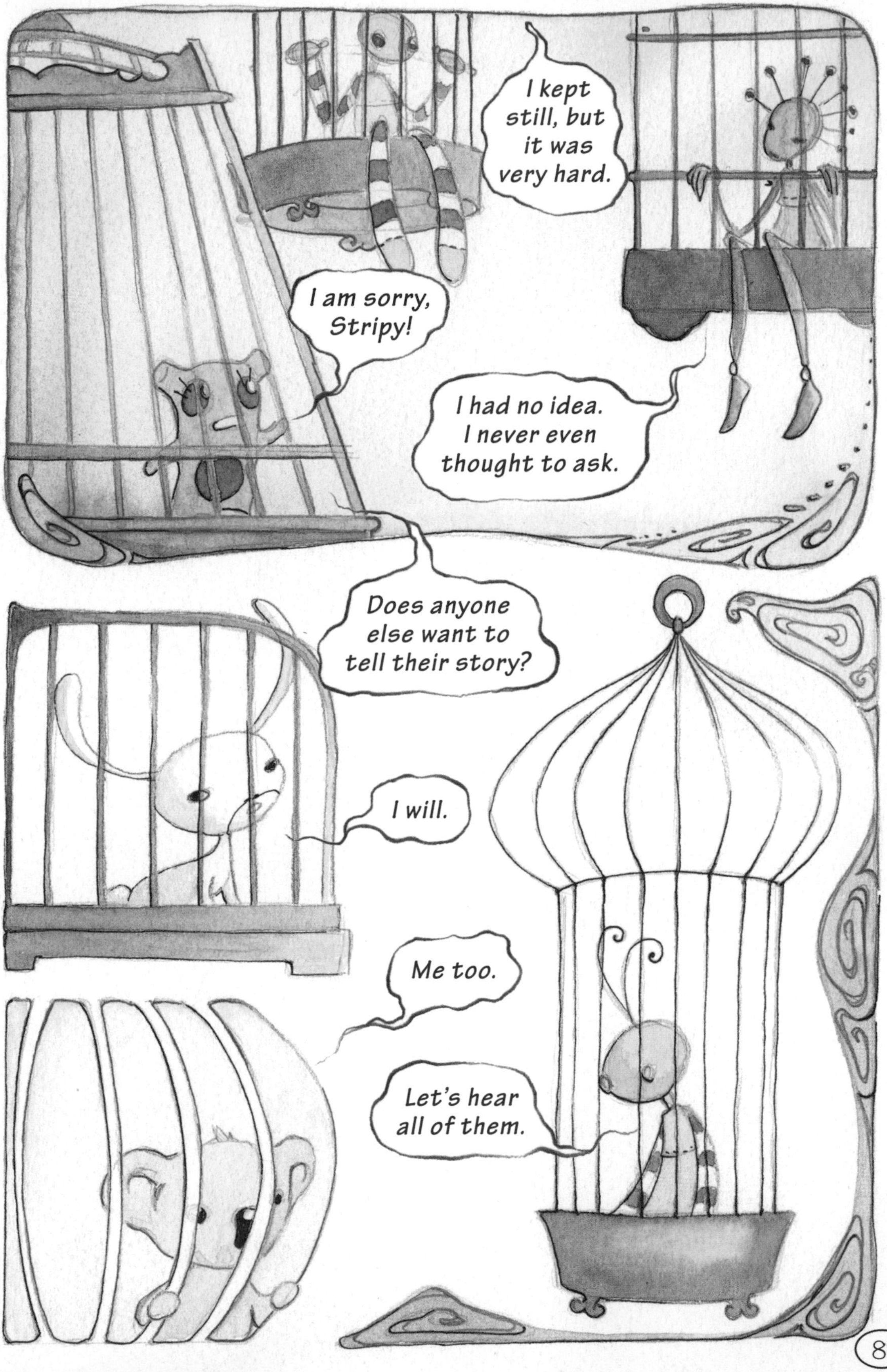
I kept still, but it was very hard.
I am sorry, Stripy!
I had no idea. I never even thought to ask.
Does anyone else want to tell their story?
I will.
Me too.
Let's hear all of them.

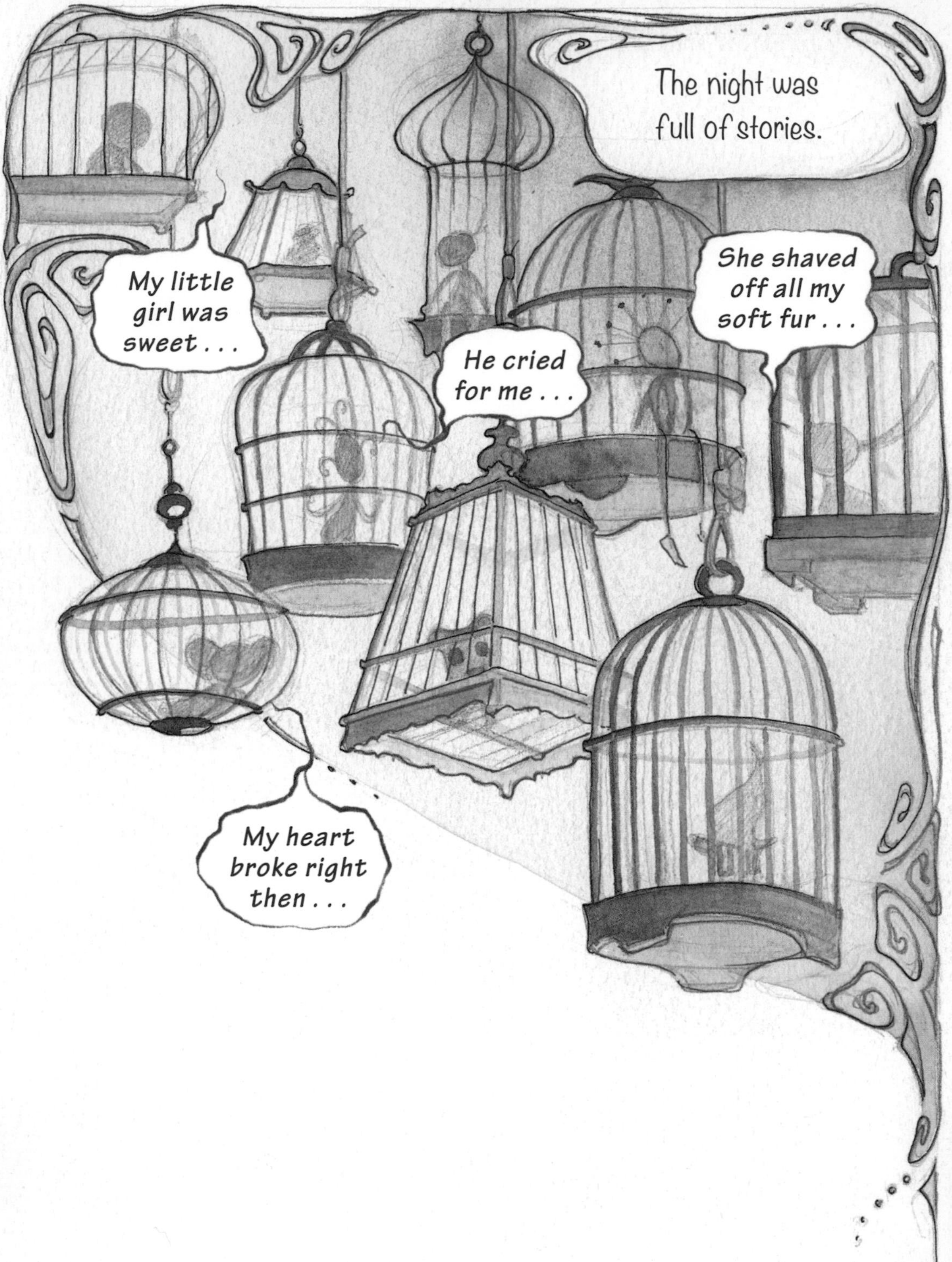
The night was full of stories.
My little girl was sweet . . .
He cried for me . . .
She shaved off all my soft fur . . .
My heart broke right then . . .

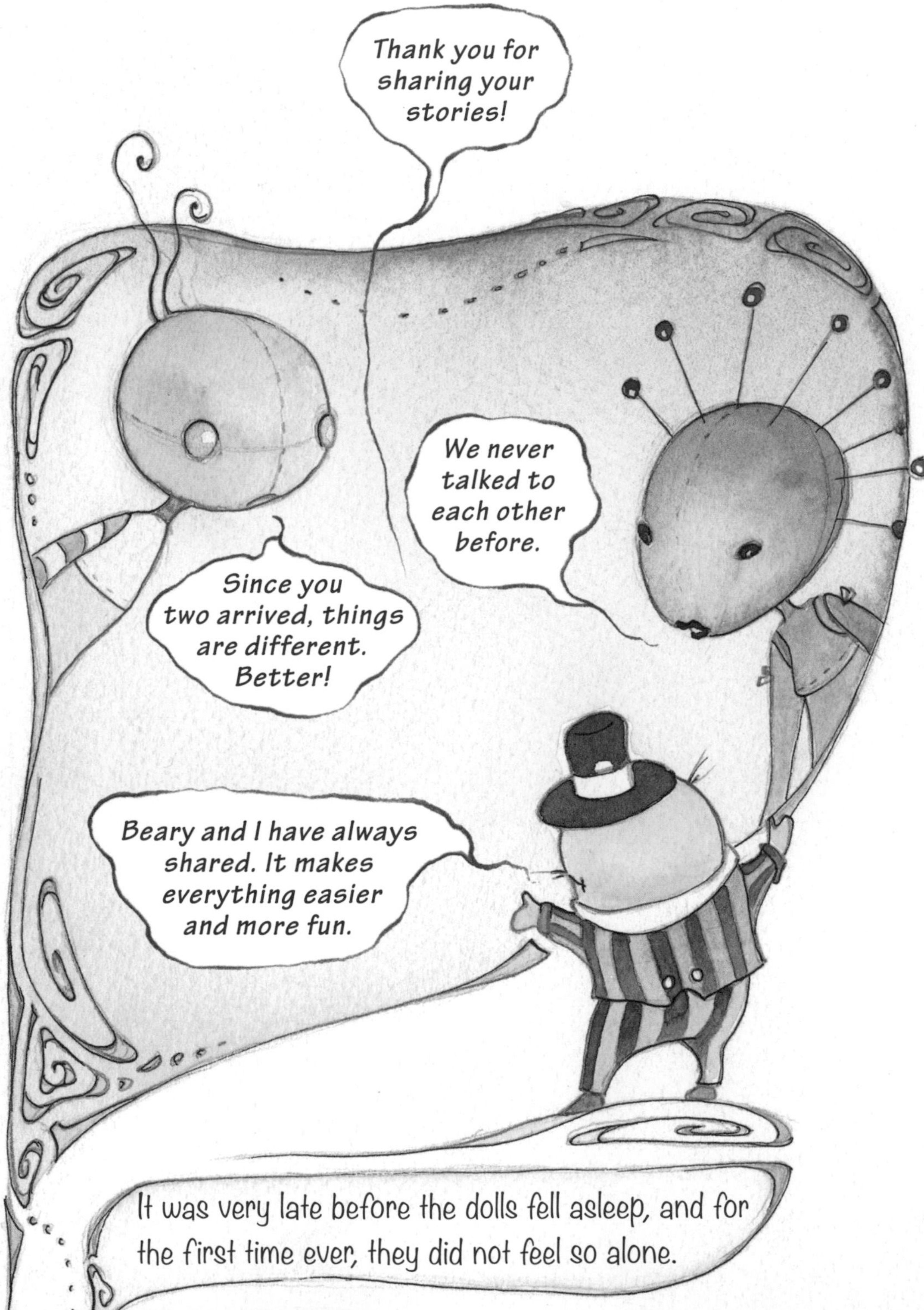
Thank you for sharing your stories!
We never talked to each other before.
Since you two arrived, things are different. Better!
Beary and I have always shared. It makes everything easier and more fun.
It was very late before the dolls fell asleep, and for the first time ever, they did not feel so alone.

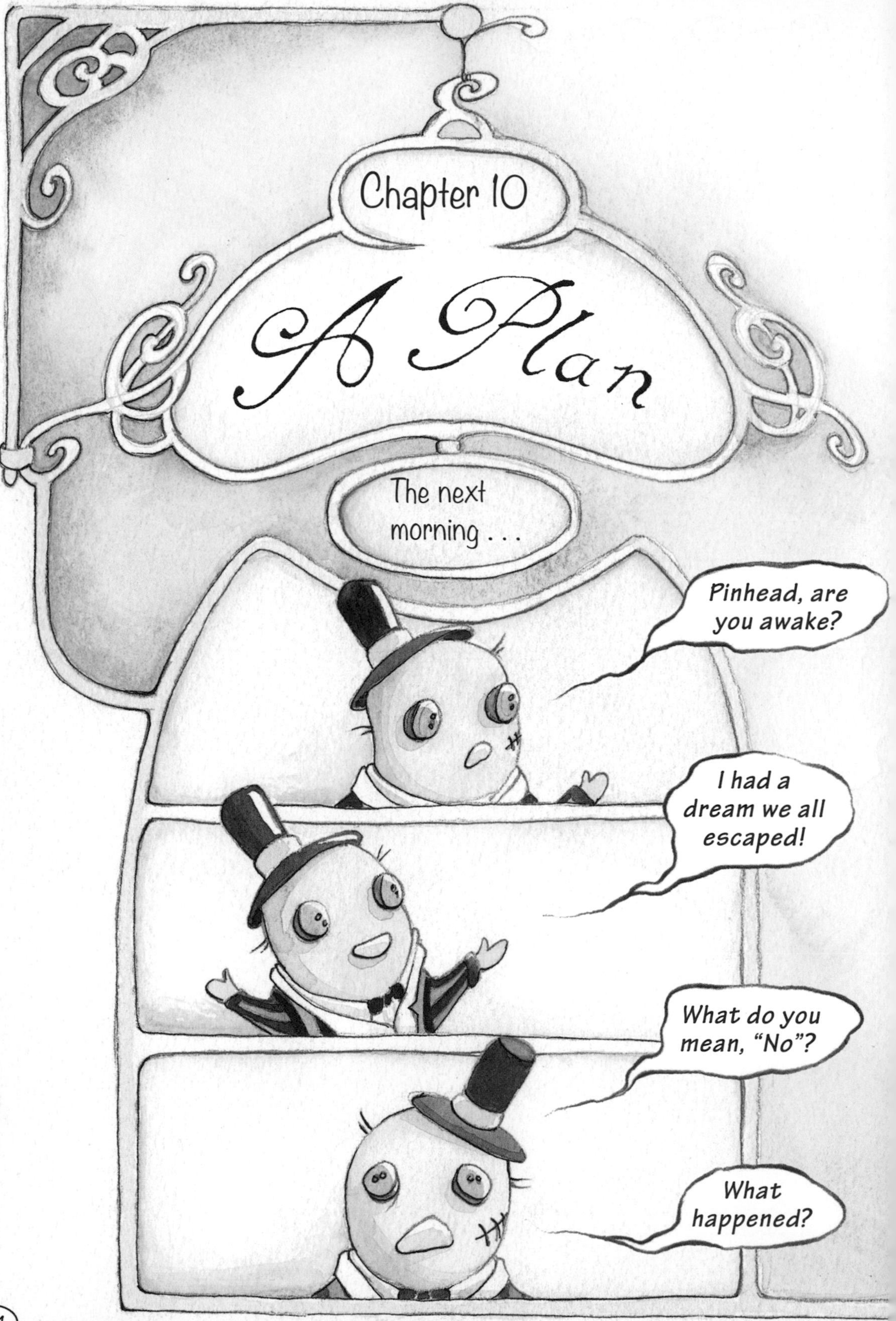
Chapter 10
A Plan
The next morning . . .
Pinhead, are you awake?
I had a dream we all escaped!
What do you mean, "No"?
What happened?

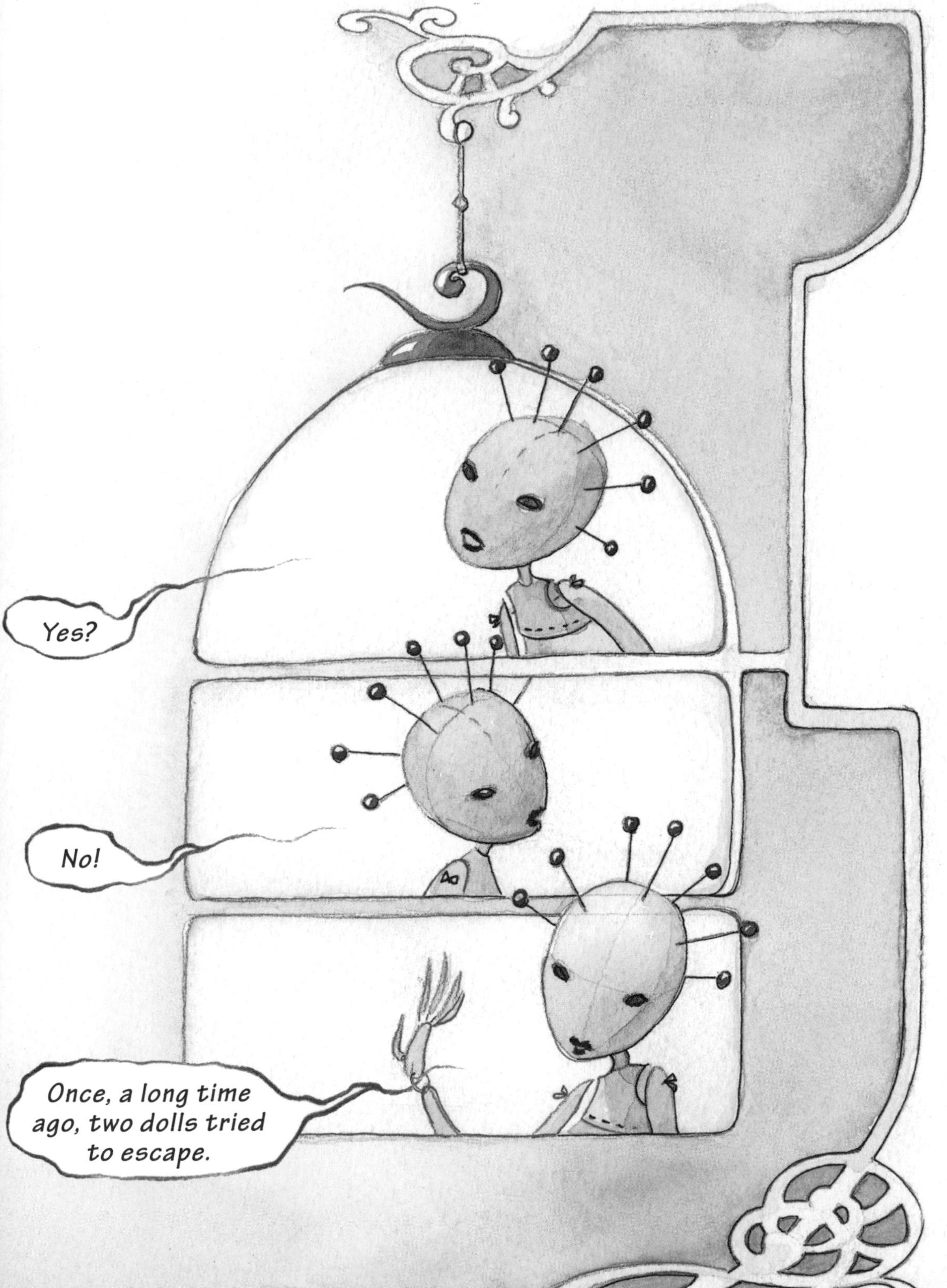
Yes?
No!
Once, a long time ago, two dolls tried to escape.

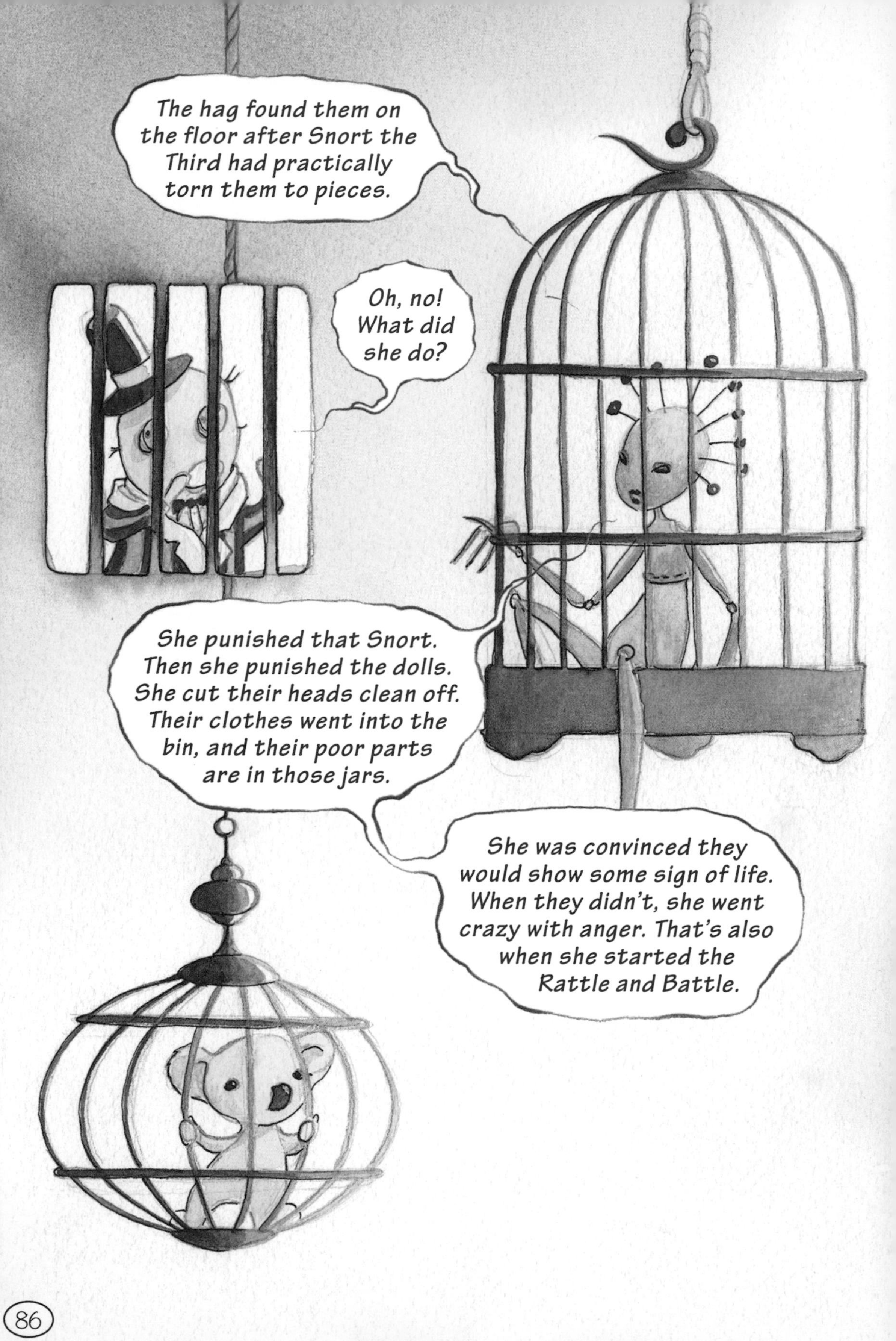
The hag found them on the floor after Snort the Third had practically torn them to pieces.
Oh, no! What did she do?
She punished that Snort. Then she punished the dolls. She cut their heads clean off. Their clothes went into the bin, and their poor parts are in those jars.
She was convinced they would show some sign of life. When they didn't, she went crazy with anger. That's also when she started the Rattle and Battle.

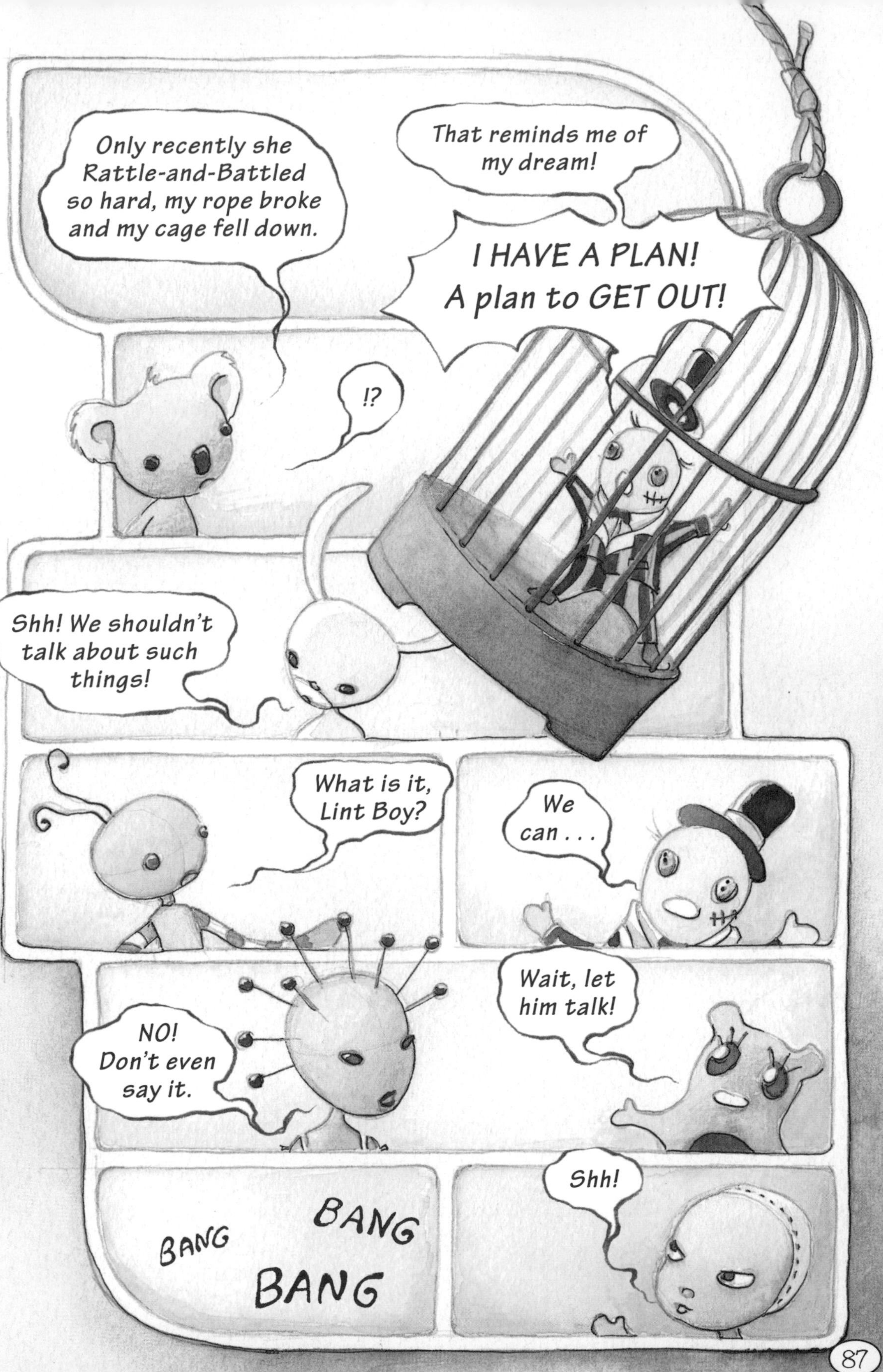
Only recently she Rattle-and-Battled so hard, my rope broke and my cage fell down.
That reminds me of my dream!
I HAVE A PLAN! A plan to GET OUT!
!?
Shh! We shouldn't talk about such things!
What is it, Lint Boy?
We can . . .
NO! Don't even say it.
Wait, let him talk!
BANG
BANG
BANG
Shh!

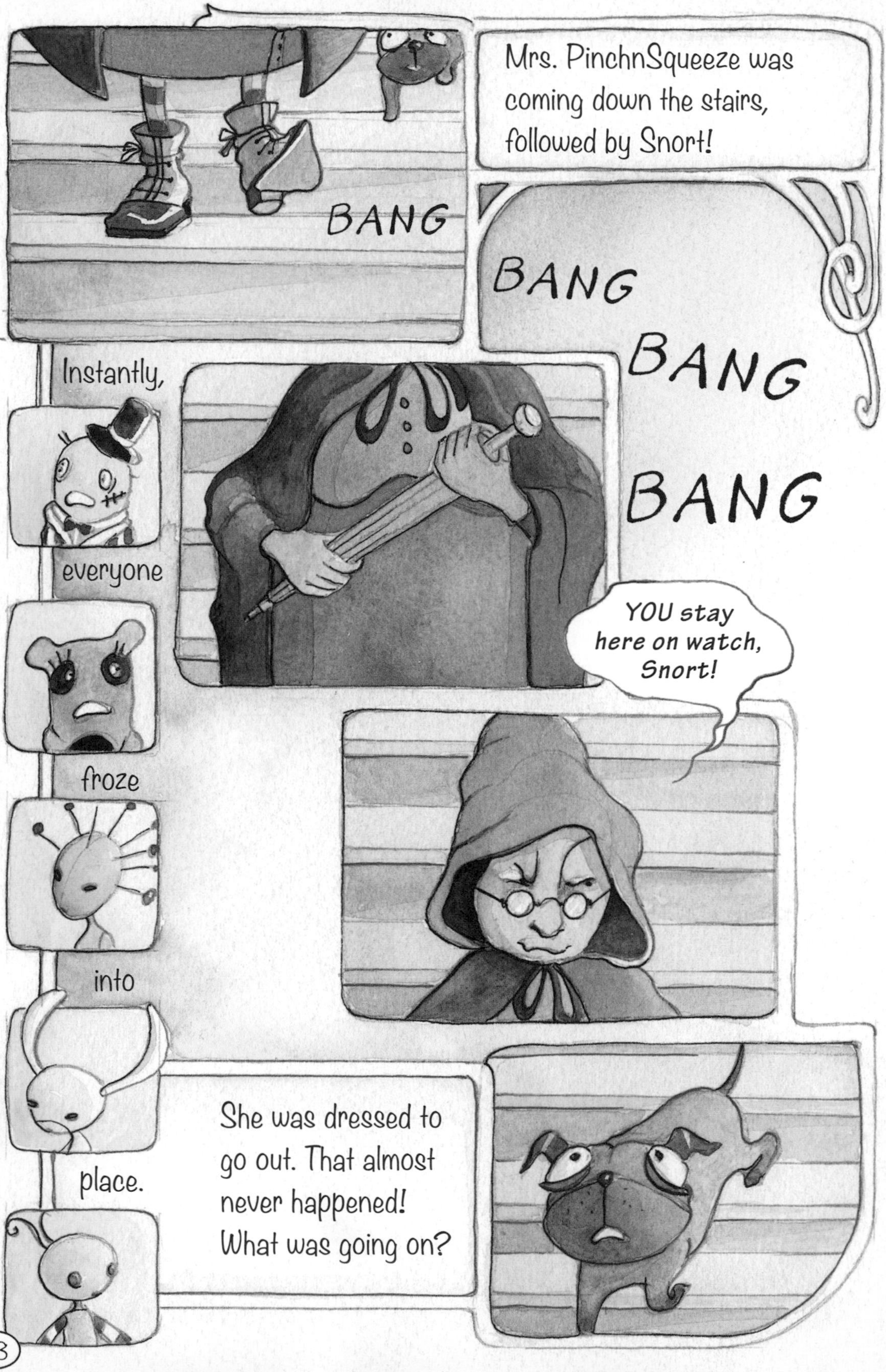
Mrs. PinchnSqueeze was coming down the stairs, followed by Snort!
BANG
BANG
BANG
BANG
Instantly,
everyone
froze
into
place.
YOU stay here on watch, Snort!
She was dressed to go out. That almost never happened! What was going on?

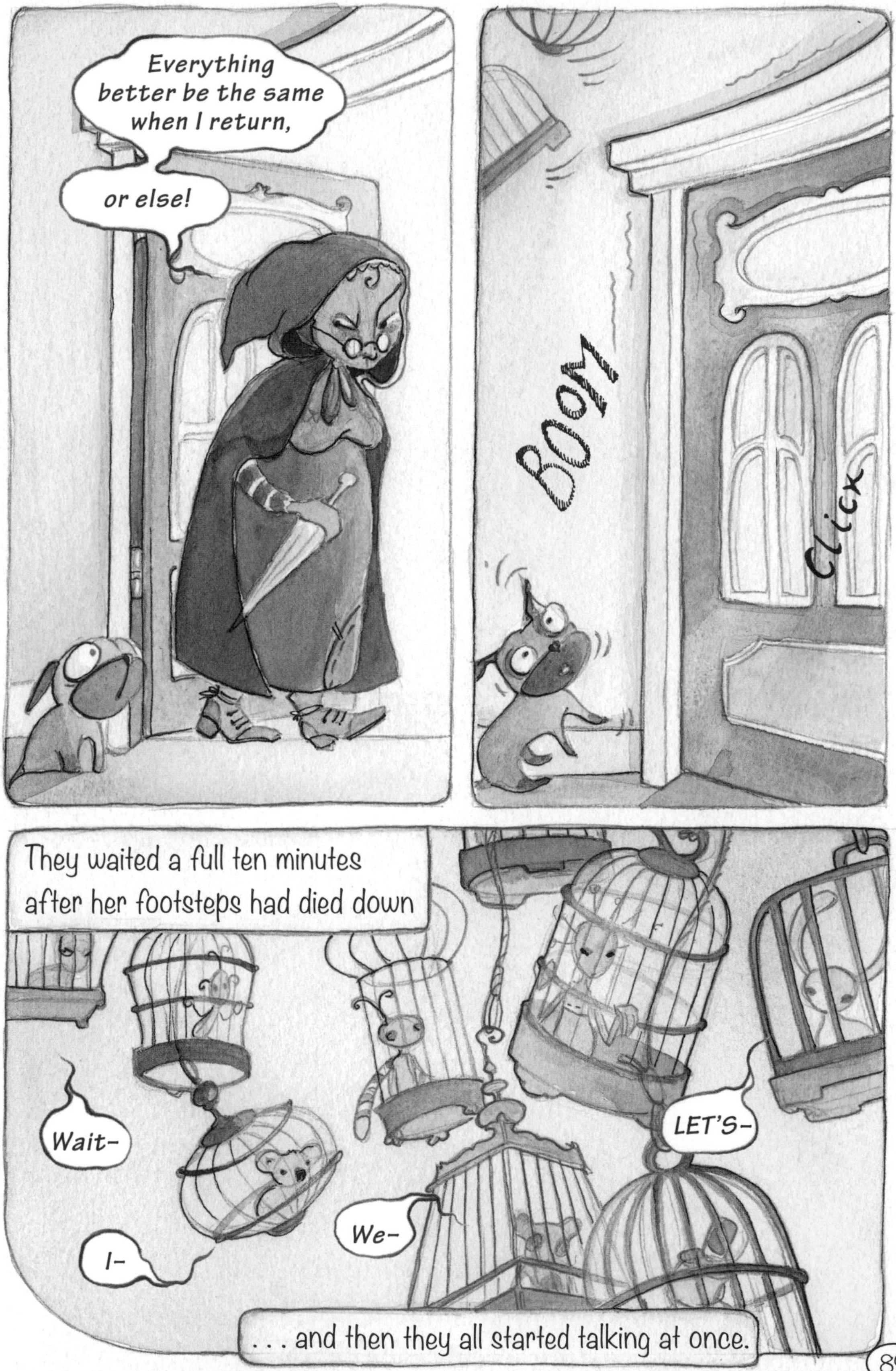
Everything better be the same when I return,
or else!
BOOM
Click
They waited a full ten minutes after her footsteps had died down
Wait-
I-
We-
LET'S-
. . . and then they all started talking at once.

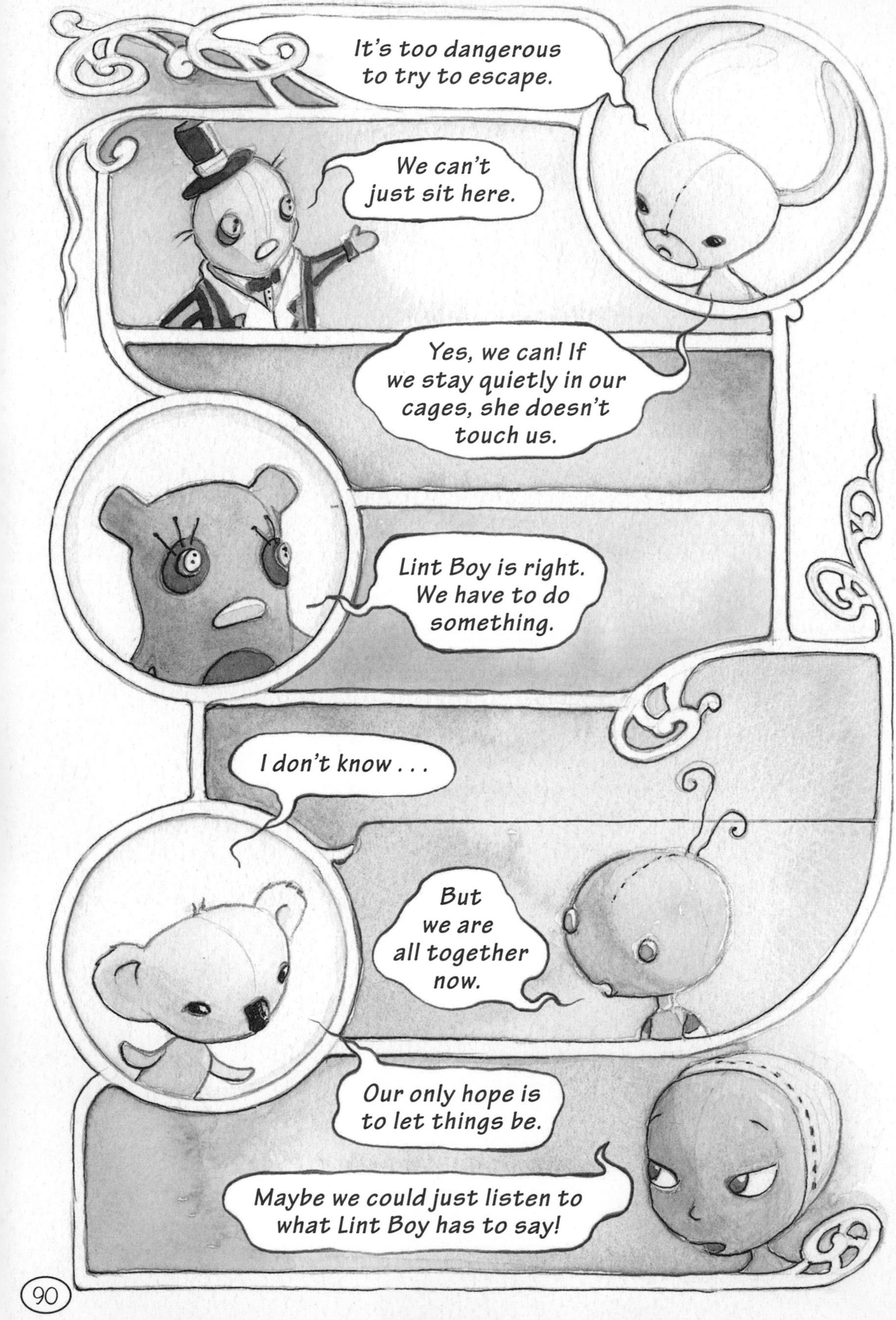

It's too dangerous to try to escape.
We can't just sit here.
Yes, we can! If we stay quietly in our cages, she doesn't touch us.
Lint Boy is right. We have to do something.
I don't know . . .
But we are all together now.
Our only hope is to let things be.
Maybe we could just listen to what Lint Boy has to say!

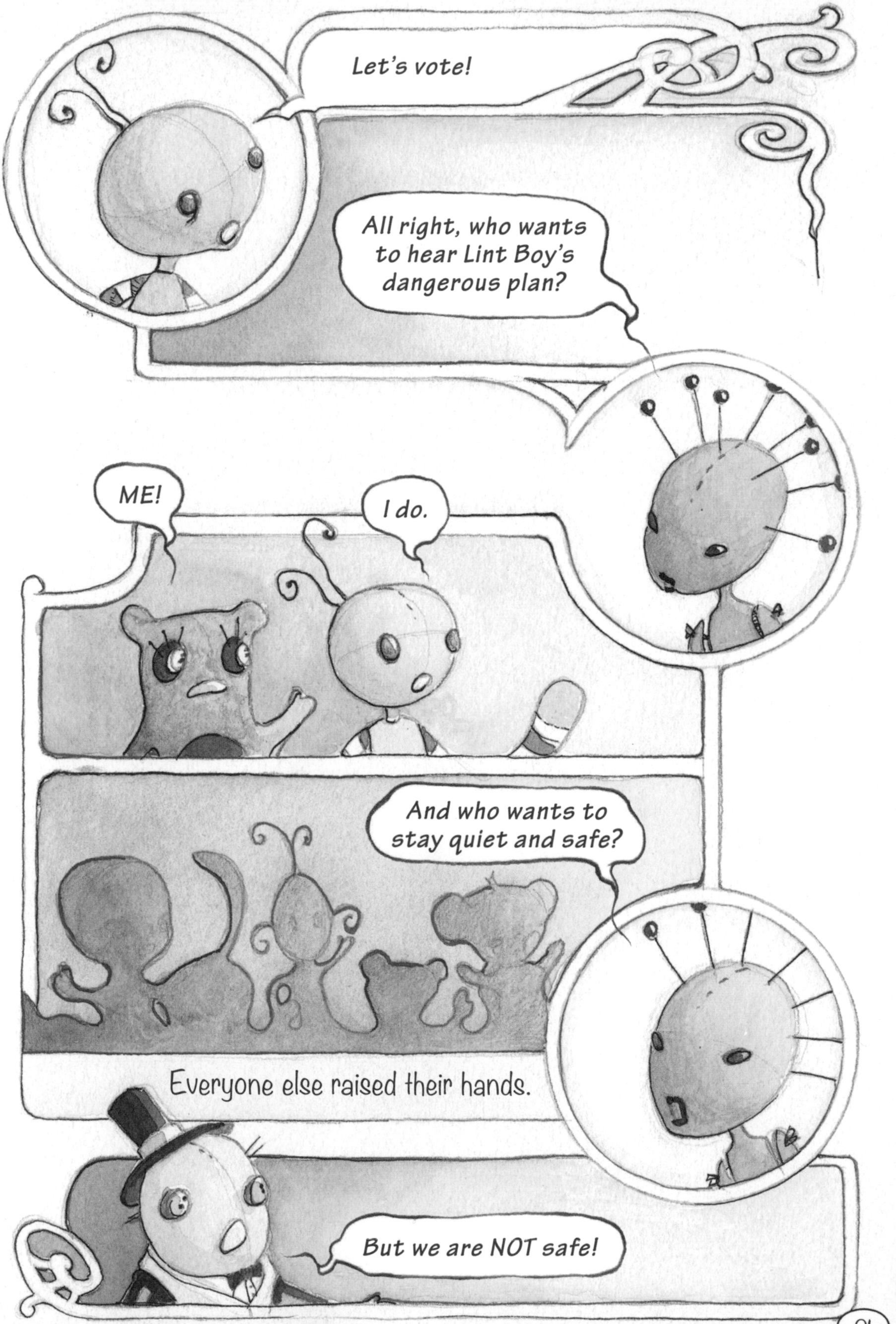
Let's vote!
All right, who wants to hear Lint Boy's dangerous plan?
ME!
I do.
And who wants to stay quiet and safe?
Everyone else raised their hands.
But we are NOT safe!

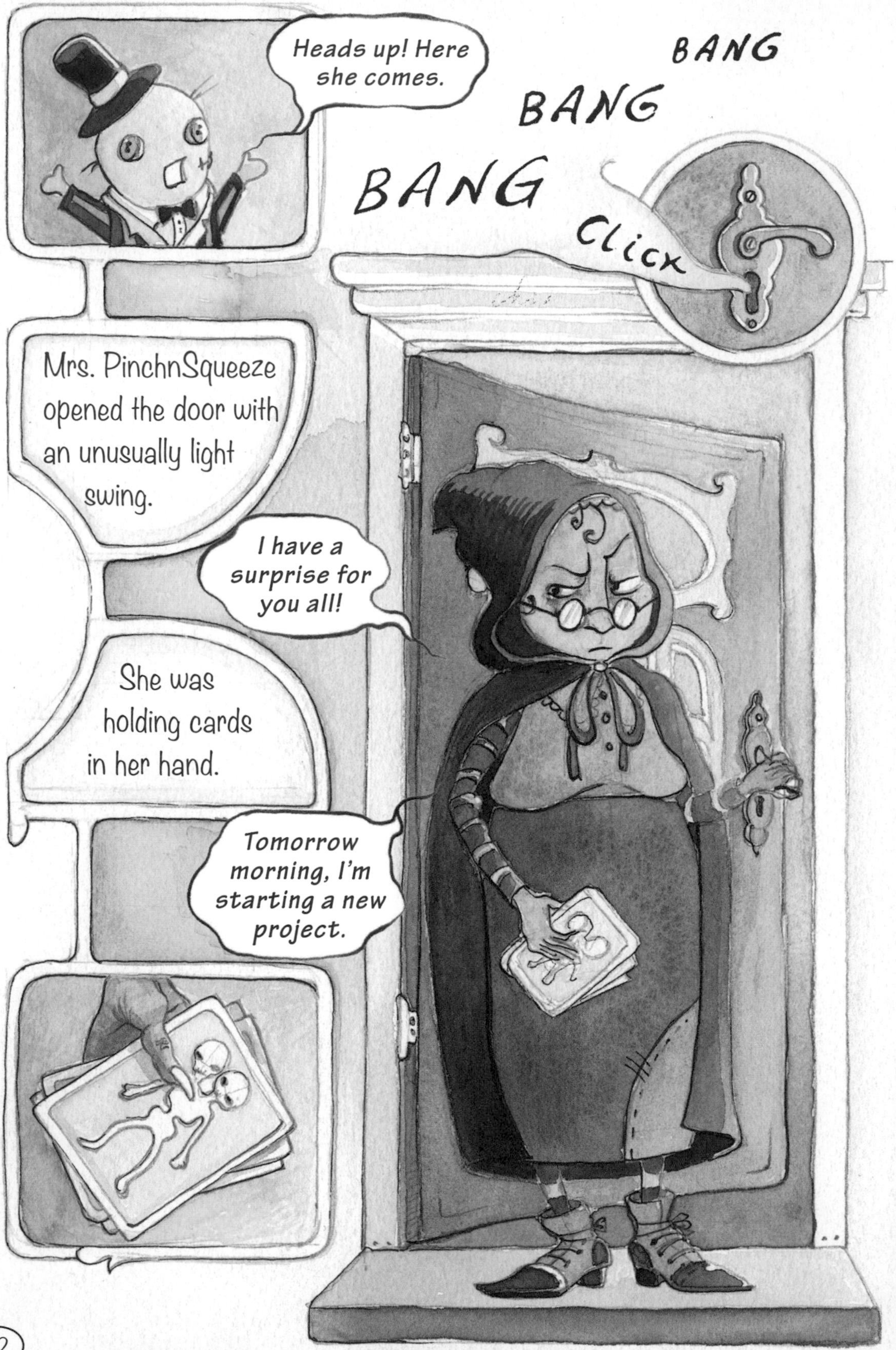
Heads up! Here she comes.
BANG
BANG
BANG
Click
Mrs. PinchnSqueeze opened the door with an unusually light swing.
I have a surprise for you all!
She was holding cards in her hand.
Tomorrow morning, I'm starting a new project.

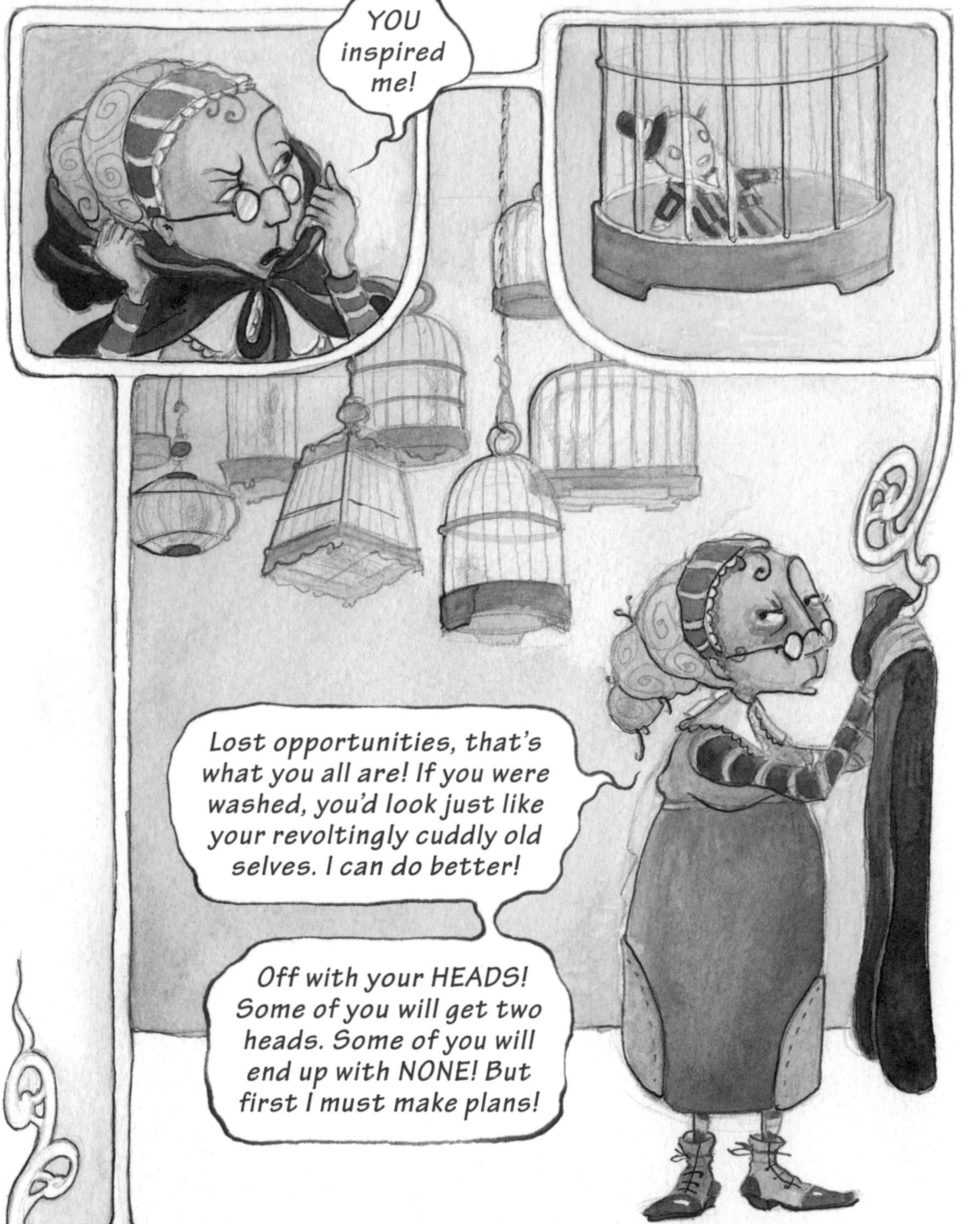
YOU inspired me!
Lost opportunities, that's what you all are! If you were washed, you'd look just like your revoltingly cuddly old selves. I can do better!
Off with your HEADS! Some of you will get two heads. Some of you will end up with NONE! But first I must make plans!

For the rest of the afternoon the old hag sat, read, and made notes and outlines of odd-looking creatures. Finally, long after dark, she got up, grabbed Snort by the tail, and stomped up the stairs.

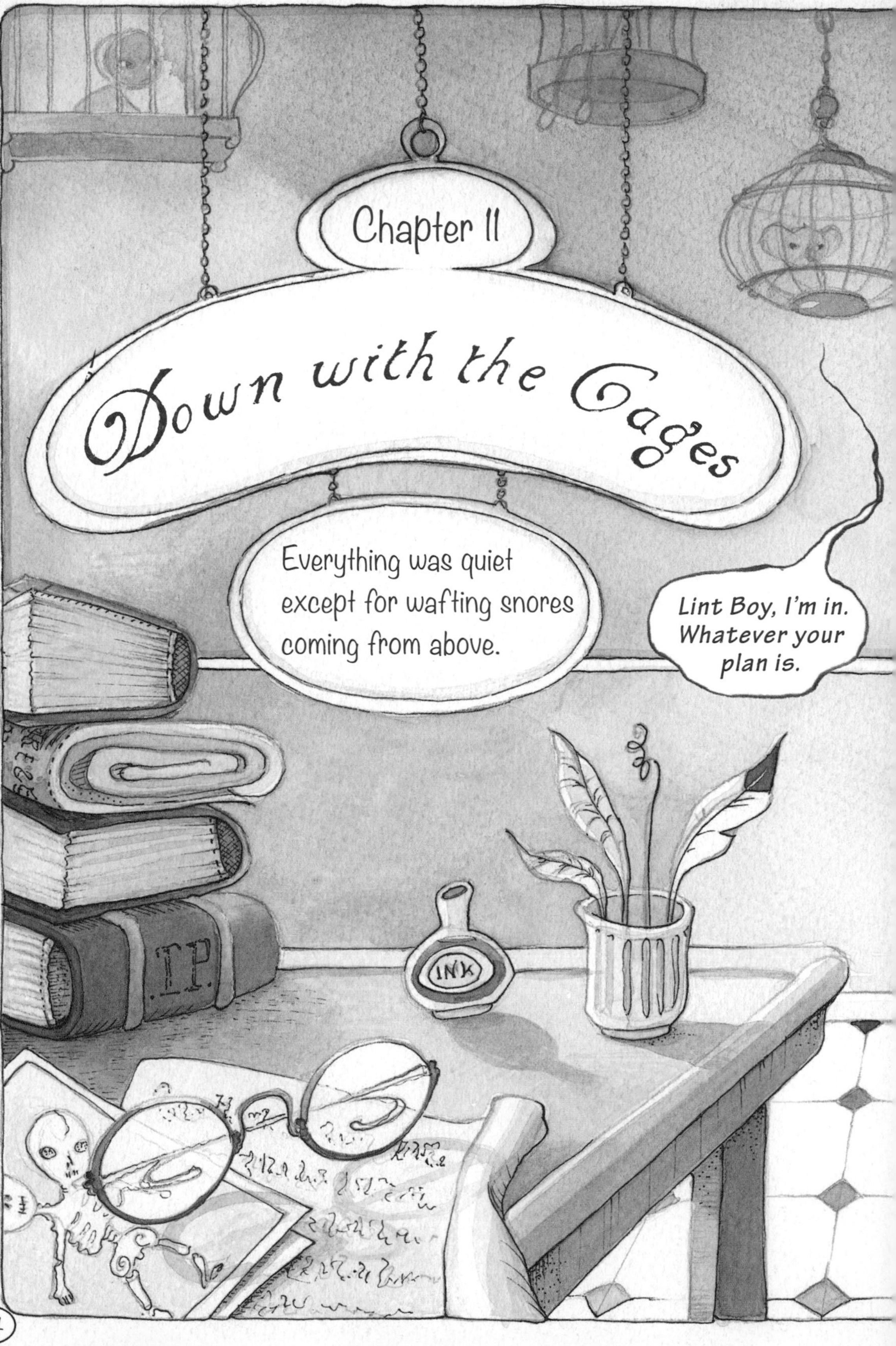
Chapter 11
Down with the Cages
Everything was quiet except for wafting snores coming from above.
Lint Boy, I'm in. Whatever your plan is.
INK
T.P.

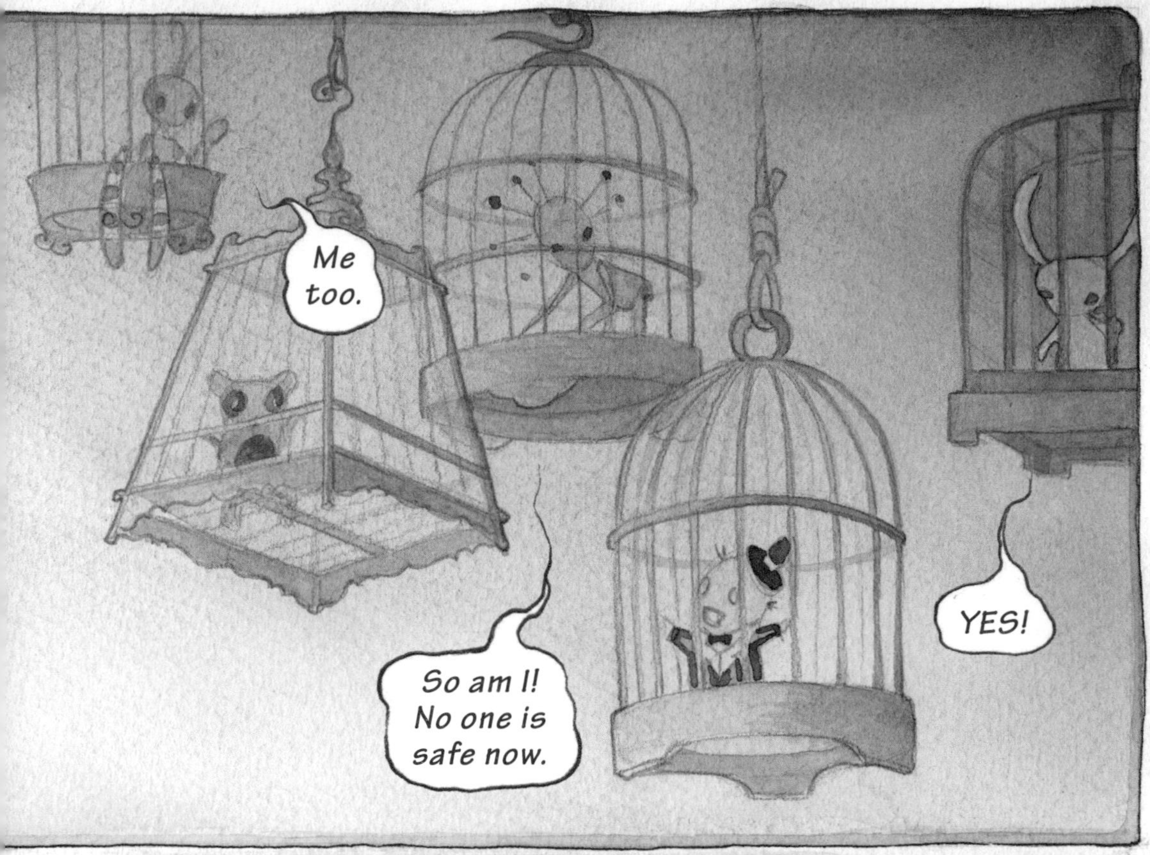
Me too.
So am I! No one is safe now.
YES!

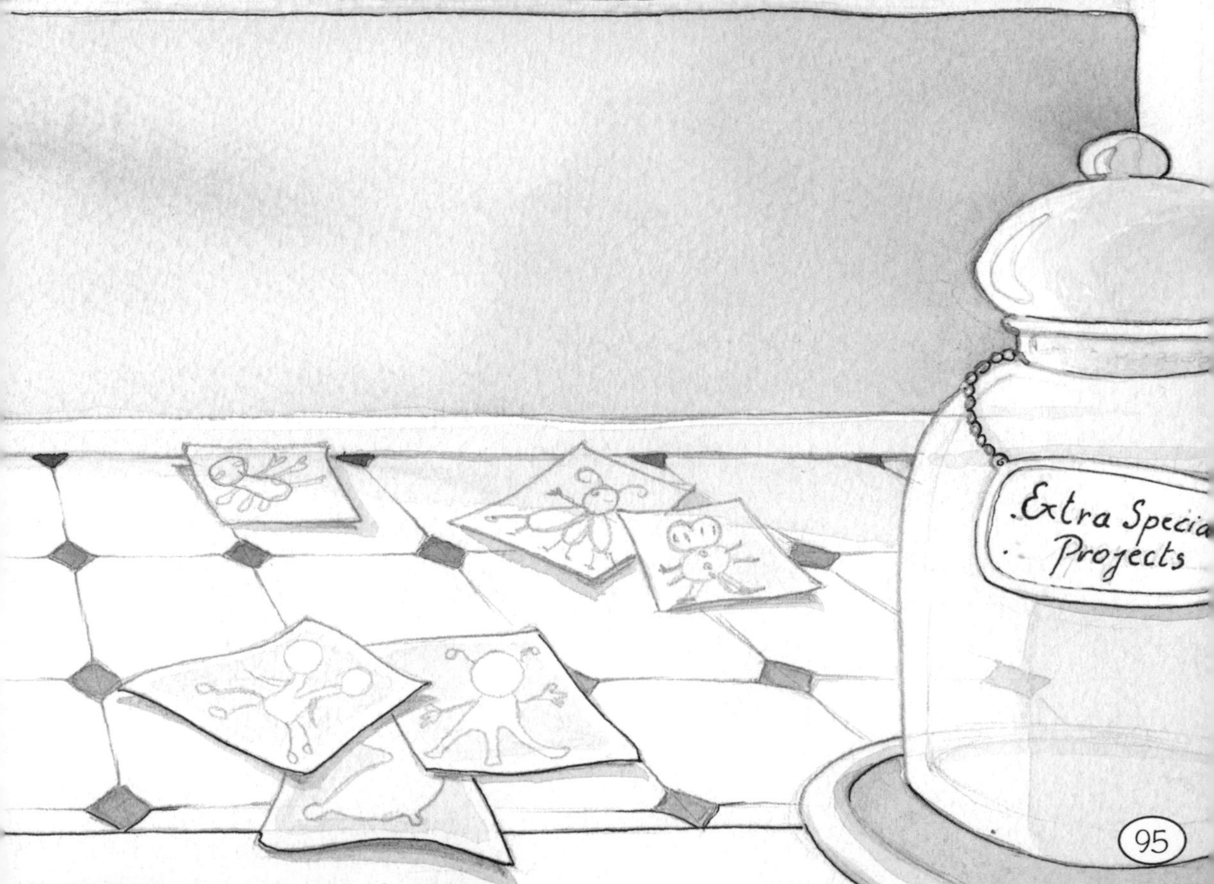
Extra Special Projects

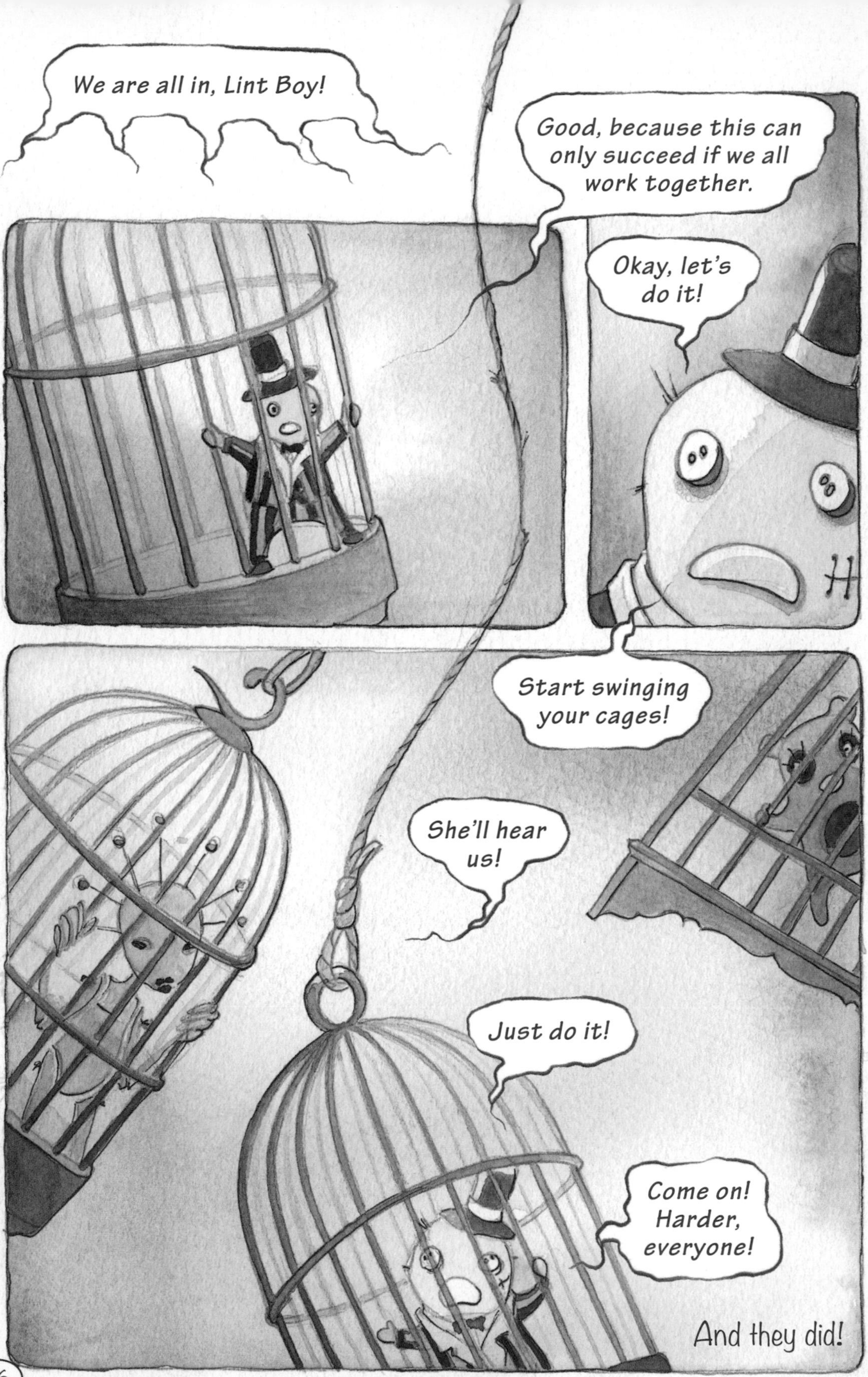
We are all in, Lint Boy!
Good, because this can only succeed if we all work together.
Okay, let's do it!
Start swinging your cages!
She'll hear us!
Just do it!
Come on! Harder, everyone!
And they did!

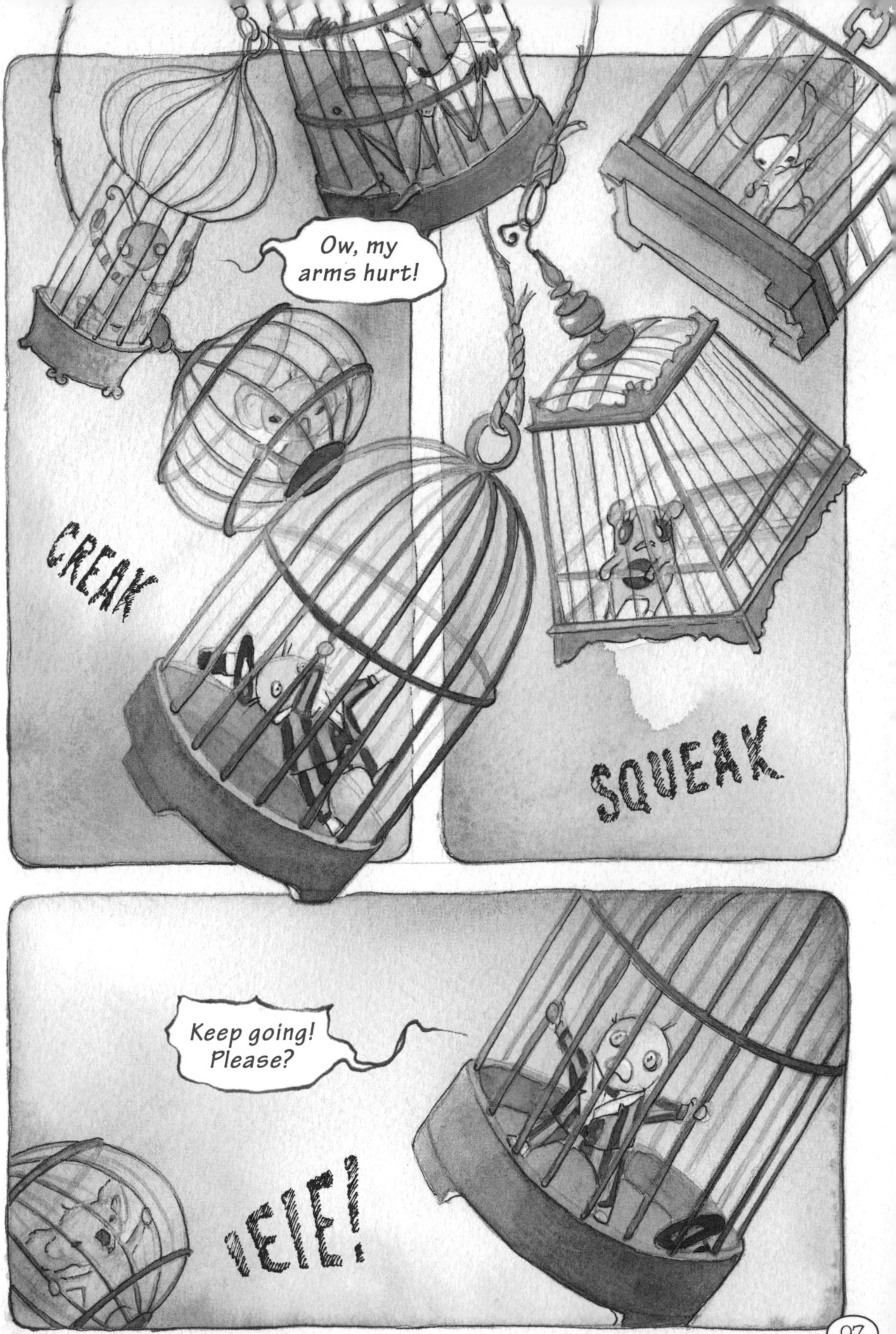
Ow, my arms hurt!
CREAK
SQUEAK
Keep going! Please?

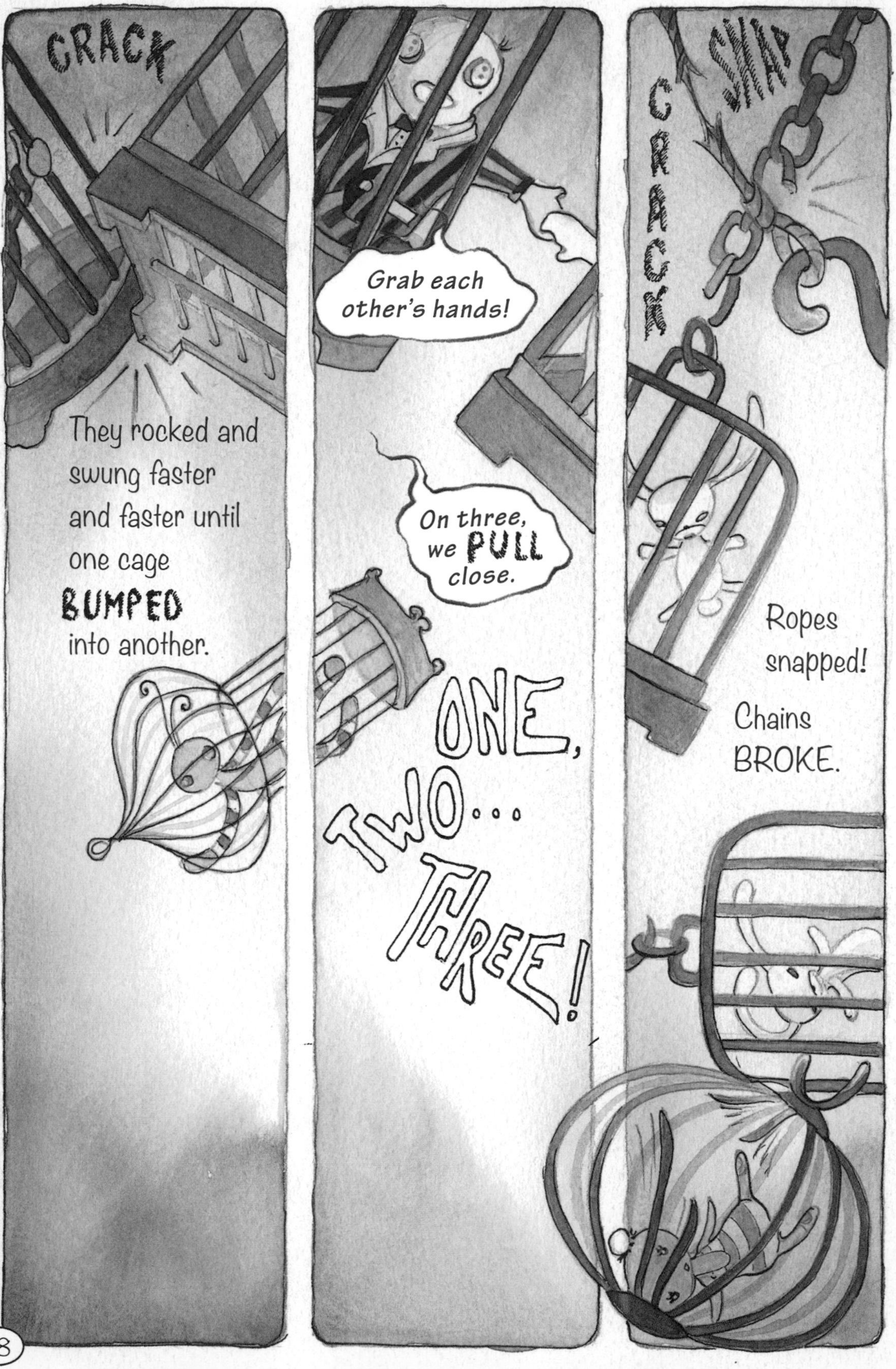
CRACK
They rocked and swung faster and faster until one cage BUMPED into another.
Grab each other's hands!
On three, we PULL close.
ONE, TWO... THREE!
CRACK
SNAP
Ropes snapped!
Chains BROKE.

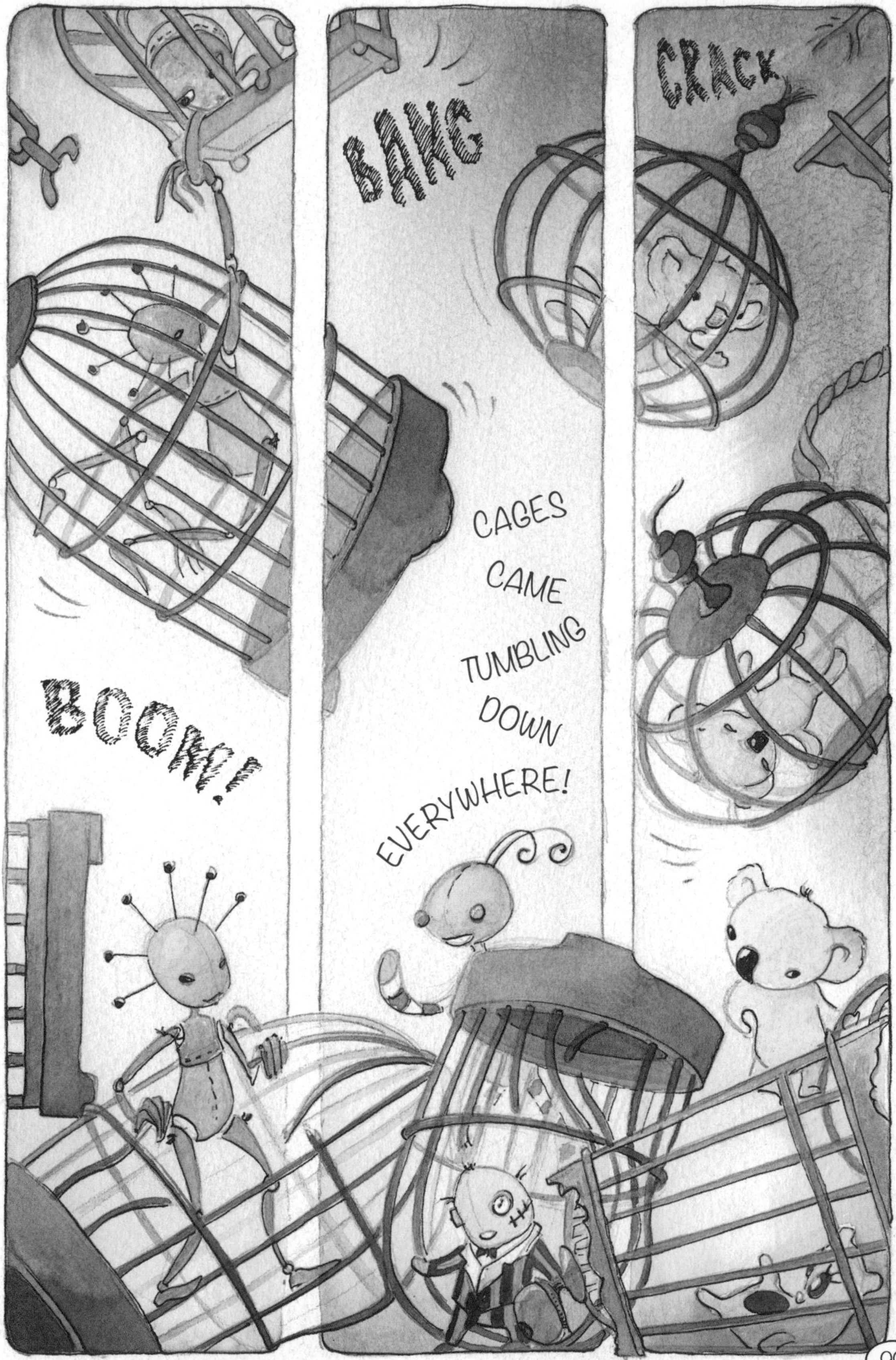
BOOM!
BANG
CAGES
CAME
TUMBLING
DOWN
EVERYWHERE!
CRACK

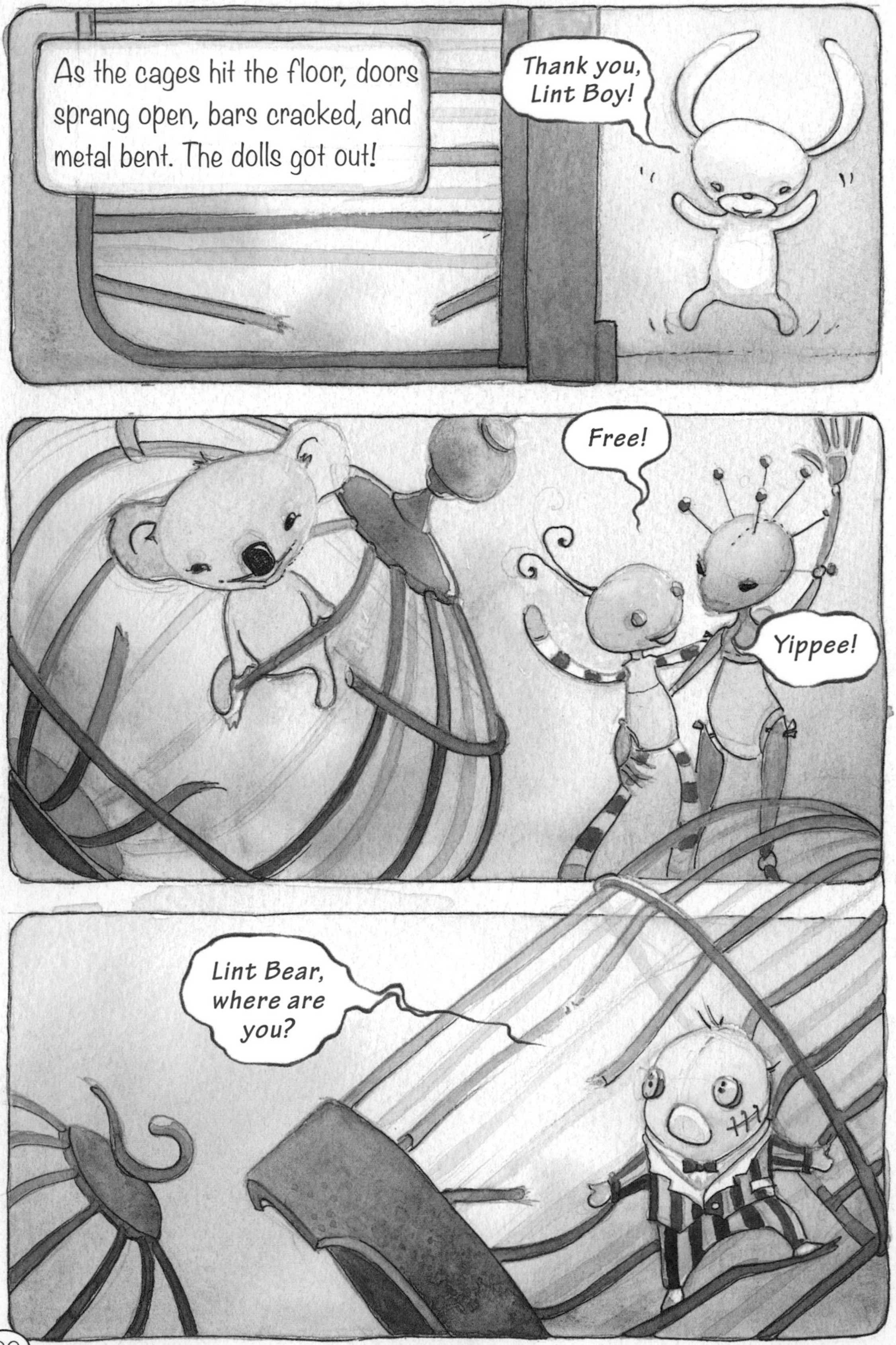
As the cages hit the floor, doors sprang open, bars cracked, and metal bent. The dolls got out!
Thank you, Lint Boy!
Free!
Yippee!
Lint Bear, where are you?

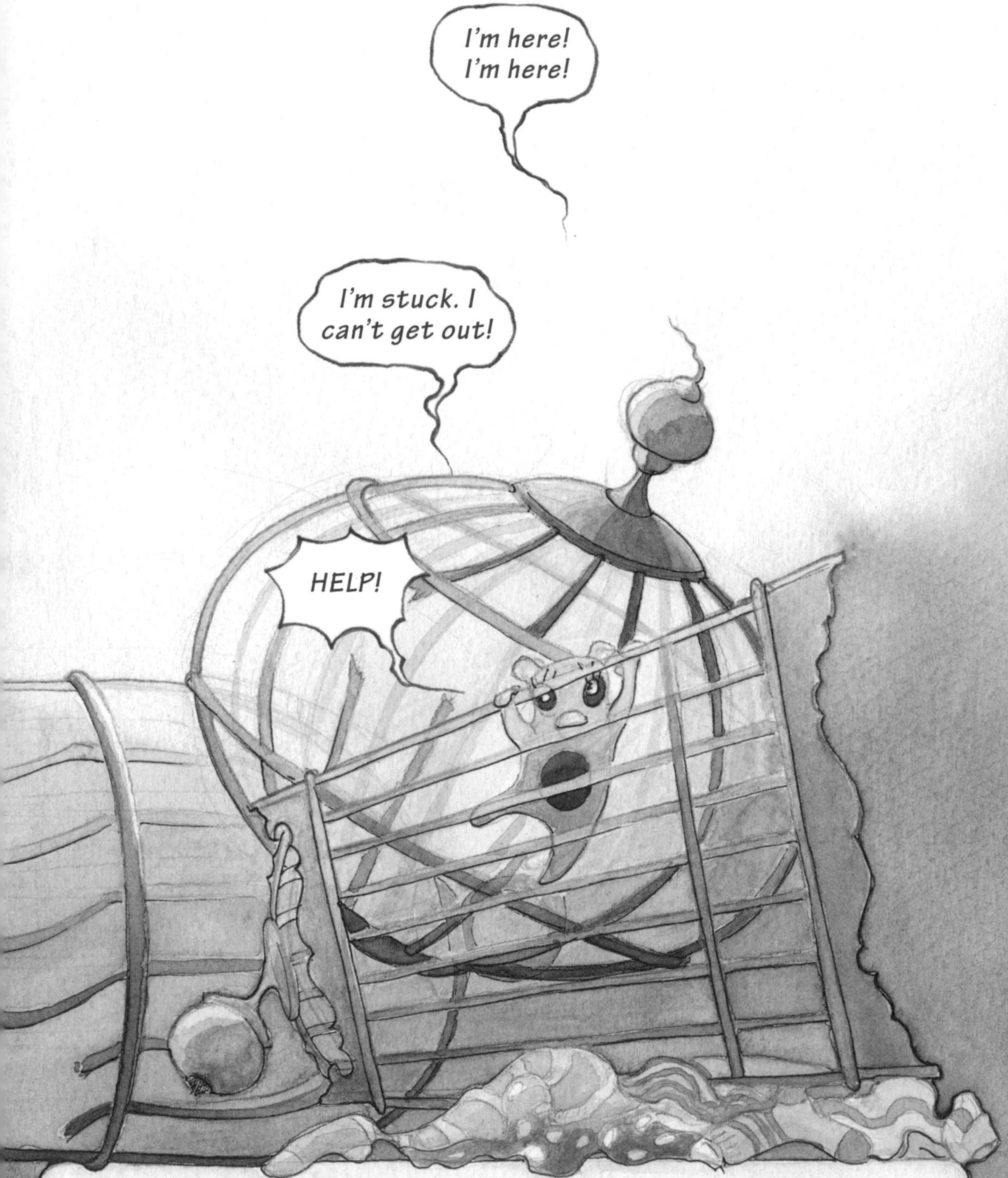
I'm here!
I'm here!
I'm stuck. I
can't get out!
HELP!

Lint Bear's cage had fallen on something soft and was the only one that remained locked.

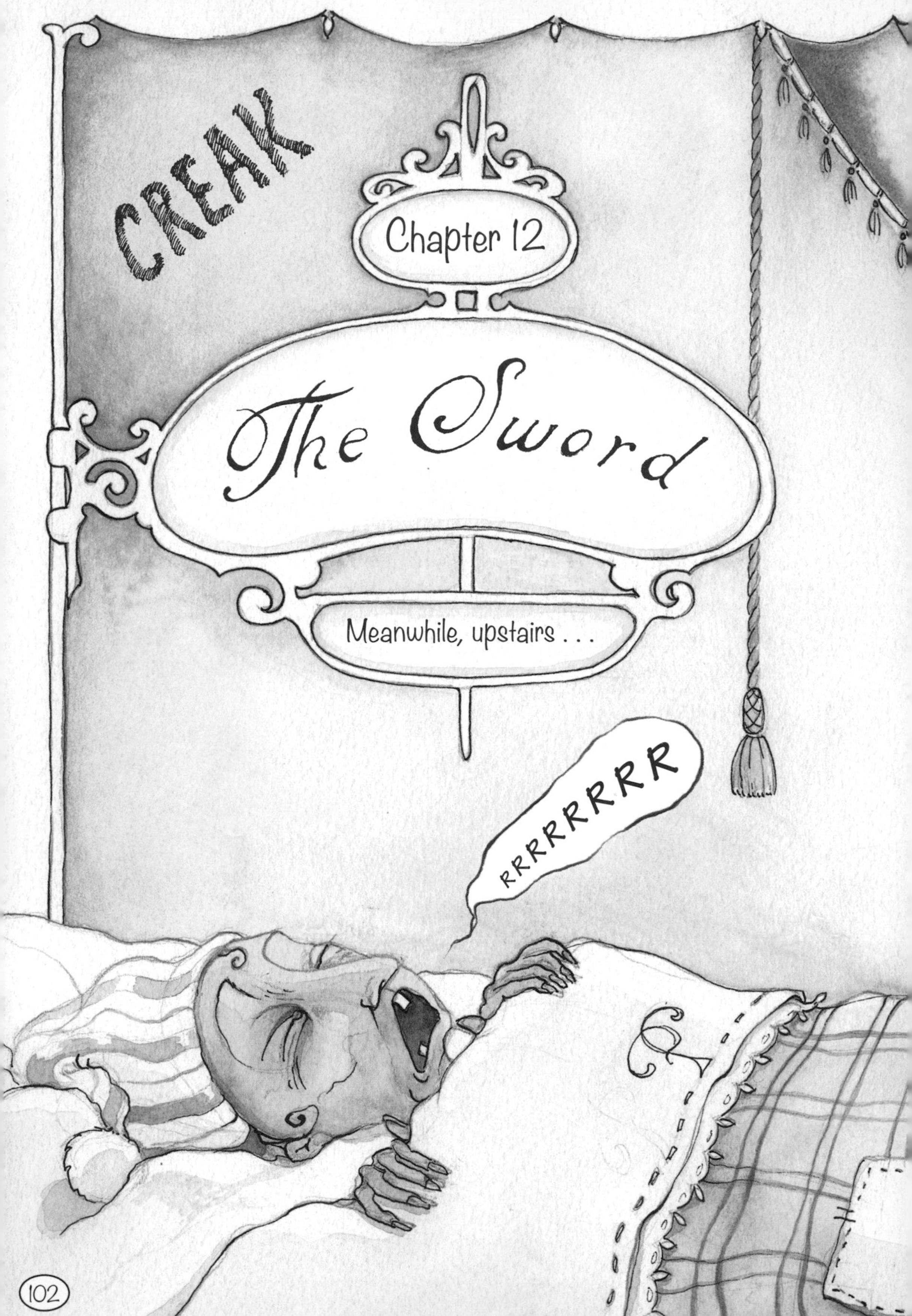
CREAK
Chapter 12
The Sword
Meanwhile, upstairs . . .
RRRRRRRRR

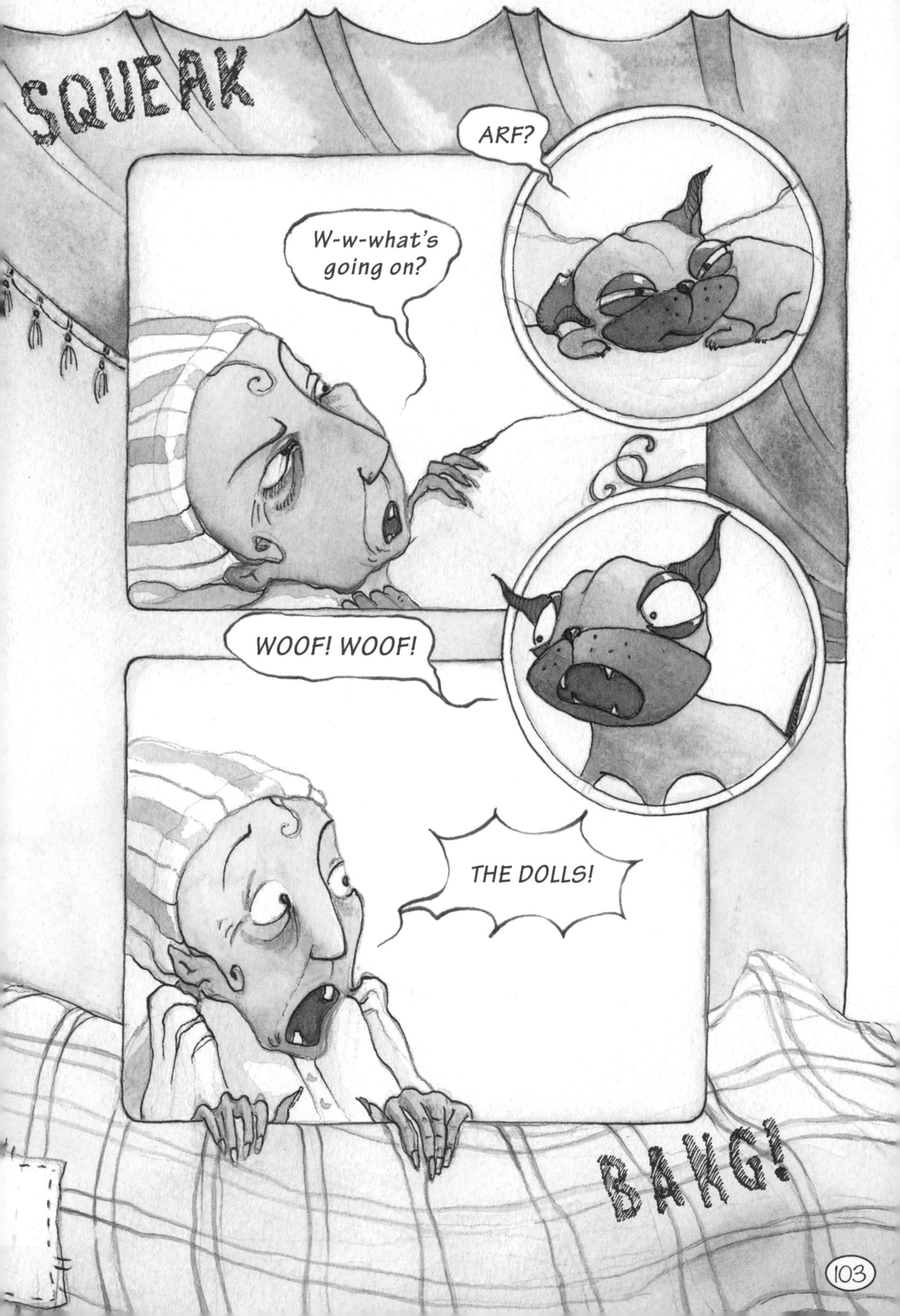
SQUEAK
ARF?
W-w-what's going on?
WOOF! WOOF!
THE DOLLS!
BANG!

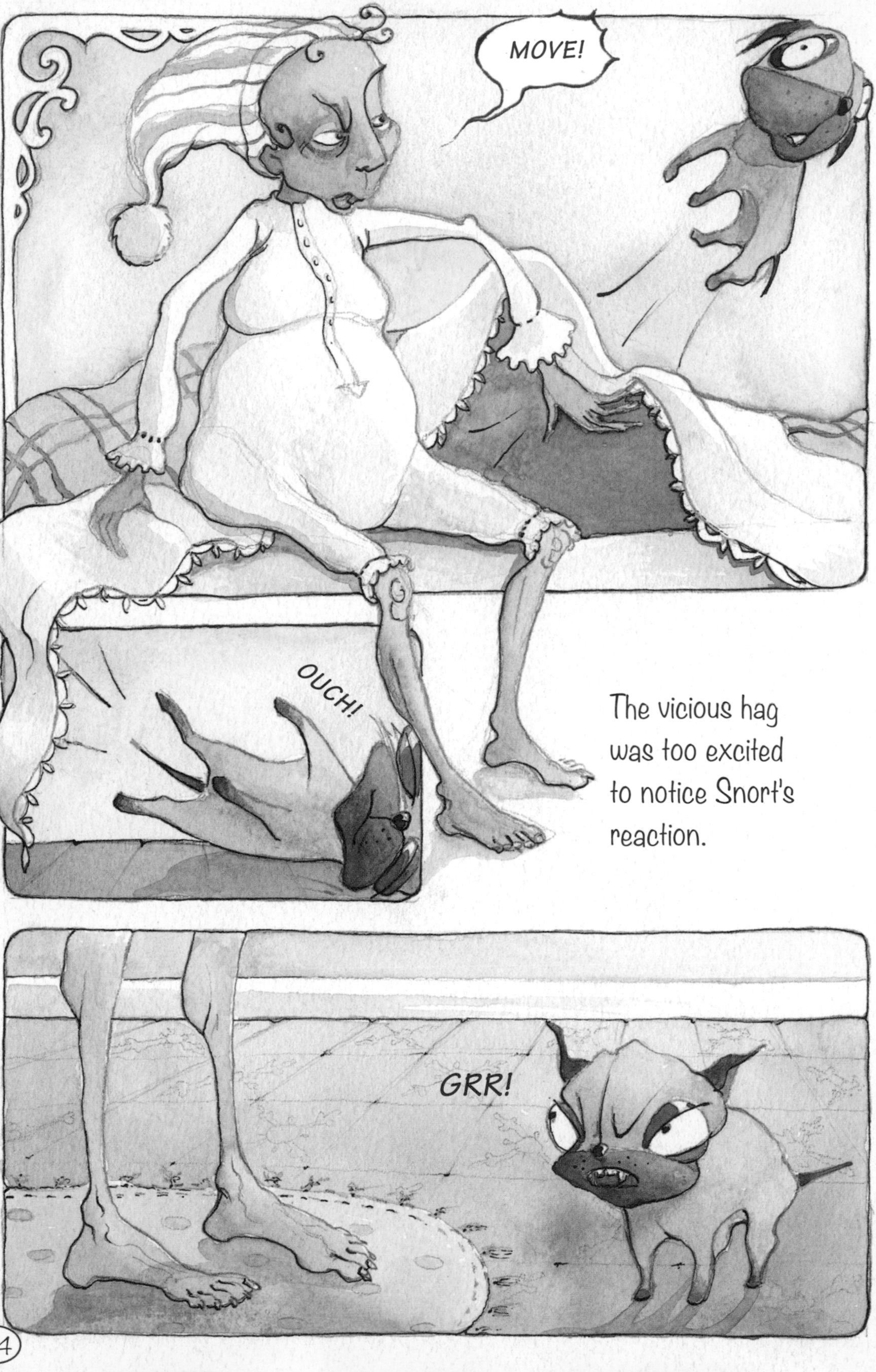
MOVE!
OUCH!
The vicious hag was too excited to notice Snort's reaction.
GRR!

Downstairs . . .

HELP ME FREE LINT BEAR!

BANG

BANG

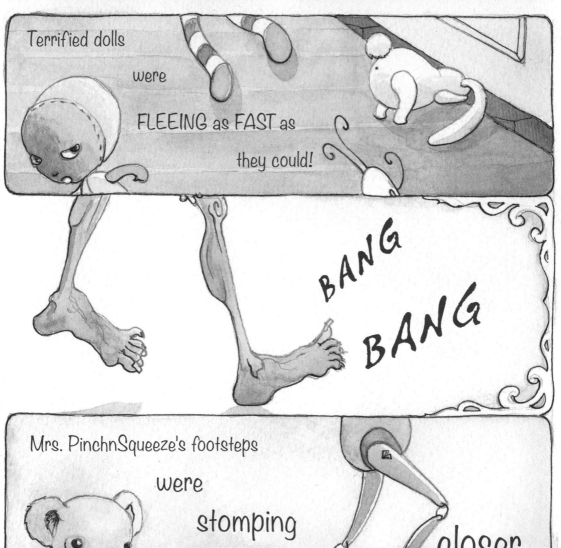

Terrified dolls

were

FLEEING as FAST as

they could!

BANG

BANG

Mrs. PinchnSqueeze's footsteps

were

stomping

closer.

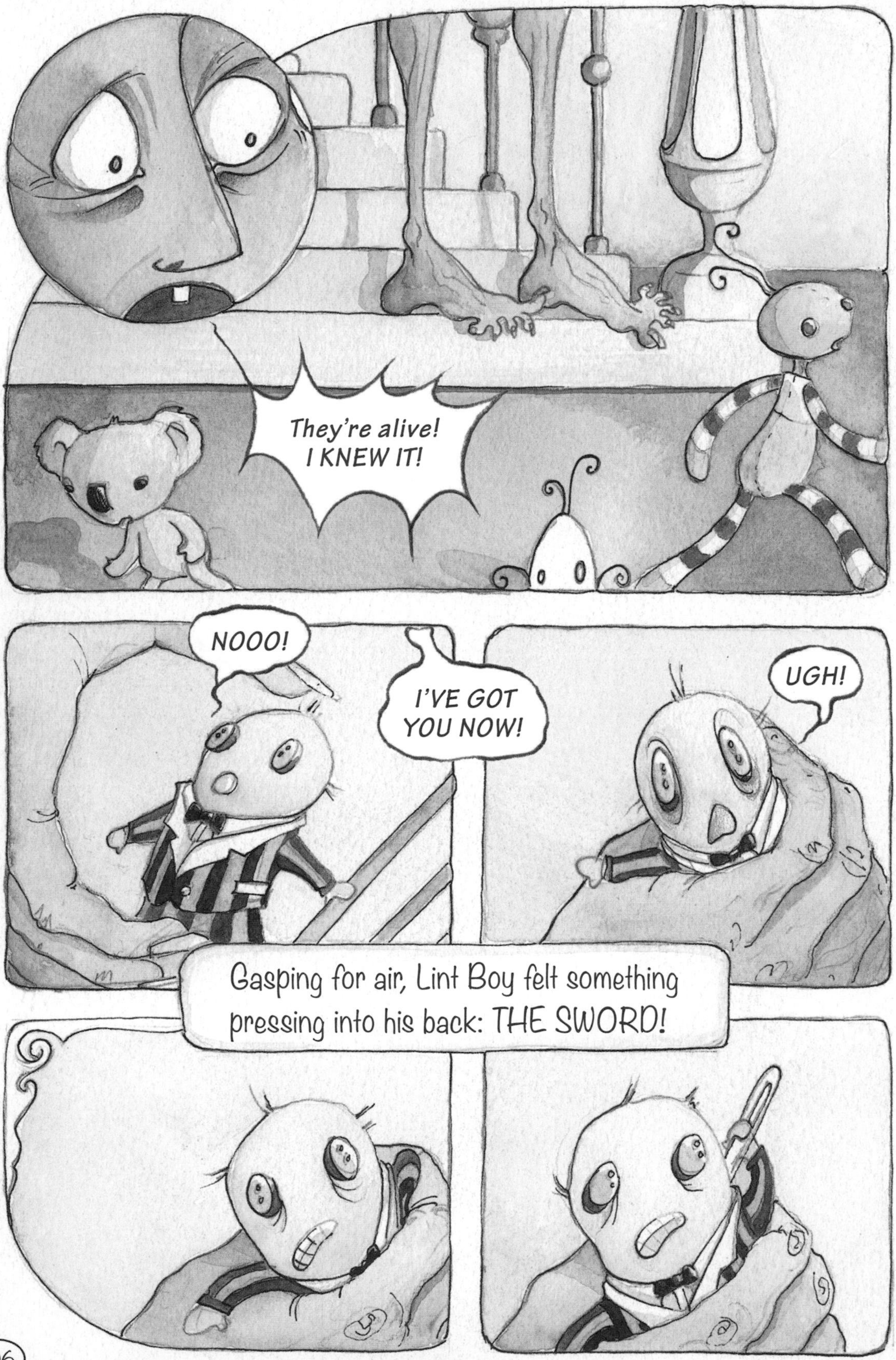
They're alive!
I KNEW IT!
NOOO!
I'VE GOT YOU NOW!
UGH!
Gasping for air, Lint Boy felt something pressing into his back: THE SWORD!

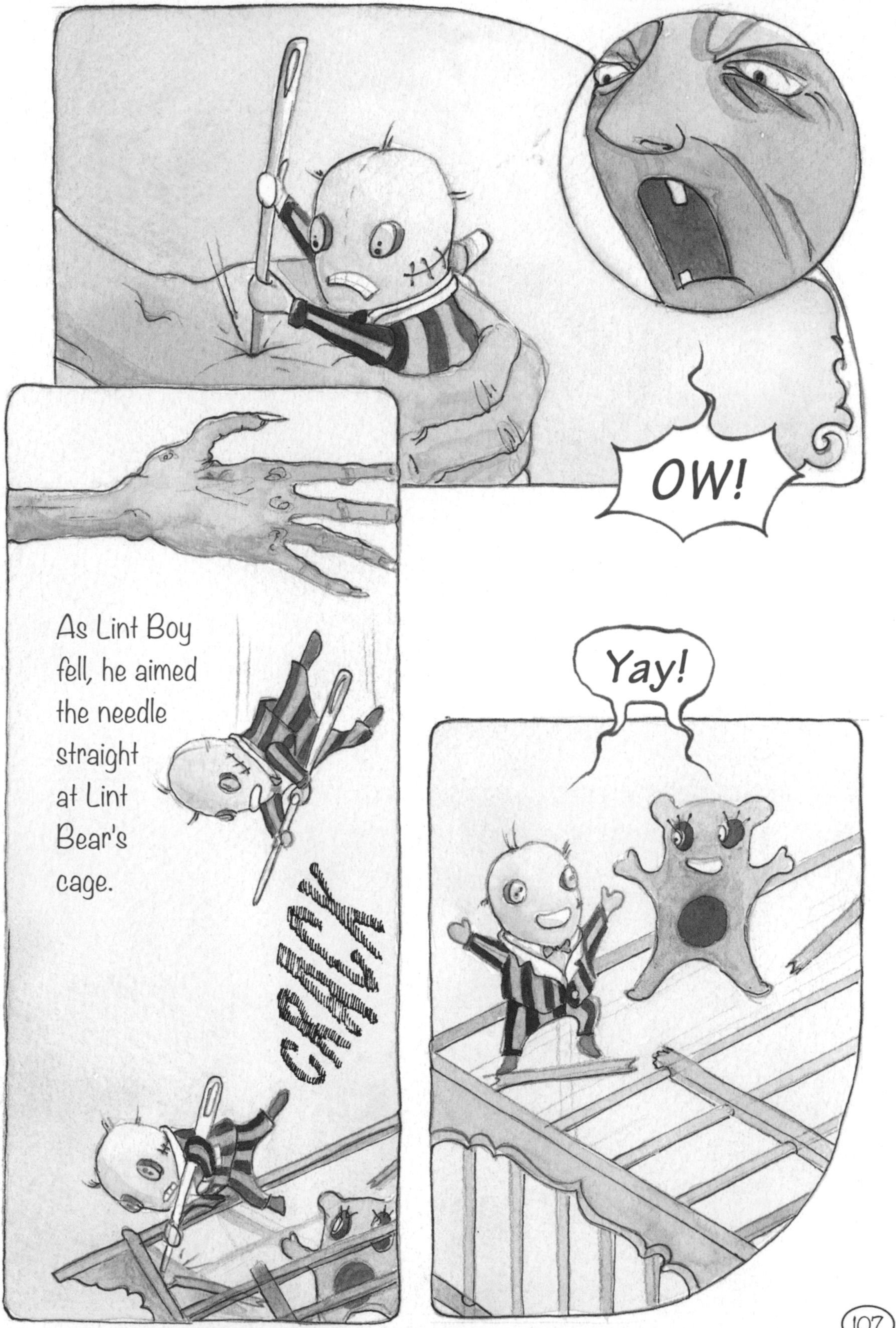
OW!
As Lint Boy fell, he aimed the needle straight at Lint Bear's cage.
CRACK
Yay!

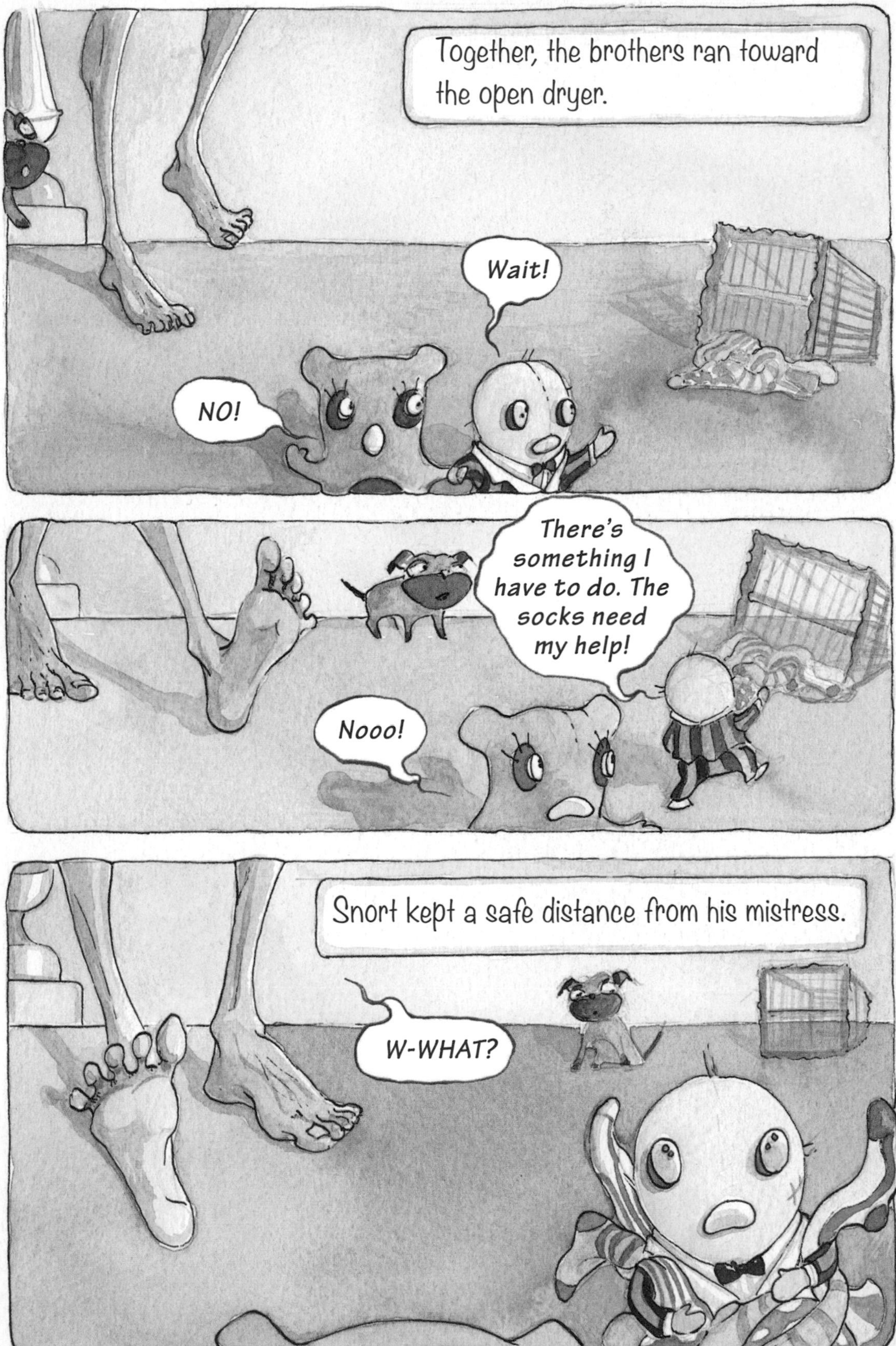
Together, the brothers ran toward the open dryer.
Wait!
NO!
There's something I have to do. The socks need my help!
Nooo!
Snort kept a safe distance from his mistress.
W-WHAT?

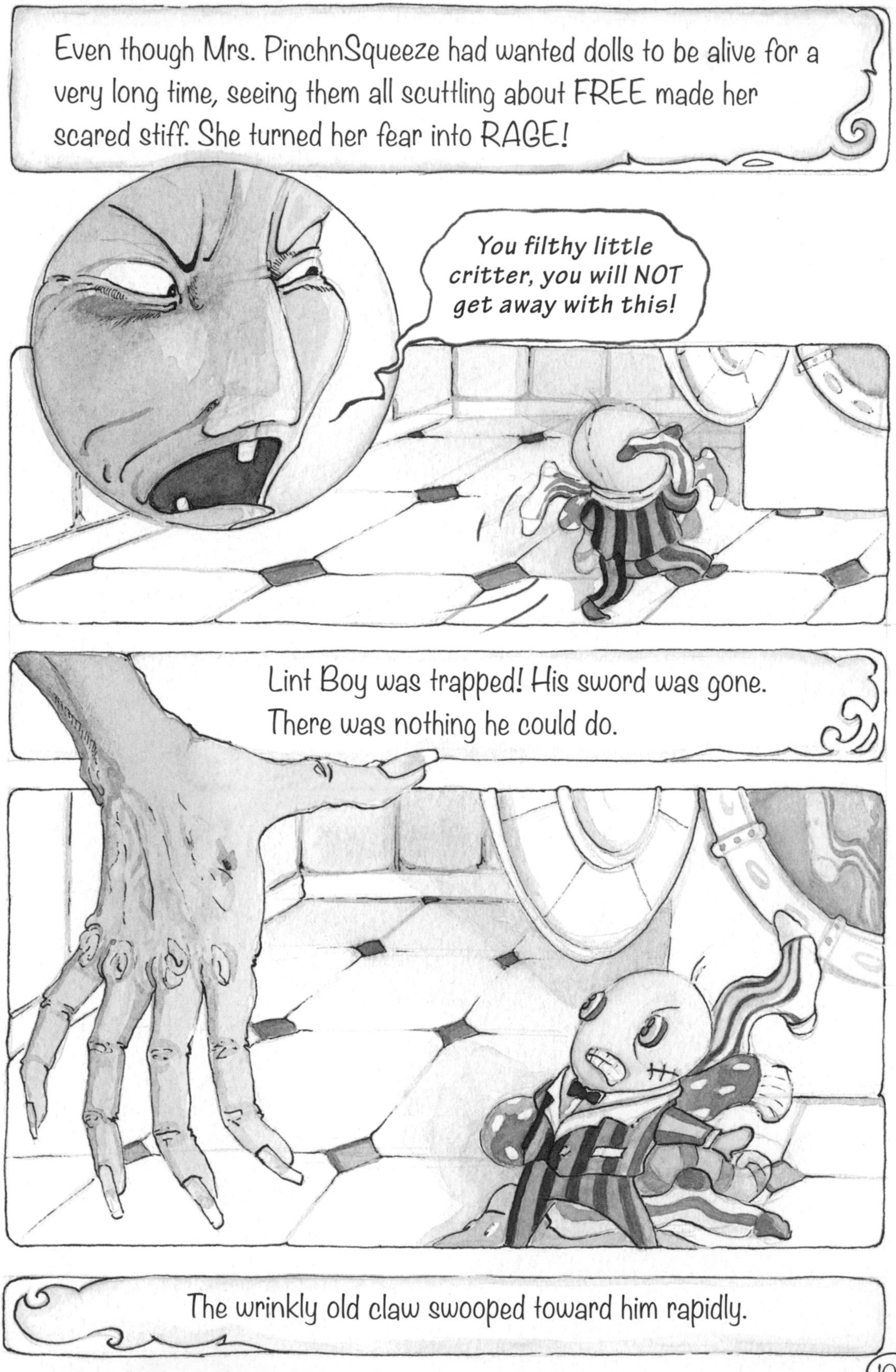
Even though Mrs. PinchnSqueeze had wanted dolls to be alive for a very long time, seeing them all scuttling about FREE made her scared stiff. She turned her fear into RAGE!
You filthy little critter, you will NOT get away with this!
Lint Boy was trapped! His sword was gone. There was nothing he could do.
The wrinkly old claw swooped toward him rapidly.

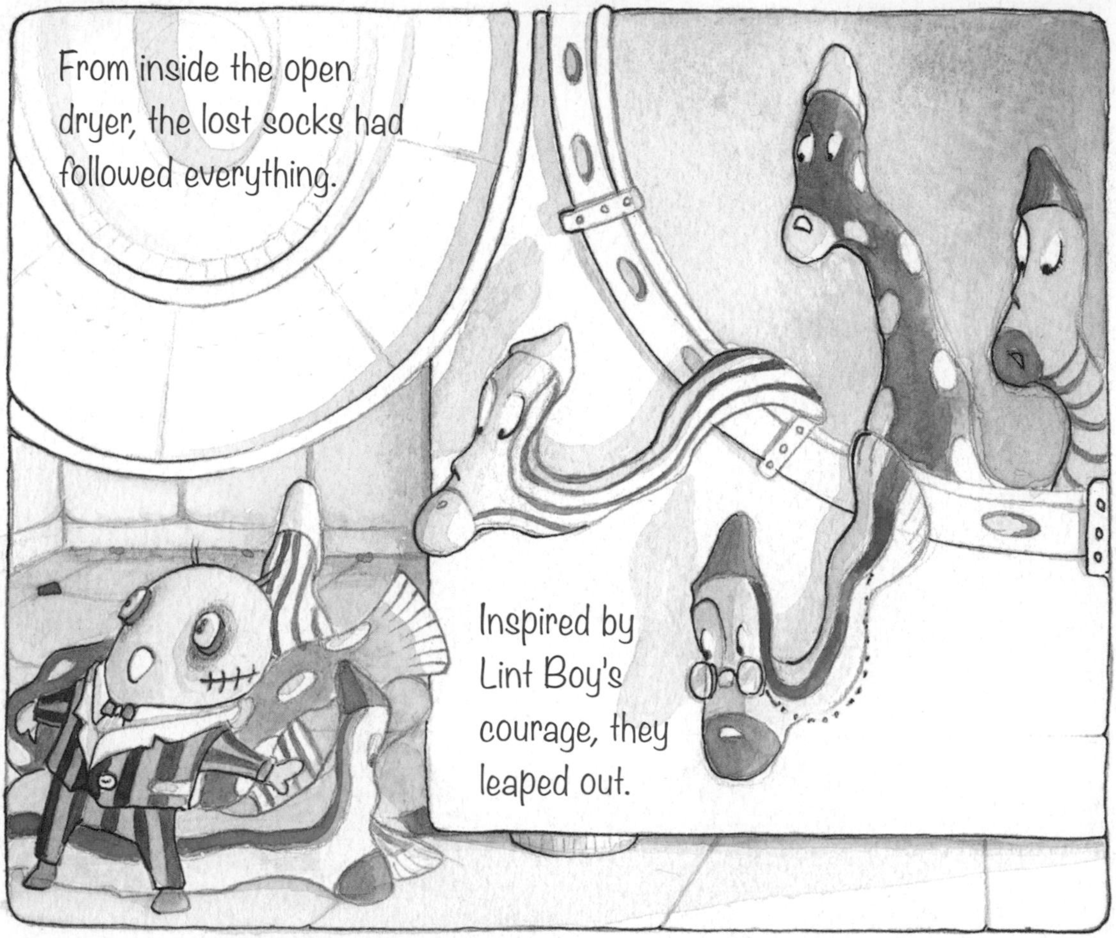
From inside the open dryer, the lost socks had followed everything.
Inspired by Lint Boy's courage, they leaped out.

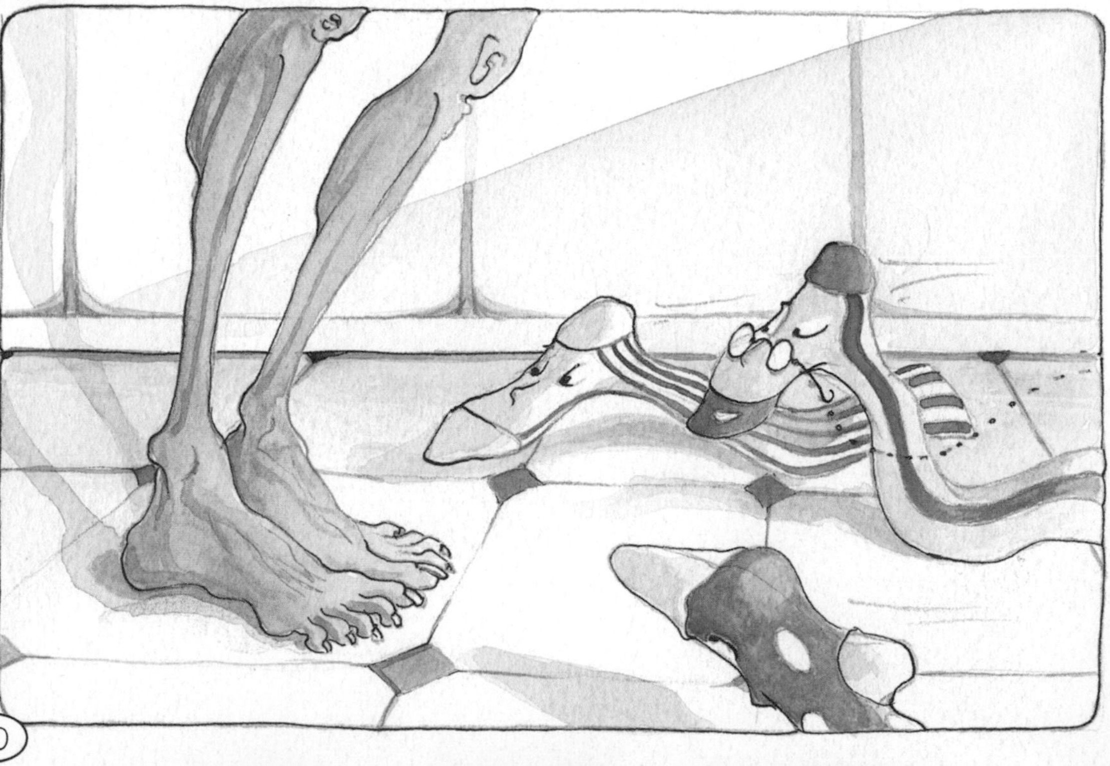

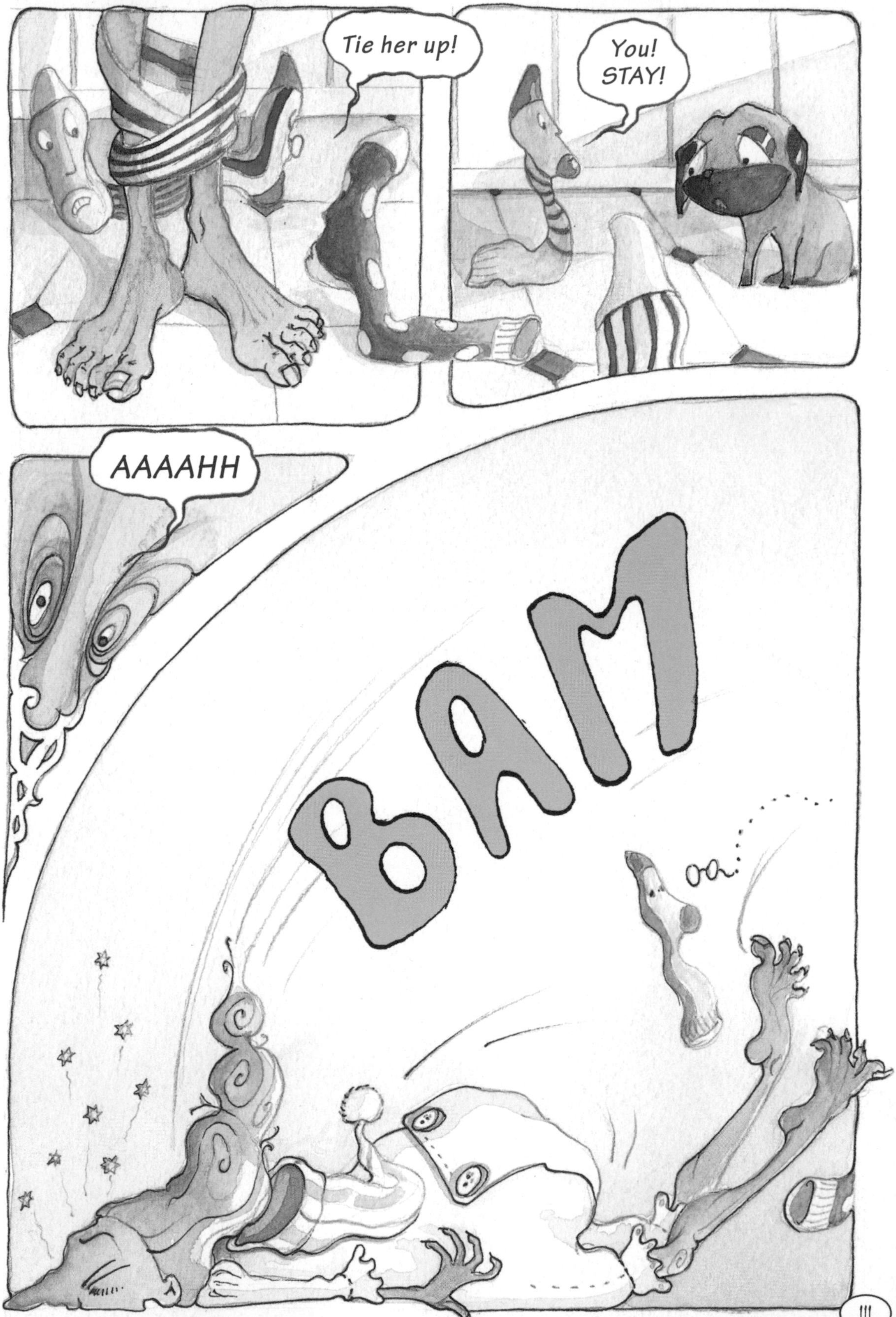
Tie her up!
You! STAY!
AAAAHH
BAM
oa...

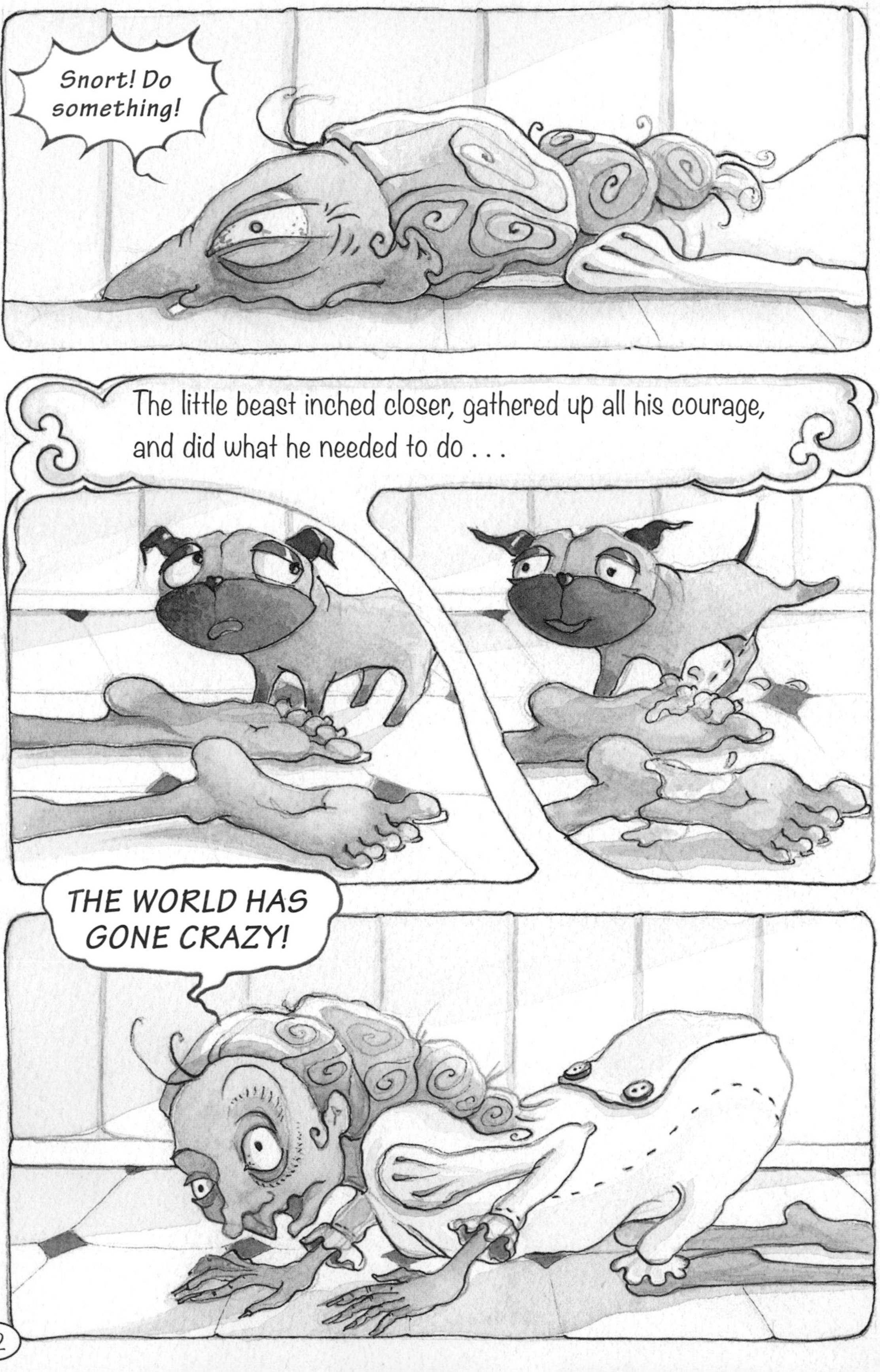
Snort! Do something!
The little beast inched closer, gathered up all his courage, and did what he needed to do . . .
THE WORLD HAS GONE CRAZY!

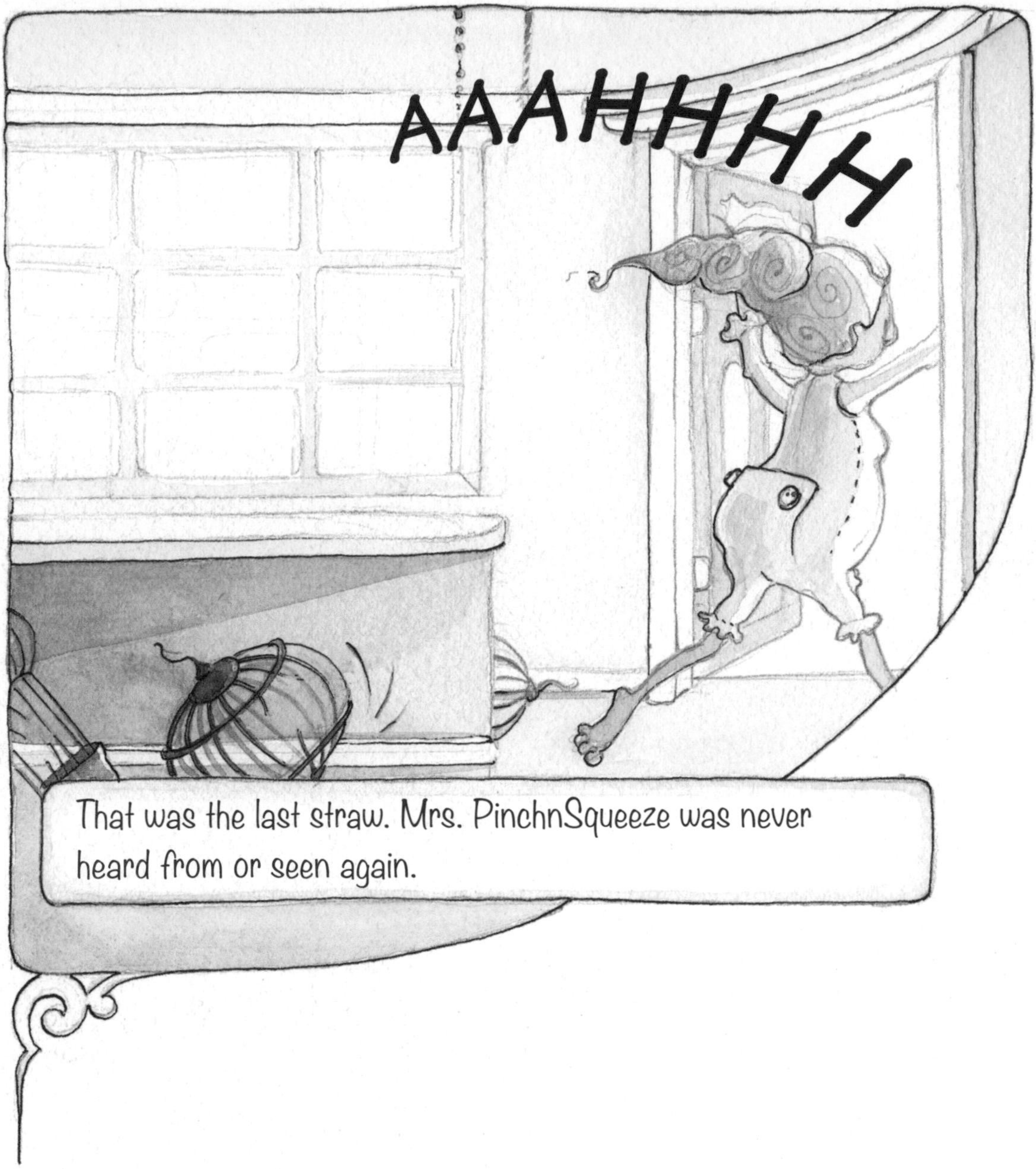
AAAHHHH

That was the last straw. Mrs. PinchnSqueeze was never heard from or seen again.

Chapter 13

Reunited

The lost socks were all reunited. They nuzzled and krumped and formed matching pairs. Lint Boy and Lint Bear couldn't stop smiling.

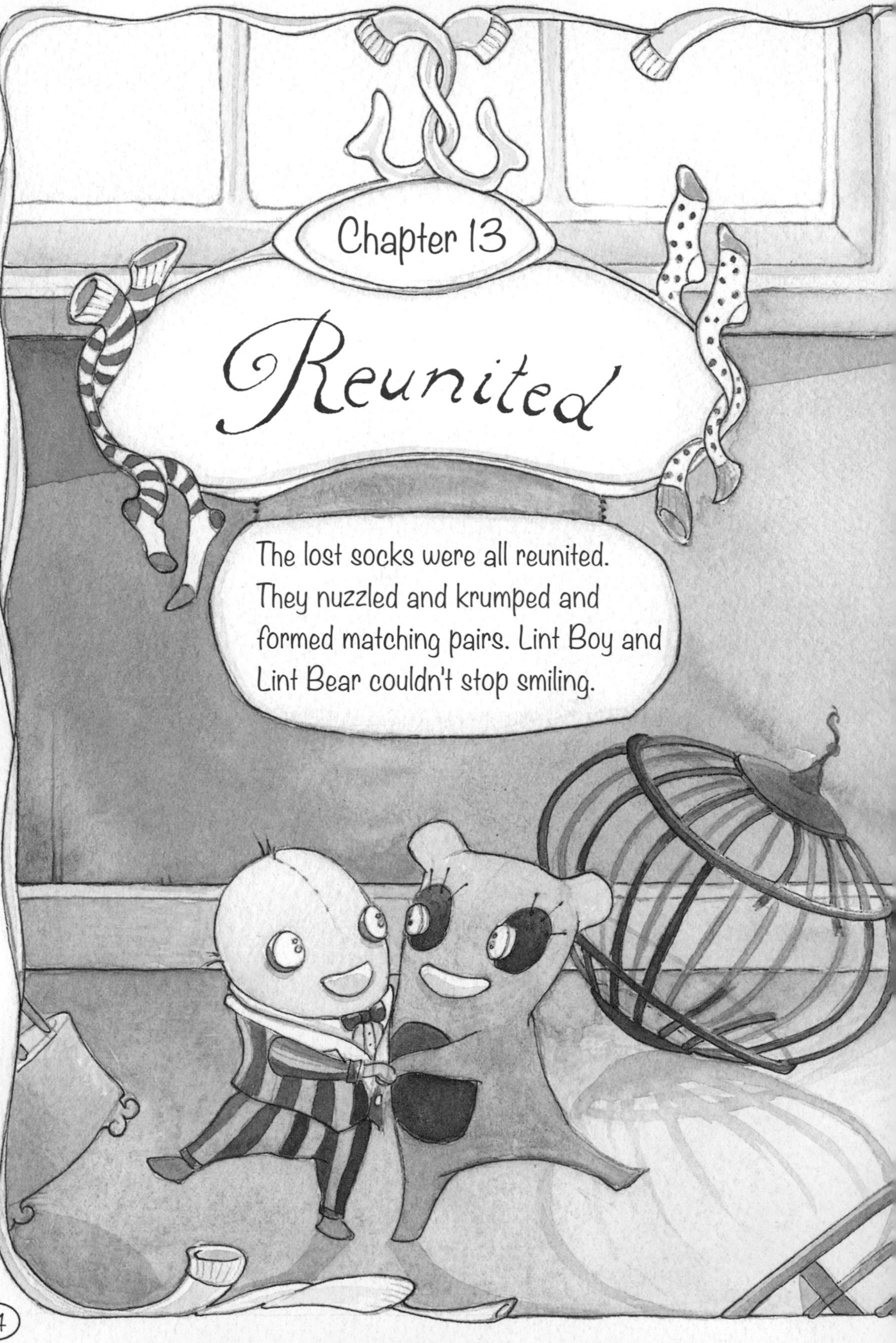

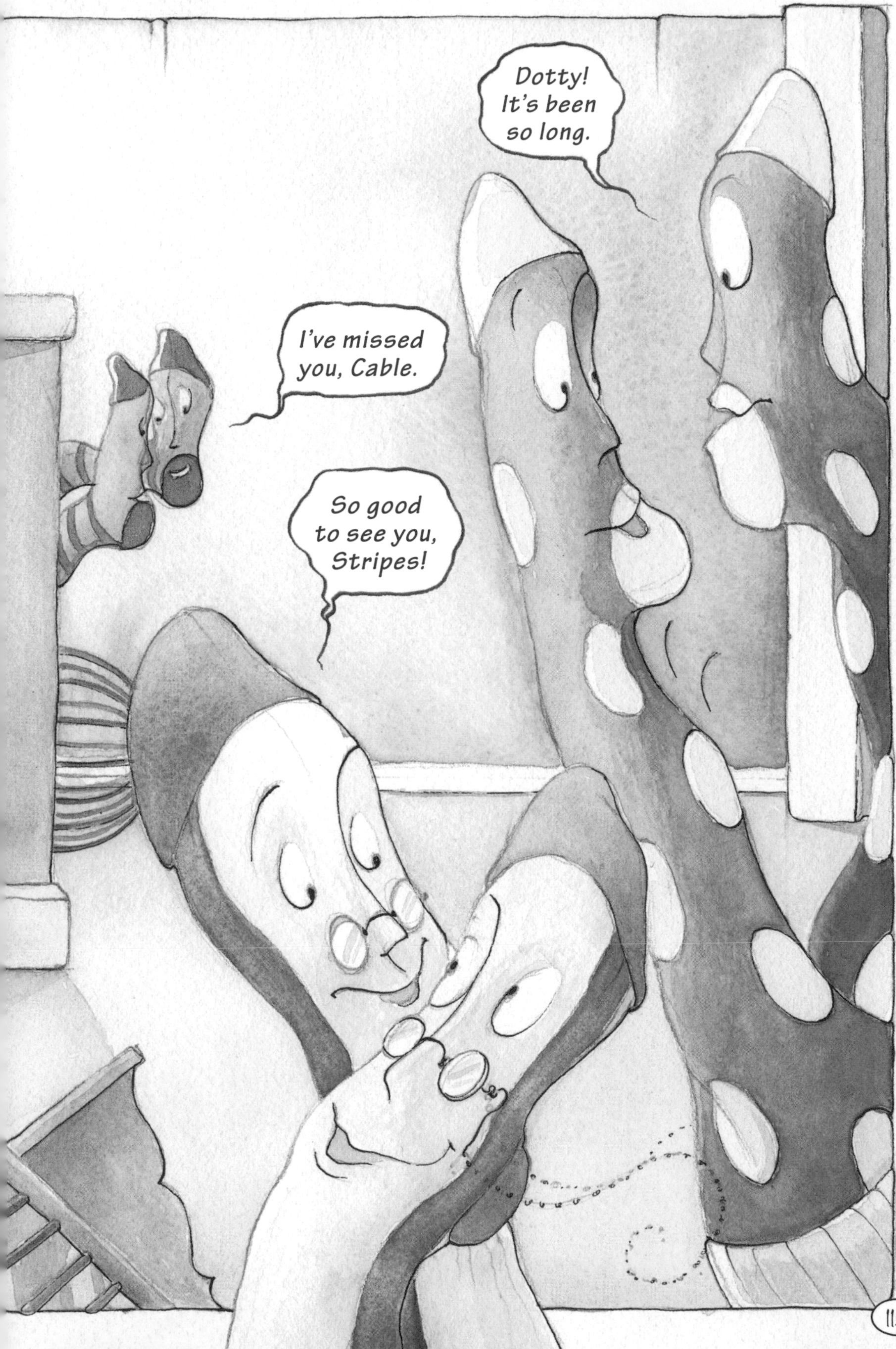
Dotty! It's been so long.
I've missed you, Cable.
So good to see you, Stripes!

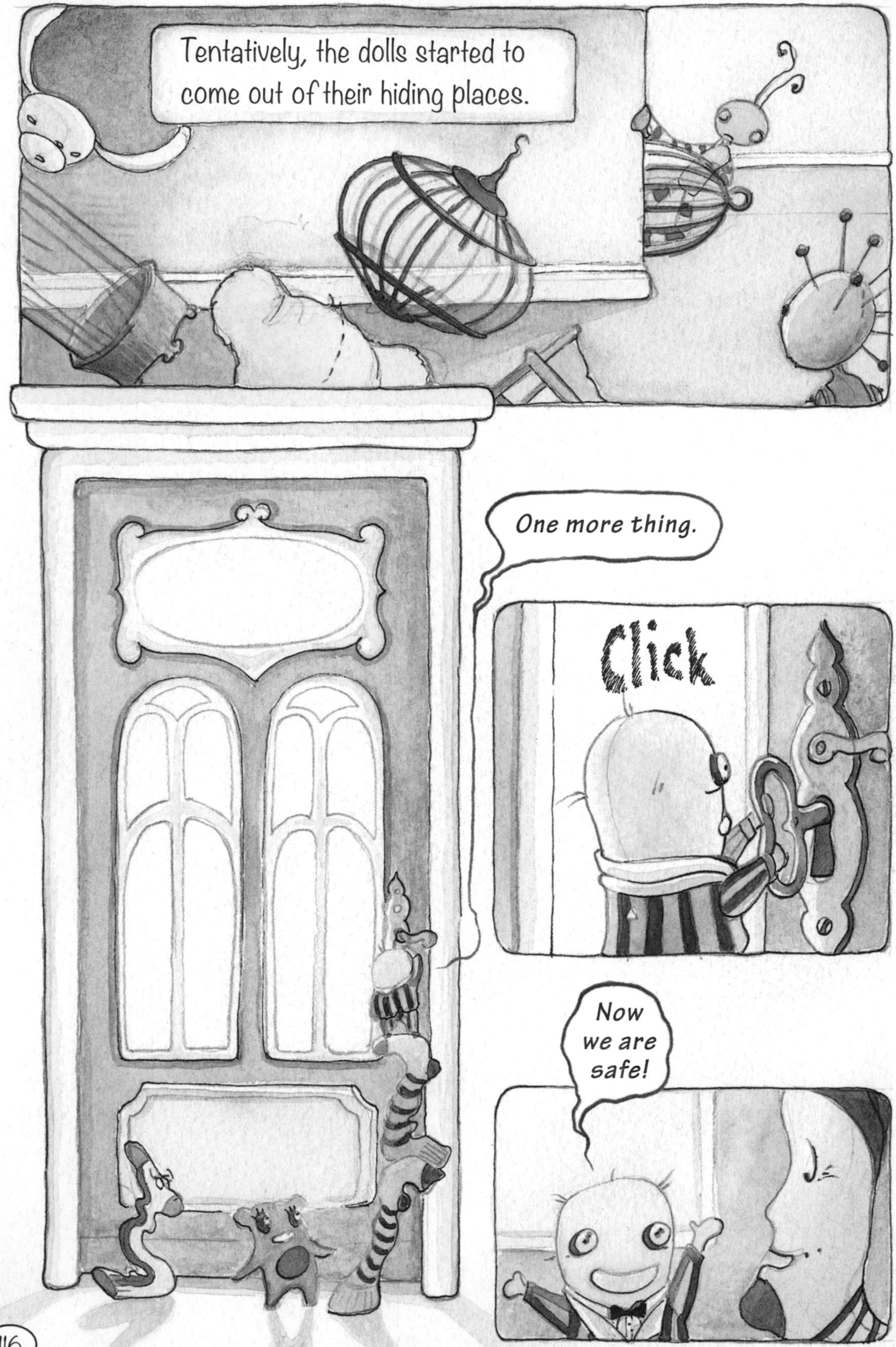
Tentatively, the dolls started to come out of their hiding places.
One more thing.
Click
Now we are safe!

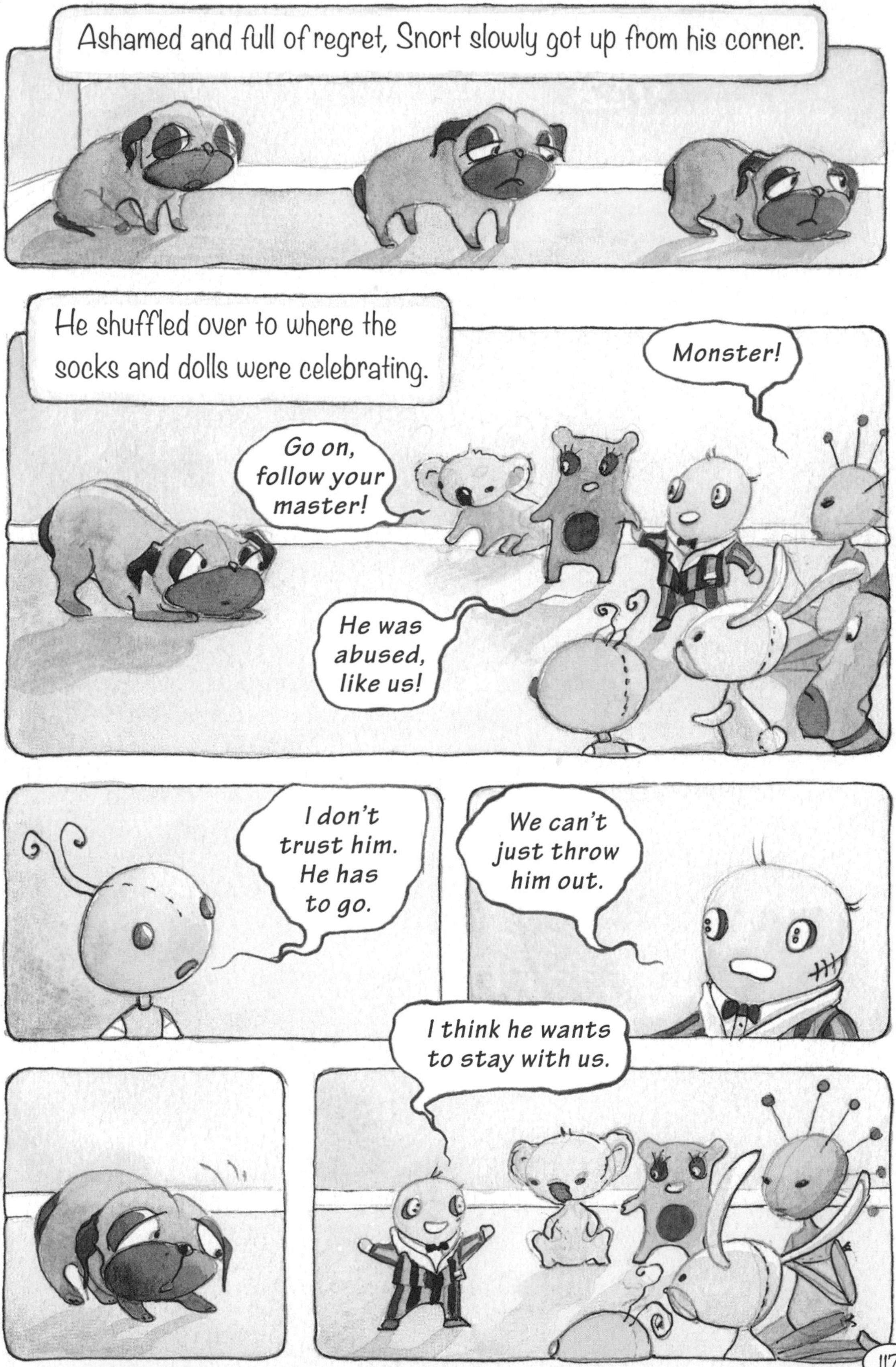

Ashamed and full of regret, Snort slowly got up from his corner.
He shuffled over to where the socks and dolls were celebrating.
Monster!
Go on, follow your master!
He was abused, like us!
I don't trust him. He has to go.
We can't just throw him out.
I think he wants to stay with us.

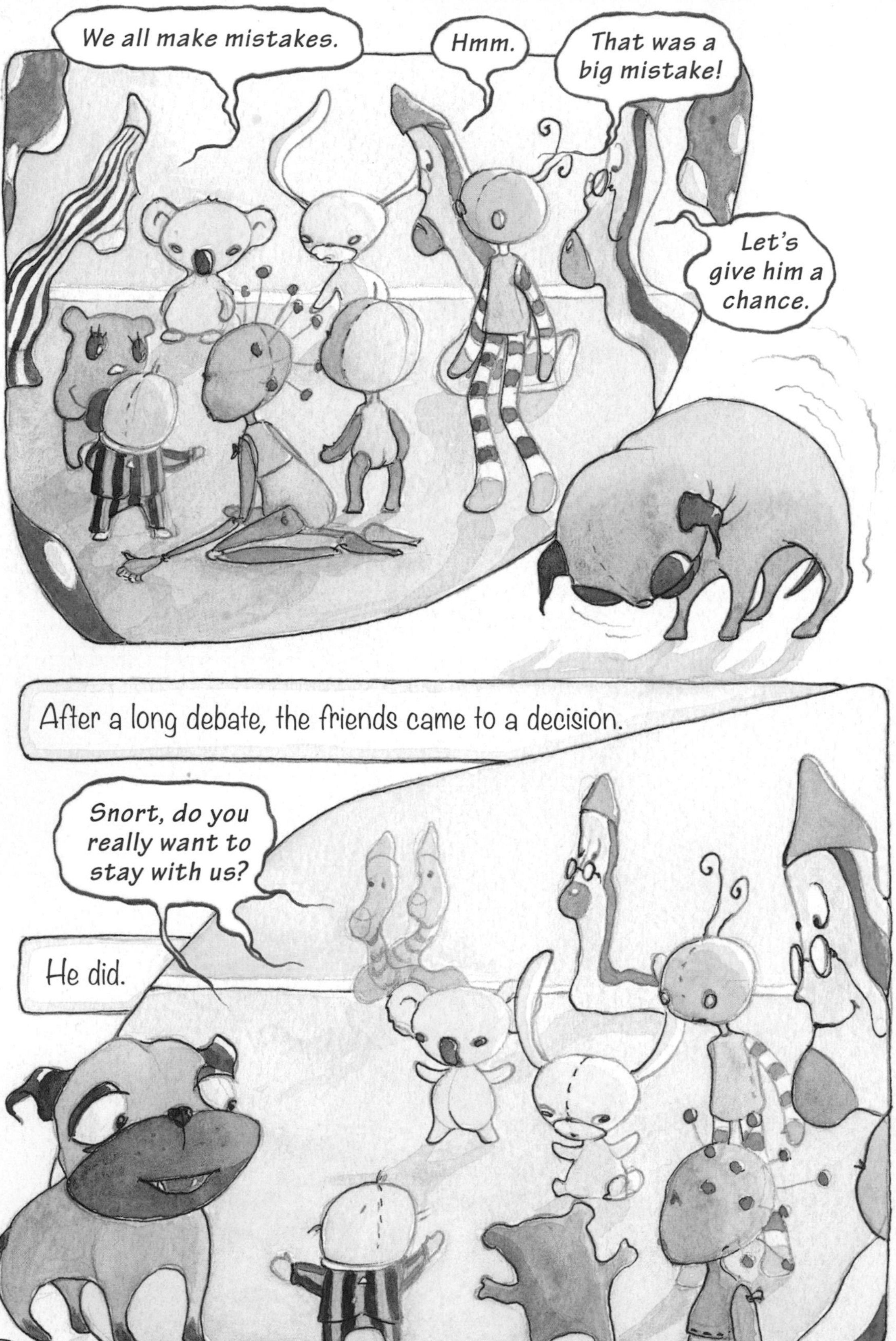
We all make mistakes.
Hmm.
That was a big mistake!
Let's give him a chance.
After a long debate, the friends came to a decision.
Snort, do you really want to stay with us?
He did.

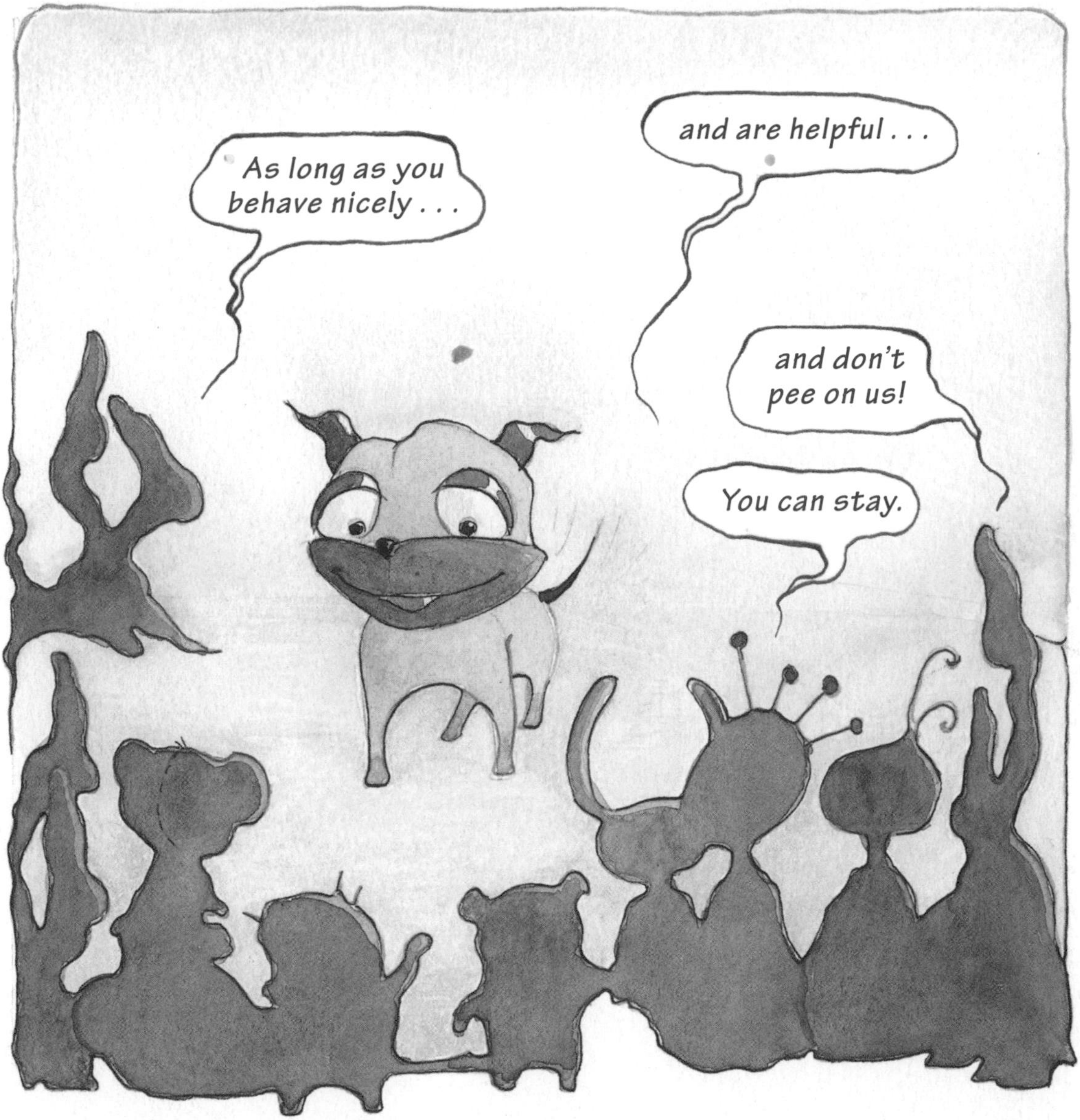
As long as you behave nicely . . .
and are helpful . . .
and don't pee on us!
You can stay.

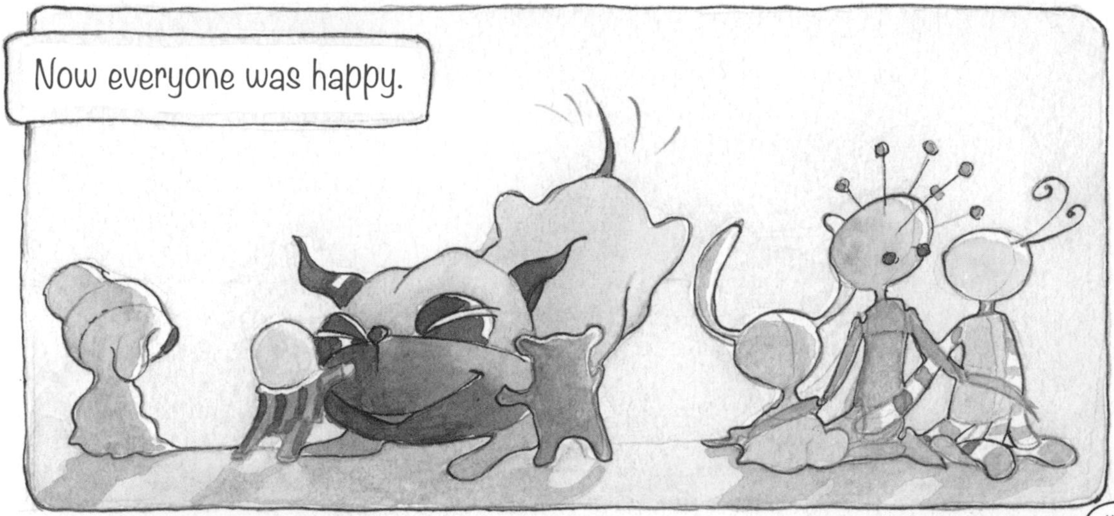
Now everyone was happy.

The grime-dipped toys enjoyed a gentle cycle in the washer, and the torture table became a joyful destination.

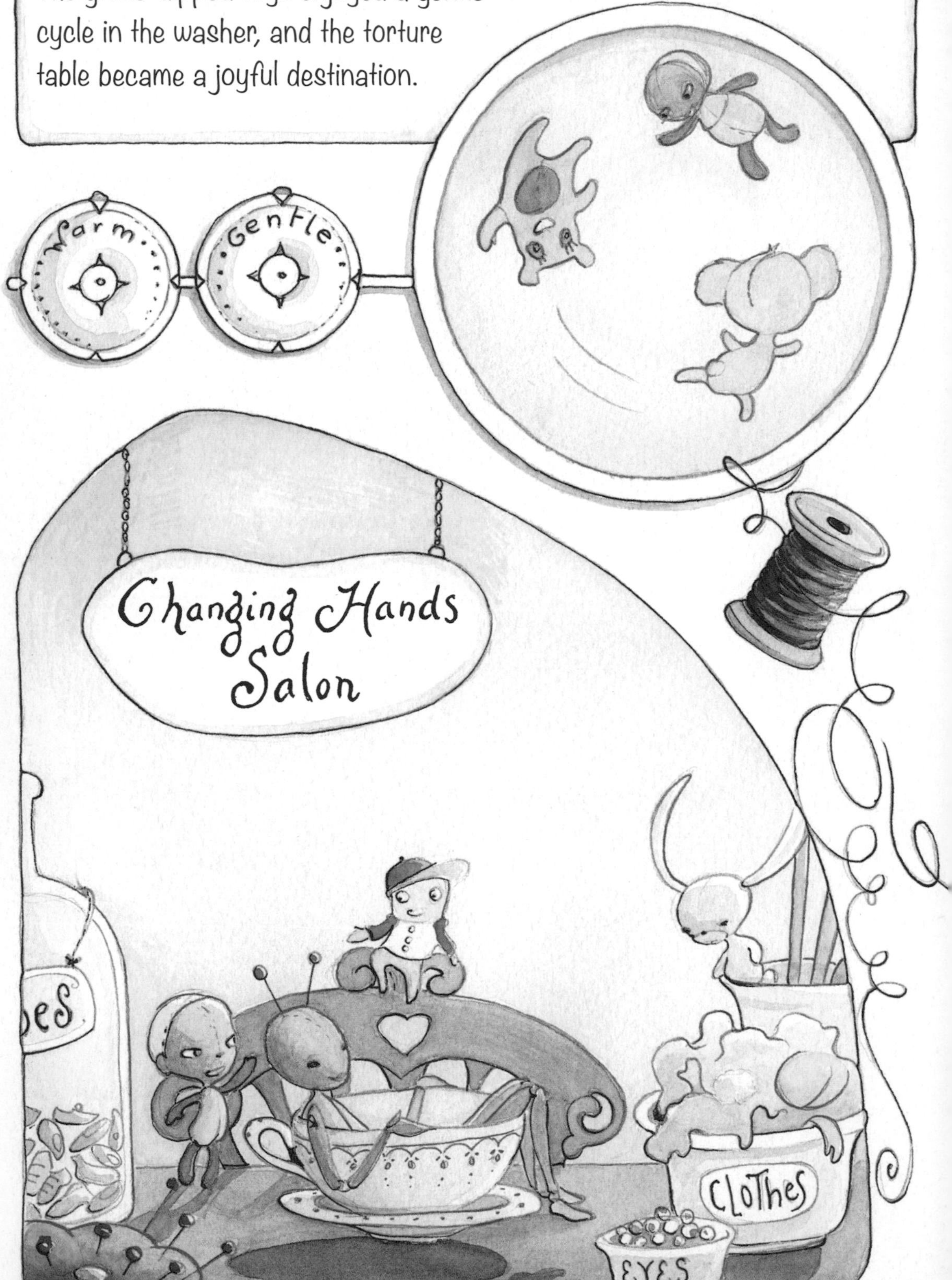
Warm
Gentle
Changing Hands Salon
Clothes
Eyes

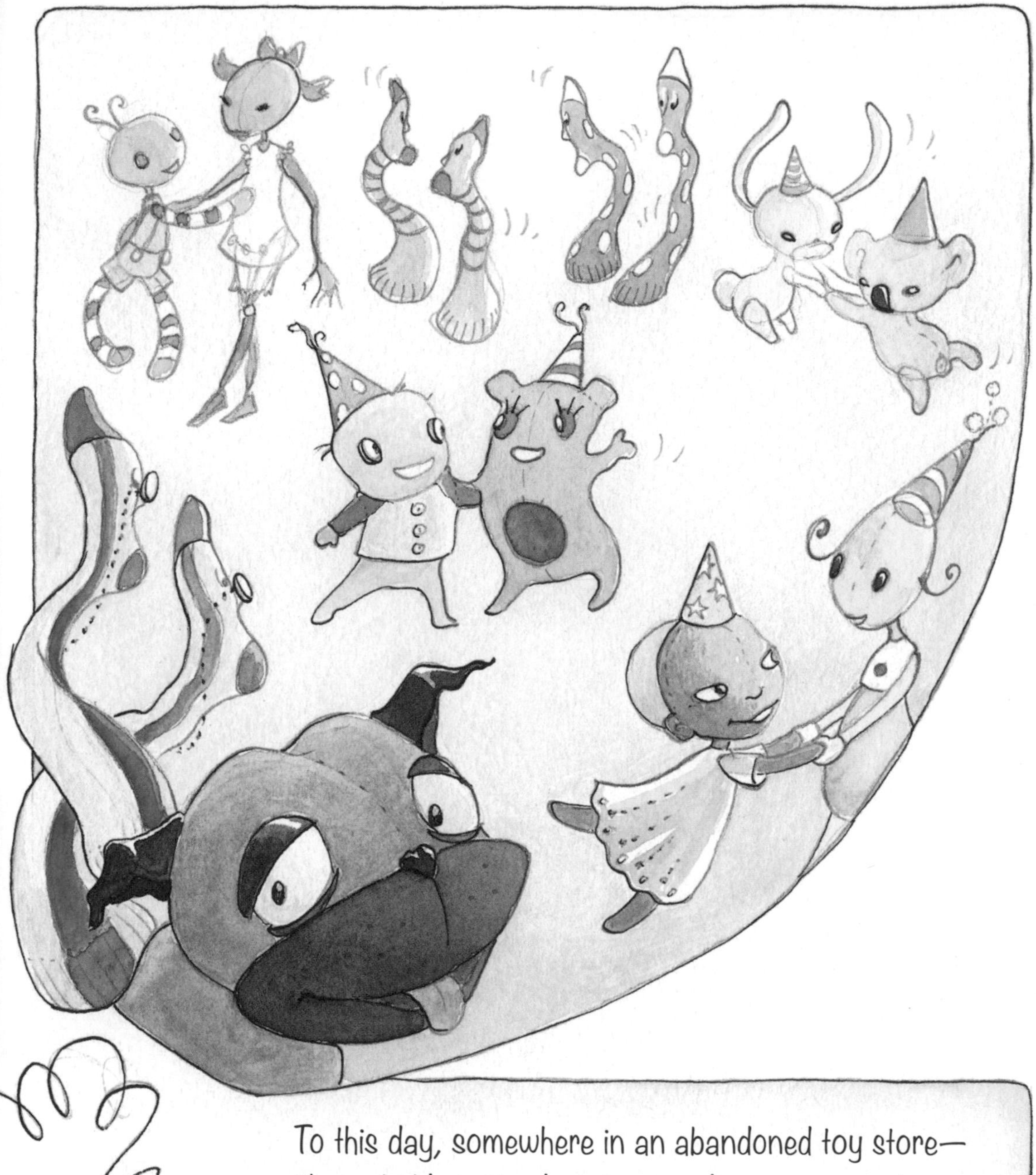

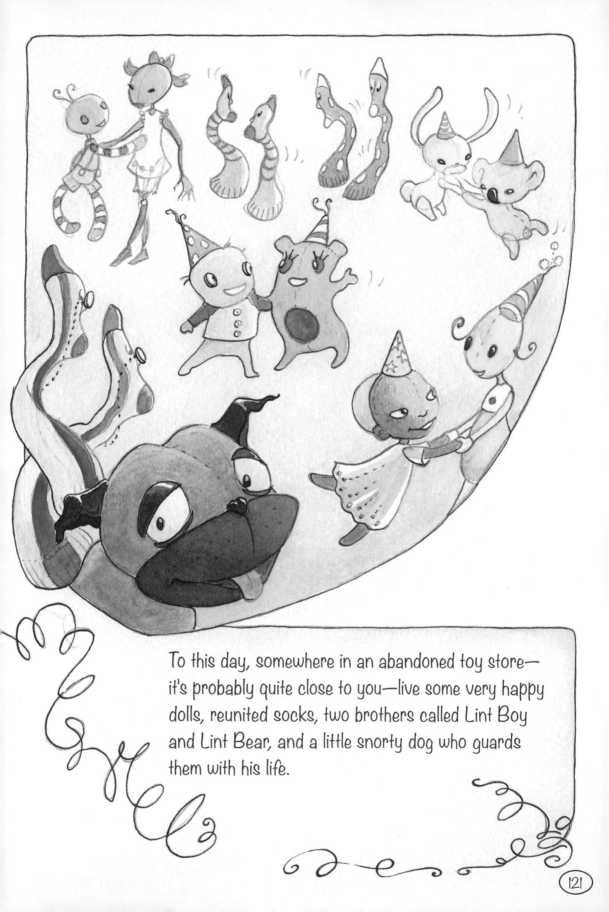

To this day, somewhere in an abandoned toy store—it's probably quite close to you—live some very happy dolls, reunited socks, two brothers called Lint Boy and Lint Bear, and a little snorty dog who guards them with his life.

The End